Raves for *THE SAGITTARIUS COMMAND*:

"Nostalgia-minded readers who yearn for the days of Doc Smith's Lensman books will enjoy the third of Meluch's barely modernized space opera series. Assassinations, the threat of civil war and a canonically evil villain all keep things hopping in this fast-paced space adventure." —*Publishers Weekly*

"Enough action and suspense for three novels. Meluch's wry, realistic wit finds the ludicrons in the military, sex, sex in the military, and a dozen other matters. A treat for military SF buffs with a sense of humor."—*Booklist*

And for the rest of the *Tour of the Merrimack* series:

"This is grand old-fashioned space opera, so toss your disbelief out the nearest airlock and dive in."
                    —*Publishers Weekly* (Starred Review)

"A fast-paced, space-action novel . . . Meluch's zany streak and slightly barbed wit help her round out the characters. Just how many Merrimack books Meluch and DAW plan hasn't been specified. Let us hope that it is a good many."   —*Booklist*

"Like *Myriad*, this one is grand space opera. You will enjoy it."   —*Analog*

"An action-packed space opera. For readers who like romps through outer space, lots of battles with gooey horrific insects, and character sexplotation, *The Myriad* delivers. The novel is full of action, tough military talk, and space-opera war."   —*SciFi.com*

"Vaguely reminiscent of Robert A. Heinlein's *Starship Troopers* (specifically, the relentless alien antagonists and the over-the-top, gung-ho characters), *The Myriad* is lighthearted, fast-paced fun. This novel will prove thoroughly enjoyable to fans of military science fiction authors like David Weber and David Drake."
                    —*The Barnes & Noble Review*

R. M. Meluch's
TOUR OF THE MERRIMACK:

THE MYRIAD
WOLF STAR
THE SAGITTARIUS COMMAND
STRENGTH AND HONOR

THE SAGITTARIUS COMMAND

A Novel of the Merrimack

R. M. MELUCH

DAW BOOKS, INC.

DONALD A. WOLLHEIM, FOUNDER

375 Hudson Street, New York, NY 10014

ELIZABETH R. WOLLHEIM
SHEILA E. GILBERT
PUBLISHERS

http://www.dawbooks.com

First Paperback Printing, November 2008
1   2   3   4   5   6   7   8   9

To Jim.

PART ONE

Emergence

1

THE HARSH WHITE SUN and the softer yellow day star shone directly overhead. Herius Asinius squinted against their combined light, searching for something wrong. Commander of Legion LXXI Draconis, Herius Asinius had a finely honed sense of wrongness.

Saw it. A smudge on the sky way up high among the icy streaks of cirrus clouds. More than one smudge. And they were moving.

Like veils of smoke or torn shreds of netting, they undulated in the lofty winds.

Sheets of the stuff rippled, furled, and spread back out, slowly falling. An edge of a broad sheet slipped, spilled the wind, dipped down quickly, caught the air, and spread itself out yet again.

Lower, closer, the cloudy sheets took on dimension, bigger, peppered, more like a swarm of gnats blowing in from a lake.

The lower they descended, the clearer it became that each gnat was a meter wide and haloed in tentacles.

Herius Asinius, on the stone rampart of the Roman fortress, lifted his wrist com, swearing and shouting into it for someone to identify the descending clouds. But he already knew what they were.

Mostly they were called gorgons or, altogether, the Hive, as the gorgons in their countless millions seemed to compose one organized whole. A single vast alien entity characterized by an inexhaustible, indiscriminate capacity to eat organic matter.

And Herius Asinius threatened all ships in orbit with crucifixion for not alerting him to this latest wave's coming.

Someone should have detected the gorgons' distinctive spheres approaching the planet Thaleia before the damn things hit atmosphere.

No one answered from above.

The ships' coms could be out.

Or everyone up there could be dead.

The very first appearance of Hive swarms on Thaleia days ago might be excused as wholly unexpected. The Americans had led Rome to believe that the Hive could not possibly arrive in Near space for another hundred years.

But gorgons were here, on the Roman planet Thaleia, right now, less than fifty parsecs from Palatine. Been here for days.

Was it only days? How many? Felt closer to an eternity. How time crawls when you are in hell.

And how in bloody hell had *more* gorgons come to the planet without warning from the lookouts in orbit?

Herius did not care if Rome was desperately short of soldiers; someone was going to die for this. Someone besides Herius Asinius, who was pretty sure he was not getting out of this alive anyway. Whoever let gorgons approach Thaleia needed to hang on a cross for a while and have his children killed before his eyes, *then* get eaten by gorgons.

Herius roared orders to his legionaries as he hefted a beam cannon onto his shoulder, and trained it on those clouds. Fired.

The netted clouds were elusive. The gorgons splayed themselves flat, tentacles fanned wide to make themselves into a net of parachutes. Under fire, they split apart into individual parachutes, drifting on the wind. They fell in spidered rain, tipping and dodging, darting in the air currents like minnows. The fortress gunners scribbled the sky with fire. Oh, you hit some, but it was like trying to prevent every drop of rain from touching the ground.

Early in the siege, Legion Draconis had scorched a wide ring of land around the Roman fortress and brought all the residents from the surrounding region inside these stone walls. The burned fields around this place made it unattractive to the ravenous aliens.

Despite all the beam fire from the high ramparts, the rain of gorgons made landfall by the hundreds of thousands in the forested hills beyond the burn area.

The fortress was an ancient style structure, made of local red stone. The buildings within its thick walls were roofed in terra-cotta. It was a historical re-creation, never meant to serve as a real shelter in *Anno Domini* 2445. But when the invading aliens caused computerized systems to fail and made automated defenses turn on their makers, these primitive walls of stone became the place of last refuge.

The monsters continued to fall in the surrounding hills. The legionaries fired beam cannons until the sky was empty and all was dead quiet on the blackened perimeter.

Green birds came over the hills in a wheeling flock. Alighted on the ramparts, chattering, their double wings flicking.

Herius Asinius lowered his beam cannon from his shoulder. Dropped into a crouch on his heels, let his head hang. His back ached. His soul ached.

He had thought his legionaries were getting ahead of the monsters. Until this. A rain of gorgons.

How in the hell?

Heard footsteps on the catwalk. The sound halted a few paces away from him. "Are you hurt, *Domni*?"

Herius Asinius shook his bowed head and waved off whoever it was. The footsteps continued along the wall, paused once. The legionary fired a single shot over the wall. Walked on. It was a sometime dream of Herius Asinius to be the one to stand between Rome and its most deadly peril. In his dream, however, he had all the resources he needed to win the desperate battle.

Troops in the Deep End—two thousand parsecs away from here, on the far side of the abyss between galactic arms—those troops had weapons with which to combat these aliens. Legion Draconis did not. Legion Draconis was equipped to battle conventional enemies in Near space with modern weapons. Herius Asinius had never been trained in—or armed for—combat against gorgons. He felt set up, cheated. A naked slave thrown to the lions.

And he could not run—take his Legion, withdraw to his ship *Horatius*, and abandon the planet Thaleia to the predators.

It was unRoman.

It was unthinkable.

Herius Asinius was going to die here.

Sometimes certain death gave soldiers a weird sense of elation. Herius had seen that buoyant fire in the recordings of the last stand of the Roman 10th cohort of the Praetorian Guard at Corindahlor. The famed 300. Their faces damn near glowed. Some of them laughed. And died to a man.

The battle for the bridge at Corindahlor had been a defeat that opened the way to planetary victory. A defeat like Thermopylae, Masada, the Alamo. A defeat that made the 10th immortal.

Herius Asinius was not going down to immortality. His Dracs were just going to be eaten like sixty-four other Legions before his.

He stood up, stared at his own grave, this planet Thaleia.

The enemy was here. Now. And if here on Thaleia, they could be at the Roman capital Palatine within the year.

It fell to him to stop them.

It was too late for Herius Asinius to be careful what he wished for.

A voice sounding from his wrist startled him: "*Ave, Domni. Vivas tu*?" It was his ship's commander, his cousin Marcus.

Lifting his wrist com to his mouth—too hurriedly— Herius hit himself in the brow with his beam cannon.

Stinging, furious, he rasped into the com in Latin, "Yes, I'm still alive, hang you! Where have you been!"

"The gorgons shut down the ship's systems," Marcus returned. "It's true what they say. With mobs of gorgons clustered on the shields, they shut down almost everything. We had to dive into the atmosphere to burn them off. We didn't have enough sharp objects to kill the ones that got on board."

The Americans had told them the only weapons that worked against gorgons were fire and a sharp edge, and even a sharp edge wouldn't cut the white ones.

"We set fires on two decks," said Marcus. "Oh, Heri, I messed up your ship."

Herius Asinius touched the rising welt on his forehead. It was bleeding. He had not slept. Anger sapped out of him. Remembered to worry about his younger cousin. "Are you okay?" Herius used the American word *okay*. Everyone did. Every nation on Earth. Every alien colony of Rome. Everyone knew that okay meant okay.

"I am—" Marcus could not say he was okay. Finished instead, "—unhurt."

A sudden boom split the quiet with a roar of heated wind. A rumbling vibration rolled through the ground. The noise thundered through everything, pounding.

No Roman ever took to space without sonic filters implanted in his ears, so the sound did not deafen Herius Asinius. But it dropped him into a crouch and knocked a chunk of the stone rampart over the edge.

"What is that!?!" Marcus' voice shouted from Herius' wrist com. "*Domni*, are you there!"

Herius stood up, turned toward the north where a blazing cloud mounted higher and higher above the horizon. He tried to remember the map of this side of the world. "The Ephesian munitions factory, I think."

Nothing edible in the factory, but masses of gorgons corrupted automated controls. Everything on this world was automated.

That's why we're hiding in this relic.

"Which way are the winds blowing?" Marcus demanded quickly.

"Northerly," said Herius. Away from the fortress. "There's a break."

"That's a first," said Marcus, sour.

Herius nodded. Marcus would know he was nodding. "Before you roasted my ship, Marcus, did you see gorgon spheres on approach?"

"No. There's nothing more coming."

"A million or more just fell."

Marcus was unintelligible for several moments. Finally choked: "Are you in danger?"

"Not immediately. They fell outside the burn area." And on the Ephesian munitions factory apparently. "Are you still blind up there, Marcus?"

"No, *Domni*. The systems came back on after we burned our gorgons off."

"What do you see coming toward the planet now?"

"Nothing! I didn't see anything before, and I don't see anything now! The Americans never told us gorgons could sneak up like that." Marcus sounded defensive. "They said gorgons travel through space in *spheres!*"

"There's a lot the Yanks didn't tell us," said Herius, watching the tower of fire in the distance. The gorgons had taken out a munitions factory. Convenient for the Americans.

"Heri? When is the last time you slept?"

Herius Asinius stammered in a fog. Admitted at last, "I'm due. I'm due. I'm overdue."

He would be of no use to anyone if he ran himself into the ground.

"I have your sky," said Marcus.

Herius glanced up. A silver glint passed overhead, horizon to horizon. His ship, the mighty *Horatius*.

"Marcus, check on my tribunes." Herius had split his Legion into its ten cohorts to defend the major population centers of Thaleia. Draconis, like most of the modern Legions, only numbered 3000—ten cohorts of 300 each—in addition to the crew of the *Horatius*.

Fortunately, Thaleia hadn't much of a population. The Dracs had gathered the citizenry into six refugee centers. Herius had no idea what was happening to them. "The other refugee centers—"

"I've *got* you, Heri," said Marcus.

Let go, Herius told himself. Herius Asinius never delegated well.

And it was not till dusk that Herius actually dragged himself down the ladder into the fortress. He set out on foot up the via Praetoria toward the center of the forty-acre complex.

Dazed refugees, wrenched from their automated homes, looked quite lost in the open air amid the stone buildings. The whole complex murmured fear, soft crying, a worried tone to all the muted voices.

God or gods, how had it come to this? How did we get treed like scared animals?

It began with the disappearance of a ship. The *Sulla*. At first few people even knew she was gone. *Sulla* was about secret business.

And those who knew kept the secret. Tried to. Rome never advertised its difficulties. The matter was to be handled quietly, done without anyone ever knowing there had been an incident in the Deep.

Rumors of *Sulla* got out. A shadow tale. A ghost story. The ship that never returned. You could not hear the name *Sulla* without a spectral cold lifting the hairs on your neck.

What had found *Sulla* then found more Roman ships. It destroyed warships, exterminated Legions, consumed worlds. Crushed the might of the star-spanning Roman Empire so that this proud people had to crawl under the heel of their hated enemy, the United States of America, to survive.

Hiding behind stone walls.

On one of the cross streets inside the legionary fortress, a hunched-over young woman, her mouse-colored hair hanging in front of her mouse-colored eyes, clutched a landing disk to her chest. Herius did not know where she thought she was going with that. Nobody was displacing off this world. No one ever displaced at all without a collar—and she did not have one.

"Drop it!" Herius barked.

The woman shied behind her mousy hair, quickly set the landing disk down, and scurried away.

"Pick up a sword!" Herius shouted after her.

Unlikely she would need one. The fortress was a secure place, unattractive to gorgons.

But just in case, his legionaries had hauled reproduction catapults and ballistae onto the ramparts of the reproduction legionary fortress.

Everyone had heard the stories. If the Hive moves on you, you will be thrown back into the most primitive warfare you can imagine.

The reproduction siege engines were constructed of massive beams of wood—real wood from imported Earth trees. There was nothing remotely like wood growing native on Thaleia. Those giant-stalked spongy, corky, sinewy, rubbery things that sprouted leaves and passed for trees on this world did not make for suitable building material.

However, the native vines' twisted sinews served very well for the ballistae's torsion springs in place of horsehair, and sharpened native ironreeds could serve as projectiles for the ballistae.

Heavy round stones stood stacked next to the catapults in their historical role. But hurled stones were useless against gorgons. You can't crush a gorgon.

But you could set them on fire. So the Dracs and the refugees had wound strips of native saptrees tight into highly flammable balls, which could be catapulted at gorgons. Pressure-operated fire suppressants would keep the operators from torching their own catapults. If it came to that.

It could not come to that, Herius told himself. There was too much vegetation out there for gorgons to bother crossing the fields of ash to get at these stone walls.

This has got to be the safest place in the world.

In the fading double light, the battlements drew a surreal horizon against the alien sky.

Stars appeared quickly, winking behind wispy clouds. Two very bright ones were part of this solar system.

MuCygni. The portside wing tip of the Swan as seen from Earth.

Herius Asinius came to the Principia at the center of the fortress. His standards were grounded here, the silver eagle staked beside his Legion colors, the gray dragon on a scarlet ground.

His men had prepared the commander's house for him.

Knew he had to sleep. Real sleep. The jack drugs would only carry him for so long before the nerve damage started.

The room was fittingly Spartan. A simple fresco of an ancient hunting scene on the walls. A simple mosaic on the floor. A single window.

A pernicious native vine had wedged itself between the window jamb and the sill with the slow force of plants everywhere. All native species of Thaleia were pernicious. Made terraforming difficult. In fact, terraforming had not really happened on Thaleia. Native life trumped the fragile imports.

Life emerged to survive conditions present.

Conditions on Thaleia were pernicious.

Herius did not undress. He stretched out on the plain chaff-stuffed linen pallet, his boots still on. Closed stinging eyes. Lay rigid and twitching.

It was hot. There were no climate controls. Alien smells carried on a thin breeze through the open window. He heard the quiet whir of the transports. Voices. Footsteps. Loading and unloading. Strange spiraling song of the green birds.

Insectoids, the kind called rotifers, flew in and out of the open window, keeping themselves aloft by means of a single flagellum like tiny copters. Rotifers normally made a humming sound, which became a whine when the creatures felt randy.

The room was filled with whining.

Herius bunched a chaff-stuffed pillow around his ears.

2

WOKE FLAILING FROM a sleep he did not remember falling into. The rotifers were in a milling chaos. They bounced off his face. Sounded like tiny buzz saws. Their little copter whip-wings stung.

Crashed into his own aides in the doorway as they came to wake him. Blare of a general alarm filled the fortress.

It was dawn. Maybe. The sky had clouded over during the night.

Beam fire knifed down through the cloud bank and drew a circle around the legionary fortress.

Herius shouted into his com: "Marcus, what are you shooting at? What is happening!"

"Gorgons. They're massing. Looks like a coordinated attack on all refugee centers planetwide. Gorgons have surrounded every one. The numbers are crippling. When they close in, you won't be able to shoot."

"You have got to be—" Herius cut himself off. Kidding? No. "Which way are they coming at us here?"

"*All* sides. They're massing over the hills. You should be able to see them in the next several minutes. Our last beam salvo had no effect."

Herius knew the gorgons could generate a weak deflection field when formed in a sphere, but never singly on the ground. "How can that be?"

"Heri, you won't believe how much they look like a Roman tortoise right now. And—" Marcus' voice cut off. Herius could hear someone else speaking in the background. Marcus came back on the com, "The ship is under attack."

Herius caught himself about to demand how. If Marcus had seen the attack coming, it would not have happened.

Asked instead: "*Any* word of reinforcements?"

"No, *Domni,*" Marcus said. His tone said, *Of course not.*

The United States of America, the League of Earth Nations, and most individual member nations of Earth had all promised aid to Thaleia. But they mobilized as fast as any other slug. All the really useful weapons were in the Deep End—where the gorgons were supposed to be. As for the Roman home guard, Legion Draconis was it. The Dracs were on their own.

"Marcus, get the ship cleaned off, then assist where you can at your discretion. *Valere.*"

Herius waved down a transport on the via Praetoria. The party of soldiers on board squeezed together to make room for him, caught his arms as he leaped aboard, running. The transport sped to the front gate.

Herius scrambled up the ladder to the rampart in time to see a black mass shroud the dawn hills. He got out the order to open fire just before the coms died.

Beam fire from the ramparts affected nothing, glancing harmlessly off the top of the approaching mass. But beam fire from the ground, aimed at tentacle-level, killed the approaching gorgons.

For a moment it looked as if this would be easy.

Dracs stationed before the gates mowed down row on advancing row. Monsters stumbled over monsters, no end to them. The black sea flooded closer and closer, splashing in the remains of their own dead.

When the burn area was filled with nothing but black bodies and thrashing tentacles, the beam cannon would not fire anymore, and it became difficult to breathe.

Herius Asinius had been told about soldiers suffocating—or feeling like they were suffocating—when surrounded by crushing numbers of gorgons.

Herius issued orders for his gunners to fall back inside the fortress.

The massive wooden gates boomed shut. Legionaries took to the ancient weapons on the ramparts.

Stationed on the towers were men with crossbows, charged with repelling the enemy from the fortress' most vulnerable part, its edible gates.

Herius prowled the top of the walls, exhorted his men to keep fighting, and keep inhaling and exhaling. He reminded them the airless sensation was not real.

It felt real as hell.

Flaming balls tore from the catapulta with a screeching hiss and rain of sparks. Plunged into the sea of gorgons.

The monsters fanned in rings, scrambling on top of each other to get away from the flames. And kept coming.

Storms of crossbow bolts, flaming arrows, javelins, spears, and fragmentation grenades rained from the stone walls.

Odor of burning lead drifted in foul clouds. The legionaries had cauldrons of the stuff bubbling ready on the ramparts should the gorgons make it to the walls.

And they would.

We cannot win like this.

A ballista near Herius Asinius on the rampart let loose, its wooden arms slamming forward on twisted sinew, reverberated. The ironreed bolt hissed through the air. Tore through several gorgons before stabbing the ground.

The ballista's two-man team did not watch it go. Already they turned the winch, dragging the massive wooden arms back again, creaking, pulling the slide back in its channel. One man leaned heavily on the winch; the other secured the hook, set another bolt into the slide. The man at the winch, a hulking blond, scarcely got clear as the other, the broad dusky one, pulled the lever. The great wooden arms slammed forward again. Another bolt ripped the air. There was no aiming. There was no shortage of targets.

Too many. Too many.

An acrid smell of friction-burned sinew rolled off the ballista.

The two men had become part of the machine. Launch, wind, hook, load, launch.

The air was thin. Of moisture, there was none.

One of the men, the hulking blond, fell off the winch, his face bright red, his body shaking in huge spasms, overheated and dehydrated nearly to death.

Herius shouted for a hydrator and a medicus. The blonde crawled toward the shadows as the darker man labored at the winch. Herius took up the other side of the wheel himself.

Till the other soldier fell, too, his dehydrated body rebelling in tremors.

Herius muscled round the heavy winch alone.

Behind him, he heard someone else engage the iron hook for him and drop a bolt into the slide. Herius stepped away. Barked, "Fire!"

Heard the clack of the lever, the burning screech of the loosed bolt, the thunk of enormous wooden arms slamming forward. He seized the winch and started hauling the crank around again.

It became a mindless sequence, turn the wheel, listen for the lock, jump clear, wait for the bolt to fly, fall back on the wheel again.

His lungs burned. His muscles shook. He could not stop to rest with that hideous blackness closing in. Fired, cranked, locked, waited for another bolt to fall in the slide.

Waited. No bolt materialized in the slide.

Herius turned, snarling, "For your life, you idiot!"

It was the first time he had actually looked at his assistant. Saw why he got no help from him turning the winch.

A child. A civilian. Not even old enough to be a child soldier.

The crate behind the machine, which had been filled

with ironweed bolts, lay empty. The boy was struggling to drag another crate of bolts along the catwalk.

Herius strode back, heaved the crate onto his shoulder. "What's your name, soldier?"

"Titus, *Domni*. Titus Vitruvius."

"Bring us some water, soldier," Herius ordered. "And hydrators if there are any left."

The curly-haired head nodded. Dashed away.

Herius turned toward the enemy. Face crinkled, twitching as if about to cry. Filled with a fierce pride. He loved Rome.

By now, it was apparent the hour of his death was at hand. It would be a Roman death. He only wished he could get Titus out of here.

Farther along the ramparts he glimpsed the cauldrons tilting. An angry sizzle and acrid metallic stench drifted his way.

The enemy were at the wall.

A splintering, shredding noise let him know they were also at the gates, chewing.

Shouts spiked from within the fortress. Herius caught a few words out of the uproar.

The gorgons were coming up the sewers.

They were in.

Herius was a twenty-fifth-century Roman. He barely knew what a sewer was. Never thought to secure them. Cursed any god that might be listening. This, *this* was so far beyond fair. Someone just *had* to re-create the fornicating *sewers*!

An ominous scritching sounded on the stones, very near, just below the ramparts. The gorgons were climbing.

There was no shooting straight down with a ballista.

The boy, Titus, returned with hydrators. Jammed one each into the necks of the fallen men, and presented another one to Herius Asinius, along with a slingshot.

The slingshot was technology right down there with sewers, but Herius could figure out how to work it. He shot himself with the hydrator, and accepted the slingshot. "Good man." Took up a bolt and climbed atop the ballista to look over the rampart.

Mouths looked back up, right *there* reaching on hell-black stalks.

Then the world began to shake.

Herius teetered, pitched toward the writhing blackness. He clutched at the ballista's wooden arm. Gorgon mouths snapped at his kicking feet. Reached.

Lost grip. The gorgon fell, flailing, knocking other gorgons off the wall.

But there were more rising.

Herius swung from the ballista's arm. Let go. Landed on the catwalk.

He pulled back the slingshot, bolt ready for whatever came over the wall.

Deep sounds rose from somewhere—below, above, around, echoing off the hills, rolling inside the low clouds like uneasy thunder. Without direction. A rhythm to it, arriving in a dopplered mash, sound over sound. A thumping baseline Herius felt up through the fortress stones.

Music.

Tremendously loud and coming closer.

A turbulence swirled the moody clouds.

Then a shape like the fin of an inverted shark tore at the cloud layer, music blaring.

"It's the cavalry!" someone shouted.

"That's not the cavalry—" someone else yelled. "It's bloody Judgment Day!"

More of the fin appeared, a goliath metal wedge. It was a spaceship's lower sail.

Slowly, the whole space battleship descended below the cloud layer. A spearhead shape—two wings, and an upper and lower sail round a single fuselage. *Monitor* class. The flag emblazoned on its hull was red, white, and blue.

The ship made a low pass over the fortress, then opened gunports and jetted hydrogen fire at the alien hordes on the ground. Mowed them back in a rolling burning wave.

The boy Titus jumped up, pointing at the ship. *"Merrimack! Merrimack!"*

The Americans had come to the rescue.

Down below, from within the fortress, cheers erupted.

Cheers for the most damned of ships. That was John Farragut's U.S.S. *Merrimack*.

Merrimack circled and made another pass like a fire-breathing dragon, scouring the gorgons, music booming.

Americans loved to make noise. So did Romans, but this was distinctly American noise in this Roman sky.

And Romans were cheering.

Gorgons died in the tens of thousands in the tsunami of fire. A wall of heat rolled up to the ramparts. Hit like a hammer, crouched you back behind the stone ramparts, shut your eyes against the blast.

And still gorgons climbed the walls. Herius could hear them scritching as the furnace blast subsided.

Merrimack could not dare fire on the walls.

Herius' young assistant Titus was not paying attention. The child's face was upturned and rapt as if beholding an angel.

Gorgon tentacles surmounted the wall, looped around the ballista. Titus shrieked. Herius thought he'd lost the boy to panic, but there was still a bolt in the ballista's slide, and as the gorgon paused to take bites from the ballista's massive wooden supports, Titus yanked the lever.

The bolt ripped through the black sack of a body. Wooden arms catapulted the remains into the air. Three torn tentacles remained clutching the ballista for a moment, then dissolved into heated brown slime.

Herius was staring at the steaming ooze dripping down the wooden supports, when another gorgon sprang up from the wall, spiderlike, onto the top of the ballista. The monster was a greasy-looking, black, shapeless sack the size of a pig, tentacles sprouting from all parts of it, each tentacle as thick as Herius' thumb, but more than a meter long and flexible, like a hose, each tentacle terminating in an open maw ringed with row within row of sharp teeth. The mouths tore at the twisted sinew of the ballista's firing mechanism.

Herius still had the slingshot in his hands. Loosed a bolt into the monster.

The bolt pierced the sack, in one side, out the other. The neat puncture wounds self-healed. The shot had done nothing but move the gorgon's interest from the ballista to Herius. The gorgon grappled over the arms of the ballista to get at the man with the slingshot.

Herius shot more bolts at the gorgon, two and three at a time. The gorgon tumbled down from the machine, dragged itself toward him by its tentacles, spilling its liquid insides.

Herius shot it again. The gorgon melted onto the catwalk.

Seven more gorgons clambered over the rampart.

Herius roared at Titus, "Fall back! Get down the ladder!" Backing away from the nests of tentacles, no bolts within reach.

Felt a hissing rip the air, ruffle his dark hair. The gorgon nearest him swayed. Another hiss sang over his shoulder. Another rupture appeared on either side of the gorgon and the one behind it.

The archers on the wall had spotted him. They ripped gorgons open with barbed arrows. The monsters splashed down dead round Herius Asinius.

And in the sky, *Merrimack* made another sweeping pass round the fortress.

Abruptly, he could breathe again. Then heard the wondrous sound of beam fire reports. The beam cannons were operational again. Legionaries were slapping powerpacks back into their hand cannons faster than a gorgon could jump.

This was a modern battle again.

Overhead, the enormous spearhead shape of the space battleship rose slowly, nearly vertically into the clouds in a grandstanding exit.

It was left to the legionaries now to shoot the remaining monsters that were scrambling to get out. They leaped from the high walls. Squashed flat on the ground and rebounded, unhurt, unless they hit the upturned stakes in the trench.

Herius climbed atop the rampart. Heat radiated up from the hard-baked ground, glassy now, like a kiln. The horizon was moving, black with the retreating multitude. An evil shadow withdrawing.

So many of them. So many of them still out there.

In time Herius' wrist com came back to life with reports from his centurions defending the other refugees centers around Thaleia:

Merrimack! Merrimack is here!

It was dusk when all the refugee centers reported in, secure for the moment.

In the moody twilight, the time of day called *inter canem et lupem*—between the dog and the wolf—Herius Asinius sat atop the rampart and watched the suns set, sharing a bottle of mead with his cousin Marcus. The mead was fairly nasty, but after four or five you didn't mind so much.

Herius felt protective of his younger kinsman. Never mind that Marcus was commander of his legion carrier *Horatius*. He was still little Marcus.

Marcus was taller, lighter skinned, his hair nearly blond. Gray-eyed, his cheekbones carved high. Handsome. There were no ugly Romans.

Herius had been a wild seed, spawned from a good lay. Marcus had been engineered. "That's why I'm better looking," Marcus always said.

Herius had a raw masculinity which genetic engineers could not encode. In a world where good looks were commonplace, it was Herius who captured attention.

The sounds rising within the ancient fortress were cheerful, citizens slopping through the disgusting remains. Voices of comaraderie and survival. Laughter. There was too much celebration down there, when we are where we were yesterday—only bloody now and robbed of several good lives. This was not a victory. Gorgons were still eating at Thaleia, still thriving on Rome's doorstep, poised to eat the heart out of the Empire. Herius did not want to go down there and have to smile for his people. He could not go down there and ruin their high morale.

His cousin knew his heart. Marcus was not smiling either. "If anybody had bothered to equip *Horatius* with hydrogen jets, we could have done that," Marcus said, nodding up where *Merrimack* had made its grand entrance.

"All hail John Farragut." Herius raised a flat toast and took a deep gulp of mead. Grimaced at the taste. "What took him so long?"

"So *long*?" Marcus pulled back in surprise. "How did he get here so *fast*? *Merrimack* is supposed to be in the Deep End!"

Herius nodded. "In the nick of time, was it not? A real *deus ex machina*, was it not?"

A god from the machine.

In stage plays in ancient times, near the end of a tragedy when all hope was lost, a god would be lowered onto the stage on a pulley to set the hopeless mess right.

Salvation came to Thaleia in a machine, but that was no god.

"*Merrimack* waited just long enough for us to get into shit deeper than our nostrils. The Americans staged that exactly right to make us look stupid."

"Heri!" Marcus' voice suddenly hushed, "You honestly think this was *planned?*"

"It could not be anything else." Herius hawked, spat over the wall into a brown puddle of deceased gorgon far, far below. "We were set up."

3

THE PERSONNEL LANDER MADE its teeth-rattling, spine-knocking descent into atmosphere; the Marines on board questioning the pilot's skill, parentage, and relationship with domestic livestock all the way down.

Weren't happy to begin with. Seven hundred and twenty U.S. Marines descending to a Roman world to give the Romans aid. Just wasn't natural.

And the Lander allowed more inertia than anyone was accustomed to, between the high winds and the pilot's warped sense of humor.

Made you pull the restraints tighter and hold on.

Knocked the language module out of one Marine's head—a she-dog from Baker Team. She unfastened her restraints and fished around on the bucking deck where her module rolled among Marines' boots. Caught it between Cole Darby's feet. Used Darby's knee to haul herself back up. "What you writing there, Darb?"

"Nothin'."

February 3, 2445
So here's Alpha Team, jammed into this space bus with two full companies of the 89th.
There's Flight Leader Ranza Espinoza. She started with Alpha a year ago, same time I did, but Ranza's on

her fourth tour so she had an easy entry. They never called her a CWAG (Civilian with a Gun).

The guy Ranza replaced got eaten by gorgons. Southern gentleman, third-generation military type named Hazard Sewell. Hazard didn't like trench mouths, so to honor his memory Ranza curses us out if we talk like soldiers. Her own mouth belongs in the head, so I think she's using that as an excuse to clean up. Arms and shoulders like a stevedore. Looks like she could bench-press Dak Shepard. I don't think she actually can, but I know for a fact she can bench-press me, and I'm 180 pounds.

Ranza has these extraordinary gray eyes. They're narrow and you can barely see them under those thick exotic lashes. You'd swear she had them enhanced, but the rest of Ranza is so raw you just know this man-jane would never sit still to have herself prettied up.

She talks like a baboon, but don't try and feed her a load of moon cheese. She'll smell it right away and ram it back up your moon.

The Personnel Lander gave a violent lurch that yanked everyone against his straps and sent up a howl and made Cole Darby clutch at his stylus.

Ranza has actually been married a couple times. I got a real hard time picturing that. (Those guys musta been looking at her eyes.) She even has some kids, back Earthside with their grandmom.

Dak Shepard laughed, swaying with the Lander's bucks and yaws. "Wish I coulda seen those lupes' faces when they saw the *Mack* come down from heaven. I'da paid money to see that. *Mack* comes plowing through all those gorgons. Like Noah parting the Red Sea. Yeah, I got their Roman superiority right here."

F/S Dak Shepard. Alpha Two. Reminds me of my old Neuf. I miss that dog. Dak don't drool like a Neuf, but he sweats, so either way you're real moist around a big happy guy. Horn toad. But who isn't? Strong guy.

Great to have him on the team. Dak is an ox. Smart as one, too.

Reg Monroe had gone quiet. Her eyes shut. Her black face greenish at the moment. Her midriff gave a little heave, followed by a very hard swallow.

"Ho! No, no, no." Carly Delgado pointed warningly across the tight aisle. "Reggie? Listen to me, Reggie. No upthrowing in the box!"

F/S Regina Monroe. Alpha Three. Reg is not a lifer. She's just in the Fleet Marines so she can get into college. Short gal. Bow heavy. (Nothing wrong with that.) Cute face. Cute voice. Wants to be an engineer. She's the Smart One of us. Not saying the rest are stupid. They are so not. Except maybe Dak. They're just a different breed of real smart.

Carly was pulling her feet as far under the bench as she could, watching Reg go into the quick swallows.

F/S Carly Delgado. Alpha Five. Carly is the pointiest man jack or jane I have ever met. Woman is all elbows. Tough, vicious. Quick, quick, quick. You want Carly on your side. Carly plays with knives. Plays well. Maybe I've been out here too long, but Carly is starting to look fine.

Twitch Fuentes rummaged under the bench. Dug a weather hood out of a duffel bag and handed it across the aisle to Reggie just in time.

Of course it wasn't Twitch's duffel bag and it wasn't Twitch's hood. It was Dak's.

Carly is pretty tight with F/S Twitch Fuentes. I'm not sure I ever heard Twitch say much of anything besides, "Yes, sir," and "Alpha Four, aye."

Has a real sneaky sense of humor for a guy who don't talk. But in a furball, you can trust him at your back, and I guess that's all you need to know about a guy.

"Hey, Darb." That was Ranza. Motioned sideways with her head, "Go forward and relieve that foat-gucker at the controls."

"Aye, sir. I'll get right on that," said Darb. "Right after I walk the plank."

Me, I replaced the most popular man in the Company. A real cowboy named Cowboy. And you just try and tell me that didn't make for a fine welcome aboard the Merrimack, Cole Darby. Most everyone has forgiven me for being here instead of him by now.

The Lander gave a violent roll and yaw. The pilot's laughter carried all the way to the back. Sounds of mutiny carried all the way to the front.

Kerry Blue was not afraid or sick or angry. Kerry Blue was asleep, her face mashed against Dak Shepard's bulging bicep.

And what can I say about Kerry Blue? (I mean after she got over me replacing Cowboy.) Once the woman decides you're okay, she makes a man feel right at home, amen.

Easy Kerry Blue was a port in anyone's storm. The ship's cherry picker. Not that she was collecting. Young men just threw themselves at her. Because, unless a man was a complete pervenoid, Kerry Blue was kind. She did not post ratings, and a man never heard a performance review in the locker room when he fell down on the job. She wasn't any voluptuous wonder like the virtual babes a man could experience in a dreambox. But if you liked it real, Kerry Blue was as real as they came.

She had a light stride for a Marine in combat boots. She didn't stand in a stack. Rather, she walked as if her body were suspended from her shoulders. It gave her a free-swinging gait, which drew the Y-chromosomed eye and made a man want to fall in step.

Made Colonel TR Steele wish dead every man who looked at Kerry Blue.

Kerry Blue lived in the right here right now. Made
her a superior soldier. Kerry Blue reacted in the moment. Never looked beyond her own horizon. Kept her
from freezing up in anticipation in combat. Allowed her
to fall asleep during the Lander's turbulent descent.

Kept her from figuring out the obvious.

Like why, whenever possible, Colonel Steele kept her
out of his sight.

*Our CO is Lieutenant Colonel TR Steele. Don't ask me
what the TR stands for. TR Steele is a real hard brand of
macho. You could bruise yourself just looking at him.
White. Real white. Ice-blue eyes. His white-blond hair is
cut short and flat enough to set your drink down on. My
team dared me to do that once. Even I ain't that dumb.
Steele is commander of our half Bat of the mighty 89th,
the Bull Mastiffs. Hoo ra.*

*I did something to make Steele want me dead. I got no
idea what.*

The Lander made a sudden surge up with its dropping of one railroad-sized cargo car filled with equipment.

The Lander made a quick roller coaster arc, and im-
mediately chunked down on the ground. All the
Marines bowed as far as their restraints would let them.
Blessed the pilot.

Kerry Blue woke up. The folds in Dak's sleeve were
imprinted on her cheek. "Are we there?"

Cole Darby snapped shut his notepad and stylus.
Stuffed them into a deep pocket of his cargo pants.

The hatch opened. Harsh sunlight and hot air spilled
in. The ramp extended.

Colonel Steele bellowed, "Red Squad! Forward Battery! Fall out!"

Blue and Green Squads and the Rear Battery
begged to be let out, too. In the alternative, requested
permission to let the pilot out.

Ranza Espinoza led the way, descending the ramp at
a draft horse clomp.

Reg disembarked unsteadily, Darb right behind her, keeping Reg's field pack balanced on her back so she wouldn't weave off the ramp.

Dak Shepard paused in the hatchway to spread his arms wide to the world. "Thaleia, behold your saviors! The 89th is here!"

Kerry Blue waited behind Dak. Her sleepy face was looking way too feminine for her to be allowed to stay in this Lander another instant.

Steele snarled at Dak. "Move your divine ass, soldier." Gave him a push.

Kerry Blue stopped in the hatchway, blinking at the sunlight.

Kerry Blue had kissed Steele once. But that was back when everyone thought Steele was going to die, so it didn't really count as a kiss.

That had been a year—a lifetime—ago, in a cold dark Roman hangar. Steele was going to a hero's death. And Kerry, like the Lady of the Lake, gave him a sword for his final battle. Okay, it was a red crowbar, but it got the job done.

It was a moment out of time. Her cold hands, either side of his head, drew him down to her and kissed him on the mouth.

He should have died there. But TR Steele found a ferocious will to live.

The woman owned him from the first moment he saw her.

"Marine, we are on a schedule!" he bellowed at her.

Kept scowling until the hatch shut her safely away from him.

Told the pilot to move it.

"Would you look at that!"

Kerry Blue had dropped her field pack and stood gawking at the hulking legionary fortress. The red stone walls, the crenellated battlements, the fanged trench, the massive wooden doors kind of chewed up around their iron bracing.

The Personnel Lander was lifting off, swirling ash

high into the air under Thaleia's brutal suns, making the fortress look like it was on fire.

"Who lives there?" Darb shaded his eyes. "Ben Hur?"

Ranza Espinoza gave him a shove from behind, knocked him off-balance. "You looking for a tour guide, Marine? Get to work."

Auto loaders were moving skids out of the cargo car. Marines off-loaded crates from the skids. The Marines had brought swords, pikes, flamethrowers, and fragmentation grenades to Thaleia, along with frictionless face shields and acid-resistant clothing. "For our protectorate," said Carly Delgado sourly.

"Ha!" said Twitch Fuentes.

"We are arming our enemy, *why?*" Any one of the Marines could have said that. They were all thinking it.

"Rome is our ally," someone else said.

"Why don't we just turn a neutron hose on the whole planet and have done with it?"

"Can't. The Roman civilians won't evacuate."

"So?"

There really wasn't a good answer to that question.

Kerry Blue lost her grip on the handle of a crate, dropped her side of it. Darb, holding up the other side, said, "Gravity too strong for you, Blue?"

Kerry was still getting her land legs. Shipboard artificial gravity was not entirely consistent. And it was entirely unpredictable. Kerry was not accustomed to standing on ground that didn't move. Or gravity that didn't lose strength unexpectedly. She kept catching herself against burbles that never happened.

Cracks led out in a spray where one corner of her crate had hit ground. "What's with the dirt here?" It was hard, shiny, ceramic, an uneven color of red brown, coated with ash. Kerry kicked at it with her heel. "What *is* this stuff?"

"It's fired clay," said Darb. "We did that. *Merrimack* did. With the hydrogen jets."

A low sound started. From within the towering stone walls. Rhythmic as alternately firing pistons. A *tramp tramp tramp tramp* like hundreds of marching soldiers.

The Marines stopped unloading their skiffs to stare at the fortress.

Deep metallic thunk of crossbars pulling back. The massive wooden doors of the fortress parted, groaning from their own weight.

Out filed hundreds of marching soldiers.

They came in perfect martial precision. Could suspect they were androids, but there was emotion in the stomps. Reined ferocity and smoldering hatred.

You immediately counted them. Six hundred of them to one hundred twenty of us. In crisp formation. Disciplined. They moved in unison in their knife-edge columns and dead straight ranks.

They were not wearing any armor, but each carried a beam cannon. Heads snapped left as one. Turned.

They wore field uniforms—loose cargo trousers with lots of pockets like any sensible modern soldier. Except theirs were black and covered with dust, where the Marines' trousers came from the factory already dust-colored. The Roman shirts were actually short, belted, black tunics. The legionaries wore their gun sights fixed either side of their eye sockets like Marines, but theirs had shapes—like fangs or wings—instead of plain black GI boxes.

The six hundred came to a halt with a stomp and a shout. Stood before the Marines, a sea of hostility. Dust and ash drifting up from the ceramic ground.

Into the pit of silence a Marine muttered, sardonic, "Yeah, that was pretty."

And there's Ranza, coming out slinging orders like she owned the fort, which she just about did as the ranking Marine here at the moment.

"Who's the guy in charge? Okay, *you*." Ranza singled one out. Man on the right front. Muscular, not yet thirty years old, or maybe just. Romans bred for strength and looks. This one had both. He was perfectly proportioned. Big, but not outsized. Had loosely curled dark locks and smoky sultry brown eyes. And he had a presence. Bare-armed as he was, you could see his mark: *SPQR*. Not a tattoo on this one. This was a brand burned into his flesh.

Tough guy. No one in the Roman company was wearing any rank insignia. But you didn't need a red-crested helmet to single out this one. Leader of the pack and sure of it. You could always spot them.

Ranza started in on him. She spoke fast and she spoke in English and didn't give a good squat who didn't habla.

"We are going to contain and destroy the alien threat. This here is the only gorgon outbreak in Near space! There are none on Earth and it's gonna *stay that way!* The enemy *will not leave* this planet!"

Ranza stalked along the expressionless first rank, bellowing.

"You *will* ID, locate, and disable all automated equipment! That means for the whole world, understand? You will get a census, then locate and secure the population of this planet."

Here the Roman commander interrupted her to demand, "Why do you need the census of a Roman territory?"

"I don't," said Ranza stalking back to him. "And I don't give a skat, 'kay? The census is for you. Account for all your guys. Or don't. The gorgons can eat all of yous for all I care, 'kay?"

A rotifer bounced off the Roman's face. He did not blink.

Ranza turned round to her Marines, who were standing about, slouching, in disorderly fashion around their crates of equipment, just watching the show.

Ranza shouted, "Hey, nobody told yous to stop working! Yous already know what you're doing!"

They knew. Just didn't like it. Resentfully continued off-loading equipment for their dubious allies.

Ranza turned back to the Roman legionaries.

"You will be getting tools for the job at hand. All your fancy Roman weapons with your range finders and target locks and nanosecond adjustments are worthless in a concentration of gorgons! Gorgons can adjust your weapons to target your own guys. Yeah, they've learned how to do that, and first thing you tell these almighty

Roman legionaries is to disable your fancy Tau sixties and do they listen? No! That's why most of them are dead and good riddance, too! DOES ANYONE HAVE AN INTACT TAU SIXTY HERE?"

The Roman ranks were motionless as a solid wall but for the breeze on their tunics.

"We are not morons," said the Legion commander.

"Well ain't chu just a Roman first," said Ranza. "What chu called?"

"I am the legate, Herius Asinius."

"'Kay, Hairy Ass. My men are unloading weapons and training materials for those weapons. You'll be getting V masks to train yous how to use a sword."

Herius walked over to a crate, picked up a sword from it. Presented the sword dangling, its tip held between his thumb and forefinger. "This is the pointy end."

"Yeah?" said Ranza. "What the V mask is going to teach you—and I don't give a rat's ass if you learn it or not—is how *not* to kill each other in close combat. You are also getting fragmentation grenades." She paused, made eye contact with the legate. "You throw them."

Herius nodded. He got that part.

"At the enemy," Ranza added. "Watch the timing, 'cause the gorgons'll try to kick 'em back. Good thing gorgons can't throw. And you can just forget about setting minefields. Gorgons can smell 'em—or whatever it is gorgons do to sense 'em. Gorgons step around mines."

He may have heard someone say, "U.S. mines stink." But Ranza just kept on talking.

"Don't get predictable. Whatever you develop, the gorgons will come up with a countermeasure to it. The only thing that always works is slicing them open. Connecting the cutter to the cuttee is always the problem. Gorgons are smart in a swarm. By themselves, they ain't yet smarted a way to dodge a sword any better than you can. So in hand-to-tentacle combat, unless you're exhausted, you have a slight edge. But gorgons always have superior numbers, so you get exhausted and then you are uffed."

Another ship passed over the fortress.

Ranza glanced up at the sound. Commented, "Green guys are here." League of Earth Nations. The LEN flag was green. The LEN had remained neutral during the U.S./Roman hostilities. "They're here to evacuate your civilians."

"Our people are not leaving our world," said Herius Asinius.

Ranza already knew that. Might as well try to get a moray eel out of its hole.

"Good," said Ranza with a shrug of her broad shoulders. "We got nowhere to put yous."

Herius Asinius declared, "We leave Thaleia, we leave it like Telecore."

Rome had taken a neutron hose to its own colonial planet, Telecore. Left the world dead, utterly sterile.

"Don't get your nuts in a cracker, Hairy Ass." Ranza waved her hand aside dismissively. "So how did the gorgons get here?"

Herius stared, dumbstruck, at the she-ape with the striking silver eyes. If Herius Asinius had seen the gorgons coming, the gorgons would not have been allowed to approach the planet. He found his voice. "*Yous* told us to watch for *spheres*!"

Ranza shrugged. " 'Kay. So how many spheres we got here?"

Herius opened his mouth. Could not speak for another second. *She is as stupid as she thinks I am.* "None."

"Then how'd they get here?"

Herius shook his head. *I am talking to a brick.* "You tell me."

"Any gluies?" Ranza asked. Got ash on her lips. Spat on the ground.

Herius had been expecting a different question. Got lost on the turn.

Gluies. The most horrible of the three kinds of gorgons. White. Hideous.

Herius collected his wits. Answered, "We have seen nothing that matches the description of a gluie."

"That's good. They're the worst. When I said slicing

them open always works? I lied. You can't slice a gluie. Your sword just gets stuck. You can burn them."

Ranza turned to another crate. "You're getting hand-held flamethrowers with backpacks. These are new. Never used 'em on shipboard. You can field test these. Let me know if they work. You're going to have to teach yourselves. We can't stay and babysit."

She walked away from the legate, fists on her hips, beautiful eyes narrowed appraisingly at the fortress walls. "You got a pretty good site here. I'm surprised the gorgons even attacked a place like this before they ran out of other stuff to eat. Did you resonate or something to bring 'em here?"

"No," said Herius, insulted. "We have all heard that gorgons can home in on a resonant pulse."

"Yeah. They do that. Don't know how they get a loc on something that ain't got a loc, but they do that. 'Kay, Hairy Ass, that's all I got for you. My Marines are going to secure this here refugee center. We'll kill everything you missed. Then we got the rest of the planet to clean. Captain Farragut will be down here to give you your orders." And she yelled past him to his legionaries: "Fall out!"

Herius Asinius stood very still. Felt the stares of his legionaries on him like a physical thing. Stunned, offended at how that U.S. grunt talked to their commander. Angry. Embarrassed.

The Americans were quick to invade the fortress. They moved their junk in beneath the Legion's silver eagle and the Legion colors—the gray dragon on a scarlet ground.

If they try to run up Stars and Stripes, I will have to shoot someone.

Herius' cousin Marcus had taken a shuttle down from *Horatius* to the planet surface. He came to Herius now, holding one of the U.S. flamethrowers, disgusted. "We could have fabricated all this."

Herius did not seem to hear him. Lost somewhere inside himself.

Captain Farragut will be down here to give you your orders.

So John Farragut meant to put Legion Draconis under his own command. The American could do that under the terms of the surrender.

It was nearly a year ago now that Captain John Alexander Farragut had taken Rome's surrender from Caesar Magnus.

After the Hive had reduced Rome to scant shreds of its former might, Caesar had been forced to crawl to Rome's worst enemy for help.

Help had come at an awful price.

John Farragut had insisted on the Subjugation.

Legion Draconis had not numbered among the honored dead in Rome's desperate battle against the Hive. Herius Asinius and his Dracs were alive to walk under the arch of spears in humiliation. The surrender had put Rome's military forces under U.S. control.

The Americans had never enacted the provision of direct control in Near Space before now.

How convenient for the Americans to have gorgons here in Near space. How convenient the excuse to invade Thaleia.

Thaleia was home to PanGalactic Automated Industries.

Suspicion, rooted deep, grew, pernicious as a Thaleian vine. Herius spoke his thoughts: "The U.S. imported the gorgons here to give them an excuse to come marching in and steal our technology."

"You think so?" said Marcus, naive as only an honorable man could be. "They would bring gorgons within seventy-one light-years of Earth? It's a stupid and dangerous thing to do."

"Americans are stupid and dangerous. *Ergo* . . ."

"Very well, Heri. Suppose, *arguendo*, the Yanks brought the gorgons here. How did they *pack* them without getting eaten by their own cargo!"

"Marcus, I don't know."

"Anyway, only a perfect madman would use gorgons as a weapon," said Marcus.

"And, of course, there is no such thing as a perfect madman," said Herius. "There was never a Nero. Never a Tiberius. And Caligula never made his horse a Senator. And we cannot forget the local king, Constantine the Great of Thaleia. I think that colossal statue of his goddess mother is still here somewhere."

"Heri, I concede the existence of perfect madmen," said Marcus. "But you are suggesting that someone was clever enough, powerful enough, stupid enough, and mad enough to bring the gorgons into Near Space and endanger all human life."

Herius was looking toward a cluster of Yanks who were comparing their surveillance maps to the local maps. Herius knew what the Americans were looking for. And it was not civilians to rescue.

"No, Marcus, I am not suggesting. I am telling you that is exactly what happened here."

4

ONCE UPON A VERY recent time, rings and rings of sentinel satellites had defended Thaleia against outsiders. Thaleia was a Roman world. Because it lay closer to Earth than to Palatine, Thaleia had been heavily defended. Its sentinel satellites automatically destroyed any Earth ship foolish enough to enter the MuCyg solar system, no matter the Earth ship's nationality or internationality. No Earth ship could get permission to approach Thaleia even in an emergency. The sentinels recognized no exceptions.

That was until the arrival of the Hive. The Hive had caused all of Thaleia's rings and rings of sentinels to self-destruct.

The world was now open to everyone and his dog. All the nations of Earth were here now. They all came ostensibly to help. And all, except the dogs, asked the same stupid question: "How did the gorgons get here?"

As if they didn't know.

A shuttle descended—red, white, and blue—outside the walls of the legionary fortress. Marines nodded up, told Herius Asinius, "Farragut is here."

"Oh, happy day. John Farragut is here," Herius said.

Shuttles were a slow and cumbersome way to get about, and vulnerable to gorgon attack. Still, the shuttles were safer than displacement. Displacement was a precise operation. Gorgons could easily foul displacement sensors and next thing you knew you were mashed potatoes on Alpha Centauri.

Herius Asinius considered waiting here and making Captain Farragut come to him. But he was not in the mood for games. Wanted to get this over with. Marched out of the fortress to where the red, white, and blue thing set down on the hard glassy ground.

The hatch opened. First thing Herius Asinius saw was the smile. And it didn't stay still. The big guy who belonged to the smile came bounding down the ramp. An instantly attractive presence—the light colors, blue eyes, blond hair, white teeth, and sparkling energy.

Farragut must have been briefed, because he knew the Roman legate on sight, seized Herius' hand and the better part of his arm. And he was full of praises for the Dracs holding the fort and acknowledged how hard it had been for them.

In the onrush of seductive warmth and comaraderie, Herius Asinius just wanted to tell Captain John Farragut to go suck a squid.

Should not have let him start talking.

Farragut was talking heroics and grand purpose. "For the first time in the history of humanity, all the sons and daughters of Earth are on *one side*. United in a single purpose. It's awesome and humbling. It's a moment in history I'm glad I didn't miss."

Of course, Herius thought. *You're in charge.* Said aloud: "United but not unified. You realize we are together for one purpose only."

"Yeah." Farragut came back down to ground level, but still smiling.

This man wielded authority as a birthright. It was only in the natural progression of things for him—a rite of passage—like body hair, lower voice, stiff dick, wisdom teeth, command rank. For John Farragut, it was simply inevitable. The lack of it would cause more notice than the attaining of it. The universe was unfolding as it should.

And here comes the question. Herius steeled himself for it.

Just say it. I have a knife. Say it.

But out of John Farragut's mouth came not the hated, insulting, *How did the gorgons get here?*

"What can you tell me?" Farragut asked. And then waited, attentive. Brightness in his gaze. Alert and absolutely here.

Struck Herius dumb. Such an amazing question. The question assumed nothing. Demanded no more than Herius had to give. And Farragut was *listening*.

Herius had a natural loathing to give any information, including the time of day, to the enemy. But this was military necessity. Caesar had put all of Rome into this man's hands. Herius told the American his observations of the Hive.

Farragut's was an expressive face. Herius saw surprise in it at his description of self-parachuting gorgons. Farragut was amazed by the gorgons' tortoise formation and the beam fire deflecting off the top of it.

John Farragut listening to you transformed you to the center of the universe. He was intent on everything Herius had to say. The Roman ballistae and the catapults intrigued him. Farragut looked up toward the ramparts. "I gotta see those later," he said, like a boy promised new toys.

He was a big man, his frame carrying more weight than he ought. But it suited him. John Farragut, larger than life.

Herius could see why people gushed over him. Not so much the blue eyes and the white teeth. It was the life behind them.

A hail sounded from Farragut's wrist com. The captain looked honestly vexed at the interruption, told the caller, "Something better be on fire."

"Captain, you have a call from Earth."

Earth was in a 13-billion-person uproar. Of course there would be calls from Earth. Farragut said, "Unless it's President Johnson, don't bother us."

Herius supposed that was meant to make him feel important.

"It's the Chief Justice of the Supreme Court of the State of Kentucky, sir."

Farragut looked to Herius, chagrined. "I'm sorry." And he moved a few paces apart to take the call.

Chief Justice John K. Farragut would rather die than initiate contact with his son, Captain John A. Farragut. People came to the Chief Justice. The Chief Justice did not seek people out. And not his own boy.

Captain Farragut's chest felt tight. Wondered who had died. Spoke into the com: "Yes, sir."

There was no hello. The Justice came right to the point: "Should I be sending your mother and the young folk to the outer colonies?"

Captain Farragut closed his eyes and silently thanked God. The family was okay. He answered, "No, sir."

"You sure about that? The gorgons are on the doorstep!"

"We are talkin' about my mother, sir."

"Hmph." It was a mollified *hmph*. "That's what your sister Catherine said. But she's a politician. I want it straight from the front. If it all goes to hell, all the boats will be taken. You know those gorgons will be coming to Earth next."

"If it ever comes to that, I'll come and move y'all myself," said Captain Farragut.

"I have your word on that?"

"By God, yes."

"Well, then." The Justice grumped for something to say. "Carry on."

Farragut returned to the Roman commander, apologizing. "Sorry. My dad. Do y'all have bighorn sheep on Palatine?"

Wasn't a question Herius Asinius was ready for. "No," he said hesitantly. "I know what they are."

Farragut brought his fists together knuckle to knuckle. "They bash heads."

"I'm told you can hear them for miles," said Herius.

Farragut shook his head, no. "For light-years, son," he corrected him. "For light-years."

John Farragut and his father as bighorn sheep. The American was trying to make a human connection with Herius Asinius.

Don't call me "son." There was not a full decade between them. *I walked in Subjugation. I will never forgive you.*

Because Farragut used his hands to talk, Herius could not help but notice the surgical gauntlets encasing both of Farragut's forearms. His eyes followed them involuntarily. Herius guessed at them. "Gorgon wounds?"

Farragut gave a very sheepish smile. Shook his head. "Sword. Friendly hacking. Both hands. Zing." Re-enacted the astonishment of watching his hands fly away from him. "You can't believe what that looks like. Just before *all* the blood leaves your head. Oh, we got chewed *all* to pieces. Turned out to be a blessing in deep cover. That's why we were on Earth for a refit—me and the *Mack*. It put us close when y'all came under attack here. The boffins slapped us back together and here we are. I'm sorry I couldn't get here sooner. Not as late as it would have been if we hadn't got mauled first. This could have been a *lot* worse."

Farragut walked a circle around a stain on the ground. Obviously, he would recognize the mark of a deceased gorgon. "I should have known that something that could gut the Roman Empire would not be easy to kill. Still, I really thought I should have been able to save the universe by now and it's torquing me off to holy Jesus that I haven't done it." He clasped Herius on the shoulder like a brother-in-arms. "We'll get them."

Herius remained rigid. *I walked in Subjugation.*

"Sir?" said Herius thickly, in English. He would not call this American *Domnus.* "I have a request."

John Farragut listened.

"Do not raise the Stars and Stripes on Thaleia."

Farragut gave a long thoughtful pause. Herius silently invoked damnations on him. Knew it. Knew it.

The American hero was going to claim the planet and plant his colors on Thaleia.

Farragut countered, "We may fly our flags from our transports on the ground."

The vessels themselves were not Roman ground, though they were *on* Roman ground. Made them rather like consulates. Herius allowed the compromise, "Fair."

"Done," said Farragut, and was immediately talking into his com to someone named "TR" regarding flag protocol. And back to Herius, "Is that it?"

Herius could not resist: "How did the gorgons get here?"

The impossible question did not offend Captain Farragut. "Now ain't that the question I can't afford to be holding the I-don't-know to? Just when I think I know the enemy, I don't. And I need to find that out *yesterday*."

Herius Asinius almost believed him.

The most sensitive of the insect telltales inside the legionary fortress did not settle until the sewers were cleared of crusted black lumps, which the Romans had not recognized as dormant gorgons.

"I came to a Roman planet to clean a Roman sewer?" F/S Reggie Monroe's high voice wailed up from the depths. Reg was small enough to fit into the sewers. "There is something not right about this! Who surrendered to whom? Yo! Is anyone listening to me? I'm filing a complaint with somebody! This ain't right!"

Once the legionary fortress was pronounced secure, the U.S. Marines prepared to move on to the civilian centers to make them safe for the civilians to go home.

"You want to move out of here, too," a Marine told Herius Asinius. This Marine was the she-ape Ranza Espinoza's superior, a big white bull named Lieutenant Colonel TR Steele. None of the captain's bonhomie in this one. This one radiated hatred.

"Why do I want that?" said Herius. And just how many of John Farragut's minions did he have to listen to?

"Not just you," said Steele. "All your legionaries. Get them out of here. You fired beams at the falling gorgons from your refugee centers. You got the gorgons' attention. When you make enough of them die, gorgons will leave off chewing on the closest thing and gang up on whatever is killing them. You brought them here. If you had just left the civilians alone in the fortress with the scorched earth around it and done your shooting from somewhere else, they would have been safe till we got here."

TR Steele left Herius stunned.

Marcus came to Herius' side. He was never far away. Marcus had heard all of it.

"He's saying we screwed up," Herius murmured.

"Well not exactly, no—" Marcus started.

"He's saying we screwed up."

Marcus struggled for explanations. Finally had to allow: "I think that's what he's saying."

Herius' mouth had gone sour and dry, colors gone flat before his eyes. *I screwed up*.

As the Marines were leaving the fortress, Flight Leader Ranza Espinoza paid a visit to Herius Asinius where he was going over his centurions' reports. She smiled a jarring, gap-toothed smile. "Gotcha a couple a going away presents, Hairy Ass."

Herius looked up from his field table. Said flatly, "I didn't get you anything."

"Shucks," said Ranza.

She set an ant farm on his table.

"You're on your own, Hairy Ass. Keep your eyes on your bugs, 'kay? All bugs react to gorgons. Some of 'em start shaking and shouting if they're in the same atmo. Some of 'em have to be in your time zone. Ants will get antsy if they're within a couple klicks." She tapped the ant farm with a surprisingly dainty finger.

"And these?" Ranza slapped down a clear canister of inert bugs onto the legate's field table. Picked it back up, gave the canister a shake to make sure the contents were still alive. Banged it down again.

Pale yellow-white Zakan moths fluttered briefly inside the canister, then went back to sleep.

"These are your best friends," said Ranza. "When these guys make a sound? Get out of the house."

5

THE CIVILIAN CENTER WAS called Antipolis. Looking at it from a distance, the Marines hesitated to call it a city. Antipolis looked like a titanic termite hill.

"That's not it!" cried Dak Shepard. "We're in the wrong place!"

The pictures Red Squad had seen in their briefing showed a wondrous place of fantastical spires, rainbow colors, enormous arched windows, flying buttresses, and roof gardens. There had been big graceful trees swaying, and tame exotic animals peacefully wandering by a dazzling waterfall that splashed down hundreds of feet from a tower into a glittering moat.

"This is the place," said Ranza.

This was Antipolis with the power turned off. A compact cloistered ziggurat perhaps a mile in diameter, spiraling five hundred feet high, with very few windows.

"The rest was just light dressing."

"Ugh," said Kerry Blue. "Put its clothes back on."

"This isn't a sightseeing tour," said Ranza. "We're here to kill things. We need to see exactly what we're doing."

The Dracs had sent a drone reconnaissance squad in ahead of the Marines. Romans used a lot of remote-controlled, unmanned craft.

"We call that skeet," Ranza had told the Roman Vee jock who had done the recon on Antipolis.

"Never lost a pilot," said the Roman pilot, just before his audio and video went black in a flurry of tentacles.

The pilot shrugged, signed out another recon drone.

Recon indicated a "residual" gorgon presence inside Antipolis. No more than fifty hostile units.

Red Squad was dispatched to eradicate the gorgon presence.

"Fourteen United States Fleet Marines against fifty gorgons," Carly Delgado sniffed. "Hardly worth our time."

The briefing had stressed that Antipolis was a civilian establishment. It was vital that the Marines get all the gorgons. "Do not miss one. Not one."

The objective was to secure Antipolis so the civilian refugees in the legionary fortress could go home.

"Well, there's a priority," said Reg Monroe. "How many million gorgons on this planet and we're gunning for fifty? I'll tell you one thing. I am *not* doing the sewers."

"It's a modern city," said Darb. "There aren't any sewers."

"I'm just telling you," said Reg, slapping at the insects that orbited her head.

The shuttle had put down one klick to the east of the city. Scrub vegetation persisted here. The gorgons, when they had attacked Antipolis, appeared to have descended on the ziggurat from above, then moved off to the west. The western ground was eaten to the dust.

Sounds carried on the scorching breezes. The Marines could hear the gorgons in the distance, countless bladed teeth in millions of mouths, crunching their way westward.

The Marines started walking toward the ziggurat.

"You gotta wonder why gorgons would choose to land on a structure this—this—" Darb waved his hand in the air as if a word would fall into it. "*Appetizing*. I mean, it's a sand castle. All the hologramic froufrou wouldn't have confused the gorgons. Someone in there must have resonated."

"A lot of someones," said Ranza. "This colony is a hundred fifty light-years from Palatine. You gots to know the Thaleians aren't sending messages home by passenger pigeon."

Resonance originating from the ziggurat would have attracted the Hive in its swarms.

"So why didn't the gorgons go to Palatine first?"

Ranza stopped. Darb stopped. Both of them stared at Kerry Blue.

"What?" said Kerry. "What'd I say? Palatine's closer to the Deep End, isn't it? Palatine is swapping res pulses with Thaleia. Shouldn't the gorgons have stopped to eat Palatine first?"

Resonance exists everywhere at once, on infinite harmonics. Touch one harmonic, and no one will know unless he is tuned to listen on that precise harmonic—in which case the listener will pick up the pulse instantly. But the listener will not be able to trace the pulse back to its source, because resonance exists everywhere at once.

Unless the listener was a gorgon. Gorgons were drawn to resonant senders and receivers on any harmonic.

Gorgons had come to Thaleia and not to Palatine.

Why didn't the gorgons go to Palatine first?

"That's a hell of a question, Blue," said Darb.

The Hive seemed to have hopped straight over the Roman capital world. And gorgons never pass up a meal.

The Marines approached the city warily, taking care to step around the Thaleian mines. None of the Marines wore a personal force field, because the PFs did not work against gorgons. The force fields worked well against beam weapons, but were designed to allow low-velocity objects to penetrate—things like air. The PF allowed your feet to contact the ground, allowed your hand to draw your sword. Did not allow lethal projectiles or beam fire through.

Gorgons had learned at exactly what speed a personal force field would permit a tentacle through. They learned that a long time ago. Probably on board the *Sulla*.

And PFs would probably not protect the Marines against the Thaleian mines anyway. The mines were actually native plants. Chameleon-colored vegetation, the mine splayed its leaves flat to the ground, and it looked like the ground. But you step on it, and up come the nettled leaves, wrapped around your calf. If you're barelegged, you are now screaming and bleeding. If you are in field fatigues, you're cursing and cutting the flat hairy leaves loose from your pant leg with your sword or knife, and— with gloved hands—peeling pieces of leaves off your fatigues with a sound like Velcro separating, then trying to get the leaves off your gloves. Then shooting the roots with your beam pistol-you're-not-supposed-to-be-carrying, just 'cause you feel like it.

"No wonder we let the lupes have this planet," said Carly, sheathing her knife.

"The whole world isn't like this," said Darb.

"Yeah, this is the garden spot," said Reg.

A place of scathing sun, searing air, vicious plants, and worse insects.

Insects darted and caromed round them.

Hive sign was ever present.

In the small, self-contained world that was a spaceship, any Hive sign meant you were in immediate mortal danger. The Marines were not accustomed to having panicked insects around them constantly. So here on the planet, they existed in nerve-scraping anxiety.

They carried canisters of Zakan moths wherever they went. The moths were natural Hive proximity detectors.

A canister hung from each Marine's belt. You checked your canister every ten paces to keep your sanity. If your moths were quiet, you probably weren't in imminent danger of being eaten.

But if your moths were quiet, you caught yourself worrying that they might be dead, so you were still on high alert.

Ranza sent Baker Team around to a southern entrance of the yellow-brown ziggurat. Took Alpha to the north side herself.

Alpha Team entered the enclosed city through an air lock, like a ship.

The inner door opened to cool soft air and total darkness. The Marines illuminated their lanterns.

The first chamber was as featureless as the outside of the ziggurat. But there were no insects banging around in here.

Kerry Blue sighed, ran her hand back through her sweaty hair. "That's better."

The place was silent.

Except for the Zakan moths fluttering and squeaking in the Marines' canisters.

"Heads up. Swords out," Ranza ordered, her lantern directed every which way. "Somebody's home. Keep your wits about you."

Darb muttered, "Let's see, I got my nitwit, my half-wit, my dimwit and my twit. All here. Ooof." Took an elbow in the kidney. Felt like Carly's.

Ranza said into her com, "Baker Leader, this is Alpha Leader. We have Hive sign."

"Roger that, Alpha Leader."

"I'll take first point," said Ranza. "Darb, you're ass end Charlie. The rest of yous, don't bunch up! We know they're here."

Alpha Team set out under low ceilings and featureless walls.

Ranks of doors all along the spiral corridor led into tight pigeonholes of living compartments. This sector of the ziggurat appeared to be a dormitory of sorts, with shared kitchen, dining, and bath facilities.

Romans were different. This was all unAmerican.

The Marines moved up the corridor, dorm room by little dorm room. All with low ceilings and no windows. Made the compartments easy to search.

They came to a compartment furnished with little more than a hammock of some synthetic weave that felt just like cotton sailcloth, and a small table that looked like woven cane but couldn't be, because there was not a single bite mark on it. There was one closet, which had quite a bit of storage space in it now that the gorgons had eaten all the natural-fibered clothes from it. They had also cleaned out the bar.

"How can anyone live this way?" said Kerry Blue, boots crunching on broken wine bottles, just as Carly turned on what looked like a light switch.

Gentle daylight filled the claustrophobic space, and the stuffy compartment was transformed. It breathed ocean air. Soft breezes and subtle sounds gave the sensation of great space. The Marines were now on a balcony under an open sky.

They looked out to an empty beach. Snowy white seagulls squalled. Sunshine glittered on the great expanse of emerald-blue water. Rush of gentle breakers sounded as if coming from below.

"Okay, well, that's how," said Kerry.

Twitch Fuentes tried to lean on the white railing that wasn't really there, pitched forward and banged his head against the sky.

Ranza barked, "Hurry it up. I don't want to be here all day."

"I do!" said Dak, trying out the hammock. Knew that was real.

Carly turned off the holoimages, tipped Dak out of the hammock. "Compartment secure."

Ranza tagged the door. "Move on."

They checked for monsters under all the beds and in all the closets of all the rooms. All the tiny living quarters could transform into illusions of space, luxury, romance, or serenity. Or the tree fort, obviously a young boy's space. "Damn, I wish I'd had one of these!" Darb said.

The room illusions were a source of endless fascination. Until Ranza ended it, promising to bring up on charges the next Marine who powered one up.

Baker Team, on the far side of the ziggurat, had brought a rat terrier with them. A small, rat-looking thing named Godzilla. Godzilla had been set loose in the ziggurat's vent system. Alpha Team could hear Godzilla's little claws tippy tapping through the extensive ductwork.

"I *hope* that's God," said Dak on second thought.

They all listened. It was a definite four-footed tapping, not a gorgon blunder.

They had started taking the compartments two at a time. Three Marines in each, one keeping watch in the corridor.

"Who *built* all this?" said Kerry Blue, slapping a tag on yet another door.

"Automatons," said Cole Darby. "This planet is headquarters of PanGalactic Automated Industries. Haven't you ever heard of Constantine Siculus?"

"Sure," said Kerry. One of those historical names everyone had heard of but did not necessarily know anything about.

In the last century, Constantine Siculus had founded PanGalactic Automated Industries, a core of machines that could design and build other machines or entire factories that would manufacture whatever you needed made. PanGalactic did not invent, but it could engineer or reverse engineer, and organize your entire supply chain from raw materials to working product. "All you do is decide what you want done, you pay up, and you get your—your—" Darb searched for an example. He stooped to pick up a silver disk the size of a dinner plate lying in the corridor. Presented it like a finished product: "You get your landing disk."

"You can keep that one." Kerry curled her lip and pushed the offered LD away from her.

Alpha Team had found quite a few of the Roman landing disks in the ziggurat. Roman LD's were smaller than U.S. make. They lacked the reassuring heft of government issue.

Marines displaced all the time, so they stopped thinking about how dangerous and precise an operation displacement was until faced with someone else's equipment. Then your first thought was: You will never catch me on one of those.

Safe displacement required three signal termini. One signal from the sending station. One at the destination—which was normally a landing disk (LD) like this one. And a third signal on the thing in transit—for human beings that was the displacement collar. U.S. Marines wore dog collars. Romans wore torques. For cargo you used a strap.

Neglect the displacement strap on your cargo, you had better own the insurance company.

Nothing in God's own galaxy could make a U.S. Marine trust a Roman landing disk.

Alpha Team took to bowling the flimsy silvery disks down the ramps until Ranza stopped that, too.

Beam fire resounded somewhere within the hollow ziggurat.

Ranza spoke into her com. "Baker Leader. This is Alpha Leader. What is your status?"

"Little busy here, Alpha Bitch!"

From the com you could hear swords meeting stone walls. Grunts and snarls as Marines swung at the enemy.

"Do you need assistance, Baker?"

"Negative. Get your own."

Ranza clicked off. "Baker got first ooze."

"Oh, shhhhhh—" Kerry started in disappointment, met Ranza's warning scowl. Finished, "—inbone."

A frantically paced tap-tap-tapping and a loud yap-yap-yapping blurred together in the ductwork.

Sounds of a rat terrier moving near light speed.

"God!" cried Dak Shepard. "Where is God?"

There was also a blundering, thumping and thrashing in the vents. The sound seemed to be everywhere.

Gorgon.

Godzilla had shared sewer duty with Reg Monroe in the legionary fortress. Reg shouted, terrified, "Godzilla?"

Dak yanked off the nearest vent cover, called, "Here, God! Here, God!"

Carly turned her head sideways, trying to separate out the sounds. "Where is he?"

"Here, boy!" Dak called.

The fast-clattering toenails sounded closer and closer.

"Here he comes."

A white football of dog rocketed out of the open vent, sailed into Dak's arms. The rest of the team had swords drawn. Hacked down the tentacles that bloomed from the opening.

The dog quivered, licking Dak's face.

Ranza spoke into her com: "Hey, Baker. We got your dog."

The dog was wagging itself.

A pat on the head, pop him into the vent, and Godzilla was clicky-clacking back into the hunt.

Darb walked point now.

Rounding a bend in the spiraling ziggurat, Cole Darby suddenly stopped with a gasp. Sounded no warning, just stopped there.

Kerry moved up behind him. Looked round the bend.

A young woman with an impish smile and blue-gray gaze, which met Darb's with seemingly genuine interest, spoke in a light, pretty voice, "*Ave*. May I help you find something?"

The woman spoke Latin. Kerry Blue knew what she'd said because Kerry was wearing a language module.

Darb gawked at the woman, could not talk.

Kerry could. "Yeah, gorgons," she answered in English, at the same time that Ranza came stalking round the bend, "Darb, you afthole, what kind of point man are y— *Lady, what are you doing here!*"

The woman, clad in pastel mufti, tilted her head and asked, in English this time, "Oh, have you mistaken me for a human being?"

Alpha Team had never seen Ranza speechless before.

Kerry answered for her, "Uh, well, *yeah*."

"Uh," said Darb.

When Ranza found her voice, she had no time for the

questions of fake people. Demanded, "Do you know what a gorgon is, chicky?"

"Yes," the gynoid said pleasantly. "One of the monsters."

Ranza hauled the gynoid about-face and gave her a push up the corridor. "You can help us find the *monsters*."

"Well, most of them left the city," the gynoid said as she might apologize for being out of Ranza's brand of beer. "But I think we might be able to find some for you. This way, if you like."

The gynoid led the way, her hips rolling, skirt swishing. She had a soft, civilian shape to her.

"Hey. Hey, you. Girl thing." Dak moved up the column. "What are you called?"

The gynoid glanced back with a pretty smile. "I am Kayle."

Carly scrunched her face. "Like the vegetable?"

"K-A-Y-L-E," said Kayle.

"She's really well made." Dak poked at the soft supple skin of Kayle's arm. "Who makes them this good?"

"PanGalactic Automated Industries," Kayle said brightly.

Reg called from the rear, "How do we know she won't lead us into a trap?"

"Trap," said Kayle. "That would mean you don't know the monsters are there." She turned round to ask, smiling, "Do you want to be surprised?"

Ranza seized the gynoid's arm, hauled her round, gave her a shove. "Find the gorgons, chicky. Sing out when you see 'em."

Sniggering, muttering among the Marines. Speculating on what the perky gynoid's song choice might be. Maybe *Mary Had A Little Lamb*?

"Oh, here we have a nice surprise," said Kayle.

A nightmare shape hurtled down a fire ladder from above.

Kayle moved out of the way. The gorgon rushed past Kayle, and leaped at the Marines.

Skewered itself on Ranza's barbed pike, knocking the

pike out of Ranza's hands. Fell to the floor and thrashed itself to death on the barbs.

A round bite wound the size of a quarter bled on Ranza's cheek. She batted away Darb's attempt at first aid.

"Ranza, it's gonna scar. You have a nice face."

"Oh, get blown up," said Ranza.

Ranza's was a strong, square face. The top line of her nose described a graceful aquiline curve, but without the aquiline hook on the end. Her thick eyebrows were not quite a unibrow, but the two were very friendly.

Ranza rubbed the blood off her cheek against her shoulder, picked up her pike, and cleaned the melted gorgon's remains off it with Kayle's pastel skirt.

Kayle watched with an expression of well-isn't-that-nice on her face.

Alpha Team's U.S. insignia did not seem to disturb Kayle either.

Never having Americans on her world, Kayle did not recognize Rome's enemies when she was guiding them on a tour of her masters' citadel.

"She's not wondering why we're wearing U.S. uniforms," Kerry Blue muttered aside to Reg.

"It's a machine," said Reg. "It don't *wonder*."

Ranza batted them both up backside the head. "Spread out! You bunched up for a group photo shoot? Move. Move. Bring the arugula."

It was nightfall by the time the Marines secured the ziggurat from the last gorgon presence. They had also cleared all the outbuildings.

A large stable outside the complex had been eaten clean of leathers. But there were no horse teeth in any of the stalls. Someone had thought to let the horses out before all the people fled to the legionary fortress.

Another cluster of buildings, furnished with very small furniture, had to be a boarding school. "Oh, they're so cute." Reg held up a child's chair.

"Baby Romans," said Carly. Spat on the schoolroom floor.

Another enclosure, dotted with beautiful statuary,

turned out to be a necropolis. Modern Romans practiced cremation, so none of graves had been dug up by hungry monsters, though something had eaten all the flowers.

Alpha Team met up with Baker Team inside the ziggurat. Lay on the ground of a faux outdoor mall, gazing up at a faux sky full of faux stars. The air was mild and smelled of grass, though the gorgons had eaten all the real grass. The Zakan moths lay quiet in their canisters.

Dak liked cute things. Could not get Reggie to sit on his chest, so God was sitting on Dak's chest, licking his face.

Reggie had curled up next to Dak, asleep, her cute face smooth, her big breasts stacked one on the other.

The stars overhead looked much the same as they did from Earth. Thaleia was only seventy-one light-years off-center from Sol.

Notably different in the star patterns was a bright yellow star, prominent in the false heaven, probably brighter than it ought to have been at a distance of seventy-one light-years. "Is that us?" Ranza pointed at the yellow star.

Darb nodded. "Yeah. That would be Sol."

"Why Sol? Why would Romans want to look at our sun in their fake sky?"

"Earth is Rome's home world," said Darb. "They want it back."

"Over my rotting carcass," said Ranza.

Kerry Blue and Big Richard from Baker Team had gone off to try out one of the fantasy bedrooms.

"Why do they call him Big Richard?" Darb asked, rankled at Kerry's choice of partners in her little expedition. "His name is Lawrence."

"Well, he don't have a big *Larry*," said Carly, her head resting on Twitch Fuentes' belly. "Figure it out."

Ranza Espinoza clicked on her com, signaled Legion Draconis. Told Herius Asinius he was clear to start sending the refugees back to Antipolis. "And nobody resonate, Hairy Ass, or I'll eat you myself!"

* * *

John Farragut stood in deep shadow within a vast crater. The shade was desert cold and dry. Native insectoids, the kind called cannibals, were thick down here. The cannibals' diet consisted solely of each other, just not their own brood. They would eat other broods, then seek out and inseminate their eggs.

The earth down here was a thin layer of windblown debris on top of bedrock, so little vegetation of any size grew on it. Some mobile blue-gray plants had wandered down, stuck their roots to the bedrock, and trolled for insects with their sticky, ciliate stalks. They feasted on cannibals.

Farragut's Marine guard watched him from the rim. Farragut had no real military purpose for being in the crater. But there was something about a crater that made you want to climb down into it.

And this crater was not supposed to be here.

Farragut checked and rechecked his map before hailing *Merrimack*. "Gypsy, I need a xeno. Can you put one on the com?"

He got two of them on the com. Doctors Weng and Sidowski.

"Gentlemen," Farragut announced. "I am standing in the middle of a big ol' crater a few miles across, and I am holding a surveillance map that shows a factory town at these coordinates. Now I think I'm reading this map right, and I think I'm reading my coordinates right, and I think I should be standing in the middle of a Pan-Galactic factory and I'm not. Any idea why I don't see a factory?"

"It's-ay one-gay." said Doctor Weng.

"Ot-nay ere-thay, aptain-cay," said Doctor Sidowski.

"Gentlemen, why are you speaking pig Latin?"

"It's a Roman world," said Weng.

"And all Romans are pigs," said Ski.

"When in Rome," said Weng.

"Y'all can belay that kind of talk as long as the truce holds," said Captain Farragut. "Clear?"

"Yes, sir."

"Yes, sir."

"Why does my map show a factory town here?"

"Old surveillance, sir," said Ski.

"Your survey was taken before the sentinel satellites and jammers went into orbit sixty years ago," said Weng.

"Sixty-one years ago," said Ski.

"But there was a town here sixty years ago?" Farragut asked.

"Sixty-one years ago," said Ski.

"Yes," said Weng.

"And now there is a crater," said Farragut. "Was there an asteroid impact here?"

"Negative," said Weng. "There is no mineral evidence of shock metamorphism. No concentric ridges round the point of supposed impact. No trees knocked over outside the crater."

"There aren't any native trees on Thaleia," Ski muttered.

"No debris fallout. No melt rocks. No fragments of ejecta in the surrounding area. No ash."

"Not an asteroid," Ski cut to the conclusion.

"Bomb?" Farragut guessed again.

"Negative," said Weng. "No burn layer. No residual radiation. No ash."

"Cleanly done," said Ski.

"Cleanly done by what?" said Farragut.

Murmurs of consultation on the other end of the com.

"Continental Knife," said Weng.

"Continental Knife," said Ski.

Farragut was astonished. "Was this some covert operation of *ours?*" Hijacking an entire factory town would certain qualify as industrial espionage taken to weird levels. Yet Farragut would not put it past the CIA to launch such an expedition.

"If it were covert, how would we know about it?" said Ski.

"However," Weng interjected. Could always count on these guys for a however. "It has the look of Roman work. Your crater is round. A U.S. Knife makes a more ovate footprint."

"Sixty-one years ago was the floruit of Constantine Siculus," Ski offered for consideration.

"End of floruit," said Weng.

"Rome gated him," said Ski.

Whether pearly ones or those of hell, Rome had shown Constantine Siculus a gate.

"With a Continental Knife?" said Farragut.

"The guy *was* PanGalactic Automated Industries. Brilliant man," said Weng.

"Yeah, real brilliant turning your empire into a stack of dominoes," said Ski, sarcastic. "It was a design flaw in PanGalactic's killer bots that allowed the Hive to detonate all the bots and kill *Legions*."

"Constantine Siculus had the power to knock over those dominoes himself," said Weng. "Maybe the domino flaw was intentional. And maybe that's why Constantine had to go. The Empire would have to feel well and truly threatened to rob itself of a brain like that."

"I don't think Rome killed Constantine with a Continental Knife," said Ski. "I think Rome used the knife to take Constantine's factory away from him."

Farragut cut in: "Gentlemen, it is not that I don't find Roman history and intrigue interesting. I do. But that's not what I'm doing in this crater. Just tell me: Can I cross this site off my list of human habitats to secure?"

"Pretty sure," said Weng.

"It's a hole, sir," said Ski.

Titus Vitruvius curled up in his own bed. Home at last. In Antipolis.

The air smelled of pine needles. Holoimages transformed the tiny compartment into a wooden tree fort. The night sky was always starry outside the window in his room. The moon above the trees was always full. It cast a gentle blue light in the pitch-darkness.

It had been a noisy night with a lot of thunder. A storm without clouds. He couldn't sleep.

He kept an ant farm by his bed, just like Legate Herius Asinius told him to.

He watched the ants pouring out of their tunnels.

And those boring, dead-looking Zakan moths, in the clear canister the legate had given him, stirred, fluttered.

Whining.

6

KERRY BLUE KICKED from a dream of gorgons to twilight awareness. Not sure where she was. Recognized the confines of her sleep pod, ship sounds and smells. She was on board *Merrimack*. Ranza was shaking her and bellowing: "We're going back to Antipolis *yesterday!*"

Kerry moaned into her pillow, already falling back to sleep. This had to be part of her gorgon dream. "We already secured Antipolis."

"It's under siege by gorgons. From the inside!"

Woke her up.

Stepped on Reggie as she fell out of her pod.

The ziggurat spouted smoke from many fires. The residents had tried to defend themselves. Legion Draconis was here by now. Legionaries with swords stood outside the ruin, thoroughly oozed.

The legate, Herius Asinius, was here. A boy, latched on to him tighter'n a tick, must be his son. The baby face at the legate's waist was fixed, grim. Dark eyes were wide and dry.

Colonel Steele was here, too. Looked like a UXB. Fair face red as fire, his scalp blazing red through white-blond buzz cut hair.

Steele roared down Ranza's throat as Red Squad arrived, "How could any troops of mine uf a site this bad!"

Ranza could not answer.

Kerry spoke up. Someone had to. May as well be Kerry Blue, 'cause Steele already hated her anyway. "Sir, we did it by the book. There weren't any gorgons here when we left. The dogs missed 'em. The *moths* missed 'em. *They weren't here.*"

Steele did not even look at her. Ordered: "Blue, back to the ship. Guard duty. Lower engine room."

Oh, yeah. Of course. Kerry snapped to attention. "Aye, sir!" *You just had to talk at him, didn'tcha, Blue? Why don't I just move my locker down to the bottom sail?*

Ranza Espinoza held her chin forward, her lips tight. Vibration in her throat betrayed that she was scared or pissed or both. Steele drilled her: "Where'd you mess up?"

Ranza's eyes were so narrow all you saw was a gleaming silver sliver between thick black lashes. "We were good, sir."

Steele shifted his glower to Baker Leader, who confirmed, "We were, sir. We were good."

And Steele nodded. Still mad, but not at his Marines anymore.

Because Steele was one of them. He picked up his Marines' dead albatross and wore it with them. "They got us," Steele growled. "Espinoza, find out how this happened. Report back to me. And I'll tell you this—it's not happening again. You got that!"

"Sir! Yes, sir!"

And—oh, no—here comes that man you really really don't want to face right now with an up screw this big.

Captain John Farragut moved in like a storm front. He looked big as a bull, his nostrils flaring. He was all but snorting.

The ziggurat belched black smoke, survivors huddled outside the settlement, crying. They had been safe inside the legionary fortress. They had been safe until the U.S. Fleet Marines had told them to go home.

Farragut's voice started very quiet. Worse than his roars.

"This is unforgivable." Farragut paced in front of Red Squad, turned round again. "Not just a lapse of security. This is titanic."

Colonel Steele stood like a stone. "Yes, sir."

The legate, Herius Asinius, unwound the boy's arms from his waist. Smoothed down the boy's curls, and sent him away.

Farragut was still pacing, outraged. "This site was pronounced clear. I come back to find gorgons *inside* the complex, eating their way *out*. That suggests there were gorgons *in* there when we left it, doesn't it?"

"Yes, sir," said Steele.

"And?"

"Sir. My Marines report that the Zakan moths, the resident automatons, the dogs, and my Marines all failed to detect any sign of Hive. The gorgons must be doing something new."

Farragut looked skyward. Nodded. "Gorgons threw a curve ball." Everyone already knew that gorgons were adaptable. "What exactly did they do to fox us? They can hide from the insects now? If they can do that, TR, we are hosed."

"Don't know, sir."

"Know." That was an order.

A crack like a thunderclap split the air. Came from somewhere inside the ziggurat. Not an explosion. Farragut had a long-practiced ear. Knew that sound at once.

Farragut hailed his exec on board *Merrimack*. "Mr. Dent. Identify whichever ship is making displacements to the surface, and escort it out of the solar system, please."

Commander Gypsy Dent's alto voice sounded from the com. "Aye, Captain."

Then Farragut called to anyone within earshot: "Did anyone get a direction on that? I'm going to clap someone in irons for that." And to Steele, "Do we have irons?"

The captain was probably not kidding. Steele said, "We could fabricate some."

The boy, who had not gone far from the legate's side, returned to Herius Asinius at a trot. Tugged on his tunic for attention.

The boy was holding a jar of Zakan moths.

The whole jar fluttered and whined.

"Holy God," someone said.

One of the Marines broke ranks to run apart from the others and throw up.

Captain Farragut met Herius Asinius' gaze. Farragut had his answer. The last answer he ever wanted.

It was an unspeakable horror.

The gates of hell were open. Gorgons had learned to displace.

The gorgons could displace from the Deep. They could go anywhere.

They could be home in a heartbeat.

Farragut's thoughts turned to his family. His mother, his father, his twenty brothers and sisters.

John Farragut had promised his father he would evacuate the family if he had to.

But there was nowhere in the universe to run.

7

*B*E CAREFUL WHAT YOU wish for, Herius
Asinius.
   He had wanted to see the American brought
low, as low as the Legions of Rome.
   *So, John Farragut, welcome to a hopeless battle. A plan-
etary siege with endless hordes that killed Legions. Welcome to despair, you who expected to save the universe.*
   A U.S. Marine, dismissed from the others, walked
past Herius Asinius, making her way toward a shuttle
set to leave the planet. Herius spoke at her in English,
"Go on, American girl. You can always get in your ship
and run. That tactic has always worked for the *Merrimack.*"
   Kerry Blue shrugged. Never gave much mind to what
a Roman thought of her. The worse the better. And actually what the Roman said was true. *Mack* could always outrun a gorgon swarm. And Kerry Blue never
had a problem with that tactic.
   Mack wasn't running this time.
   Problem here was, as Dak was saying: "Gorgons are
on the five-yard line. Can't let 'em in the end zone."
   "Yeah, that's profound, Marine," said Ranza, whack-
ing Dak upside the head. "Ugly up, ladies, we got things
to kill."
   Kerry turned and called back to Steele. "Colonel!
Can I stay and fight?"

Strange expressions moved across his red face. She thought he was going to shoot her. Steele roared: "NO!"

A Roman legionary approached the Americans upwind of the smoke. A very young legionary, no more than sixteen years old. He came at a run. Stopped well short of Captain Farragut and his guards. Announced: "The legate's compliments, Captain Farragut. There is something you need to see."

Captain Farragut let himself and his Marines be led to a cluster of buildings up on the hillside apart from the ziggurat on what used to be a grassy knoll, eaten bald.

Merrimack's civilian adviser, Jose Maria de Cordillera, came with them, looking out of place. A Terra Rican nobleman, Jose Maria dressed like Terra Rican aristocracy, in muted colors, simple lines, and the finest fabrics. Under Thaleia's harsh white sun he wore a flat-crowned broadbrim black hat, its silken cord drawn under his chin. Jose Maria was a wasp-waisted, trim, and striking man for all his sixty years. He wore his long glossy black hair held back in a silver clasp.

Merrimack's crew had long since stopped thinking of Jose Maria as a civilian. He was their *Don* Cordillera. Nobel laureate, microbiologist, expert swordsman, wealthy Renaissance man. Jose Maria was *Merrimack*'s sword master, the captain's confidant.

Jose Maria de Cordillera had joined the *Merrimack* on a personal mission to see the Hive exterminated.

Farragut was glad to have Jose Maria with him right now. He slowed the pace as he saw where he was headed, where the legate waited.

From the adjacent playground, the complex of low buildings on the hill looked ominously like a boarding school.

John Farragut knew he did not want to see this. But it happened under his protection, so he was obligated to look. Heard Jose Maria's murmur. Sounded like a benediction. This was going to be horrible.

And the Roman legate, burned, covered in soot and gorgon ooze, looked as if he were chewing venom.

Herius Asinius waited next to a bunker that had been built against tornado, fire, or bomb. The bunker's metal hatch had been pried up, its stout metal hinges pulled off as if a giant starfish had torn open a steel-and-concrete clam.

Hive work.

Outside the twisted hatch lay a Roman helmet, a kevlar vest, some shredded synthetic cloth, black as a legionary's uniform. A pair of legionary boots ripped to pieces. A scatter of brass buttons. A kevlar glove. A Roman projectile side arm, its magazine spent. A sword.

The bare ground around the bunker was wet and muddy with puddles of brown ooze. What dead gorgons looked like.

The monsters had not got into the bunker without a fight.

Three Marines went down the concrete steps ahead of the captain. They came back out of the ground, their faces colorless, and pronounced the bunker clear in unsteady voices. They advised against the captain going down.

I don't want to see this. I have to see this.

Farragut descended into the bunker.

There were no torn boots or cloth down here. The victims must have been wearing natural fibers. There was little to see.

Only the scatter of shiny little pearls on the floor.

Tiny teeth.

Farragut knelt and gathered them. Saw the tremor in his own hand.

One of the Marine guards, who had followed the captain down, slung his weapon across his back and knelt down to help. The other stood watch, squinting up the steps, his mouth twitching.

Farragut rose, mounted the steps stiffly.

"Jose Maria, do you have a handkerchief?"

Don Cordillera produced a fine linen cloth. Farragut emptied his hands into it.

"Madre de Dios," Jose Maria murmured, folding the pitiful collection up gently.

Farragut excused himself and marched up the hill toward the school buildings, as if there were something he needed to check up there and only he could do it.

He marched round the back of one of the sand-colored buildings.

Alone, he fell back against a windowless wall, turned his face up at the pitiless blue sky. Tears fell like rain.

He slid down the wall into a crouch. His face wrinkled up. Had not felt this low since he had given *Merrimack*'s surrender to the Roman General Numa Pompeii.

Baby teeth. They should be under pillows, one at a time. Where was the love of God?

He swallowed sobs, fighting to stay silent. Breathed and breathed until he could breathe without sobbing, and he could hold his hand steady again.

A shadow crossed his hand. He had not heard anyone follow him up here.

He looked up. A long way up to a lean, tall figure. The man looked very lean because he was clad in black. Looked tall because he was very tall. He was six foot eight at least, his stony features, strong and regular, but too hollow, too taut and forbidding to be attractive. He stood over Captain Farragut, imperially proud, bitter, closemouthed.

Dignitos. The Romans owned that word, and this man had it. The power and the glory. His dignitos would have made him imposing. Even if he were not really, really tall.

"I didn't know anyone was here," said Farragut, voice gone gravelly.

"How do you live with yourself after this?"

The thought startled Farragut. Ought he to be feeling suicidal? "I have a job to do."

"No guilt?"

"It's just not helpful, Augustus." Farragut got to his feet.

Caesar Magnus had given Augustus to Farragut a year ago. Farragut had promptly given Augustus over to Naval Intelligence.

Farragut had not seen Augustus since.

The patterner's cables were hanging loose just now, disconnected, his wrist sockets empty. Nothing plugged in behind his neck.

Farragut did not know too much about the workings of patterners. Knew they could line up a shot that could pass through a space battleship's forward force field, or could ram a cannon barrel up a ship's gunport at speed without wrinkling the vessel that carried it.

Patterners were wicked creations, and you had to wonder why the Empire didn't make thousands of them. It could only be that the Empire *couldn't* make a lot of them. Probably couldn't make many of them, because these things were at least half human. And God knew *those* were always dicey to control.

Farragut was pretty sure patterners were *not* Pan-Galactic products.

He smeared his sleeve across his wet face, blurring the tear tracks. His eyes felt puffy, probably red, his lashes wet. He dragged the heel of his palm under his eyes, preparing to face his men.

The patterner stood like a critical tree.

"How do I look?" said Farragut.

"Like shit," said Augustus.

There was nothing for it. There were worse things than being caught crying for dead children. Farragut moved out of hiding with a squint like someone who has drunk too much, slept too little, or just run out of tears. He returned to the bunker.

Crouched next to the helmet and torn boots, searching in the caustic mud for an ID. Found it.

Decurion Melissa Asinius Atticus.

He collected her teeth. Picked up a kevlar glove, mostly empty. Felt like there might be a couple of bones left in the fingers. He held the remains in his two hands as if a person were attached, and he was holding Melissa's hand.

"Hero-making, John Farragut?" Augustus' voice sounded over his head. The patterner had followed him here.

Farragut murmured, "Seems to me she did that all by herself."

"She," said Augustus, *"died."*

"Something against heroes, Augustus?" He fished about in the mud for more of Melissa's teeth.

"I understand dying for your duty. The deification is useless to the dead and a danger to the living."

Farragut murmured to the teeth, as if Melissa still had ears. "You gave all you had. Sleep easy now. I'll see you home."

"She can't hear you," said Augustus.

"You speak for the dead, Augustus?"

"I have an insight you don't."

Irritated, Farragut retorted, rising to stand. "You having died when?"

"In my past life."

Farragut did not know what to make of the remark. Said, "This is my life."

"Good for you."

"I should like the respect of the dead."

"The dead are dead," said Augustus.

Farragut did not accept it. He repeated quietly, more to himself than to Augustus, "I should like the dead to think well of me."

He carefully gave over the glove, the teeth, and the ID into Herius Asinius' hands. "Make sure Caesar Magnus knows of this."

Herius nodded, conflicting expressions on his face, attempting, badly, to maintain no expression.

"Melissa Asinius Atticus," said Farragut. "Was she kin?"

Herius Asinius glanced at him as if Farragut had made a foul joke. The legate summoned his legionaries and left Captain Farragut with Jose Maria de Cordillera, the Marines, and Augustus.

"What did I say? Why did Herius look at me like that?"

"His kin," said Augustus, "are legion."

"Legion Draconis—"

"Is almost entirely from *gens* Asinius. There are millions of Romans named Asinius. Almost as many as there are Flavians."

An acrid cloud of black smoke scudded from the ruined ziggurat, up the bald hillock. Made Farragut cough.

Augustus said, "It is your fault this happened."

That rocked Farragut. "Fine. Yes. And where the hell have Naval Intelligence been!"

"I wouldn't know," said Augustus.

How could Augustus not know? Farragut had given Augustus to Naval Intelligence a year ago.

Farragut gazed back toward the smoldering ziggurat. Under his watch. This had happened under his watch.

The gorgons were displacing. Displacing *here*. Why here?

Know your enemy. Couldn't.

"The Hive makes no sense," he said aloud.

"Yes, that would be of paramount concern when the universe was creating itself that it make sense to John Farragut," said Augustus.

"It makes sense to *you*?" Farragut challenged.

"It's all entropy," said Augustus. "The Hive. The universe. Entropy is a fundamental condition of the universe. It makes perfect sense," said Augustus. "It is the rest of this idiot's tale that signifies nothing."

Farragut demanded, tired of this, "Augustus, why are you here?"

As if in answer, Augustus flicked something at him. Farragut caught it on reflex. A lightweight, flimsy metal disk. The kind of thing that passed for a landing disk in Rome. John Farragut regarded the disk in his hand. Looked up at Augustus. "Can I have a more comprehensive answer?"

"Destroy them. All of them," said Augustus. He followed that command up with a message capsule, purportedly from the U.S. Joint Chiefs, instructing John Farragut to organize the destruction of all landing disks (LDs) manufactured by PanGalactic Automated Industries.

"I don't understand. Destroy all LDs? All LDs where? On the whole planet?"

"All that there are," said Augustus.

That raised all the eyebrows in the Marine guard.

The realization hit hard. "The gorgons are using our equipment," said Farragut.

"No. They arc using *our* equipment," said Augustus. PanGalactic was a Roman firm. Roman displacement equipment was incompatible with U.S. equipment. "Do not miss any. Those in space. Those in orbit. All of them. And not just deactivate. Not just turn off. Destroy."

Farragut did a double-take. *Those in orbit?* "Who put LDs in orbit?"

"How very little you know."

"Augustus, we have been collecting data on the Hive for a solid year, and you are supposed to be a miracle machine at synthesizing data, so why *don't* we know?"

"No, John Farragut. I mean how little *tu* know."

Te was "you" singular in Latin, not *vos*, "you" plural.

Augustus was not saying that any collection of Americans was lacking in intelligence. He had said how little you—John Farragut—know.

Farragut kept his temper in check. He had a long fuse to begin with. And he had just let a civilian Roman settlement under his protection get eaten. He was willing to give the Roman a few miles of leeway. "Glory be, Augustus, just tell me what I don't know."

"Caesar Magnus thought he was serving Rome by giving me into your hands. Rome surrendered to you. *Te*. It was your responsibility to use—or not use—what you were given."

The com on the back of Augustus' hand began blinking. "My keepers summon." Augustus dismissed himself.

A Marine offered, "Brig the son of a bitch, sir?"

Farragut shook his head. Handed the Marine the orders from the JC. "Verify these orders, then start collecting PanGalactic landing disks."

He watched the tall bitter Roman go.

There was something he did not know.

8

WHAT WAS MAKING THE war in the Deep End near impossible was the inexhaustible numbers of gorgons out there. And, with displacement capability, gorgon numbers could become inexhaustible in Near Space as well.

But now the gorgons' invasion route to Near Space was known. The defense plan became simple: destroy the landing disks. That would end the invasion and limit the battle to those gorgons already in Near Space.

Thaleia was PanGalactic Automated Industries' headquarters. PanGalactic's central database contained a catalog of every PanGalactic landing disk ever manufactured. So locating every last one of the LDs was not impossible. Landing disks were made to be found. It was just a matter of doing it. Over and over and over.

There were over one billion units in circulation throughout the Roman Empire.

Caesar Magnus assisted in the collection and destruction by issuing a decree making it a capital offense for any Roman to maintain a PanGalactic LD.

At the same time, Caesar also declared that any bid coming from outside the Empire for the design and manufacture of replacement displacement equipment would not be considered. No outsider was going to benefit from "the sacrifice Rome makes in the name of human defense."

"Rome's sacrifice? Oh, my Aunt Fanny!" Kerry Blue cried, returned from her stint on guard duty in the ship's armpit. "The Romans bring 'em here, we clean up their mess!"

"You didn't have to do sewers," said Reg.

The landing disks were everywhere on Thaleia, which could be expected on their matrix world, but the LDs were in odd places. Under the sea. In the arctic. And yes, landing disks had somehow ended up in orbit around Thaleia.

The Marines did not even need to participate in the roundup of LDs on Thaleia. By now everyone and his squid had come to Thaleia to defend Near Space from the gorgons' invasion. Ships from all the nations of Earth, individually, and collectively from the League of Earth Nations came. The U.S. National Guard from all eighty-three United States was here. Citizen volunteers from Palatine came. From every Near Space colony and independent neutral world, people came.

The alien Vwakikikikik sent three ships. No one had ever known squid to make war, so their ships were not battleships. And the Vwakikikikik had no soldiers. What the squid sent to Thaleia were welders, equipped to burn the gorgons under the sea, and to collect the Roman LDs from the ocean floor.

"I never knew squid were friends of Rome," said Kerry Blue.

"They're not," said Cole Darby. "The war is coming home. They're practicing enlightened self-interest."

"Squids are enlightened?" said Dak.

No one found any sign that the gorgons were using either displacement collars or cargo straps in transit, which meant that the gorgons were not displacing safely.

There was no telling how many attempted displacements they had botched.

"Not enough," everyone agreed.

But if all landing disks were removed, the gorgons could never arrive at all. Displacement without a destination was unsuccessful one hundred percent of the time.

In hindsight, it made sense that it would be Roman equipment the Hive chose to use. PanGalactic displacement equipment had a resonant component, which would have attracted Hive interest, where U.S. displacement equipment would not.

U.S. displacement did not involve resonance, which limited U.S. displacement range to well below one light-second. There was the one huge exception to that. The Fort Roosevelt/Fort Eisenhower Shotgun. The Shotgun did employ resonance to move ships across the two kiloparsecs from Near Space to the Deep End.

Any resonance attracted the Hive.

And Hive swarms were steadily closing in on Fort Eisenhower in the Deep End.

Unless the Hive was destroyed, Fort Eisenhower had five years to evacuate everyone from the Deep, and destroy the Shotgun after them. Even with that, humankind would not be safe from the Hive for more than two generations.

Jose Maria de Cordillera conferred with Captain Farragut. "Though I am heartily encouraged that we may be able to control this present Near Space invasion, it is a fleeting victory. I am gravely disturbed by this development of Hive displacement."

"As are we all, Jose Maria," said John Farragut.

"No, young Captain. Not just the act itself disturbs. It is the implication of a creative leap not seen before in the monster. It is one thing to cause Roman killer bots to detonate. That is the mere flipping of a switch. Quite another for the gorgon to link a displacement unit to a distant landing disk and *somehow* decide to send itself and then, *somehow*, do it. This is an evolution I would never believe, if it were not happening. In fact—no. I do not believe it. This is not happening."

"That's real scientific, Jose Maria." Farragut hazarded a smile.

"It is, actually. The conclusions we make now are based upon insufficient or flawed data. I aver: this is not happening."

"Bet?" said Farragut. "A case of Kentucky bourbon against—?"

"A case of Spanish brandy." Jose Maria clasped Farragut's hand.

"And I really wish you could win, Jose Maria, 'cause I really *really* hate the idea of creative gorgons," said Farragut. "But I'm fixin' to drink bourbon over our fleeting victory in Near Space."

"YeeeeeeeHA! Gotcha, gorgo!" Kerry Blue's Swift bore down on her target in a strafing run.

The destruction of the PanGalactic landing disks had worked. No more gorgons were arriving on Thaleia. Their numbers diminished under concentrated human attack.

And at some point the gorgons of Thaleia realized, if gorgons can be said to realize, they were in trouble. They were too spread out to use their combined energy to fox computerized systems. With no more reinforcements arriving, the gorgons were sitting ducks.

All the ships in orbit saw it first. "The gorgons on the planet surface are swarming!"

The Fleet Marine were issued immediate orders to keep the enemy from forming up in numbers. "Break 'em up. Cut 'em down."

Swifts were not designed to operate in atmosphere. Bombs were more aerodynamic than Swifts. A Swift's cooling system was only designed to get the Swift into space or onto the ground, not to fox-trot around in the middle. You only had minutes to fox-trot, then either park it on the ground or hightail to space, else roast yourself to tastes-like-chicken.

The Marine Wing tried picking off the gorgons on the ground from orbit, but the gorgons avoided the shots. Not that gorgons moved faster than light down there in the dirt. But they appeared to be sensing the Marine's sensors. Gorgons were allergic to targeting solutions. Shots missed by inches.

"Inches count," said Carly.

The only choice was to get in close.

The Swift pilots adjusted their displacement fields forward, to keep the thickest part of the field over bow and keel. The stern was open behind the engines.

Then they dove down there on the deck to fox-trot. Shoved shots up the gorgons' tentacle noses.

The Marines were not even bothering with targeting solutions. They took the enemy down the old-fashioned way, with messy, waste-a-crapload-of-shots strafing runs.

Dak shouted over the com: "Good night, Gretaaaaa!"

Carly: "Hoo ra!"

Reg: "They got their flapping butts here. They ain't ever leaving. Got one! I got one."

"Good. Do that twenty-five hundred more times." That was Ranza.

The gorgons galloped like obscene giraffes before the Swifts.

This close to the ground, you felt the speed, because you could see it.

"Cowboy would've loved this," Kerry sent over the com.

Cowboy's replacement, Cole Darby, sent, "*I* love this. Don't I count?"

Darby Cole was no Cowboy. Kerry hesitated, sent back: "You're a nice guy, Darb."

Twitch Fuentes cackled, and Dak gave a sympathetic moan on Darb's behalf. "Hombre, you can't love the sound of *that*."

Nice. The gals called him nice. Darb protested, "Why don't you just cut off my thing, why don't you?"

Carly: "Got bigger targets. Hoo ra!" Laughed at her own joke.

Dak: "They're cruel. They're cruel."

Darb, bleating: "I don't know if I can perform like this." But Cole Darby did bag his share of gorgons. Just couldn't bring himself to shout *Hoo ra*.

If Cowboy were alive, he would have augered in by now.

Reggie chasing a gorgon: "Come on. Come on. Come on. Come onnnnnn."

"You spend any more time with that thing, you're gonna have to marry it, Reggie girl."

"Shut up, Dak." Reggie jinked with her target. This gorgon had a wobble stop no-rhythm step going for it. Reggie brought her Swift down low on it.

The gorgon leaped.

"Shiiii—" Reg banked upward. "—ingles!"

Dak sang out: "Jumpin' gretas! Did you *see* that!"

"Yeah I *saw* that big bag of legs!" Reg cried, overheating. "I gotta go to the roof."

Reggie's Swift, Alpha Three, rocketed out of the atmosphere.

Kerry dove after Reggie's gorgon. "You don't get away with that, bagalegs!"

Carly snapped on the com: "Too steep, *chica linda*. Get your nose up."

Kerry yelling through the dive: "Yeeeeeee—"

The gorgon jumped. Caught her bow.

Alpha Six plunged deep into the ground and went silent.

9

"**K**ERRY!" TOOK A MOMENT to recognize that voice on the com. Alpha Four. Twitch Fuentes.

The Swifts of Alpha Team circled the site where Alpha Six had augered in.

Smoke issued from the hole in the ground.

"Chica!"

Ranza, in the dead calm voice of dire emergency, kept repeating, "Alpha Leader to Alpha Six. Alpha Leader to Alpha Six. Respond."

Utter nothing came back on the com.

"*Merrimack. Merrimack. Merrimack.* This is Alpha Leader. Do we have a reading on Alpha Six?"

"Alpha Leader. This is *Merrimack*. We are reading a distortion field at minimal. Tactical advises she should have survived that."

Alpha Three, Reg Monroe, scorching a path back into the atmosphere, sent: "Then why ain't she talking?"

Dak sent: "Kerry, why ain't you talking?"

Ranza checked her chron. Some of her birds had been down here too long. She ordered Dak Shepard to go upstairs and grab some vacuum.

Dak Shepard streaked heavenward. Cole Darby had to make a run for the roof as well. Could not talk. He was crying.

Ranza, continued mechanically: "Alpha Six. This is Alpha Leader. Respond."

Then she stopped sending. Listened to nothing.

TR Steele listened from *Merrimack*'s command deck, turned gray-white and still as a marble headstone. Dying in the silence.

Kerry Blue. The woman had become the center of his universe. He wanted to go down there and dig her out with his bare hands.

She was a Marine. She was born to fight.

She was his life.

Reg Monroe's voice, pitched high enough to deafen a bat, scared to anger: *"Kerry, say something!"*

Steele marched to the hatch to quit the command deck. He was going down there to dig her out with his bare hands.

The com had gone gravely silent again.

A tiny voice. Carly Delgado's. *"Chica?"*

The quiet lingered.

A cough.

A small voice on the com sounded disgusted: "Oh. *Shick*elgruber."

"Kerry!" All the rest of the voices.

And Colonel Steele barking into the com: "Wing Leader to Alpha Six. Marine, what is your situation."

"I'm stuck."

Ranza: "Wing Leader. This is Alpha Leader. I've got her, Colonel."

Kerry Blue fumbled in the dark. She had been flying in daylight. Then everything had gone dark as outer space. She found the switch for her cockpit light.

In the light she saw dirt and rocks and roots pressing against her distortion field, close and weird and claustrophobic. "This is too much like being buried alive."

"Uh. You *are* buried alive." That was Marcander Vincent at tactical on board *Merrimack*. He supplied her depth at twenty feet.

"Get me outta here!" Kerry yelled.

"Well, Kerry," said Ranza. "Come out."

"I can't move."

"Have you tried backing out the way you came in, molewoman?" That was Reg Monroe.

Kerry unstrapped, turned round in her seat in the cramped cockpit to check her instrument reading with her own eyes. "No. It caved in."

"It's still the path of least resistance. Move your cowcatcher to the stern and back out."

The cowcatcher was the stoutest part of a ship's distortion field. *Merrimack*'s distortion field could hold off just about anything in the universe. The Swifts' fields were not as formidable. Loading most of the energy in the direction of travel—like a cowcatcher—offered the little spacecraft the most protection.

"Can't I just turn it off?" said Kerry. "I'm not moving, and I'm getting hot in here."

The cooling system on most spacecraft was heavily dependent on the ambient temperature outside being around three degrees Kelvin.

"Do NOT turn your field off!" Reg shrieked at her. You'll be crushed. Vent out the sides."

A silence.

"Kerry! Did you hear me?"

"Uh-oh."

"Kerry? Translate that."

"I, uh." Too long a silence. You just wanted to reach through the com and throttle her.

"I'm not alone down here."

Carly figured it out first. "The gorgon that grabbed her crate! Where's the gorgon!"

"It's, um, smashed against my nose cone." Kerry knelt up in her seat, her head brushing the canopy. Stared at her bow.

Wadded up round her Swift's nose was a squashed amorphous blob of gorgon. Tentacles led off every which way like flattened hoses.

"You can't crush a gorgon!" someone had to shout.

"Uh, yeah," said Kerry, sour as hell.

It was moving. Slowly.

It was strange-looking, distorted through her distortion field. She tried to focus on it through the distortion field. And that was it.

It was *through the distortion field*.

Or getting there.

Gorgons could do a lot of impossible things. Like travel faster than light in swarms. And move around in a vacuum.

And penetrate an impenetrable distortion field.

The gorgon was *in* the field itself. Kerry had seen this several times before on board *Merrimack*. *Insinuation* was the word the xenos used to describe how a gorgon wormed its way through an energy field.

"Kerry! Get out of there!"

It was too late.

The gorgon was part of her force field. If she moved her Swift, the gorgon was coming with her.

And it was coming inside.

"O God. O God. O God. O God."

"What?"

Fear quickly turned to anger. Kerry threw her Swift's clear canopy back hard in its slide. She eeled out of her cockpit, squeezing herself into the tight space between the hull and the distortion field.

The space battleship *Merrimack* had an enormous distortion field, with a spacious area between its field and hull. You could get out and *walk* on the *Mack*'s hull under her distortion field.

The Swift's distortion field was much thinner. Kerry had a *maximum* sixteen inches between her metal hull and a really hard energy shell in which to move.

She slithered on the hull, keeping her head low. Elbowed her way forward to where the first circular mouths were emerging from the inner surface of her force field.

Kerry pulled her knife from its sheath. Sliced the mouths off their stalks as they poked through the energy field and into her reach.

She muttered in a breathy snarl as she carved at the loathsome rings of teeth. "You couldn't cut yourself open on a sharp rock, could you? No, you foose-mucker.

You just had to stick your faces where they don't belong." She sawed through another toothy maw. The angle was awkward, upward, close to her head, with nowhere to put her elbow.

She tried to shimmy backward. "Can't you just die like a good gorgon? Oh. Oh. Oh."

The severed mouths gave off an acidic gas as they disintegrated into brown residue and dripped down. Burned her hands. Watered her eyes. Stung her nose and closed her throat. "Oh."

"Alpha Six, what is your situation." Sounded like Steele.

"Fox-trotted!" Kerry cried.

Sweat threaded along her scalp. It was hot and hard to breathe. She jabbed her blade into a mouth right over her head. Little teeth popping out like corn kernels. Peppered her hair and dissolved into acidic gore. "Oh!"

Sudden pain and screaming. Hers. Kerry kicked wildly. Banged her head on the energy plane.

A tentacle had outflanked her within the force field, reached through and sunk all its teeth into her back. Tore out a dollar's worth of flesh from over one kidney.

Kerry writhed backward at panic speed, squid-fashion. Hit her chin on the hull. Another bite. Out of her scalp. A banshee shrieking, from every direction. Kerry Blue's voice rebounding on her.

But even in the throes of wild terror she found a strange stillness inside. Some part of her had detached. Watched herself writhe and scuttle and shriek. The animal carcass howling release, while the rest of her knew what to do. Contorted her arm around and continued to carve the hell out of the mouths. Sent them to hell.

Till the gorgon had no mouths, and all she could do was scream as it died on her.

Did not realize how frightful she looked when she reported to Ops for debriefing after the sortie. Figured it out when the Naval Intelligence Officer immediately summoned a medic for her. Spooks never looked out for you. And when Cole Darby said from behind her, "Uh, Blue. You look like you've been foully murdered."

"What?" Reached behind her for a tickling itch. Brought her hand forward covered in blood. She had thought all that wetness was sweat.

Most of the blood was from the head wound. The gorgon had taken a shard out of her skull with that head bite, and had come within a millimeter of her kidney on the first chomp.

The ship's medical officer, Mohsen Shah answered the summons to Ops. He temporarily patched Kerry Blue's wounds with pink gel to hold her till he could cultivate new tissue and bone for her. Advised the interrogator, "Please be making this inquiry as short as is being possible."

The intelligence officer gave a curt nod. Put the question to all of Alpha Team: "Number of gorgons secured?"

"Pathetic," said Flight Leader Ranza Espinoza.

The IO recorded her answer.

"Observations?" the IO asked.

The Alphas glanced at each other.

"Gorgons jump," said Reg Monroe.

"Gorgons jump high," said Kerry Blue.

"Any other observations?"

"Kerry Blue discovered a wormhole," Cole Darby offered.

The IO glanced up. Asked wryly, "Confirming that using a wormhole collapses the wormhole?"

Never knew IOs to have a sense of humor.

"Yes, sir," said Kerry Blue. The blood in her hair was starting to dry and get stiff.

Just then Lieutenant Colonel TR Steele barreled into Ops with a head full of pissed off.

But he found everyone in Ops smiling.

Locked up everything he meant to say.

If he let out shouting, he may as well drop trousers and show everyone how he felt about Flight Sergeant Blue. So he forced evenness, his face immobile. Asked the Navy interrogators: "Did anyone report the unscheduled mining operation by Alpha Six?"

Kerry Blue shrank a little. Wondered how that foul-up had already got back to Colonel Steele. Wasn't a huge deal. So she buried a Swift. She and her Swift were back on board *Merrimack* and functional. What was the big thing?

The IO answered the Marine CO: "Yes, sir. We thought a Swift ought to manage a depth greater than twenty feet." More spook humor.

Steele was amused as a block of ice.

The IO finished his debriefing. Snapped his file closed. Motioned at Kerry Blue as he spoke to Dr. Mo Shah, "Your man, Mo."

Steele intervened. Demanded a moment with his Marine before giving her over to the medics. Said ominously, "This won't take long."

All of Team Alpha turned toward Kerry Blue. She could only meet the stunned gaze of one of them. Carly. Eyes round with doom.

Heard Ranza speaking, trying to, "Colonel. This is my—"

"Dismissed, Flight Leader," Steele cut her off.

Kerry's mates filed through the hatch in a funereal procession, each giving one last glance back.

Till Kerry Blue was alone with Colonel Steele.

He stalked a circle round her standing at stiff attention. She was cooling down, the pain settling in.

Colonel Steele was going to take her wings. Or transfer her. Or sack her.

This is it.

"What the hell did you think you were doing?"

"Up screwing, sir."

He nodded. An accurate assessment.

Had heard the com. Had died over and over. Heard her screaming. Feeling like being torn open and his guts spilling out on the deck.

Hurt him to see her here. Her pretty shape smeared with gore. Blood clotted her brown hair, soaked the back of her uniform. The medical gel oozed pinkly from her hideous wounds. Her girl-soft cheek was too smooth for a soldier. Her nostrils quivered in fear, pain, or anger. He couldn't tell.

He had listened to her go silent on that cannonball dive into the ground. *Yeeeeeee—*

Cowboy Carver's last words had been *Eeeeeeeha.*

Had she been following Cowboy?

Steele never figured Kerry Blue as suicidal. But she had loved that bastard Cowboy.

Apparently, she loved him still.

Damn Cowboy. Cowboy was dead.

Would he *ever* leave?

"Does it ever cross your mind—" Steele stopped, began again, "Do you ever think *you could die out here?*"

Kerry seemed startled. Answered simply, "I *will* die out here." And to his blank stare, she said, "I live out here. Where else can I die?"

Struck him dumb. He had to gesture at her, because he could not even get out the word: Dismissed.

10

THE YELLOW DAY STAR was just setting. Jose Maria de Cordillera joined a group of Marines resting under the spreading branches of an imported elm, out of the direct light of the hard white primary sun overhead.

Red Squad had been dispatched to this island in the southern hemisphere to take out an enclave of gorgons, which had fled the attacks of the Vwakikikikik in Thaleia's oceans.

Jose Maria took off his hangar, set it aside, and sat on the ground, his arms loosely circling his knees.

Flight Sergeant Dak Shepard lay on the ground, sleeping like a baby. A baby with a handsaw. You could hear Dak Shepard snore in a vacuum.

Twitch Fuentes swatted a winged something out of his face. Native insectoids were plentiful, loud, and bad tempered even without gorgons present. It was tough to tell what was Hive sign and what was normal vicious Thaleian insectoid behavior.

Cole Darby came tromping in from the sunlight, sweating like Dak. He threw himself down in the shade of the elm. Jerked his thumb back the way he had come. "Never *never* use the word *idiosyncratic* to a bunch of grunts. Now Baker Team is trying to synchronize their idiots."

"Do we have to synchronize ours?" came a mumble from the ground.

"Shut up, Dak."

Heat sizzled. In the tree branches overhead, insect noise wound up in rattling whir. It was a calm sound for all its volume. No panic about it. The gorgon population was thinning out, and some insects—those with only close-range sensitivity to the Hive—had settled into normality.

Normality in these insects was loud.

"Are we almost done here, *Don* Cordillera?" Cole Darby asked, pulling off his boots and shaking them out. He angled his feet downwind. "I'm tired of dirt, and I wanna go home."

Home was the *Merrimack*.

Jose Maria nodded. "We are close."

Thaleia was nearly free of gorgons. The battle for Near Space was just about won.

There remained countless hordes in the Deep, closing in on the far colonies and on Fort Eisenhower.

"So what we gotta do to get this done?" Ranza asked, rolling up on her elbows. "Kill the queen?"

Jose Maria demurred with a tilt of his head. Even in the shade his glossy black hair reflected a rich sheen. "That suggestion is based on a misunderstanding of the role of the queen in any hive. The queen does not rule. The queen does not make decisions. The queen is not the brain. The queen is the egg layer. She is also replaceable. Unlike a brain."

"Maybe *your* brain, *Don* Cordillera," said Carly Delgado. "We're not sure about Dak's."

"Hey," said Dak.

"So let's take out the brain," said Cole Darby.

"No!" Dak cried, hands protectively round his head.

"There is no brain," said Jose Maria.

"Yeah, there is!" Dak yelped.

"I apologize, Flight Sergeant Shepard," said Jose Maria, smiling. "I meant in the Hive. The Hive has no brain. Despite the obvious adaptability, there is no evidence of higher intelligence in the Hive."

"They seem pretty smart to *me,*" said Kerry, picking at a bite scab on her arm till Carly slapped her to leave it alone.

Jose Maria explained, "Certain organisms change their behavior in groups, according to circumstance. But survival mechanisms should not be mistaken for intelligence."

"Then what *is* it?" said Ranza Espinoza.

"Emergent behavior," said Jose Maria.

"Yeah," said Ranza. "And I still don't know what it is."

Jose Maria bowed his head, abashed. He often spoke above his audience, but never intended insult. "Emergence refers to the spontaneous formation of complex systems from simple organisms obeying simple rules."

"Nope." Ranza wagged her head side to side. "The Hive don't have a brain. I got that far. How's it do what it does?"

"The Hive . . . cooperates. Consider the Portuguese man-of-war. To see its top bladders and its cluster of long stinging tentacles, you would think you were looking at a single animal—a jellyfish. But the Portuguese man-of-war is a cooperative colony of specialized entities. Were you to push a Portuguese man-of-war through a sieve, it would re-form."

"Woolly Bully!" said Dak. "Can we try that!"

"Fortunately—I mean, alas, I do not believe *Merrimack* carries a Portuguese man-of-war on board," said Jose Maria.

Darb said, "Okay, so forget the brain. I've heard a theory that if we find the gorgons' res harmonic, we can uf *their* functions just like they uf ours."

Jose Maria gave a hesitant sideways nod. "It is not quite a theory. It is still a hypothesis. A very attractive hypothesis. If the Hive indeed owes its coherence to resonance, that would make it vulnerable in a way that no other life-form is. Human life—in fact all life excluding the Hive—is protected by its diversity and its degrees of separation."

"In English, doc?" Carly suggested. "Or Spanish?"

Jose Maria started over: "Consider a virus. Let us assume one of us carries a virus."

"Do not!" Kerry Blue cried. "It's a lie."

"A cold virus," Jose Maria specified. "One of us has a cold. The virus requires a vector—a means of transportation—to spread itself from its current host to someone else. The vector could be as simple as a sneeze. Now we—by 'we' I mean this convivial gathering underneath the kindly boughs of this elm tree—at one degree of separation from each other, we could all be exposed to the virus with a single sneeze from the infected person."

Cole Darby nudged Dak with his bare foot. "Cover your mouth next time."

"Though we may be infected, not all of us will express symptoms," Jose Maria continued. "Because of our varied genetics, some of us will clear the disease without ever knowing we were infected. That is the strength of a sexual species—our diversity. Now, instead of a cold virus, consider one of the extinct deadly viruses—"

"But it's extinct," said Kerry. "How can it do anything?"

"We are going back in time for this illustration, Kerry Blue. Back when there were such things as deadly viruses. Consider one for which the most common vector was a mosquito. Let us assume I am infected with the virus. A mosquito bites me, then lands on one of you. Or all of you."

The Marines were seized by an unconscious need to brush imagined pinpricks off their arms and backs.

"None of you will become infected," said Jose Maria.

"Why not?" Darb argued. "Mosquitoes pass blood from person to person."

"Mosquitoes do carry blood from person to person, and might spread a virus with it, but only if the mosquito ingested a virus along with my blood. The mosquito that bit me did not pick up a virus with her bite."

"And we're really really sure of this—why?" said Ranza.

"Because the concentration of this virus in the human bloodstream—or in the bloodstream of any mammal—is very very low. The mosquito only withdraws a small drop of blood from me. The chance of the mosquito ingesting even a single virus with that particular drop of blood is remote. So the mosquito cannot pass the virus from me to you. This virus does not pass from person to person."

"Then how did *you* get it in the first place?"

"Not from another person. The mosquito that infected me may have bitten an infected jay first. The viremia of our subject virus in the bloodstream of a jay or in any of the *corvidae* was great. When the mosquito bites the infected jay, the mosquito has a one-hundred-percent chance of ingesting the virus. But that mosquito may carry the virus to a dead end instead of to a fertile reservoir. When I mentioned degrees of separation, I refer to the number of links required to connect one individual to another. Only one degree separates you and me. We are linked because we know each other."

"So I'm like one degree separated from Dak, but I'm ninety-five-hundred degrees separated from the President of the United States," Reg Monroe said.

"Two degrees actually," said Jose Maria. "I had dinner with President Johnson last month. Two degrees separate you from the President."

"*Well*, then!" said Reg, straightening her back importantly.

"Returning to our deadly, mosquito-borne virus, our one degree of separation is an impassable canyon. The virus cannot negotiate our link. It cannot spread from person to person. So even before we exterminated the deadly viruses, life on Earth already had certain natural walls against the rampant spread of most viruses."

"Why didn't we kill off *all* the viruses—and mosquitoes!—while we were at it?" said Ranza.

"Extinction must be undertaken with only the most profound consideration," Jose Maria said gravely.

"The Hive," said Darb. "We *are* going to exterminate the Hive, aren't we?"

"After profound consideration, yes. The Hive is bound for extinction by my own hand, if no one else accomplishes it first—and anyone may beat me to it with all my love and blessings."

"You're gonna do it with a virus," Reg guessed.

Jose Maria nodded. "Of a sort. The Hive has no degrees of separation and no diversity. Because the Hive is cohered by resonance, and resonance is everywhere at once, the Hive is more like a computer network without firewalls than it is like any organic system. One well-coded computer-type virus could infect the entire Hive instantly, and, as Flight Sergeant Darby suggests, we could uf their functions quite thoroughly. That is a hypothesis I pray to God I may test."

Reg blurted, "*Don* Cordillera, you are so beautiful. Can I bear your child?"

Jose Maria chuckled.

Kerry Blue suddenly jumped up onto her heels in a crouch. "Holes!" she said, casting about her on the ground on all sides. There were a lot of the holes pocking the ground under the scrub grass, holes the size of a finger. Smaller than a gorgon's mouth, but lots of them. "What's in all these foxtrotting holes!"

Jose Maria put out a calming hand. "Nothing, Kerry Blue. Everything is already out."

"*What!*" Kerry screeched. "What came out!"

Jose Maria pointed up into the shady elm boughs over their heads. "The sounds you have been hearing." He paused as an insect sound wound up, became loud. "Seventeen-year locusts."

Jose Maria turned to Ranza. "Now *this*, Ranza Espinoza, this is emergent behavior. The spontaneous organization of simple organisms with no leader. For seventeen years these insects burrow in the ground, dark, silent, solitary, wormlike. Then comes the night when the entire brood, in its millions, crawls to the surface and changes form." He plucked an empty locust husk off the elm tree trunk. "And our isolated, mute, ground dweller transforms into a noisemaking, gregarious creature, swarming together with others of its kind in an insectoid Mardi Gras for a few brief weeks out in the light."

"They change into something slinky and throw an orgy every seventeen years," said Kerry Blue.

"Once, Kerry Blue. Only once. The offspring of these locusts will organize the next orgy in another seventeen years—all without a leader or a communal brain. There is your emergence. There is your Hive."

Ranza said only: "What Roman squid-for-brains imported uffing locusts to one of their own colonies?"

"It has the look of a mistake," said Jose Maria with a sigh, sitting back against the elm. "The locusts likely arrived inside the roots of imported trees like this one," he patted the elm's stout trunk. "This world was terraformed by a coarse and clumsy hand. Not the way my Mercedes would have done."

Jose Maria de Cordillera had first come aboard *Merrimack* on a quest to find his wife. Dr. Mercedes de Cordillera, an expert xenobotanist, had worked on a secret Roman terraforming project deep in the Deep End. A planet called Telecore by those who knew of its existence.

On her homeward voyage, Mercedes disappeared in the Deep with the Roman ship *Sulla*.

Rome kept the disappearance secret for a long time. Jose Maria's attempt to get information ran aground. Because even Rome's feared Imperial Intelligence did not know what had become of *Sulla*.

And then they discovered other secrets too terrible to tell.

Now it was clear that the crew and passengers of *Sulla* must have been the first human casualties of the Hive.

Sulla was never found.

"This planet was trench-terraformed," said Jose Maria, setting aside his locust shell. "A clumsy, reckless method. But the developer of Thaleia was a self-serving man."

"Constantine Siculus," Cole Darby named the self-serving man. "Founder of PanGalactic Automated Industries. Set himself up as Caesar of Thaleia. Then he decided he was God, so Rome dared him to resurrect himself."

Reg frowned, confused, missing a step. Her pert nose wrinkled up. "Resurrect? Wouldn't that mean he had to die first?"

"Oh, yeah," said Darb. "Rome killed him good."

"Didn't happen, then?" Reg guessed. "The resurrection part?"

"No. It did not."

Kerry Blue cranked her head round to stare at Darby as if her comrade-in-arms had grown a second nose. "Darb, how do you know all this stuff?"

"Our Darb knows lots of stuff," said Carly. "None of it very useful. You know, like Reggie's stuff. But he knows stuff."

Ranza's silver eyes lifted to some point beyond the shade of the elm tree. "You got company, *Don* Cordillera."

Jose Maria did not even look to see who was coming. Gave a secret smile. "I do not believe this visit is for me."

A big figure hove into view. Captain John Farragut, hiking up the hill. Motioned the Marines of Alpha Team down as they made to stand up. That big sunny smile on the captain's face was all for Reg Monroe.

Reg's breath caught with a little gasp. She started up on hands and knees. Farragut's grin got brighter. "Mail call, Mister Monroe."

Farragut noticed every sparrow that fell on his boat, and he knew his Marines by name. And knew that Flight Sergeant Regina Monroe was a short timer with applications out at several schools.

The vid stat in his hand showed the seal of the University of Southern California.

Reg's eyes tried to escape her head. Her face was as pale as a black woman's could be. She was utterly terrified.

Farragut arrived at the elm tree, held out the stat to Reg. "Congratulations, Flight Sergeant Monroe."

Reg sprang straight up with an ear-piercing squeal. She did a little dance that included jumping into Captain Farragut's arms. And him catching her and just chuckling like Saint Nick.

Dak frowned, confused. "What just happened?"

"I'm guessing our little Reggie girl got into college," said Darb.

Reg's face was awash with tears. She squeaked over and over, "USC! USC!"

"Hey, I heard of them," said Dak. "That's a real school. They got a football team."

Reg had only ever enlisted in the Fleet Marine so she could get an education on Uncle Sam's card. There were church mice with more spending money than Reg Monroe had.

Reg had spent four years with John Farragut in front of the front line and waded through gallons of gorgon guts to get here. But she had arrived. College bound. A scant one month and seventy-one light-years from home.

Flight Sergeant Reg Monroe was the happiest she-dog in the known galaxy.

"I own you for another month," Farragut told Reg. "You watch your stern. That's an order."

League of Earth Nations inspectors declared Thaleia free of gorgons, from pole to pole, ionosphere to bottom of the seas.

Celebrations and memorials and thanksgivings were held all across Near Space. It was the first time a planet had ever been cleared of Hive presence without killing the planet.

For Herius Asinius, victory had a bitter edge.

Once again, John Farragut had got off easy. The battle for Thaleia had not been the same as the desperate Roman battles in the Deep. There were no endless hordes of gorgons on Thaleia. No gluies.

There were endless hordes of *humans* here.

The gorgons' line of transportation had been cut. Their reinforcements completely blocked—thanks to *Roman* intelligence, did you mark that, John Farragut?

Legion Draconis had been sent in without tools to do the job. Left it to John Farragut to save the day. Herius still swore that the fireman had set this fire.

Captain Farragut thanked Herius Asinius and released Legion Draconis to continue its former duty on the Roman home guard.

Herius took it as an insult. As if Draconis were still not worthy of Deep End responsibility.

Herius toured every settlement on this Roman world before leaving. He bade farewell to the boy Titus Vitruvius at Antipolis. Titus Vitruvius was his one bright memory of this hole.

Herius felt a startlingly ferocious paternal bond with the child. Valiant little Titus Vitruvius, who desperately wanted to come with him and serve in Legion Draconis.

But the boy had a mother.

Most Romans began life in a petri dish.

Herius Asinius himself took pride in having been conceived in passion. His life began in a womb, even if he hadn't stayed there for the duration. An incubator had finished the job. Titus did him one better. This child had been born of woman. You don't break up a set like that this early.

Pretty sure Titus' mother would murder him if he accepted his enlistment.

Herius dropped on one knee to look up at Titus' teary eyes. "Not that I couldn't use a man like you, you understand, but you already have a duty." And ordered the boy to stand his post and protect his mother. Legion Draconis would wait.

Herius, with his cousin Marcus, returned to the ancient-style fortress where he had made his first stand against the gorgons just months ago. He had aged five lifetimes since then.

Marcus halted the skimmer, short of the fortress, where the road was blocked. Herius and Marcus both climbed out of the skimmer to stare at the construction.

Automatons of PanGalactic Automated Industries were at work building a monumental structure that spanned the approach road to the fortress.

"What the hell is that?"

"Heri!" Marcus seized his cousin's arm. "It's a triumphal arch!"

Herius blinked. The dead last thing he expected. "I'll be damned."

He walked toward it. Marcus ran ahead, round to the other side of the huge stone structure.

Marcus' face changed. Strange unreadable expressions.

Marcus picked up a clod of mud and hurled it at the towering arch.

That certainly boded ill. Herius continued at a measured walk, made the turn to face the thing.

Looked up.

Oh. By. Jove.

Read the inscription on the architrave. *I shan't be damned,* he thought. *I am already in hell.*

S P Q R
IMP CAES MAGNVS
IOHN FARRAGVT AMERICANO
QVOD CVM EXERCITV EST ARMIS IVSTIS
VIC HOSTES ALIENIGENOS
ARCVM TRIVMPHIS FAC CVR H L

PART TWO

The Ides Of August

11

THE FACE ON THE RES com screen registered astonishment.

"John!"

A perfect face. Without its frame of long lush chestnut hair—here pulled severely back—the face was naked, perfect. Almond eyes. Sultry. Elegant.

Hard to take seriously.

Captain Callista Carmel, former executive officer of the space battleship *Merrimack* had a beauty to open doors. It also shut them. Beauty was Calli Carmel's last choice for a weapon, but she never threw away a weapon.

Captain Carmel had to drop her ship *Wolfhound* down from FTL to collect a coherent res message from a stationary caller. Resonance exists everywhere at once, but when a caller's time is relative to the receiver of the message, only the mess gets through.

Calli's ship operated in Deep Space, on the far side of the Abyss, so Calli was surprised when John Farragut's image resolved on her res caller. She knew he was fighting the Near Space gorgons. She thought he had that battle won. Now this call. Scared her. She was accustomed to bad news over the resonator. Something had gone wrong. "John, what is it?"

"Cal. I need my Roman expert."

Calli almost laughed. "You're on a Roman planet.

Aren't there one or two genuine Romans there you can consult?"

"Lots of 'em. Lookin' at me like I burned their ranch, stole their horses, and shot their dog."

"What'd you do?"

"Has something to do with this big ol' arch, like something you'd see in Paris, but this one is outside the legionary fortress here on Thaleia, and it has my name on it. I'm turning you round here. Stay with me. Here it is. Can you see this? Stop saying Omigod Omigod and tell me what this is."

"John, this is huge."

"Almost seventy foot high."

"No. I mean it's, it's, it's the Congressional Medal of Honor. Only greater."

"Honor doesn't get any greater."

"Oh, yes it does. You have to have done something like—well, like save Palatine. Which I guess you just did. There's a crown that goes with that."

"Oh—" Wanted to say all kinds of words. Said instead, "Shouldn't Caesar might maybe oughta've *told* me about this?"

"I don't know."

"Why not! You're my Roman expert!"

"Triumphs are rare. I was on Palatine during the peace." Calli had grown up in the U.S. Embassy on Palatine and had attended the Imperial Military Institute. "I don't know how these are done. And there's something else. Stop pacing. You're making me nauseous. Bring that image back. There. You see?"

Farragut looked back up at the arch. "No."

"Look for what's not there."

"Cal, I can't really read it. Romans use more abbreviations and acronyms and alphabet mash than even the U.S. Navy."

" '*Caesar Magnus and the Senate and People of Rome dedicate this triumphal arch in this place to John Farragut Americano, because he conquered the alien enemy with his army.*' Isn't Legion Draconis there with you?"

"Yes. Herius Asinius' boys. They've been here since the beginning."

"They're not mentioned on the arch."

"Oh, for Jesus." That explained much. "Is Magnus trying to get me murdered?"

"Any other Roman, I'd say maybe. But that's not Magnus' way. But he did slip something in there. 'John Farragut Americano.' "

"That doesn't just mean I'm from America?"

"No. That would have read 'John Farragut of the U.S.A.' This is styled as part of your name. Tacitly, it claims you as a citizen of Rome from the Roman province of America. Ever since the end of the Long Silence, Rome has insisted that the U.S. is a Roman colony, not the other way around, so it's not a new idea. But here it is set in stone, so to say."

"All right. That's it. I'm getting myself posted to the Deep End right now." The image of the arch disappeared from Calli's res caller.

"John, *don't* refuse the triumph," Calli said seriously. Would have been an order had she been his senior. "We can't do a two-front war. With Near Space secured, it's *our* colonies out here in the Deep who will be eaten first."

"It's Rome who can't afford to open the war back up," said Farragut, dead certain.

"What Rome can afford to do and what Rome *will* do for the sake of pride aren't necessarily one and the same."

Farragut reconsidered. Death before dishonor was a distinctly Roman notion.

And a large—nay, *huge*—segment of the Roman population was almighty pissed at John Farragut for insisting on the Subjugation.

Very well, it was the entire Empire.

"Hell, Cal, if Magnus wanted to thank me, why didn't he get me World Series tickets?"

"Accept the Triumph, John."

"I'll think about it."

Did not sound sincere. The only thing he was thinking about was how to word a polite refusal.

Until he received orders to accept. From his Commander in Chief, Marissa Johnson, President of the United States of America.

Julius Caesar Magnus on the vid. Looked old. Haggard. The weight of his ravaged Empire on him. He carried it like a cross.

The white on his temples had taken over his entire head of thinning hair. His cheeks had sunk. The jowls belonged on a bloodhound.

Saving his Empire meant stabbing himself in the heart, and Caesar Magnus had done it. Caesar Magnus had surrendered Rome to the hated United States of America. It was a living death.

Magnus was not holding this Triumph for John Farragut out of gratitude. It was a public claiming of the American as a Roman. Made America less of a conqueror and more of an estranged relative you really hated to ask for help.

Behold the Roman Empire, prodigal sons and all, standing together against the deadly alien menace from the Deep.

John Farragut had not faced Magnus since the surrender. Saw what he expected. Resentment. Crushing duty.

And there was no love going back the other way from Farragut. But the two men understood each other.

Magnus' voice had lost all its color. Sounded papery. "Because you are a plainspoken man, I will be plain. I do not expect you to walk up the Via Triumphalis. Someone would take a shot at you, and it is not my intention that you be shot."

Plain enough. "I appreciate that, Caesar."

"At the end of the triumphal procession, you in your *Merrimack* will pass over Roma Nova with the Imperial home guard. You will be required to disembark from your *Merrimack* to accept the *obsidionalis* from my hand."

Note to self: ask Cal what an *obsidionalis* is.

"That ceremony will take place in Fortress Aeyrie

where we can control the attendees and eliminate any chance of sabotage. Yes, I realize you are not universally loved. Neither am I. A protocol officer will instruct you and your Vice President on all you need to know."

The Roman protocol officer informed Captain John Farragut that weapons could not be brought into Fortress Aeyrie, and that the captain would not be permitted a Marine guard. Farragut was allowed one officer to accompany him.

"What's Reed allowed?" Farragut demanded.

"The Vice President of the United States of America is permitted six attendants," the liaison said loftily. Status conscious. Put Farragut in his place. "Unarmed."

No wonder President Johnson passed on this circus.

"*You* may have one attendant," the liaison repeated.

Yeah, I'm just the guy getting the crown, Farragut thought, the warmth of his enthusiasm slipping into degrees below absolute zero.

Farragut's choice of a companion was immediate and obvious. He signaled *Wolfhound* again in Deep space.

Surprised to find Captain Carmel not on board.

Calli Carmel had come through the Shotgun on a Long Range Shuttle. She was now in Near Space, at Fort Theodore Roosevelt.

And she had already been invited to the ceremony. Not as a military officer. She was attending as consort to Caesar's son, Romulus.

"You're Romulus' *date?*" Farragut yelled into the com.

"Well, yes. That is the sordid truth," Calli sent back.

"What were you thinking!"

"I was thinking I should report the invite to Admiral Mishindi. Which I did. And next thing I know, the Joint Chiefs are on my resonator. All of them. And *they* were thinking it would be good to get another Naval officer in Fortress Aeyrie any way they could."

"They ordered you to accept!"

"They strongly advised it. This is good, John. It means they trust me upstairs."

"Cal, you never had a good thing to say about Romulus."

"I still don't."

Caesar's son Romulus had attended the Imperial Military Institute with Calli Carmel. Calli was the extraordinary beauty who always said no. Made her a must have.

Farragut said, "Some terms I remember, let's see, self-serving, cunning, opportunist. Shallow as pond scum. . . ."

"That was half a lifetime ago, and people change," said Calli. "But not that much. You're right. I don't think Romulus ever learned that the word 'no' can apply to him, too. I may have to stab him at the end of the evening."

"With what? We're not allowed weapons inside Fortress Aeyrie."

"With hair sticks," Calli retorted. "I'll find something. I could hit him with Sampson Reed's chin."

Vice President Sampson Reed had an absurdly deep, manly block of a chin with a deep dimple in it, and enormous white teeth above.

Farragut had to smile. "I'm glad you'll be there, Cal. Watch out for me."

"There can't be any trouble. Security can't get any tighter."

"It's *their* security."

"Their security is better than ours," said Calli. Comments like that got her in trouble with U.S. authorities, who were often allergic to the truth. So yes, it was good to see the Joint Chiefs trusting her with the enemy. But John Farragut did not trust the enemy with her.

"Cal, have I ever cried wolf?"

"Not without there being a wolf," Calli admitted.

"Well, listen to me: Wolf. Wolf. If I could get out of this, I would. When we get into Fortress Aeyrie, *their* security is going to grab you, me, and Sampson, truss us up onto one of those big ol' Roman altars and open up our throats for Caesar."

"That is not Magnus' way," said Calli reasonably.

"It'll be a surprise present from Romulus to his daddy," said Farragut.

"*Their* security doesn't allow surprises to Magnus. Anyway, if my throat were getting cut, Numa Pompeii would want to be there, and he's not coming."

Meant as a jest, but it was a comforting argument. Both Farragut and Calli Carmel had history with the Triumphalis, General Numa Pompeii. Numa Pompeii would not miss Farragut's and Carmel's executions for anything in the universe.

Numa wasn't coming. So maybe this ceremony truly was the presentation of a crown to John Farragut after all.

"What's an *obsidionalis?*" Farragut remembered to ask.

"It's a grass crown given to Roman victors who have rescued a place from a siege," said Calli.

Farragut considered this. Said at last: "What kind of grass?"

12

THE WOLF STAR WAS A white main sequence star with a wide orbiting white companion two hundred light-years distant from Sol in the constellation of the Southern Crown. Were the crown to be worn, the Wolf Star would present over the wearer's left ear.

The planet Palatine orbited the main star at 1.12 astronomical units.

Roma Nova had been founded on a river in the northern temperate zone. An exquisite city, orderly, textured, artistic. Rich with color—the deep browns and golds of its stone and stucco, terra-cotta red of its tiled roofs, varying greens of its trees and gardens. There were typically Roman arches and domes, villas, fountains, viaducts, classical colonnades and temples. There was also the best of every alien style the Empire could borrow, for nothing was more Roman than adopting someone else's good idea and someone else's gods. The soaring bright Kwindaqqin spires were of questionable artistry—Kwindaqqin pricks, their critics called them—but Rome was nothing without its vulgar side.

Palatine, and every planet in the Roman Empire, kept its own local calendar, calculated to the planetary motions of its solar system. On Palatine the local year was 2856 *ab urbi condita*—2856 local years from the original foundation of old Rome back on Earth.

In addition to local reckoning, Rome also maintained a common calendar across all planets of the empire, much as all of Earth kept Greenwich Meridian Time even though little of Earth's population actually lived in the Greenwich Time zone. No matter where you were, there was one uniform date everyone could reference.

Because Rome claimed Earth as part of its Empire, the official time and date of the Roman Empire was the time and date at Greenwich, England, Earth.

So when *Merrimack* swung into orbit around Palatine, the date here and everywhere was the 15th of August 2445 C.E.

New among Roma Nova's monumental public artworks was the Monument to the Conciliation.

Conciliation was the official name of the Subjugation, that pride-crushing moment when Caesar and his surviving Legions walked beneath an arch of crossed spears in surrender.

The term Conciliation only ever came out of official mouths. Everyone else still called it the Subjugation. When John Farragut took Rome's surrender over a year ago.

The Monument ignored that, and celebrated the joining of bitter enemies for the common human good. The soaring graceful sculpture formed two eagles, one bald, one golden, flying wing tip to wing tip.

Romans hated it.

The monument had even angered most of Earth. All the nations of Earth other than the USA were left completely out of it, even though many Earth nations were friends of Rome.

It was always the worst prodigal who got the fatted calf.

In emergency, Rome turned not to its friends but to its most powerful enemy for help.

What *Merrimack* saw from above that could not be seen from the ground, or even from the palace on its hill, because of the tilt of the eagles' wings, was that someone had egged the back of the bald eagle. Farragut wondered how many times a day PanGalactic automatons had to clean that off.

"Let me down there," said the specialist at the tactical station, oldest man in the control room. "I bet I could lob some dog exhaust onto the golden eagle."

"That will do, Mr. Vincent."

Marcander Vincent was forty-three years old. He had been at the same grade for ten years now. Would probably retire there.

Planetside, crowds gathered round the Capitoline. Whether because Caesar commanded or because this promised to be a hell of a spectacle, the Roman citizenry was there.

In space, waiting their turn, the crew of the *Merrimack* watched on its many monitors a Legion of really pissed-off Dracs leading the procession. There should have been a crown on their standard. There wasn't. Following Legion Draconis came formations of flag bearers, prancing horses, elephants, camels, giraffes, griffins, centaurs, and sphinxes. Physical things, not holoimages.

Qord Johnson, the cryptotech, looked from the sphinxes to Captain Farragut on the command deck. "PanGalactic products?"

"Without a doubt," said Farragut.

Then clouds rolled in with astonishing swiftness, covering the sky over Roma Nova.

"Is that real?" Farragut asked Tactical.

"No, sir," said Marcander Vincent. "Holo."

"Get me a bounce of the ground. I want to see what this looks like from down there."

Menacing clouds billowed miles high. Darkened the Eternal City. Jagged lightning darted horizon to horizon. Snaking trees of blue and red scorched angry tracks across the heavens.

Then a bright shining golden crack split the darkness. The glowering black clouds parted, and the gleaming golden chariot of the Sun appeared, pulled by fiery horses.

As up from the ground a fountain of opalescent water spouted, towering a thousand feet high. Leaping dolphins danced at the crests of the shining waters. The spume spread miles wide, shimmering all colors, and casting triple rainbows in the sunlight.

The billowing clouds had turned a snowy, scintillating white. In the midst of them a ghostly shimmering triumphal arch appeared like a gateway to eternity.

While on the ground, in the procession, sixty-four fallen Legions marched. These were holoimages of the dead. Legionaries who had fallen to the gorgons before the surrender.

The legionaries looked perfectly real and whole, carrying their colors. Crowns on their standards.

And rank by rank the ghost legionaries stepped into the air on an unseen wide spiral stairway. The legionaries grew in size as they climbed, become ethereal, the size of titans, their faces turned downward as if searching the ground for someone left behind.

Apparently, the images were masterworks of accuracy, expression, gesture, and nuance, because everywhere in the crowd people burst into tears, shrieked, pointed, and waved at beloved images.

The spectral legions marched a wide spiral skyward. At the shining archway, a ghostly she-wolf waited, her teats heavy, her mouth spread in lupine smile. She greeted each of her sons at the arch. And each specter turned for a last look back at a special someone before passing through to the shining hills beyond.

After all the Legions had ascended to the home of heroes—and the crowd was completely blinded by tears—it came *Merrimack*'s turn.

Merrimack descended into atmosphere, joined up with the Legion carrier *Horatius* to pass slowly, wing tip to wing tip, up the Via Triumphalis in the tracks of the dead.

As nothing was permitted to fly directly over the Capitoline, when the two ships arrived at the Monument of the Conciliation, the American and the Roman split left and right.

Exactly what's going to happen the moment the Hive is dead, thought John Farragut.

The display ended with ground-shaking, sky-burning fireworks—real ones that boomed and sizzled and left a gunpowder haze over the dispersing crowds.

The spectacle struck Farragut as more a public funeral than a triumph. A reminder to the Romans of what they had lost. A justification of what Caesar had done to preserve the survivors.

That had been the easy part. What Farragut dreaded was still to come.

Spaceship Two was already at Fortress Aeyrie in orbit around Palatine when *Merrimack* made rendezvous.

Merrimack's companies of Marines of the 89th Battalion were barking furious not to be allowed to go with their captain into the wolf's lair.

"No weapons! What kind of Roman guano is that?" Kerry Blue squawked. "Does Reed get guards?"

Sampson Reed, Vice President of the United States.

"Reed gets an honor guard," Cole Darby answered. "But they're not armed either."

"Oh!" Kerry Blue gestured outrage in the air. *"Colonel!"* Begging with just his name.

White-blond head nodded. Square jaw set hard. TR Steele was in complete sympathy with his mutinous Marines but could say nothing.

Steele had insisted that he be the one to accompany the captain into Fortress Aeyrie. He had been denied.

"So who's going with?" Kerry demanded.

Steele could not answer her. Was afraid he would babble. She derailed every thought in his skull.

Ranza answered, "Mr. Dent."

Commander Egypt ("Gypsy") Dent was imposing. Had a bold bone structure with bold musculature over that, head to heel. Gypsy was black. Blacker than Reg. Way blacker than Dak. Gypsy Dent looked like she could break you down quicker than you could break down your field piece, though she was usually pretty mellow. The enemy never saw Commander Dent mellow.

Kerry nodded approval to that at least. "Yeah, she'd be my pick to take with."

Commander Dent had come over from Captain

Carmel's *Wolfhound* after *Merrimack* lost her short-lived Executive Officer Sebastian Gray. Mr. Gray had gone missing, presumed eaten, in a battle with gorgons over a year ago.

Mr. Dent had a real bad start on *Merrimack*. First thing, straight off, one of the ship's dogs ate the new XO's cat.

Someone shoulda warned the new Exec about the sheer volume of doggage on board *Merrimack*. And not a whole lot in the way of cattage. In fact, there were no pets on *Merrimack*, except for the lizard plant Kerry Blue had picked up in the Myriad, but that passed as a plant because it had leaves.

For the demise of Mr. Dent's cat, it had been a Doberman named Inga what done the deed. Not the brightest of the breed, Inga had just wanted to play. Bluebeard had not.

It was probably the ragdoll shake rather than the launch into the bulkhead that snapped the cat's neck.

Captain Farragut had apologized to Commander Dent, but you could tell the captain wasn't all that upset. Inga was crew. Bluebeard was a cat. And you could tell Egypt Dent was all kinds of smoked about it.

That was for starters. Next thing, Farragut ordered Mr. Dent to lose the hair.

Gypsy Dent had come aboard the *Mack* with this Medusan thing on her head. The hair was a work of art. The hair was scary. Coils of woven dreadlocks, each ending in a gold snake head.

Gypsy already had a device for removing and reattaching the headdress hair by hair, so the order was not hard to obey.

It was insulting.

"*That* is not serving on my command deck," had been the captain's words.

So when Farragut requested Commander Dent accompany him to his crowning on Fortress Aeyrie, Gypsy asked, "May I wear my hair?"

"Mr. Dent, I would be pleased all to Jesus if you would wear your hair."

And Kerry Blue decided, yeah, Farragut and Dent will be okay.

That left Lieutenant Commander Glenn (Hamster) Hamilton in charge of the *Mack* while the captain and the exec were on Fortress Aeryie.

The Hamster was thrilled. This never happened. Never had both the captain and the XO been off the boat at the same time. Everyone could just hear Hamster's husband Patrick saying to his wife, "Maybe something will happen to the captain and the exec, and you'll get to keep command."

Captain Farragut couldn't quite blame Patrick Hamilton for wanting him dead. It wasn't quite the secret Farragut hoped it was that Farragut was too fond of Dr. Patrick Hamilton's wife.

Glenn Hamilton was petite, polished, smart. Had a big attitude. Stood no taller than Farragut's chin. Could handle this boat. Only needed more mileage on her. Glenn Hamilton was not yet thirty years old.

"Do you trust me?" Hamster asked as the captain prepared to depart.

"With everything I have," said Farragut. "Keep the guns ready and stay on high alert."

"John, are you expecting trouble?"

When Captain Farragut was uneasy, it made everyone uneasy.

He said, "It's just fixin' to be pomp and circumstance. There won't be any shooting."

Those were his words, but Hamster heard his thoughts: Something—*something*—is fixin' to go south.

Hamster said, "Anything goes wrong, you can smite them all with the jawbone of the Vice President."

Got half a snicker out of him. Little more than a breath out the nose.

Glenn reached up to fix his collar. It seemed a natural thing for a woman to do for a man. Natural to do for a man she was intimate with, not for her captain. Her hands were behind his neck before she realized what she was doing. Burned with a sudden blush.

So did he.

There would not be any shooting unless Patrick Hamilton walked in on this.

Hamster bowed her head, gave her captain's broad chest a pat with a guilty smile. She moved back away from him to check her work. "You clean up pretty, John Farragut."

And she left him figuring out how to lose this wood before he boarded Fortress Aeyrie.

Took a look at Gypsy's hair. All's well again. Loved that hair.

The boffins had planted a rover in Gypsy's snaky headdress so the command deck on *Merrimack* would see everything Gypsy saw. Both the captain and the XO wore earpieces and collar phones, so they could hear the command deck and whisper back.

Both officers were tricked out in full dress blues, plenty of fruit salad on their chests. Hats tucked under arms.

A skiff ferried them into the spaceborne mountain that was Caesar's mobile palace, Fortress Aeyrie. The skiff was forbidden armament, but the Marines inside it bristled like pirates, carrying everything but knives between their teeth.

Kerry Blue tried to clench a blade between her teeth. Did not care for the sensation of metal against enamel *at all*. Made her teeth curl.

The Roman guards who met them at the dock were also armed. They allowed only Farragut and Dent to disembark. Checked them for weapons.

Most American men carried a pocketknife, if only because their daddies gave it to them. The guards at the dock confiscated Farragut's. Checked the snake heads in Gypsy's headdress for venom before admitting them to the inner fortress.

A ceremonial guard in ancient-style armor provided escort in from the dock, their faces more expressionless than automatons. They did not carry weapons.

Met up with a protocol officer who led Captain Farragut and Commander Dent through the fortress with chilly professionalism.

Caesar's audience hall had changed appearance since last time Farragut had been here. Where there had been a bridge and bottomless crevasse was now a spacious solid floor to accommodate many many dignitaries.

Everyone was standing. The only chairs in the entire hall were in front, behind a long table with a snowy cloth, and up in the balcony for the musicians.

The protocol officer stationed Captain Farragut and Commander Dent in the back. Farragut could see he was going to make a long walk up the center aisle to the raised dais in front to collect his crown.

Gypsy turned her head slowly to show the monitors on *Merrimack* the lay of the land.

From the front of the wide hall, two ramps led up both sides to a balcony in back. Unarmed guards in ceremonial regalia were posted throughout. There were no weapons to be had here. Nothing that could be used against its bearer. Not even ceremonial swords. God knew John Farragut could use a sword.

Most of the attendees here were Senators, garbed in ancient-style togas, and provincial governors wearing anything from suits to lion skins.

Gypsy paused her sweep of the room when Legate Herius Asinius came into her line of sight. Let the command crew get a long look at him.

"Now there's a man who looks like he took one hard up the stern," Farragut heard Hamster's voice in his earpiece.

Muttered back: "He did."

Herius did not look back at Farragut's entrance.

Farragut glanced over his own shoulder, encouraged to see no one parked behind him. What he'd felt looming back there was a statue of a beautiful Roman youth holding out a golden orb in its alabaster palm. Farragut had a boyish urge to pick up the orb, it being between the size of a baseball and a softball, and it really looked like it wasn't fastened down. He resisted. Faced forward.

"There's no LEN there," Hamster's voice sounded again.

"Don't see any," Farragut murmured back. Gypsy made a slow scan of the upper level, which revealed no League of Earth Nations guests there either.

The League participated in the defense of Thaleia. They were not being recognized for it here.

"No squid either," Farragut observed.

The Vwakikikikik had done a splendid job eliminating the gorgons in the sea. It hadn't been easy for them. Thaleian seawater was harsh on squid skin.

But the Vwakikikikik did not even know they'd been slighted. It was tough to offend a squid. Which was why there were no squid armed forces.

Farragut muttered into his com, "I shoulda made Augustus come here."

Augustus, more than anyone, had stopped the Hive incursion into Near Space.

"I'm sure Augustus would enjoy this every bit as much as I am."

"There!" said Hamster suddenly. "Commander Dent, hold it."

Farragut looked in the direction of Gypsy's line of sight.

"The man standing to the right of the head table," said Hamster. "Colonel Steele doesn't like him."

The target was a dignified older gentleman. His seamed face had gone to seed. He looked extremely uncomfortable. But there were a lot of people like that. Most of them in Senatorial robes.

There were several U.S. Senators here. But not Catherine. Catherine had taken her husband's name, so maybe the Romans didn't know she was a Farragut. Or, perhaps they realized they would need a bigger room if they started inviting John Farragut's brothers and sisters.

Invited but not in attendance was the Chief Justice of the Supreme Court of Kentucky. The press of business prevented His Honor from attending.

"Must be something very important to keep him away," the protocol officer had observed.

"Yes, the Judge is a very important man," Captain Farragut had told him.

Vice President Sampson Reed had a prominent place in front, seated behind the table. There were speeches to be made and decrees to be signed.

Beside Vice President Reed was seated the Roman Senator Gaius Bruccius Eleutherius Americanus. A stately man. Gaius had aged well. Calli Carmel confessed to having a crush on Gaius Americanus in her Imperial Military Institute days. Gaius was American born. Had risen to power the hard way. From American ex-con to Roman slave to freeman to general to Senator. Now Gaius Americanus was regarded as the second man in the empire. Of a different *gens* but the same mind as Julius Caesar Magnus.

Farragut was relieved not to see the Triumphalis General Numa Pompeii in attendance. The fourth man in the Empire. Ostensibly Numa's duties defending Rome in the Deep kept him away. Truth was Numa would rather eat gorgon tentacles than watch John Farragut be crowned in triumph.

Standing in front, off to the right, was Caesar's son Romulus, a younger man of dark indulgent good looks. Gorgeous, really. And decorating Romulus' arm was one of the true beauties of this or any universe, Callista Carmel, looking spectacular in mufti—a simple floor-length gown, strapless, empire-waisted, cut from rich fabric of the color called black emerald. A side slit flashed a great length of smooth leg. Emeralds shone at her throat. Farragut could hear voices in his earpiece from *Merrimack*'s command deck, "Holy mother-of-pearl! Look at Mr. Carmel!"

Romulus looked altogether smug and possessive, proud as a Caesar. A vain man, Romulus would need to be seen with a woman of Calli's voltage. The emeralds were probably his, because last time Farragut looked, Calli didn't own any.

Almost laughed out loud when he noticed she was wearing hair sticks.

There was the weedy crown waiting on a stand beside the altar. There was no way out of it. Farragut settled into resignation.

Trumpets blared from the balcony. Those dignitaries seated at the front table rose to their feet for the entrance of Julius Caesar Magnus.

Caesar wore a plain toga and a simple laurel wreath. Real laurel, not gold. He moved like a very old man.

There was a religious offering involving incense and a very small flame on the altar, a chorus of resonant male basso voices and an ethereal feminine counterpoint. Figures of ancestors appeared in the flames as the incense was tossed onto the altar with requests for benediction.

Then there were decrees to be signed, validating the Conciliation, recognizing America's assistance in the deliverance of Thaleia from the gorgons.

The Vice President of the United States, a handful of U.S. Senators, and a handful of Roman Senators took their seats with Caesar at the table. Parchments were read aloud and laid out for signature.

The man TR Steele didn't like was presenting the signatories with their pens. Pens were important at such occasions. These were destined to become museum pieces or part of someone's private collection or auctioned for stupid amounts of money.

Farragut's gaze wandered upward to the brilliant illusion of wide-open sky overhead.

So he didn't see the pen plunge into Caesar's eye socket.

13

HEARD THE SCREAMS. Saw the blood, the slumping body. Heard Lieutenant Commander Glenn Hamilton's voice in his ear calling *Merrimack* to general quarters. Commander Dent instructing the skiff to prepare for departure.

Farragut's eyes followed the running man pushing his way up the right-hand ramp to the upper level.

The man Steele didn't like.

Farragut made a reflexive reach for a sidearm that was not there. There were no weapons here.

Nothing built as a weapon.

But there was a golden orb in the alabaster hand of the statue behind him. And it turned out to be detachable.

John Farragut had briefly pitched minor league for the Akron Aeros. Never made the majors because he had only one pitch.

Still had it. Fast ball.

Low and way inside. Heard the crunch a split second before the animal screech. Dropped the assassin in an anguished heap on the ramp, curled round his shattered knee.

Wasn't a lethal hit, but the man was well and truly dead by the time the guards hauled him up, blue poison spilling from his slack mouth.

The man had to have known he had only the smallest chance of getting out of here. He had been ready for capture.

An authoritative booming voice demanded calm and order. Quickly brought the clamor down to a murmur.

Romulus.

Romulus summoning medics to resurrect his father.

Romulus calling on guards to seek out the assassin's family and associates immediately.

Gaius Americanus had run up the ramp and was calling for medics to make haste to revive the assailant. It went without saying that Gaius wanted the man alive and talking, but without the saying, Romulus seized the opportunity to take a verbal stab at the man Magnus had elevated above his own son. "Oh, yes, tend to the health of my father's attacker if you must, Gaius Americanus."

Romulus met Captain Farragut's eyes across the great hall. Told him the ceremony would not continue. "You should leave now." Sounded concerned for his safety.

"Not arguing," said Farragut.

The Roman mood in Caesar's hall, already foul, became menacing.

There were a lot of pens left.

Romulus also advised Vice President Sampson Reed and the U.S. Senators to go. They were already clotted around the forward exit, behind a half ring of Secret Service agents.

For everyone to hear, Romulus announced, "Hysteria and blind vengeance would be easy, but I do not imagine the United States were involved in a plot against my father. Our guests will leave. Until my father is revived, this is what I expect—"

As Romulus told his people his expectations, the Secret Service agents hustled the Vice President out of the chamber.

Calli Carmel took off her high heels and sprinted through the crowd to John Farragut, who had his jacket off and over her bare shoulders as soon as she joined up with him and Gypsy.

"I'm not cold, John," said Calli as his jacket surrounded her.

"I want that prick to see Navy colors and captain's stars when he watches you go out the door."

Calli did not pretend not to know who the prick was. "Romulus has no time to look at me."

Gypsy glanced back, corrected Calli as she followed the captains out the door. "Oh, yes, he does."

Farragut, Carmel, and Dent made it to the skiff and cleared Fortress Aeyrie without incident. Farragut did not count the gun pointed in his face at the dock as an incident worth noting. It was bluff and posture to see if the American hero would blink. He didn't. Neither did he tell the man to go ahead and shoot, because gunmen tend to obey you when you say that.

Farragut asked for his pocketknife back.

Once the skiff cleared Fortress Aeyrie's force field, *Merrimack* looped out an energy hook to enfold the little craft into its own protection.

In transit, Farragut ordered over the com, "Hamster, hail Spacecraft Two. Stay in contact. Advise them *Merrimack* will provide escort back to Earth. Then get me Admiral Mishindi at the Pentagon."

Glanced aside to a Marine staring at him. A rough sort of pretty gal. Everyone knew Kerry Blue. "Flight Sergeant Blue?" Farragut prompted.

"You didn't get your crown," said Kerry Blue.

"Sure didn't," said Farragut.

"Maybe that was the idea," Calli Carmel suggested. She pulled out her hair sticks and let fall her shining chestnut tresses. All the other Marines were staring at Captain Carmel. "Someone couldn't bear the thought of you with a crown."

Farragut shook his head. "Then why wasn't it *me?*"

As soon as the skiff was in dock and the hatch opened, Farragut exited like a cannonball. Nearly took out his Marine commander barreling up the ramp tunnel. "TR! You were dead on with the guy you didn't like. I shoulda listened harder."

TR Steele was true as the family dog. Just like Lily should have listened to the Farragut family dog when she went off and married that bum Eddie Ray. Doesn't do to ignore the dog. Didn't take a lot of intelligence to have a truckload of good sense. Bull mastiffs and TR Steele could sense bad faith.

"With respect, sir," said Colonel Steele, keeping up with the captain's charge up to his command deck, "I changed my mind. I like him a lot."

"TR, what is happening here—this is *not* good."

Farragut arrived on his command deck in his shirt-sleeves just as the Roman legion carrier *Horatius* cut across *Merrimack*'s bow.

"What the hell was that?" Hamster cried, giving over the command to Farragut.

"Saber rattling," said Farragut, watching *Horatius*' pass on the monitors.

"Roman Legion carrier is coming round again," Tactical advised.

"Oh, for—!" Farragut started, more exasperated than anything. "Punch us to the gate. Threshold velocity. Execute now."

The great battleship shot forward. Cut off *Horatius*' attempted maneuver. Came close to skinning the Legion carrier's nose.

Farragut opened a com channel. Used to be the Roman channel. The Romans had probably changed it by now, but Farragut sent anyway: "Marcus, you try that again, I'll drop you." Clicked off.

"What was he *thinking?*" Glenn Hamilton said, watching *Horatius* on the tac screen. The ship was turning back toward Fortress Aeyrie.

"I don't know," said Farragut, unprovoked. "What would you do if someone dropped President Johnson?"

"Drop Sampson Reed?" Tactical suggested.

"I did not hear that, Mr. Vincent."

Marcander Vincent had a habit of inappropriateness. *Merrimack* had to keep her six engines at threshold to stay with Spacecraft Two, which had departed

Fortress Aeyrie like solar ejecta. Even at that, the *Mack* was not going to catch up until Spacecraft Two came within range of the Earth home guard.

Merrimack took up a position on the Vice Presidential ship's stern, several light-years behind, and settled there for a two-day journey.

A maelstrom of messages whirled round the settled region of the galaxy.

At threshold speed, the only messages *Merrimack* sent or received were res pulses, and only messages in which the whole message could be conveyed in a single instant. Mostly that meant written text. *Mack* could converse well enough with Spacecraft Two, which was moving at the same pace, but voice messages from *Mack* arrived on Earth in a compressed mash, while Earth's messages to *Mack* were strung out in bits.

So the Joint Chiefs at the Pentagon got text answers to their questions mere instants after they asked them, while on board *Merrimack*, waiting for the next question from the JC was like watching a rock erode.

John Farragut and Gypsy Dent had missed dinner, so they went to the captain's Mess while they waited for the next grain of sand to fall off the rock.

It was the middle watch, ship's night. *Merrimack* stepped down from high alert, back into her normal routines. The lighting was subdued most decks, dark in the forecastle. Quiet as she ever got. The ship was never silent. Sounds had a comforting familiarity, hisses and clanks, the deep hum of the six mammoth engines, footsteps, voices carrying through metal decks and thin partitions. Thumping of joggers' feet on the elevated track. Air moving in conduits. Water in pipes.

Chef Zack got out of bed to feed the captain and the XO. Was disappointed that the officers could not tell him about the banquet. The food on Fortress Aeyrie was legendary and Zack had been expecting a full report.

Calli showed up at the Mess, clad in a badly fitting borrowed dress-down uniform. Gave Farragut his dress jacket back.

She offered to tell Chef Zack about the food in Fortress Aeyrie if he would feed her, too. "Rom took me to the galley when they were preparing for the banquet," she said, sliding into a chair at the captain's table. "It was overwhelming."

Farragut's brows lifted like a dog's ears. "Rom?" said Farragut. "*Rom?*"

Gypsy's dark, heavy-lidded eyes narrowed at her former CO, Captain Carmel. Gypsy had two young sons back on Earth, so she had the mom look down cold. "And what did you think you were doing in the kitchen with Rom?"

"He was showing off," said Calli.

"Like 'You play your cards right, all of this could be yours' kind of showing off?" Gypsy suggested.

Calli let her head fall to one side, thinking. "I don't know. He has either grown up into a responsible man or he has turned into a perfect psychopath."

"That was some surprising statesmanship back there," said Farragut.

"Yes, it was," said Calli. "Surprising."

"So why was it Romulus instead of Gaius calling the shots?" said Farragut. "Isn't Gaius Americanus the Second Man in Rome?"

Calli shook her head. "Romulus just grabbed the wheel first. He was quick. He made Gaius look like an ass."

"He did that very well," said Farragut. "Cheap shot about the attacker's health. But it worked. And your Gaius didn't try to argue with him."

"Gaius doesn't answer cheap shots. And he doesn't make snap decisions when he knows he's missing strategic facts. Gaius will wait to see how things fall. If Magnus can be resuscitated, then Rom's sniping back there won't matter much."

"Did he know?" said Gypsy.

Calli's smooth face pinched at the edges of her almond eyes, her full lips. "Rom? Oh, yes. While we were getting it human in the kitchen he told me he bribed one of his father's friends to stab him in the eye."

"Sarcasm does not look attractive on you, Captain Carmel," said Gypsy.

"Romulus did talk like he's expecting Magnus to survive," said Farragut. "Did y'all notice that?"

"'Until my father is revived, this is what I expect,'" Gypsy recited. "That was a nice touch. Not what you'd expect a parricide to say."

It was either the natural refusal of a son to assume the worst or the calculated facade of a perfect psychopath.

On a sudden thought Calli fished in the pocket of her baggy uniform. Produced an emerald necklace. It sparkled in the low light, dangling from her long fingers. "Can I get a courier to send these back to Rom?"

Big brother to many, Farragut had long practice ordering, "Cal, I don't want you seeing that boy anymore."

Gypsy positioned herself shoulder to shoulder with him, her arms crossed, like the other disapproving parent. "Calli, honey, you know we only want what's best for you."

"Know your enemy," said Calli.

Gypsy frowned. "Honey, you don't need to know him that well."

The resonator finally coughed up a message dot, automatically slotting it into the player. All three officers leaned forward. Farragut's blue eyes moved quickly back and forth across the text of the Joint Chiefs' latest message.

"Caesar is dead."

Caesar died and stayed dead. Roman medicine could repair a lot of damage to the human body. But in this case it was the ink—injected directly into the brain—that prevented resuscitation.

Neither had the Roman medics been able to revive the assassin. The Americans had to wonder at that. In the assassin's case the poison had not been injected directly into his brain. Either he had been a very clever assassin or the medics had not been trying hard enough.

By the middle of the second day of the voyage home,

the crew of the *Merrimack* had learned that the assassin had already lost his children to the Hive, and that his wife left him a long time ago in a truly bitter divorce, so there was no Roman vengeance to be had.

The lack of a suicide note or of a shouted declaration as he struck Caesar down left the motive muddy. Unless the death of his children drove the man to it. He had already suffered in the worst way, so might he just as well commit a crime equal to it? And if his ex-wife were executed on his account, so much the better?

The investigation unearthed a dirty little secret in the assassin's excessive admiration of young girls. But killing Caesar was no way to keep that a secret, so blackmail seemed an unlikely motive.

A Sargasson autopsy found no brain alteration that might have affected his behavior—no alteration other than the poison that killed him, and a mild sedative he had taken that morning.

The why of it appeared unknowable. But lack of evidence did not hinder the proliferation of theories and accusations in the least.

There was speculation that Magnus had arranged his own assassination to soothe his empire's wounded pride. Magnus, so the theory went, had made a pact with his trusted adviser to do the deed, using someone who had no family to suffer for his apparent disloyalty.

But in a society that valued honorable death, that idea was perfectly alien and was more popular on Earth than anywhere in the Roman Empire.

Romulus wasted no time on speculation and witch hunts. The assassin was dead and that would do for now.

For now, Romulus kept a firm hand on his disrupted empire. He showed a poise and gravitas not seen before in Magnus' callow late-born son. Romulus had risen to the occasion.

And kept rising.

Succession in the empire was not hereditary. Magnus had never publicly announced a successor. Romulus had just assumed the interim rule. And for his boldness, his decisiveness, his restraint, the Roman Senate let him.

Romulus left Magnus' last testament sealed. Magnus may have named a successor in the sealed testament, but that successor could not be vested in the office without the vote of the Senate. That could wait.

Now, said Romulus, was not the time for political dissension and debate. The future of Rome should not be decided in haste during a crisis. Rome must deal with the Hive first, then, in safety, unseal Caesar's last wishes and decide the path of the empire.

It was a bald power grab. Everyone knew that Romulus' name was probably not in that sealed testament. Especially Romulus. Romulus would also know that the one at the helm at the end of the storm had a high likelihood of keeping the job.

Many Romans considered Magnus' death an assassination waiting to happen.

The wrath of the conquered empire, if not abated, was mollified with the death of its betraying ruler who sold them into Subjugation. Romulus, in an address to the Empire—appearing very handsome, grave, and imperial—stated that he disagreed with the Subjugation, but that he loved and honored his father, and that second-guessing the past was not the way to move forward.

Neat trick, thought Farragut. To be in alliance with the U.S. without taking the blame for the act that got Rome there. Romulus had not made the agonizing decision. Magnus had. But Romulus reaped the benefit.

Magnus had died to save Rome.

Or had he?

Had fury at the Subjugation been the motive behind the killing? Seemed obvious.

But there was someone more responsible for the Subjugation than Magnus. Magnus had only submitted to it. Someone else had demanded it. Someone who left Fortress Aeyrie alive.

The question came back again and again:
Why wasn't it me?

Merrimack arrived at Earth hot on the stern of Spacecraft Two. The emeralds were on their way back to

Fortress Aeyrie. And Calli Carmel was back in her own uniform.

John Farragut saw her to the Kansas spaceport, where a military transport would take her to Fort Roosevelt. From there it would be through the Shotgun and back to her own ship *Wolfhound* in the Deep.

Calli could not get out of Near Space fast enough.

A sidebar to the media circus *sans* bread that surrounded Caesar's assassination was an unfortunate plethora of video of Calli Carmel on Romulus' arm.

Calli was not a celebrity in her own right, but she had stellar looks and she was with the new emperor—so the media were calling Romulus—and that made her video fodder.

"Be careful going through Fort Ted," Farragut told her.

Calli, surprised and perplexed, said, "It's *our* fort."

"Gypsy wanted to make sure you saw this."

Handed her a vid sheet. She opened it.

The image of Calli and Romulus jumped out at her. The caption read: EMPRESS CALLI.

Calli left her mouth open for quite a few moments. Finally she said to John Farragut, "Oh, for Jesus."

14

ADMIRAL MISHINDI HAD LET himself age outwardly. The brindled hair, the seamed face, gave him an air of wisdom and authority. But the old man could run John Farragut round a squash court and smash that little green ball like a man half John Farragut's age.

Mishindi appeared sedate and venerable behind his desk in his office at the Pentagon.

Like Mishindi, the Pentagon had been much rejuvenated on the inside. The admiral's chamber might have been a compartment on a spaceship, except that the ceilings were higher, the furniture was not bolted down, and the hatch appeared like a door, though it sealed as securely as any hatch.

"Captain Farragut, the Joint Chiefs have determined because the Hive has adapted to our current tactics that a change of tactics is in order. Single ships have become more and more vulnerable. We are organizing our forces into Attack Groups. To that end, the *Merrimack* will be flagship of Attack Group One, comprising *Gladiator*, *Wolfhound*, *Rio Grande* . . ."

Farragut had shut his eyes at the word flagship and kept them shut. The honor from the Black Lagoon. It meant some damned admiral was fixing to plant his flag on John Farragut's command deck, while John Farragut, captain of the *Merrimack*, became a passenger on his own ship. He tried not to look crushed but that was difficult to do with his eyes shut.

Until Admiral Mishindi spoke into John Farragut's darkness, "Congratulations, Commodore Farragut."

Farragut's eyes flew open. Mishindi was slyly grinning.

"Me! I'm the damned admiral!"

"How damned you are, I cannot say. It is a field promotion, mind you."

Farragut spoke thickly past the lump in his throat. "Thank you, sir."

Mishindi looked impish. "Did I scare you?"

Farragut wanted to bluster *No*. But the admiral had him cold. "A little," Farragut admitted.

Mishindi sniggered, devilish.

"Okay. A *lot*," Farragut cried. "I'll get you for that, Mishindi."

The admiral cackled out loud.

Farragut said, "Well, seeing as how I just shipped Cal back to the Deep to rejoin *Wolfhound* instead of *Wolfhound* coming here, can I assume my theater of operations is the Deep?"

"You can, Commodore. The mission objective is to detect, locate, isolate, and prosecute the Hive nexus."

"Hive nexus? There is such a thing?"

"Newly uncovered evidence suggests there is."

"'Newly uncovered' means we've had the intelligence and someone's been sitting on it."

Mishindi sighed, folded his hands across his middle and sat back in his chair. "Information sharing has never been our country's long suit. The CIA just decided to share that."

"I gave Naval Intelligence a Roman patterner a year ago. Why don't we have our own answers?"

"Augustus is no longer with Naval Intelligence."

"What!" Farragut came out of his chair. Then, sitting back down, "Sir."

Mishindi allowed the outburst. Pained him to admit, "Augustus reports to the CIA."

Farragut about swallowed his tongue. Kept his voice

level addressing his admiral, "How did the CIA get him?"

Mishindi's face pinched in pain. "Admiral Klein."

"What about Admiral Klein?"

"He hit him," said Mishindi.

"Augustus *hit* Admiral Klein!" Farragut could not believe it.

"No." Mishindi's face knotted up entirely. "Former Admiral Klein hit Augustus."

Farragut's blue eyes popped wide.

Mishindi continued, "Your patterner has a talent for igniting people and causing careers to spontaneously combust."

Farragut instantly knew what the CIA had done with Augustus from there. The spooks would be more concerned with limiting Augustus' access to U.S. data than using him to consolidate the data. The power of a patterner was his ability to synthesize great masses of disparate information. Augustus' great power had been squandered in the clutches of the CIA.

John Farragut was on the edge of his chair, nearly on top of Mishindi's desk. "Get him back, sir. *I'll* take him. Patterners are amazing. We can't just piss him away because he's pissy. We need to use him. *I* need to use him."

For Jesus, no wonder Augustus hated him. Augustus' venom made sense now. *How little you know.*

"Do remember, John, this is the man—if you can call him a man—who shut down Fleet communications several years ago."

The patterner had discovered that sending the complement of a resonant harmonic whites out both harmonics. Augustus had got hold of the Fleet common harmonic and generated its complement at random intervals. Because some messages got through, the Fleet were slow to realize that other messages were not, and still slower to actually believe it could be happening.

"This is that guy," said Mishindi. "*Not* friendly."

"I know what he is."

"The CIA does not trust you, John. Something about 'idiot ideas of fair play.'"

"Idiot ideas of fair play are why the *Mack* is still alive. That patterner had a clean shot at my stern."

"And sorely regrets not taking the shot," Mishindi finished for him.

"He says that. But it's a Roman creed—if you win the battle and lose your honor, what have you won?"

Mishindi's dark face purpled, exasperated. Fingers curled as if to cage the air and throttle it. "John, *I* would have taken the shot!"

"You're not Roman."

"It's also a fact that Romans are the sneakiest, most self-serving, back-stabbing bastards in the known galaxy."

"I got the right Roman," said Farragut.

Mishindi shook his head, reluctant, relenting. "I can get you Augustus. But I don't know about getting you the files he wants. The CIA says that Augustus is trying to know his enemy."

"God bless America!" Farragut roared like a curse. "That's what he's for!"

"Us," said Mishindi. "They're afraid he will know *us*. Knowledge is power, and no one knows that better than the children of the wolf. There's a reason the CIA is mighty tightfisted about their information."

"Then cut off their fists. I mean it. We can't fight the Hive blindfolded."

"Here's the thing, John. What they're afraid of— What *I'm* afraid of— Are you listening to this part, John? We're afraid that your patterner will figure out how the Hive is getting a loc on a res pulse."

Before humankind's first encounter with the Hive, getting a location on a resonant pulse's point of transmission or reception was widely accepted as impossible. It was simple fact. But the Hive did it and most insects did it. And the United States needed to do it before the Romans.

"Yes, this is the guy who can figure that out," Farragut agreed. "And best he figures it out while we're still allied, 'cause otherwise he'll just figure it out after the Hive is gone and he's working only for Rome again."

Mishindi rolled the suggestion around. Said finally, "That argument has *some* merit. You do know that Augustus is a five-star monster when he is enabled?"

"Glory, I sure hope so, 'cause that's what I need to step in the ring with the Hive."

The admiral spread his hands, giving in. "I have never regretted taking a risk on you. I will requisition your patterner immediately. Mind you, this is not Androcles' lion you're getting here. You stuck the thorn *in* his paw."

Captain Farragut took delivery of the patterner in Mishindi's office.

Augustus. A stone basilisk who had refused the invitation to sit. Standing, Augustus could use his imposing height to intimidate.

Someone had provided him with U.S. drab to wear instead of the Roman black Farragut had always seen Augustus in, but still the patterner looked dark and forbidding. He had been given the rank of colonel, but was not a line officer.

Admiral Mishindi told Captain Farragut that information was being provided to *Merrimack*'s data banks. Copies of certain Pentagon databases were being sanitized, and irrelevant files omitted.

"You are no judge of relevance," said the patterner.

Mishindi countered, crossly, "What *is* relevant—and we haven't been able to *get*—are the Thaleia files. Thaleia is a Roman world. Your people are protective of their proprietary information. And Romulus won't release the information."

"Romulus?" Augustus echoed. Little expression, but Farragut sensed confusion and unease from him. Augustus asked carefully, "And what does Caesar say?"

A pall held the chamber. Even Mishindi was mortified.

Someone with a gift for making sense of data had been given less than none.

He doesn't even know Caesar is dead!

Farragut, mouth dry, asked, "Augustus, what information did the CIA give you access to?"

The head turned robotically, dark, dark eyes directed at him like weapons. The wrath.

Augustus finally spoke, soft as a whisper, gentle as a sadist before he cuts you. "Apparently even less than I thought. Where is Caesar?"

Silence fell thick and stayed.

Augustus waited.

Farragut answered at last, *"Ad patres."*

Gone to his forefathers.

Gone light speed. Gone from this life.

Augustus gave no reaction. In truth, it was the only answer Augustus could have expected after that long a silence.

Without expression, Augustus said/asked, "Assassination."

"Yes," said Farragut.

"How did you know?" Mishindi challenged.

"After Caesar acceded to the Subjugation, and without me there, it became only a question of when. Who?"

Mishindi supplied the name. Augustus dismissed it at once. "Who else?"

"No one that we know of."

Augustus appeared skeptical of that. Of the unknowing. Of the absence of others. "If I had been with Caesar, no one could have got to him. He should never have given me away."

"It was his decision," said Farragut. "He gave you to me."

"And that killed him," said Augustus.

"Maybe there were things more important to Caesar than staying alive."

Augustus looked genuinely shocked. As at a pig quoting Shakespeare. John Farragut had said something inadvertently profound. Or was it advertent? Augustus had not expected an American to know of things more important than his own life.

"There were," said Augustus. "But Caesar would have been sorry to give his life for— Just what did Caesar give his life for?"

Farragut took responsibility for that one. He should

have checked up on Augustus. Made sure that Caesar's patterner was being used for important things.

Yet even in data starvation, Augustus had managed to puzzle together the fact that the Hive was using Pan-Galactic technology to displace to Near Space.

"Augustus, what do you need to do what you do?"

"Data."

"Exactly what data?"

"All that there is."

"Any particular format?"

"Any format."

Mishindi daunted, hesitated. "Exactly how much do you retain once you're unplugged?" He nodded toward the cables hanging from Augustus' forearms and the back of his neck.

"Things of interest," said Augustus, a dare. The look on his face said he expected to be locked away again.

"You'll have it," said Farragut. Thought he might have seen Mishindi flinch.

Spoken promises meant little to Augustus, but he said, "Then may I also request you get from the Empire anything surrounding the assassination. I could not prevent Caesar's murder. I can, at least, avenge him."

Farragut would have put a reassuring hand on the shoulder of anyone else at this point. But Augustus was remote, glacial. Farragut gave him his distance. "I'll request that information from Imperial Intelligence for you."

Augustus' wicked little Striker spacecraft had been locked down inside one of *Merrimack*'s docks. The Striker looked fast and evil, and it was. With its patterner installed, a Striker was an extraordinary war machine. The hull of this one was black and red, Flavian colors.

En route to Fort Theodore Roosevelt, the patterner was permitted to plug into *Merrimack*'s main database. Augustus' left-side forearm cable could adapt to any physical or electromagnetic dataport.

He made the connection and vanished from conscious presence. Sat. Hollow-eyed. Facial muscles slack.

Whether from pride or determination, his mouth did not hang open.

He did not eat or drink for two watches. Ignored you when you asked if he was okay. And when you persisted, he said from far away: "Don't talk to me."

The Naval Intelligence officers advised Farragut that a patterner's time sense was altered when enabled. And human speech became as whale songs with their thirty-minute-long phrases. Like listening to mud flow.

Very well if you are a whale and in no great hurry. This being was compiling unimaginable amounts of data.

Farragut looked in on him every hour. The xenos and medics came and went, observing, speculating what the cables were for. One suggested they were analogous to express lanes added to a congested highway. There were synthetic neural pathways within those armored cable sheaths.

After seven hours—Palatine hours—Augustus lifted a somnambulant arm. Reached slowly behind his head. Pulled the cables out of the sockets at the base of his skull.

Looked cadaverous.

He detached his arm cable from the dataport. Unplugged a data module from behind his ear, where most folks wore their language modules.

Tossed the module carelessly onto the console.

Stood up. Threw up. Or spit up. There was very little to throw. Lay down on the deck and passed out.

John Farragut thought they'd killed him.

The intelligence officer seized the module. Several xenos and Jose Maria de Cordillera immediately withdrew from the compartment to review the contents.

Farragut summoned the medical officer.

Doctor Mo Shah was the only man Farragut knew who could react swiftly and remain utterly serene. Mo Shah did not seem surprised to see the patterner crumpled on the deck in the data vault. Regarded the motionless figure with deep hound dog eyes. "Yes, I have been reading about this happening. Your patterner will be continuing in this state for many hours."

"This is *supposed* to happen?"

Mo tilted his head to one side then the other. "Not so much supposing to as simply happening."

"Can you do anything for him?"

"Your Roman has forbidden me to be touching him," said Mo. " '*Primum non nocere.*' "

Farragut knew that one. "First, do no harm."

"I am not knowing if moving him would be harming him."

Farragut planted his fists just behind his hipbones, and strolled a half circle round the body on the black deck grates. Blue eyes lifted. "Well, I didn't take that oath, Mo. And neither did y'all," he said to the MPs at the hatch. "Get something comfortable underneath this officer."

Farragut could not see how getting Augustus off the deck grates could hurt.

And if he died, at least he would not look as if he had been killed with a waffle iron.

Everyone who reviewed the patterner's report looked like they had found religion. They were awed. Even Jose Maria de Cordillera.

"It is an astonishing piece of work, young Captain. How someone can identify and distill all these bits of scattered evidence and disparate minutiae into a coherent pattern is beyond my comprehension."

More than the method, Augustus' conclusion hit with the force of a bomb. "The gorgons did not displace themselves. They were delivered."

"*Delivered?*"

"There was an intelligence behind the act. There had to be. The Hive are not intelligent."

"No," Farragut rejected the idea. He launched into agitated pacing, with big stalking steps and big arm motions and big voice. "Augustus can't tell me some alien intelligence is using our own technology to sling gorgons at us from the Deep!"

"No. He cannot. And he is not," Jose Maria said, composed as a cat on a windowsill. "It is a human intelligence. And the patterner has put a name on it. The difficulty is that we are ninety-nine percent certain that the man who belongs to the name is dead."

The pacing stopped. Farragut guessed, "So we're looking at the other one percent here?"

"We are ninety-nine percent sure that we are. Rome killed him sixty-one years ago on the planet Thaleia. But because death is not always prohibitive anymore, your Roman is confident in saying that the intelligence behind the Hive is the aforesaid dead man. His name is Constantine Siculus."

15

AUGUSTUS WOKE UP hours later. Lumbered like a drunken zombie—a drunken zombie with a homing beacon—through *Merrimack*'s corridors, its laddered shafts, the ramp tunnel, to the dock where his Striker was locked down.

A wicked little hornet of a spacecraft, colored red and black, the Striker crouched in the spacious dock between the bigger, placid, boxy, gray shuttles. Gave an impression of speed in the stillness, implacable anger in the dark.

The Striker's side hatch opened at Augustus' approach. Augustus climbed inside and slept some more.

Augustus' sleeping compartment was not large, but it was grand—opulent, draped deck to overhead in richly textured fabrics of deep red and brilliant gold against forest greens and browns. Very Roman. Augustus sprawled corpselike, with a brocade tapestry pulled half across him. The bed was longer than U.S. standard, built to accommodate Augustus' six-foot-eight frame. Still, he'd managed to miss the target, and one foot still hung off the end of the bed, the other off the side.

A voice intruded into his head-thumping dark: "You asleep?"

Without opening his eyes, Augustus croaked, "No."

"What's that about?"

Augustus had to crack one eye in a pained squint to see what "that" was.

Captain Farragut stood at the foot of his bed, looking straight down.

Augustus was sporting a toe tag on one bare foot.

"I woke up with it," said Augustus, voice raspy. "Not your work, then, I take it."

"No. I apologize—"

"Don't," said Augustus. The corner of his mouth made a hard curl. "I see the humor in it."

The toe tag was most likely the work of the FNG (New Guy), Flight Sergeant Cain Salvador. Replaced Reg Monroe in the Alpha Three spot. Reg Monroe had just left for home on an LRS headed from Fort Theodore Roosevelt to Earth.

Cain Salvador's new squad mates would have put him up to the tagging.

"Why are you here?" said Augustus.

"Stopped in to see if you were dead."

Augustus lifted his tagged foot. Considered. "Could be."

"Dead like Constantine?"

Augustus nodded, not lifting his head from the mattress. "About that dead."

"Anything I can do for you?"

Farragut had been advised that Augustus was dominant homosexual with sadistic inclinations, so he might have expected the reply he got.

The captain did not react to the obscenity. Just shook his head. "That won't be happening. But there's probably a dreambox programmed for that sort of thing."

"Then what do you want here?"

"Constantine Siculus."

"You have my report."

"Your report is extremely detailed."

Augustus had noted all his references and explicitly linked every miniscule point of evidence back to its conclusion.

"I came for the executive summary."

"The moron's version?" Augustus translated.

Farragut leaned back against a faux marble pilaster, crossed one ankle over the other, ready to listen to a story. "Please."

You just could not insult the man. Well, you could, but it had no effect. Your opinion of John Farragut did not change him, and he knew it.

Augustus half rolled, elbow-crawled to get all of himself onto the bed, flopped back down, his back to Farragut. "Constantine Siculus is alive and coexisting with the Hive in the Deep."

"Not possible. Gorgons have never spared anything."

"Nothing," said Augustus. "Except each other."

Heard the amazed realization at his back: "He's got the Hive harmonic. He's resonating on the Hive harmonic."

"He is," said Augustus. "Coexisting with the Hive like a clown fish inside an anemone in very deep Sagittarian space."

"Can't be," said Farragut. He knew something of Constantine Siculus. "If someone is out there, it can't be Constantine."

Constantine Siculus. Born Conrad Nelson one hundred and thirty years ago in the United States of America. His mother was a Roman mole, working in the Pentagon. She fled to Palatine with her son as she was about to be brought in for questioning. There she ditched her husband's name, and assumed her true *nomen* of Siculus, and renamed her son Constantine.

Constantine became a systems engineer. Undertook the terraforming of Thaleia, where he founded Pan-Galactic Automated Industries.

The name of his business said a lot about the man. PanGalactic—when humankind had only explored a fraction of the galaxy.

Megalomania. The word was older than Rome.

The death of Constantine's mother unhinged him. He demanded that Caesar deify her. Caesar—Caesar Daisius at that time—refused, so Constantine declared himself Caesar and ordered the citizens of Thaleia to worship his mother.

Rome dethroned him.

"Rome blew him up," said Farragut. "They found pieces of him. There was a Sargasson analysis. Those weren't cloned pieces. That was Constantine's body."

"Pieces of it," said Augustus. "You know, if you're going to stay here, I'm going to do illegal drugs."

He punched his headboard. Tubes eeled out, found their way to a vein in the crook of his elbow. Made a connection, hissed briefly, and withdrew back into the headboard.

Augustus sat up, looking marginally more human. Said, "They found an original heart, an original lung, an original kidney, and original bone of Constantine's at the blast site."

"That would make him pretty dead," said Farragut.

"There is a sublegal clinic on Palatine, which identifies its patients only by file number. It's a clone farm. Patient One thousand fifty-eight had a heart, kidney, lung, and bone replaced with cloned parts. Patient one thousand fifty-eight's stay at the clinic coincided with a time period in which no communications with Constantine were recorded on Thaleia."

"Not conclusive," said Farragut. "Lack of evidence is slim evidence."

"Patient one thousand fifty-eight was unique at the clinic for his demand to take his old parts with him."

Looked to Farragut for a return argument. There was none coming. Only astonishment.

"He was premeditating his own fake death," said Farragut.

Constantine had known Rome was gunning for him, and he'd been ready.

Augustus watched Farragut closely. "Do you remember when Numa Pompeii planted a resonator on your ship as gorgon bait?"

All resonance attracts the Hive. Numa Pompeii had found one harmonic that provoked gorgons into a ravenous frenzy to the exclusion of all else. Numa had planted a resonator on board *Merrimack* transmitting on that harmonic in order to draw gorgons off of his own ship *Gladiator*.

Farragut cracked a bright white smile and snorted. "Won't forget that unless you blow my brains out."

"Don't tempt me," said Augustus. "Ever wonder where Numa got that harmonic?"

"Are you nuts?" Of course he wondered.

"Sixty-one years ago, Imperial Intelligence found a note in Constantine's files on Thaleia with the notation: *This is the harmonic*."

Augustus watched the captain's fair face go blank, then smolder with deepening wrath. Finally, in the soft voice of complete outrage, Farragut murmured, "That bastard."

"Numa or Constantine?"

"Both, but I was talking about Constantine. How— how could any human being—"

Anger. Augustus had got white-hot anger out of John Farragut.

But it wasn't the selfish little anger of most men. It wasn't for pride or for challenged authority or threat to himself, or even blasphemy against his idea of God. It was a pure sort of anger from a man faced with an amoral monster who let tens of thousands die. May have even caused their deaths.

Farragut was just now realizing that Constantine Siculus knew about the Hive decades before *Sulla* disappeared.

Farragut was in motion, pacing, too angry to put together a sentence. "Sixty-one years ago—! And he didn't—!"

Constantine had never warned anyone about the existence of the Hive.

"Damn him," Farragut said finally, softly. "Damn him to hell."

"Trying," said Augustus.

Farragut calmed down. Shook his head, brows drawn together. "Constantine was never *in* the Deep End. How did he discover the Hive?"

"Constantine had himself a private little Deep End

terraforming project on the side. He'd been siphoning resources off Thaleia ever since he got there. He used automatons for everything. No loose lips on a machine, so he kept absolute secrecy. There was no Shotgun in those days, not that he would have been allowed to use it. So it was very slow work. But machines on board unmanned spacecraft don't mind slow work. At some point—probably when his automatons tried to transplant vegetation onto his target world, or when the automatons sent a resonant message back to their boss—Constantine Siculus discovered the Hive.

"By this time Rome was highly suspicious of Constantine. His PanGalactic products were in use across the Empire—his killer bots, his displacement equipment. He was dangerous, and he was unstable.

"Caesar Daisius sent his patterner—the patterner Secundus in that era—to Thaleia to tap into Constantine's computer network.

"Constantine was ready for that move. Probably hoping for it. He had a Trojan Horse program ready and waiting to corrupt Secundus' programming."

Farragut looked startled. "Y'all really are programmed?"

"To a degree, yes."

"If Secundus was a patterner, why didn't he see the trap?"

"No doubt Secundus was given insufficient information on Constantine before he was sent in. The technology for creating patterners was still new back then—Secundus was only the second of our kind ever made. Powerful creations that can think for themselves cause distrust. People are still very reluctant to give patterners enough information to get the job done. Did you know that?"

"I've gotten that drift, yes."

"Using information gathered by Constantine's drones in the Deep, Secundus would have divined both the provocative harmonic and the Hive's own harmonic."

"Of course," said Farragut, ironic. "A human being

couldn't have figured it out. A discovery that extraordinary must be made by one of you cyborgs."

"Yes. Except that I am not a cyborg, yes," said Augustus. "When Secundus failed to return from Thaleia—with or without Constantine's head—that prompted drastic measures. If the size of the bomb was any indication, Rome was plenty afraid of Constantine. When they found his charred organs, Imperial Intelligence assumed they got him. They had a Sargasson check the parts for authenticity. Someone should have known that Constantine got away when they found no remains of Secuncus or his Striker.

"Constantine is alive, in an area of space scummy with Hive. Your Admiral Mishindi thought it was the breeding ground or nerve center of the Beast. It's Constantine's refuge. It's Attack Group One's target in deep Sagittarian space."

"You're a patterner," said Farragut. "Why can't you come up with the Hive harmonic?"

"I don't have any of the information Secundus had from the automatons on Constantine's Deep End world. The only shred of data that Constantine left behind regarding his secret project was the harmonic that gets you the Hive's undivided attention."

Farragut nodded. "Good work, Augustus." He headed toward the hatch.

"I don't need an atta boy from John Farragut."

"Then don't take it."

"The files you gave me are incomplete," said Augustus as Farragut opened the hatch.

It had the sound of an accusation.

Farragut turned sharply. "What are those CIA weasels withholding?"

"Wrong weasel," said Augustus. "There is nothing at all in your data banks concerning Caesar's assassination."

Merrimack dropped from FTL to take a res call from Admiral Mishindi. Farragut heard disbelief in the admiral's voice, "Captain Farragut, did you put in a request to Imperial Intelligence for their files concerning Caesar Magnus' assassination? *Twice?*"

"Yes, sir. I did."

"What the hell for? Did you used to play with hornets' nests back in Kentucky? And did you take too many stings to the head while you were at it! Internal Roman politics are not within the purview of the U.S. Naval Fleet! Romulus is stinging mad!"

Farragut had not considered how his information request might look to the Romans. Did it look like he was trying to interfere in the Roman government? "I asked for it at Augustus' request. He has some conspiracy theory and thinks he could smoke out other plotters in Caesar's assassination if he had access to the data. I didn't see the point in denying him that."

"Ever consider that your patterner's search for another conspirator could be a search for *self?*" said Mishindi.

Farragut blinked. Augustus as assassin? Yes, he could see Augustus as an assassin. But as a traitor? "Not for a heartbeat, sir."

"Well, John, I am holding here—in my hand—an extradition order served on the Joint Chiefs, issued by Caesar Romulus, to arrest Augustus on suspicion of complicity in Magnus' assassination. It orders us to return Augustus to Palatine—immediately. Dead or incapacitated."

"What did the JC answer?"

"Didn't. Passed it to me. And I'm passing it to you. You have an answer to this?"

"Yes, I do, sir. The answer is no."

Farragut expected an argument, a rebuke. Instead he got an extended silence that ended in, "I accept your refusal of Caesar's order. Romulus' stated reason for wanting Augustus lacks credence. I think he just wants the patterner back for his own use. But *you* are going to have to accept Caesar's refusal to hand over the files. I'm not going to war over this."

"It was a request, sir," said Farragut. "I didn't expect a war."

* * *

Reg Monroe called the bet and raised a lot. Her shirt gapped loose as she leaned forward to push the pile of money into the pot. A tactic as old as the invention of breasts and lace. Jarred the poker faces loose.

"Who let them play!" Enzo yelped.

"No fair, Reg." Tad, the dealer, gave the player to his right a shove. "So what are you doin'? You in or you out?"

The man stared, stupidly blissful, struck senseless by the vision. Mumbled, "I have no idea."

Long Range Shuttles moved at a tedious pace. But Reg Monroe was on her way home to Earth. For good. She was flying. Whiled away the time with a couple of bull mastiffs on leave—Tad from Delta flight and Enzo from Echo, and a station rat from Fort Ted.

"I—uh—fold," the station rat said finally. "I can't compete with that."

"Dealer calls." Tad pushed his money in.

Enzo studied the huge pot. Looked hard at Reg. At her eyes. "You got nothin'." Pushed all his money in. "I wanna see 'em."

"Me, too," said the station rat, dreamily.

"That was cheap, Reg," Tad scolded.

"Cheap?" Reg straightened her back, indignant. "How dare you say that to this elegant hag. Or this elegant hag." Reg lay down the queen of diamonds. "Or this elegant hag." Queen of spades. "Or this elegant hag." Hearts.

Tad and Enzo howling misery with every hag.

A cluster of bangs, like muffled explosions, rocked the LRS. Sent the money sliding off the table. Alarms sounded. Another series of hits. Dipped the lights.

The station rat was on the deck. The Marines kept their seats.

"What did we fly into?" said Enzo.

A voice on over the loud com announced, laconic: "We are under attack by the Roman Legion carrier *Horatius*. We are about to be boarded."

The clank of a *corvus* sounded on the hull.

Reg threw down her last two cards. "Oooo, they've been itchin' for a fight since we saved their sorry little planet for them. Let's have it! Come *on!*"

"We got this, Reggie girl," said Tad, rising.

"Stay in the back, short timer," said Enzo.

"Short timer?" said Reg. "I'm *done*! I crawled in a fox-trotting Roman sewer for those folf-wuckers! The elegant hag does NOT do the *back!*"

16

SIX BELLS, AND ONE OF the guys in the forecastle was screaming as if he'd found something dead in the sleep pod with him. Some laughter sounded, too, so no one was really dying.

Flight Sergeant Cain Salvador screamed bloody murder.

Apparently the toe tag had found its way back. Cain had woken up with it. And not on his toe.

Cain pounded on the partition that separated the jacks from the janes. "Kerry Blue! This better've been you!"

Kerry giggled in her sleep pod. "'Fraid not."

Cain wailed, "Aw, no. *Lie* to me, babe!"

The other men in the forecastle were altogether creeped. Kerry Blue could hear a case of the squirms and dancing yewies like never. Sounded like the guys just wanted to crawl out of their own skins and have 'em fumigated. Didn't want to think how that tag got there. There but for the grace of God.

Flight Leader Ranza Espinoza was up and trying to muster some kind of command to order, but she was *this far* from belly laughs. Could see the guffaws moving around in her midriff like snakes. Her eyes were upturned crescents, gleaming merry tears.

Dak Shepard pleaded through the partition, "Kerry Blue, can I sleep with you tonight? I'm scared!"

The sound to general quarters ended all that, with the Marine Wing throwing on clothes and running to their Swifts.

Commodore Farragut burst onto the command deck, still dripping, carrying his clothes under his arm except for his pants which were on him. The commodore had one of the three water showers on board *Merrimack* and had been in it when the alarms sounded.

Lieutenant Colonel Steele was already on the command deck. The XO, Gypsy Dent, was there, too, demanding the nature of the threat from the Officer of the Watch, Lieutenant Glenn Hamilton.

"Not sure, sir," Glenn Hamilton confessed. "The Emergency Action Message from the Joint Chiefs called *everyone* to red alert."

"Everyone?" Commander Gypsy Dent and Commodore Farragut said at the same time.

"The United States of America. Everyone," said Hamster. "There was a Roman attack. No declaration of war. No one knows what it means."

"Oh, for—" Farragut started. Then: "Tactical, who is out there?"

"Just us chickens, Commodore. We are still fifty light-years from Fort Theodore Roosevelt and there is no one within thirty light-years of the *Mack*."

All the monitors showed nothing but stars, and Marine Swifts out there in the big dark looking for a target and nobody laughing.

"Okay, turn off that alarm and back us down to yellow," said Farragut, slightly nettled at someone giving orders to his ship from a couple dozen light-years away. "Give me that EAM."

Farragut popped the EAM into his player. Glanced up from the reader. "Has this been authenticated?"

Glenn Hamilton stiffened as if she'd been called stupid. But it was only protocol. She answered evenly, "Yes, sir."

The cryptotech, Qord Johnson, echoed, "Yes, sir."

Farragut read the Emergency Action Message while he pulled his shirt on. "This is crazy."

A U.S. Long Range Shuttle had been attacked by a Roman Legion carrier. The *Horatius*. Two light-years outside the solar system. Three Marines had been killed trying to repel boarders.

No one could say if the U.S. and Rome were at war or not. Whether this was Pearl Harbor or piracy or something else, no one seemed to know.

The Emergency Action Message ordered all armed forces everywhere to expect other attacks. Or at least be ready for them.

"Request confirmation," Farragut ordered. A single silver star glinted from either collar tab as he buttoned his shirt.

The com tech and the cryptotech acknowledged. Sent the request.

The tall, ominous figure of the Roman patterner Augustus appeared in the hatchway to the command deck. Marines flanking the hatch instantly drew arms.

Augustus halted.

Difficult to read his expression. No fear. Disdain for the Marines and their splinter guns. Some curiosity. Looked to Farragut as if for explanation.

Farragut asked, "Augustus, are we at war?"

"I can hope," said Augustus.

"Are we at war?" Farragut repeated.

"If we are, I have not been informed," said Augustus.

"Neither have I, but there's been some shooting," Farragut told him. "Confine yourself to quarters until one of us knows."

Augustus had been moved out of his Striker in the ship's dock and given quarters on board *Merrimack*.

The patterner turned smartly about-face in the hatchway.

Farragut added at his back: "Whoever knows first *will* have the courtesy to inform the other."

Augustus lifted a hand, acknowledging that. Withdrew from the hatchway.

Steele ordered the guards, "Make sure he gets to his quarters and keep him there."

Surprised to hear the commodore speak over him,

"Belay that. Stay at your posts." And to Steele, "Put a guard in the dock."

Lieutenant Colonel Steele, who never challenged orders, was trying hard to contain himself. He flushed. Looked like a tower of pink granite. Eyes of artic blue glared with accusation.

Farragut answered the unspoken objection. "TR, he's one of us right up until he's not."

Civility was vital in space warfare.

Which was why it was incomprehensible that *Horatius* would commit piracy.

Another EAM came in, summoning *Merrimack* back to the solar system.

Horatius had not responded to any hail. A pack of Rattlers in pursuit been fired upon and turned back. A request from the White House for clarification of the nations' status still awaited answer from Fortress Aeyrie.

"TR, bring your birds in," Farragut ordered. "Mr. Dent, as soon as everyone is aboard, turn this boat around."

Farragut returned to his quarters to finish his shower.

Merrimack hurtled toward Earth at threshold velocity. Covered vast distances without word from Earth. In the com silence, you had to wonder if Earth was still there.

The hard part was the not knowing.

Wondered about the Romans and Americans in the Deep End, serving side by side. Suddenly they had to watch their sides.

Updates dripped in with scant information.

Twelve hours later, the message everyone waited for came in: Rome had not declared war and had not ordered the attack.

"So what happened?" Farragut demanded as *Merrimack* dropped out of FTL at the perimeter of the solar system twenty-four hours after the first alarm.

The controller on Triton base responded by giving

Merrimack the current vector of the renegade *Horatius*, and ordered *Merrimack* to pursue and secure.

"Is this a hostage situation?" Farragut asked.

"Not precisely," the controller answered.

"Make it precise for me."

"The Dracs took possession of a Long Range Shuttle and beached the crew and passengers on Thaleia. The planetary governor on Thaleia notified us that our people are not in detention. Not in detention, but they have no way off world. Earth traffic is barred from Thaleian space."

Farragut filled in the blanks. "The governor of Thaleia didn't actively aid the Dracs but didn't do anything to prevent their getaway."

"Precisely."

"Where does Romulus stand on this?"

"Romulus isn't talking to us," said Triton Control. "He answered President Johnson—just to say that Rome had not declared war. His aide indicated to us that our failure to control military vessels wasn't any fault of Rome's and that the U.S. should handle its own affairs."

"Squid feet!" said Farragut.

"The JC are giving this to you, *Merrimack*. If we are to treat this as a mutiny, no one wants the JC to issue direct orders to *Horatius* and be ignored. Commodore Farragut, you have orders to secure the *Horatius* and Legion Draconis by any means necessary."

"Fine," said Farragut, with the com off. Clicked on: "Acknowledged, Triton Control."

Merrimack could run down just about anything near her size, and *Horatius* was not running. Not precisely.

Augustus, released from self-confinement, watched in grim amusement as *Merrimack* closed on *Horatius*. Not that Augustus found the imminent death of Romans entertaining, but he took a vicious satisfaction in the hole Farragut had dug for himself. The Subjugation had given Farragut authority to command Roman troops. Roman troops had mutinied.

How are you going to get out this, John Farragut? Kill your own?

He had to.

As *Merrimack* closed the range between ships, *Horatius* opened fire.

All ordnance slid off *Mack*'s formidable forward distortion field.

When *Merrimack* drew very close, a mere 100 klicks separating the two ships, Farragut requested the harmonic of *Horatius*' verbal com.

A cluster of bombs detonated on *Mack*'s bow, dimming all the viewports. Farragut took up the caller. "Well, darlin', you can slap my face all night, but I'm still fixin' to walk you home from this dance. Care to talk?"

No response. *Horatius* continued at speed.

Clicked on the caller again, "You can't put in at any port anywhere ever again in this lifetime unless you talk to me. So what do you have to say?"

Herius Asinius' voice sounded thick: "We do not recognize U.S. authority. We fight for Roma Eterna."

Consternation visibly washed off Farragut's face, replaced by a calm, almost smiling expression. He might have been coaching Little League, the game in the bag, and no one else could see it.

"Well, I ain't Caesar—" Farragut began.

"Thank you for acknowledging that, Captain Farragut."

"But I made some assumptions that I thought were kinda obvious. Now I know Rome isn't the United States—"

"Thank you for acknowledging that, Captain Farragut."

"But where I come from, the government doesn't fall just because an office holder dies. Before the surrender, a Roman warship had the right, under Roman rule, to commandeer any United States vessel it could. So all this would have been legal back then. But this is after the surrender now, son, and Magnus' death did not overthrow Rome or its treaties or truces."

"The law according to Captain Farragut," said Herius Asinius. "*We* serve Roma Eterna."

"Then how 'bout we ask Roma Eterna about that?" And with the com open for the Dracs to hear, Farragut told his com tech, "Mr. Hicks, hail Caesar."

Merrimack dropped out of FTL to place the resonant call.

While waiting for a response, Farragut advised Tactical, "Let me know when *Horatius* drops."

The com tech tried to get Romulus on the com, but was informed by a prickly gatekeeper that Romulus did not heel to the summons of American Naval officers. If this were a matter of State, the gatekeeper was certain that Romulus would hear of it from President Johnson.

Tactical reported quietly that the *Horatius* had dropped out of FTL and was very likely listening to the exchange. Probably smirking.

Farragut had experience dealing with stubborn, powerful people. His father was galactic champion of the I'm-too-important-to-take-your-call game.

"I'm sorry," Farragut apologized to the gatekeeper. "I negotiated the peace with Caesar Magnus, and Magnus is not there. In the absence of Magnus, Magnus' successor shall have to answer. But y'all haven't ratified anyone as Caesar. Would the qualified authority be then the Senate? Connect me with Senator Gaius Americanus."

There was a short silence and then, "Please stand by for Caesar Romulus."

Farragut knew that Romulus was already listening, so Farragut did not stand by, just started right in: "I made the truce with Rome, so I know the terms did not alter Rome's internal government. But I'm not real clear on Lex Romana, and I've got a shipload of folks on an open channel here who don't seem clear on the order of the Empire either. I need someone like a Caesar—"

"I *am* Caesar," Romulus broke his silence.

Good. "—to confirm that the Empire still stands and that the truce of Caesar Magnus holds with the full force of Rome behind it. Does it?"

So there was Romulus, backed against the wall. The

least uncertainty, hesitation, or hair-splitting in this moment would destroy him. For Romulus to disavow the surrender would be a declaration of war. And Romulus had just told President Marissa Johnson that Rome had not declared war.

Romulus snapped, "Yes, of course it does."

There was a collective exhalation on *Merrimack*'s command deck.

Roma Eterna had just put the Dracs under U.S. command.

"And just so I understand Roman law, were a combat unit to refuse a lawful order, under Roman law the penalty would be death to the soldiers and death to their kin. Even suicide would not spare their mothers, fathers, spouses, and children. Under Roman law. Is that still true?"

Farragut had the authority to command Roman troops, but Roman disobedience put them subject to the penalties of Roman law. Any executions would not be at U.S. hands.

An instant dread chill clutched the command deck.

Horatius, over the com, was deathly silent.

No one had seen that one coming.

Least of all Romulus. He answered in cold fury, "Roman law has not changed." And terminated the connection before he could be trapped into anything else.

Farragut spoke into the com, "All right, Mister Asinius. Come back here. Drop your distortion fields except for your asteroid deflector and follow me to Thaleia."

"We are to be put to death?" Herius asked, stoic.

"Why? You fixin' to break a law?"

Wordless confusion read over the com.

Farragut said, "You didn't understand the chain of command. Now you do. Now follow me to Thaleia, and tell your buddies who have my LRS to meet us there with my people, or so help me God I won't stop at their mothers and fathers and kids. I'll have their grammies, their sisters, their brothers, their dogs, and their goldfish crucified." He clicked off. Ordered *Merrimack* to turn heel.

In a moment he asked his tactical specialist, "Is *Horatius* behind us?"

"Yes, sir."

"Lining up a shot on my ass?"

"No, sir."

Farragut nodded.

Felt Augustus' eyes on him. Asked, "What?"

The patterner answered, "Not what I would have predicted."

Farragut, who had a reputation as being trigger happy—a well deserved reputation—had won this crisis without firing a shot.

"You know, it woulda been real helpful if *your* emperor had made the status of the surrender clear from the get go. He left that point just fuzzy enough for a proud, hardheaded young Roman to get creative."

"Romulus is not emperor yet. I think Romulus was rather counting on your slaughtering the Dracs."

Jolted Farragut. "Why would Romulus want the Dracs dead?"

"Wasn't the effect on the Dracs he would have wanted. It would be the effect on you. And on Romulus. The more detestable the enemy leader, the more popular your own leader."

If Farragut had done what everyone expected and secured *Horatius* the old-fashioned way, that might have caused the Romans to rally even more strongly round their new unratified Caesar, who had denounced John Farragut's Subjugation of Rome and had denied John Farragut his Triumphal crown.

"Really?" It was too much bloody political maneuvering for Farragut. "Then I'm happy to disappoint him. And you, Augustus? Are you disappointed?"

"I think too little of you for you to disappoint me. Permission to withdraw."

"Granted."

A tittering about the command deck followed Augustus' departure.

Marcander Vincent snarled into his readouts. "Caesar sent him to serve you, my Aunt Fanny."

"Be all kinds of real fine to have him on our side," said Farragut.

"Yeah, that would be fine if it ever happened," said Vincent. "Sir."

"What was that man thinking?" Farragut thought out loud to his exec as *Merrimack* approached the planet Thaleia with *Horatius* heeling like a dog. "Herius Asinius, I mean. Was he trying to start a war?"

"Maybe," Gypsy considered it. "Make a first strike and hope Rome followed his lead?"

"Yeah," said Farragut. "But it would be a strategic disaster with the Hive out there."

"You called it, sir. A proud, hotheaded young Roman. Didn't Calli say: what Rome can afford to do and what Rome will do for pride are two different things?"

Pride was the deadliest of Roman sins. And Herius Asinius' pride had taken a bloody beating.

"Or maybe he didn't want a war," Farragut searched for another motive. "He just wanted to give America a bloody nose and expected Romulus to shelter him. Romulus did give the Dracs reason to expect some kind of support. Romulus has publicly expressed disgust at the surrender without ever repudiating it."

"Hit and run?" said Gypsy. "Herius didn't run. He didn't leave the area. He let *Merrimack* get close. You got called into the street for a gunfight, Marshal. Herius wanted either to destroy the *Merrimack* or have you send him and the Dracs gloriously to the Corindahlor Bridge in hopeless battle."

Gypsy glanced up to the monitor screens as *Merrimack* approached Thaleia. Said: "In fact, it was definitely you he wanted, sir. Look."

The image of the captive LRS came into view on the screen.

"Oh, for Jesus."

Steele saw the identification numbers on the LRS and went rigid.

One of the guards at the hatch, normally mute as a statue, spoke, "Can we still string up their grannies?"

Farragut answered sympathetically, "No, son."

Steele found his voice. Asked hoarsely, "Three casualties? Marines?"

Farragut nodded.

Merrimack collected the Long Range Shuttle, its crew, cargo, passengers, and three bodies. Set the LRS back on course to Earth.

The crew and Legion of *Horatius* had orders to assemble in their cargo hold and wait with their small arms piled on the deck.

Merrimack docked with *Horatius*.

Farragut boarded *Horatius* in person, armed, but without a Marine guard, his only attendant the Roman patterner, Augustus.

As commanded, no Dracs met him at the dock.

It would have been an easy thing to go to the *Horatius*' control room and purge the cargo hold into the vacuum.

Farragut marched into the cargo hold, took a stand before the assembled Romans and did not order them to ease. Caesar's patterner stood motionless at his flank.

Commodore Farragut announced, "I am pressing this vessel into service in Attack Group One. I will beach whoever does not want to come with me. I need folks to man this boat, so I'll give y'all first shot. Do I have volunteers?"

Mumbles, with sniggers interspersed, rippled through the rigid ranks.

Farragut's voice started soft and got louder. "I am going to the Deep to kill gorgons. Not everyone is made of the same stuff as the Tenth at Corindahlor, and I don't want anyone with me who doesn't want to be there. So if you're not coming, *get off my boat*. And now that we're clear on who you're supposed to be taking orders from and that you still have a duty to defend Rome, choose a place—on the ground safe in Near

Space or on board this ship in the Deep End—pick up your weapons, and *do your goddamn duty!*"

Augustus absorbed the final verbal blast with small flinches that were more like half blinks in his otherwise basilisk face.

"DISMISSED!" Farragut ended with a roar, motioned Augustus to fall in, and stalked back to *Merrimack* without waiting for anyone's decision.

The commodore was an idiot. Naive, bright-eyed, energetic, and way too optimistic to be the man in charge of so many men of war. He led by personality. Had a face people trusted instantly. And why? Just because he was good-looking, had bright blue eyes and that glad-to-see-you smile? Or because he remembered your name and every damn thing you ever told him about yourself?

Augustus hated a fraud, and John Farragut had to be a fraud. John Farragut appeared to be the kind of man everyone wanted to exist. And they would willingly follow that image to hell.

"Permission to speak freely," said Farragut.

Augustus' brow furrowed very slightly. "I did not request it."

"Nevertheless, you have it."

"You should not have invoked Corindahlor back there," said Augustus.

"Do I sully the memory of the heroes of the Roman Tenth by speaking of them?"

"The Tenth? No, they're not sullied. And they're hardly heroes. Only an idiot enlists for ground duty in a unit of three hundred."

"What's wrong with three hundred?"

"It's a heroic number. Nations make their honor cadres in three hundreds, so when they are obliterated in hopeless battle, they are heroes. Thermopylae, the Sacred Band of Thebes at Chaironeia, the three hundred at Masada. Never join an outfit that numbers three hundred. Or a multiple of three hundred, unless you want to ride in the valley of death. Invoking Corindahlor was a cheap way to manipulate the Dracs."

"The only one I manipulated was Romulus, and he asked for it," said Farragut. "Herius and his boys just got caught in a rundown while trying to steal a base."

"A stalwart Roman Legion." Augustus' voice dripped scorn. "Their hearts changed in less than a beat."

"Sure they changed quick! Once you kick folks off the fence, it gets real clear real quick which side everyone is on, and decisions get real simple."

"Oh, the insulting, monumental arrogance of the completely dominant. You have no idea why we resent the offered help, even if we need it. Especially if we need it. You saved Rome's planetary ass. You cannot imagine how demeaning it is to be tucked under your protective wing. If not for the Hive, the United States and Rome would be enemies; and I and John Farragut would be staring down each other's guns. And maybe I would be magnanimous in your defeat, but I don't think so. I step on the weak, and that includes idiots."

And Augustus stood back, in a *so there* stance. Waited for comment or execution. When neither came, Augustus said, "Any free speaking coming back at me?"

Farragut shook his head. "Just wanted to know what was on your mind."

Carly Delgado had a scream that could detonate warheads. Did not help at all that the KIAs were getting medals.

"She didn't want no medal! She wanted to be an engineer! A *civilian* engineer!"

Kerry Blue bounced off the bulks like a caged rat. "Let me out! Let me out! I'll kill 'em all!"

"Blue! Delgado! Team Alpha! Stand down!" Steele thundered.

"No!" Carly cried.

Steele bodily took hold of Carly and slammed her up against the bulk. "Only proves you are out of control, Delgado. You're a menace to everyone. *Stand down!*" Let her drop.

She kept dropping. Kind of crumpled to sit on the deck, sobbing over her crossed legs.

Girl Marines crying tore Steele's guts out.

Echo and Delta were taking it just as hard. They had lost a man each, supposed to be on leave. Tad and Enzo. Outstanding soldiers. They were not coming back.

And Reg Monroe, going home for good. Happy as a bride.

Kerry Blue was on the deck now, next to Carly, looking like a mama bitch who lost her puppies and won't believe they're really gone. Looked up to Steele with bewildered forlorn eyes as if he could bring them back.

Kerry's tears. That face. And he could not do what she needed him to do. Never felt worse or less of a man than now.

TR Steele was going to rip the guts out of whoever killed his two big mutts and that happy little she-dog.

"*I* am *not* flying with those bastards!" Cole Darby declared.

The crew and company of *Horatius* had, to a man, volunteered to serve under Commodore Farragut in Attack Group One.

Steele had been ordered to head off talk like that. Been waiting for it. Roared at Darb, "You *are*, or you're going home with a dishonorable!" The words burned him coming out. His dogs were only saying what Steele felt. "You are *not* the only dog soldiers who ever lost mates to the wolves!"

"During a surrender we are!" Kerry cried.

Steele inhaled to bellow at her. Lost all his air.

Steele's solid shoulders slumped. He could not argue with her. Rested his hands on his hips, let his head drop forward. Spoke into the deck, "Gordy already asked Farragut if we could crucify their grannies."

Dak Shepard lifted his teary face from his hands, hopeful. "Yeah? What'd Farragut say?"

17

FORT THEODORE ROOSEVELT had been built in the star system Beta Aurigae aka Mankib Dhi-al-'Inan, The Shoulder of the Charioteer. The ancient Greeks looked up and saw a charioteer in the stars, but most American children looked up and connected those five dots into a child-drawn house. Fort Ted was at the peak of the roof, eighty-two light-years from Earth in the opposite direction from the Wolf Star.

Mankib Dhi-al-'Inan was actually three stars, two of them white subgiants that had wandered off the main sequence hand in hand. They had worked up nice helium cores but were still very hot, their photospheres still very white, not ready to blow up just yet. It would take another million years for them to become dangerous. For now they were just plain spectacular.

The two white stars swung round each other in a tight dance, eclipsing each other just about every two Earth days. So the starlight in Fort Ted varied between bright and brighter.

A third star in the system, a red dwarf, circled the other two way the hell out there at eight times the distance of Pluto to Sol. Between the two main stars and the lights of Fort Ted, the red dwarf went pretty much unseen.

Merrimack approached Theodore Roosevelt with its

flag, and all the flags in the spaceport, at half staff for the death of a head of state.

The space cav charged out to escort the Roman warship *Horatius* directly round the outskirts of the Fort to quarantine, where dwelled things infectious, explosive, suspicious, or the Roman murderers of three U.S. Marines. The snub-nosed Rattlers of the U.S. space cav always looked smoked. The Rattlers darted in close enough to set off *Horatius'* prox alarms, and ordered the Romans to shut down their distortion field and park.

A maintenance platform closed round *Horatius* and clanked against the hull. The platform generated a distortion field round the ship, and pumped an atmosphere in. The ship's hull iced over in the heated air. The platform powered up an artificial grav, and *Horatius* received orders to pop her hatches.

The maintenance platform kept a U.S. atmosphere— fifteen psi—so it made for an ear-popping moment when the Roman seventeen psi hissed loose from *Horatius*.

The platform uprights turned on the swamplights. Swamps did not cast the hard shadows of floods. The swamps gave an overall illumination like daylight for technicians to work in.

Herius Asinius, in company of his cousin Marcus, stepped outside under a weird starry black sky.

A platoon of U.S. erks stood ready to board, equipped to rip the ship to razor blades. Herius and Marcus almost called the Legion to arms, but on the platform also stood John Farragut, who announced to the erks, "This is *my* ship. These are *my* men. Treat them so."

The erks looked dubious. Farragut added, "And post this."

The erks reverently received the U.S. flag from the commodore. Farragut turned to Herius Asinius. As if waiting for an objection.

There was no way around it this time. That flag was going on Herius' ship. "Don't take down our standards," said Herius.

"No," Farragut agreed. He waved the erks in.

Big men with heavy boots stomped aboard like a wrecking crew. Herius was pretty sure they *were* a wrecking crew.

The astrarch, Marcus, asked, unsettled, "What are you doing to my ship?"

"Nothing that I didn't have done to my *Merrimack*."

Herius and Marcus still cringed at the sudden *brrr-rack!* of big drills on the bulkheads. Like undergoing surgery without an anesthetic.

"She'll live," said Farragut. "Herius, your boys are good with swords and y'all know what you're doing in front of a bunch of tentacles by now. What you don't have behind you is what it's like when the light goes out in outer space. The Hive will do that. You're getting chemical and mechanical and manual backups. And you're getting blister turrets with projectile cannon with mechanical loads. When the erks are done in there, we're going out to play with guns that go boom and shells that shred things. We've got some fiendishly realistic mock gorgons we can set loose for y'all to shoot to shingles."

Neither Roman was accustomed to such casual flippant talk from a Triumphalis. But guns that went boom did sound like fun.

Herius had known John Farragut had a sunny disposition. Had also seen that sun could burn your skin off. Farragut had blazed at him. Gave him and his Dracs a wrath-of-God thunder-and-lightning kind of talking to. And the hell of it was, Herius Asinius could not argue with a single thing the American had said. So when the moment of decision came, Herius had no choice but to pick up his hand cannon and join Commodore Farragut. He was not happy with how eagerly his men had followed his lead, in glassy-eyed hero worship of the American. All of them were here to a man.

"I mean it about the mock gorgons," said Farragut. "You will swear they're real. And you better hit all of 'em because if you miss any, they'll have you swearing a *lot*."

"Are we getting fire breathers?" Marcus asked.

As if the alternative never occurred to him, Farragut said, "You think I'd take you out there naked? You'll have what I have."

"I don't want your Marines teaching us," said Herius.

Farragut pressed his lips together, eyes to the platform. Herius sensed a refusal coming, but at last Farragut nodded. "This here is what we call a shotgun wedding. I guess I might oughta better find somebody else to teach y'all. I can keep my Marines off your ship. *But.*"

Herius steeled himself against the *but*.

"Because I need y'all to know what you're doing, and I'm not confident that you can really know something until you teach it, *you* are going to show Bambi and Twinkletoes over there how it's done after you've learned it." He gestured across an expanse of blackness to where another oasis of swamplights illuminated another maintenance platform enclosing two League of Earth Nations ships.

The LEN had added two ships to Farragut's Attack Group One. *Windward Isles* and *Sunlit Meadows*. The LEN were always naming-convention challenged.

In the war between the U.S. and Rome, the LEN had been staunchly noncommittal. In the middle was always a good place to get yourself shot. Americans and Romans regarded their delared enemies more highly than their lukewarm allies.

"I am charging you, Herius Asinius, with making sure they can hold up their end."

"Aye, Commodore," said Herius Asinius.

"Permission to come aboard."

"Good God Almighty, Dallas McDaniels. What the Sam Hill are you doing this side of the Big Dark?" Farragut crossed *Merrimack*'s starboard dock with huge strides to seize Captain McDaniels and thump him on the back, pull back beaming, and hug him and thump him again. Had expected to join up with Captain McDaniels and *Rio Grande* on the other side of the Shotgun. "Last time I saw you, you were saving Mama Farragut's favorite son from a pile of gorgons."

"John, old son, we got chewed."

"Someone I know once told me never ever let 'em aboard."

"And I was right, wasn't I?"

Dallas McDaniels, Captain of the *Rio Grande*, looked like he ought to be on a cattle drive. A tall, spare man all rawhide and whipcord, steel nerves and an easy drawl. Had a seamed, leathery face, dusty-colored hair, and keen eyes locked in a permanent squint.

"They got all the king's horses and all the king's men putting my poor *Rio* back together again. And next thing I know I'm reporting to a *junior* officer. After I saved your ass, too. You want to tell me what's fair about that?"

"Yeah, about that," said Farragut. "The ass saving. I never did get a chance to thank you."

"Well, I'm just going to hold it over your head for the rest of your natural-born days."

"That's fair, *compadre*."

"So now tell me, old son, do I salute or do I bow?"

Farragut flipped him a one-digit salute and ushered Dallas aboard, arm round his shoulders. "Come on in, I'll have Chef Zack cook up something for you."

An odd sound made Dallas lift his eyes. Dallas McDaniels thought he knew all the sounds a space battleship could make. "What is that? Sounds like a cow in labor."

"A cow in labor," Farragut answered. "We carry some livestock in case we get stranded."

"Let's not get stranded."

"Not my first, second, or third choice," said Farragut, as the cow gave a particularly painful moo.

"Are they supposed to do that?"

"Technically, no. I think someone's been screwing around in the livestock compartment."

"Sounds like that would be the cow. I think I'll pass on the veal selection."

The rhythmic thump thump thump of joggers on the

track sounded from above decks. A sudden grav burble brought stomachs to throats, bent the knees, and made the steady thump thump thump dissolve into a stagger/bumble/roll.

Dallas' eyes crinkled at the corners. "Now there's a homey sound. I'd have thought a ship of *Merrimack*'s class to have smoother artificial gravity than the rest of us peons."

"Nah," said Farragut. "My *Mack*. She has her moods."

"Don't have to tell me. *Rio*'s brought me to my knees."

"Don't they all?" said Farragut.

"Yes, sir, they do. So where's your crown, Triumphalis?"

"I didn't get it. It was grass anyway."

"Yeah?" Dallas drawled. "What kind of grass?"

John Farragut paid a visit to the Roman maintenance platform. Asked Herius Asinius, "How are the *Mountain Oyster* and the *Kumbaya* coming along?"

"We didn't name the ships," a female voice sounded from behind.

Farragut turned. A hard, thin woman smiled politely. Perhaps fifty years old, her hair a hard shade of blonde. She wore the uniform of a League of Earth Nations captain.

Farragut actually blushed, caught with a mouth full of foot. Gave a chagrined grin. "Yeah, I really said that."

He took the LEN captain's offered hand as she introduced herself and her dark companion with the wide, shiny face, "Fredrika Freiheit of the *Minnow* and this is Captain Ram Singh of the *Nightcrawler*."

"Bait," said Farragut, clueing in to the names. "You're not bait."

"And we're not LEN golf balls, Commodore," said Fredrika. "Don't judge us by the stupid names. *Sunlit Meadows* and *Windward Isles* are police ships, and we make dead with the best of them."

Farragut looked to Herius Asinius. "How are they doing?"

"Very well," said Herius formally. "I would trust the LEN ships at my back."

Farragut turned to Fredrika and Ram. "Then I'm pleased to blue peaches to have y'all in my attack group." He called past them to the erks. Motioned at the LEN ships, "Flag 'em."

Fredrika recited blandly, "LEN convention forbids a League ship from taking on the flag of any individual nation."

The erks paused, looking to Farragut for direction.

"You have your orders," said Farragut. Where his ships were going there could be only one undisputed master.

"Oh, look at the view from here," Fredrika said, turning to face the spectacular double star Mankib Dhi-al-'Inan, her back toward her ship as the Stars and Stripes were posted on her *Sunlit Meadows.*

Captain Ram Singh, a middle-sized man, well muscled, very black, stood beside her, his arms crossed. "Yes. Very nice," said Ram, as *Windward Isles* received the U.S. flag.

All space farers had ultraviolet filters implanted in their eyes, so Fred and Ram could gaze at the swollen white suns as long as it took for them not to see their ships being reflagged.

Neither LEN ship was very big. Farragut asked, "What kind of soldiers do y'all have on board?"

"Engineers," said Ram Singh. "All of us."

"You're getting Marines or Dracs," said Farragut.

"We don't fight hand-to-hand, Commodore," Fredrika Freiheit explained. "We don't board pirates. We blow them out of the vacuum."

"You're getting Marines or Dracs," Farragut said again. "We go against the Hive, you *will* be boarded. I don't care how good you make dead. There are just too many of them out there to make."

When Romulus hailed the *Merrimack*, Commodore Farragut took the call immediately. There was no waiting. John Farragut was never one to play tit for tat.

"You have the mutineers with you," Romulus said, aghast, accusing.

"The Dracs?" said Farragut. "They're not mutineers. They were confused."

"Did they pledge loyalty to me?"

"They pledged to Rome."

"They have shown their disregard for orders," said Romulus. "And you put them in your service?"

"They're all straight now."

"Could they have had a hand in my father's assassination?"

"Caesar, that's just plain dumb."

Romulus pulled back from the vid screen, offended.

"It's true and you know it," said Farragut, his voice easy, coaxing. "Those boys are loyal to Rome. If—IF—Herius Asinius had been mad enough over the Subjugation and my Triumph to kill your father, he would have charged up shouting 'Death to the Tyrant,' not stood there and watched a Julian do it for him."

"Commodore Farragut, we need to understand each other."

"I agree, sir."

Romulus held up to the vid screen a court document giving Romulus authority to retrieve Augustus from U.S. custody.

"That again," said Farragut. "The long arm of your law does not reach into my ship." And more conciliatory, "Your daddy gave that patterner to me, and I need him. If I don't use talent like that to stop the Hive, then I deserve to be eaten by gorgons."

"I do not question the importance of your mission, Commodore Farragut, so don't try to wave that around as the excuse for everything you want to do. This man, this *cyborg*, has been implicated in the death of a Caesar!"

Farragut had to laugh. "*Qui bono* wasn't Augustus!"

"Are you accusing *me* of my father's murder?"

"*I* was talking about Augustus," said Farragut. "Don't know why you tried the shoe on."

Romulus drew back, eyes flaring, outraged.

Farragut realized he had been too flippant. "Your father was murdered before your eyes. I don't see how *bono* that is for you either. I'm sorry for your loss."●

Romulus lowered his eyes, nodded, appeared to be grieving. Lifted his gaze, his voice abruptly reasonable. "Does it not strike you as odd that Augustus was conveniently absent from Fortress Aeyrie when my father was murdered?"

"No, sir. Not strange at all. Magnus could *only* have been murdered in Augustus' absence. Augustus can connect dots parsecs apart, and I've met Rottweilers less protective than Magnus' patterner."

"What has he told you about me?"

"I did not have the chance to talk with your father all that long."

"I meant Augustus. What has he told you?"

"Nothing that I can remember."

"Truly?" said Romulus, somewhere between skeptical and complete disbelief.

"I can tell you lots of things he's had to say about *me*." Farragut offered.

"And does he suspect you of killing Caesar?"

"No, not *suspect*. He came right out and told me I was guilty. By keeping him away from Caesar."

"Then you know not to trust him."

"Sir, with respect, it sounds like you don't know who to trust. And in your situation, I guess I wouldn't either. If you would let us, I could enlist Naval Intelligence to help sort this out—"

"No! You have no business in the rule of our Empire. And if you will not surrender the Roman patterner by reason or law or right or justice, then know this: you may have an assassin on board your ship, and he is at best unreliable. Excuse me now, I have a funeral to attend."

Maybe it was an overdose of paranoia, but as the call terminated, Farragut suddenly wondered if *Horatius'* attack on the LRS had not been executed under someone's orders after all.

* * *

"Romulus demanded I turn you over to him," said Farragut. Waited for the patterner's reaction.

The face did not so much as ripple. "I will go."

"No, you won't."

"If I return to Rome," said Augustus, "I will know who was behind Caesar's assassin."

"If you go back to Rome, the only thing you'll know is a bullet in the brain. Romulus is ready to kill just about anybody. You, in particular."

"That is his right."

"Got a terminal death wish, don't you, Augustus?"

"You figured that out?"

"All by myself. And you're not going."

Augustus glared at him like the Rottweiler, Farragut standing between him and his master.

Farragut held his gaze. Finally observed, curious, "Augustus, you're not refusing my order. Why?"

"I cannot. Caesar gave me to you. Damn him. Damn you."

"You want to know who killed Caesar? Well, sacrificing you to Romulus won't get the job done. Won't destroy the Hive either. Magnus gave me a powerful weapon to use, and I've thoroughly bollixed that plan to date—"

"Yes, you have."

"That'll do, Augustus. I ain't fixing to keep squandering what Magnus gave me. He gave you to me to destroy the Hive, and that's what we're doing first. So whatever you and Romulus have going on, keep it out of my way. *And* I'm giving you standing orders: Do not kill yourself so long as you are under my command."

Augustus' gaze turned murderous. He spoke slowly, "And the moment we return to a hot war?"

"Then you can go jump off a bridge."

Made Augustus blink.

18

UPON LEARNING THAT Captain Fredrika Freiheit and Captain Ram Singh had never been through the Fort Theodore Roosevelt/Fort Dwight David Eisenhower Shotgun, Commodore Farragut advised them, "Brace yourself for the biggest letdown of your life."

"Why? What's it like?" said Fredrika.

"Nothing," said Farragut. "I mean really. Nothing. They'll tell you not to move a muscle. Moose gills. It happens in an instant, and you don't even know which instant unless you're looking at the monitors. Then you'll see the stars change faster than the flip of a vid channel. Your ship is here. Then your ship is there in literal no time."

"Beats a three-month flight through the Abyss," said Ram Singh.

"Amen and hallelujah. The Shotgun has saved me a few years of my life," said Farragut. "Just didn't want y'all to go expecting a thrill ride."

Fort Eisenhower in the Deep End was smaller than Fort Theodore Roosevelt in Near Space. Fort Ike had fewer stations, but more starlight, being 2000 parsecs closer to the galactic hub. Fort Ike was wild as befit a frontier town. Gases and all the station's lights made the space fort a bright gaudy oasis in the night.

The last two ships of Attack Group One, the Roman

behemoth *Gladiator* and the old U.S.S. *Wolfhound* orbited the main station.

Fort Ike's main station was a ten mile in diameter, ten-story disk, with smaller and smaller concentric disks above and below, so that it looked like a gargantuan Christmas tree ornament.

A young woman accosted John Farragut upon his entry into the main station. Not unusual. Even before John Farragut had taken the surrender of the Roman Empire, women came on to him. He was a good-looking man in commodore's stars, and station women were particularly aggressive.

This was a pert, fit, sunshine blonde, with a neat angular little blonde beard. "Caesar Romulus sent me."

"That's a new one," said Farragut, and strode on by quickly so he wouldn't let slip something rude about the beard.

A signal from Colonel Steele caused a cadre of Fleet Marines to block the young woman's pursuit.

She was very quick, and cornered like a chipmunk. Almost got round the Marines, and Nev had to fire a splinter into her ass to make her stop.

Even at that, she turned and stared down the shooter, daring, a feral near-smile on her face, as if gauging whether he would really detonate the charge. Nev's stony return gaze told her he would, so she finally gave up.

The Marines offered to take the splinter out, but she carried her own extractor. She had been shot before.

A crowd had gathered on the main concourse.

Across a small table set up in the middle of the concourse, Captain Calli Carmel of the U.S. ship *Wolfhound* faced off with General Numa Pompeii of the Roman ship *Gladiator*.

Rows of half shots of vodka were lined up on the table, along with a glass bowl of water, and another glass bowl stacked with little red gel balls that looked like soft marbles.

All around them a crowd thickened. Lots of money

was changing lots of hands. Bets made and markers given.

Kerry Blue blurted, "O Gawd! Captain Carmel's doing hopper shots with Numa Pompeii!" And immediately shoved out a path to the front.

Numa Pompeii. General. Triumphalis. Legend.

A supremely confident and disdainful hulk. Powerfully built, big-boned, brawny. A voice big and heavy as the man. They said if Numa Pompeii, instead of the *Titanic,* had hit the iceberg, the iceberg would have gone down.

Fort Ike was a U.S. installation, and the station authorities did not allow Romans in by the pack, so there was no throng of legionaries behind him. The people behind him chanting, "*NU*ma! *NU*ma! *NU*ma!" were internationals.

Calli Carmel sat tall, a slender gazelle to Numa's water buffalo, cool and elegant. Not for long. No one looked elegant doing hopper shots.

Self-appointed guards kept a small ring clear around the table. So when someone moved close to Calli's shoulder, she glanced up startled. Did a double take. Started to rise.

John Farragut motioned her to stay where she was.

"Commodore?" said Calli. "Are you calling this off?"

"No, I'm lookin' for a bookie here."

"The smart money is on Numa," someone in the crowd advised Farragut.

Someone else countered that, "Numa to win won't pay gurzn gas. The real money is on the number of rounds. You *know* she's going down."

"Mister Carmel!" The shout in the crowd made Calli look. Marines of the 89th, the Bull Mastiffs, raised fists, gave a thunderous double woof and a Hoo ra.

Calli broke a smile, a thousand-ship-wrecking smile that caused men to walk into solid objects, each other, their own feet.

When the man running this circus signaled the betting closed, Numa and Calli each selected one red ball from the first bowl. At a mutual nod, they tossed the red balls into their mouths, clinked shot glasses, washed down the hoppers with the half shot of vodka, rapped the empty glasses upside down on the table, and shouted at each other, "Come on!"

Waited, glowering at each other. A chant started low in the crowd, "Hop. Hop. Hop. Hop."

Calli's head reared, her throat convulsed. She leaned forward and spat a little red frog into her hand. She dropped the hopper into the bowl of water, shouted "Clear!" to cheers from the crowd.

Numa spat out his little red froglet, dunked it. "Clear!" he announced to louder cheers. More of the onlookers had money on Numa for an early win.

Flight Leader Ranza Espinoza's thick brows twisted, dubious, at Calli. "They ain't gonna be calling her Empress ever again."

Flight Sergeant Cain Salvador leaned his head sideways to ask Kerry Blue, under his arm, "What are the rules?"

Cain Salvador was the new guy. Sort of new. Cain had already done two tours. Had tried the civilian gig. Not for him. So he was back. Fit in well with Team Alpha. Kerry Blue made him feel welcome. Hoo ra. Only Cain had done something to make Colonel Steele hate his guts. Had no idea what.

"The hopper has to come *up*," Kerry answered, eyes focused on the action. "You have to drink the glass empty. You're not allowed to dry swallow the hopper. If the hopper sticks in your throat, you can wash it down, but it has to be with vodka. And you have to make it go down. You're allowed to make yourself throw up or go to the head between rounds. But if you run to the head with a hopper still down, you lose. You pass out any time, you lose. You don't match a shot, you lose."

"What if the hopper dies?"

"Oh, honey, this never kills 'em. They get *out*. But if it ain't through the front gate—"

"You lose," Cain finished.

"Who made up this game?" Cole Darby yelped, truly rattled.

"I think it might've been Cowboy," said Kerry Blue.

It was really a sport as old as humankind, down there with geeks biting the heads off chickens and gladiators killing each other in the coliseum.

Calli Carmel at a table with a Roman general swallowing live animals with a crowd of hyenas egging them on.

At the table Calli was making an odd face, as if she had an ice cream headache. Eyes watering. A tiny red webbed foot flailed out one nostril of her narrow, gracefully shaped nose. She took the little foot between her thumb and forefinger and pulled the hopper out—to a huge crowd roar of delighted disgust—tossed it in the water bowl. Rather congested, she declared, "Clear!"

Darb shook his head, astonished. Like observing a baboon troop. His baboon troop. This was a U.S. Naval Captain and a Roman Triumphalis. Apparently these two had traded shots before—the kind that can kill you.

The crowd was getting thicker, more boisterous.

"Stay in there, Mister Carmel!" Carly Delgado yelled.

Cain asked in dazzled disbelief, "Carmel used to be XO of the *Mack?*"

"Yeah."

"Wish I'd been aboard then!" said Cain with a suggestive chuckle.

Got an elbow in his broad abdomen for that. Kerry Blue took Cain's thick arm from round her shoulders, and shoved it back at him.

"What?" said Cain. "What'd I do?"

"I know Carmel looks good even with a hopper hanging out her nose, but you don't ogle someone else when you're with *me.*"

Numa and Calli had taken to trying to aim their hoppers instead of spitting them into their palms. Calli got Numa a good one off his broad forehead.

Numa, in time-honored Roman tradition, availed himself of the vomitorium between rounds to get rid of some excess alcohol.

Calli, a third Numa's mass, should have and didn't.

She was too proud. She looked regal in between coughing up hoppers. But her eyes were getting misty, her lips lusciously full and pouting. Fine chestnut hairs stuck to her moist brow.

"I've never seen Mister Carmel like this," said Dak, marveling.

"Who has?"

"She can't win!" Ranza murmured. "He's a building!"

From the table came the double roar: "Come *on!*"

Numa and Calli had just thrown back number fifteen.

Numa quickly coughed his up, shouted, "Clear!" Dunked his hopper in the water bowl that was now swimming with a couple dozen red hoppers. He waited on Calli. "Trouble, Callista?"

Calli interlaced her long fingers prettily on the table. "Would it kill you to call me *Mister* Carmel?"

"Would it kill you to call me *Domnus*?"

"Yes. I think it would," said Calli. Her midriff flexed. She stuck out her tongue. On it, briefly, sat a red froglet that instantly hopped a mighty hop that cleared the table.

"Clear!" Calli plucked up another red ball. "Put it up, General."

Numa took up a red ball. "Shut up and do it."

They popped their hoppers. Clinked glasses. Threw back the half shots. Swallowed. Slammed the glasses down. Snarled across the table at each other, "Come on!"

Shortly, Numa opened his mouth, let the hopper jump out toward Calli.

Calli, sitting tall, rather primly, waited.

The crowd chant started again, very low, almost a whisper, but a lot of voices, so it was almost ominous: "Hop! Hop! Hop! Hop!"

Made Calli's stomach surge. She swallowed down nausea. Should not have done that.

Hop! Hop! Hop! Hop!

Felt the twist in her gut. She looked concerned.

Numa smirked. Ever so solicitously and kindly he asked, "Are you well, Callista?"

Calli's expression turned peculiar.

"Callista?"

Abruptly Calli kicked back her chair, pushed away from the table, setting the bowls to sloshing, and ran. The crowd made way for her. The big noise in her wake was a simultaneous descending "AWWW!" and a cheering roar, with Numa's big voice behind it all: "We have a winner!"

Only after the crowds had dispersed did Calli emerge from the head. Found Farragut waiting for her.

She leaned her forehead on his shoulder. "How many rounds did you have me for, John?"

"I didn't go for rounds, I had you to win."

She tried to walk, missed her step and wove back in to him. She sniggered. Patted his chest. "Sorry I lost you your shekels."

"Not a problem."

Farragut came from money. Could watch it ebb and flow without concern. "Nice of you to let Numa win one." Winked.

Calli had won the battles that mattered. "Oh, yeah, I planned it that way," she said with heavy insincerity. "For the unity of the Attack Group."

A Marine, Flight Sergeant Dakota Shepard, approached reverently. Advised, "Take the bilge bowl next time, Mister Carmel. I think that's what did you in."

Calli smiled wanly, an alcohol shine to her face. "Oh Flight Sergeant, there isn't going to be a next time. That has got to rank in the top two hundred dumbest things I've ever done."

"Sir?" said Dak. "You were *outstanding*."

Rob Roy Buchanan stared into his drink at a solitary table in Mad Bear O's space bar in the main station at Fort Eisenhower.

Mad Bear O's was a human bar. There was very little social mixing of species in any of the many bars inside the stations of Fort Eisenhower. Different species had different notions of what made for pleasant background sounds, what was drinkable, what was edible, what was breathable, and what temperatures and furniture were comfortable. Many aliens wore environmental suits in the main station because the partial pressures of the gases in that mix humans called "air" were toxic to them at the station's ambient pressure of fifteen psi. Then there were bodily emanations and slime trails, the acceptability of which did not transcend species.

There were no nonhumans in Mad Bear O's. Not because they were not allowed. They just didn't like it. The exceptions were the Sargassons in the aquariums. The large seaweedy aliens assumed brilliant colors that humans found beautiful, and they made soothing, languid motions in the water, which won them safe clean homes and caused humankind to spread their kind across the human-settled portion of the galaxy.

Rob Roy Buchanan was a Navy lawyer in his late thirties, though his face was utterly boyish. He was very slender, very tall, even with his boyish slouch. He'd had a hearing earlier that circadian cycle before the Admiralty, so his chin was not as scruffy as it usually was, and his face looked even younger than it usually did.

A woman wove into the bar, slid into the seat next to him. "Buy a lady a soberant?"

Rob Roy lifted his brown eyes. Stared at a vision. A drunk vision. He signaled to the bartender, who had seen her come in for her landing. Returned that flick of the eyes that said: Coming right up.

"I stink," said Calli.

"You smell flammable," said Rob Roy.

The soberant arrived promptly. Rob Roy and Calli sat a long time, not speaking. The music was American cool jazz.

Rob Roy said at last, "You know, you even look fetching with frogs crawling out your nose."

"You saw that?" Calli asked, wincing.

"I won forty shekels."

"Farragut had me to win."

Rob Roy's expression became very wry, almost bitter.

"You are still the prettiest woman I've ever seen," said Rob Roy not looking at her. "The strongest. The most courageous."

"Then why did you give me the push?"

Rob Roy opened his hands, kind of helpless. "I'm out of my depth here. You're out there going head to head with a gorilla. You beat him in battle—twice. You know you two are becoming like Patton and Rommel out here. Then you've got your John-had-me-to-win-Farragut. And last time I was with you, I watched Numa slam you against a wall and I didn't do a damn thing about it. John Farragut called him out—which is what I was supposed to do and never could. Makes a man feel pretty darn studly. AND you've got your Caesar Romulus, Empress Calli. What am I?"

"You're really stupid, Robbie. Sweet. Cute. Really intelligent, but God Bless America, are you ever dumb."

"Are you saying I have a shot here?"

Calli lightly beat her forehead against the table. It was a nod.

Sargassons have no gender.

This seaweed decided *he* wanted to be John Wayne, the twentieth century cowboy. But, just to avoid confusion with the real John Wayne, the Sargasson decided to be John Wayne's brother Steve instead.

No one knew that John Wayne was not the actor's real name, or if he ever had a brother. That was neither here nor there. The seaweed was tripping anyway. The members of Attack Group One consented to call the thing Steve "to avoid confusion."

"Thoughtful of it to clarify that," said Commander Gypsy Dent.

"Careful," Steve's handler warned. "He will be able to tell you are being sarcastic if he hears you."

"Then I'd better steer wide," said Gypsy, watching the tank float in on its hover platform, with a great length of peacock-colored vegetation undulating in the water.

Gypsy's brown eyes rolled to the commodore. "John Wayne's brother?"

Farragut kept his mouth tight shut. Nodded. If he spoke, the Sargasson would know he was laughing.

The Sargasson had been added to Attack Group One at the insistence of Naval Intelligence, with the backing of the xenos, as a secret weapon of sorts.

The idea had merits. Of sorts.

Sargassons were known for their hyperaccurate sense of physical incongruity even in alien beings. Medical examiners employed them in autopsies, because Sargassons had an uncanny talent for detecting what did not belong in a human body, or any other alien body, down to the cellular level. In a limited sense they were patterners. They could find rogue cells, but could not say what they were. They could only tell you, through a translator, what was out of place in a body.

They also looked good in a fish tank.

The Sargasson Steve Wayne was added to Attack Group One in hopes he would be able to detect physiological changes in insects when the insects were brought into proximity to the Hive. Given that the insects had to be detecting Hive resonance, the hope was that the insects' physical changes would indicate the Hive's harmonic.

"Dang," said Dallas McDaniels, staring at the tank in the commodore's Mess. "I was afraid that was the salad."

All cultures everywhere had in common one universal sign of unity, the sharing of food. So Commodore Farragut gathered the commanders of his Attack Group aboard *Merrimack* for dinner.

Chef Zack had gone into Fort Ike to the market for Deep End delicacies, so he was ready to show off.

There were no veal dishes on the menu.

The guests were still arriving when a Marine brought Commodore Farragut a message. "Some white greta with a beard gave me this to show you, sir."

The message had the Roman imperial seal on it.

"Persistent," Farragut commented. Did not take the message. "Nil it. Ask TR to come see me after dinner."

"Aye, sir."

Herius Asinius sat stiffly. Reluctant to eat or drink

anything in hell. Had to eat. It was, after all, dinner. But he drank only water, because you could not drink a toast with water. And it was impolite to push alcohol on anyone who did not request it. Herius would not have to raise his glass to anything Farragut proposed.

Calli looked imperial and sober. She drank iced mnomsadian tea. Kept a wineglass in reserve at her place for toasts.

Farragut got merry. Had most of them laughing. Exchanged tall tales with Fred and Ram.

"So we're leaving Thaleia and we didn't want to take anything Thaleian with us. You've heard of the kudzu effect?"

They all had. The danger of alien imports was not alien disease. Diseases did not jump genetic codes, so Earth life was not susceptible to alien pathogens.

The danger was the kudzu effect—where an invasive species was hardier and more aggressive than native stock, overwhelmed the ecosystem, and pushed the native life out.

"Thaleian life makes kudzu look like Gypsy's potted plants."

Commander Gypsy Dent could not keep a plant alive for love or money. Gypsy claimed that her plants were sensitive.

"So we're leaving Thaleia and we have to sanitize the ship because Lord knows what kind of Thaleian slime mold we've tracked on board. You were there, Herius."

Herius Asinius nodded, mutely.

"So we evac. Everyone. Everything. The ship's dogs, the livestock, the houseplants—except Gypsy's houseplants; they're dead anyway—the lab insects, the telltales, the hydroponic gardens, everything living.

"Now I have this chief who is— What is the word for the Og?"

"Unique," Calli supplied diplomatically.

"Oh, no, the Og is completely crackers," said Farragut. "So the chief of my boat has these two goldfish, James and Dolley. Og enlisted them. Rated them. There are erks on board *Merrimack* outranked by James and Dolley.

"Og forgot to evacuate the goldfish. And the engineers take a neutron hose to *Merrimack*."

Lifted his eyes to the overhead. "Well." Nodded. "We killed James and Dolley.

"I am down planetside squaring away all our equipment, and the Og is up here on my boat using TR Steele's Fleet Marines to hold a full military funeral for James and Dolley. Dress whites. Drum corps."

"Caskets?" Fredrika asked.

"They were this big," said Farragut, thumb and forefinger a goldfish length apart.

Fred, Ram, and Dallas were laughing themselves to tears. The alcohol helped.

"The gun salute got everyone's attention. Sure got mine."

Even Numa Pompeii was snorting guffaws. "What happened to the Og?"

"I managed to keep TR from killing him."

Herius Asinius would not even smile. Asked, "Why is this Og still in your Navy?"

Farragut's eyes sparkled as he gushed, "Oh, hell if I know!"

The commanders recovered by the time the coffee and soberants came around, and the briefing board took over one side of the Mess.

"All right, gentlemen." Farragut stood up. "Why we're here and where we're going. The capsule version.

"First task, before we cross the frontier, we're fixin' to give Steve Wayne a chance to find out what the insects are detecting."

The Sargasson in its tank spread its brilliant blue and green and gold fronds.

"*Merrimack* will approach a Hive swarm close enough for the ship's telltales to react. Steve will work his Sargasson analysis magic on the telltales. Best scenario has Augustus figuring out the Hive harmonic from analyzing Steve's impressions of the insects. We use this information to kill all the gorgons, and we all go home and start shooting at each other again."

Numa Pompeii and Dallas McDaniels thumped the table in support of that plan.

"If Augustus can't pull the information together, or if we do get the harmonic and the gorgons fail to die, we proceed to the next scenario. Attack Group One goes to find Constantine.

"Now Contantine is in a star system we're calling Sagittarius Zero. From Earth, it lies a straight shot through the Lagoon Nebula and NGC Sixty-Five Thirty, but twice the distance. That puts it thirty-five hundred light-years from here at Fort Ike, in the general direction of the galactic hub."

Dallas McDaniels gave a low whistle, and the commanders exchanged murmurs. "How in blazes did Constantine find this world?"

"PanGalactic automated scout ships, we're guessing," said Farragut.

"It would take forever for his automatons just to get there from Thaleia," said Herius.

Farragut nodded. "Six months best speed. One year round trip. The man is apparently as patient as a trapdoor spider, and he always has one eye on the escape hatch.

"Sagittarius Zero is a single formed G Two star, nearly a twin to Sol, and Planet Zero lies one astronomical unit from it in a nearly circular orbit."

"Home away from home," said Dallas.

"Way away from home. Once Attack Group One passes the frontier, we are looking at a good month's journey in total res silence. So prepare your messages home before we fly off the map, because you won't be talking with your loved ones for two months. Any messages during the dark time will be by courier missile relayed through the repeater.

"Our ships will be flying in a five hundred klick spread, connected by com filaments. We will be towing boxcars of explosives and extra ordnance."

Calli knew John Farragut liked overkill, but this seemed excessive even for him. "Sir, among the six of us, we have enough ordnance to destroy several worlds."

"There are gorgons equivalent to the masses of *many* worlds in the Sagittarius Zero system."

At the end of the buzz of whispers, Dallas McDaniels asked, "You sure we got enough box cars?"

"Fortunately, space makes us all a mote in God's eye. We can get to Sagittarius Zero without coming within five light years of a gorgon, and we won't attract notice provided we don't resonate and we keep the running lights off. At the frontier we will shut down all our displacement chambers. Ship-visiting will be by shuttle only.

"Once we reach Constantine's solar system, we will need the patterner to plot us a course in to the planet."

Caused some murmurs. Fredrika asked aloud, "The gorgons are that thick inside the solar system?"

"Best we can tell from one thousand parsecs, they're that thick. Just hope we don't need to use the boxcars to get out.

"What we do once we get to Planet Zero will depend on what we find on Planet Zero."

"A trapdoor spider?" Ram Singh suggested.

"We need to assume that Constantine will see us coming. And even with as impregnable a location as he's got, I have to expect Planet Zero also has Pan-Galactic sentinels in orbit, just like he had at Thaleia. I'm hoping he doesn't die before we get there. He's fairly old, even for a rejuv. Our mission objective is to find out how he has managed to live within a Hive presence."

"What? So we can learn to live among them?" Fredrika's tone betrayed her disgust with the usual LEN line of live and let live.

"No," said Farragut. "So we can kill them all."

Met with amens, hear-hears, and a Hoo ra.

"We depart Fort Ike at eight bells. You've got the rest of this evening to get your ships in order, watch Magnus' funeral on the res feed, let your crew go into Fort Ike, or do what you need to do."

At the meeting's end, Commodore Farragut and Jose Maria de Cordillera walked Herius Asinius and Marcus

Asinius to *Merrimack*'s displacement chamber. Caught furtive expressions of the Marine guards flanking the hatch. Some harassment that didn't happen because Farragut was there.

Jose Maria waited until the Romans were safely away and he and Farragut were out of earshot of anyone to speak. "Is it not asking much of your Marines to serve side by side with the killers of their comrades, young Commodore?"

"Hang it, Jose Maria, about all I do out here is ask folks to give more than they got! And I got no room for eyes for eyes and teeth for teeth!"

Jose Maria lowered his eyes, penitent. "I am out of line."

"No. No, you're not, Jose Maria." Punched his own palm. "If you weren't right, you couldn't have torqued me off."

Saw him in the main concourse on the eve of her leaving. Calli had heard he was here. Come to Fort Ike directly Magnus had been assassinated. Ostensibly to tour the battlefront in this time of crisis.

Calli knew it was really to avoid the long knives.

Gaius Bruccius Eleutherius Americanus.

He had brought his wife and his children.

During the last peace, Gaius had been an instructor at the Imperial Military Institute. Like Numa Pompeii, Gaius Americanus had been one of Calli's instructors. Unlike Numa, Gaius had given Calli every chance to succeed, gave her his wisdom, gave her his respect.

Calli wished she were John Farragut that she could run up and throw her arms around her old mentor in an unbridled hello. But Captain Carmel kept the bridle on. "Gaius."

Gaius looked for the source of the voice. Caught sight of Calli with a warm sad smile. Crossed to her. Took her hand in both of his. "Callista." He glanced at her uniform, its insignia. "What are we now? *Captain* Carmel?" No surprise in his voice. Entirely expected.

"Numa told me you were here," said Calli.

What Numa had actually said was, "Your patron is here." And had commented that Caesar Magnus was not even cold and here's Gaius Americanus suddenly seized of an urgent need to observe the Deep End.

Calli had refrained from commenting back that it was telling in the Roman Empire when it was safer to be closer to the Hive than to Palatine.

Gaius' face looked old, pinched with tight lines. Maybe he was even ill. "Gaius, what's wrong?"

Gaius spoke sadly, "Caesar is dead. Gorgons are mauling our ships. Roman worlds in the Deep End are being evacuated. That is not enough?"

"I would have thought you would stay in Roma Nova."

"I won't be discussing internal affairs with you, Captain Carmel," he said to be overheard. Then, for her to read between the lines: "You were always a quick study."

She nodded.

What he actually meant was that it was more difficult to arrange a Roman hit in an American space fort than to arrange one on the Roman home world.

But no more difficult than arranging a Roman hit in Fortress Aeyrie. There was no such thing as a safe place.

Gaius had been Magnus' right hand. Rumors had it that Gaius Americanus' name was written in Caesar's sealed testament, which Romulus had not opened. If Magnus had enemies, then Gaius Americanus had the same enemies.

He had fallen back to regroup, recon, collect allies, form a plan, then act. Calli knew Gaius was not one to go charging across a minefield without a map. Perhaps he meant to establish a government in exile here in the Deep. He would not be able to tell the U.S. Naval captain any of that.

Gaius studied Calli, troubled. Finally it came out, pained, "Why were you on Romulus' arm when Caesar died?"

Calli answered, "Keep your friends close."

Everyone knew the other part of that saying: Keep your enemies closer.

"Is that why you play drinking games with Numa Pompeii?"

Calli's almond eyes shut in embarrassment. "I was hoping you hadn't seen that."

Gaius could not say he hadn't.

"Do you think less of me?" Calli asked.

"Does it matter what I think?"

"Yes!" she cried in earnest.

"Why?" Gaius asked, like a Socratic teacher might.

"Because *you* matter."

"It was disappointing," Gaius confessed.

"That hurts."

"I cannot change the truth."

"I know. That's why I have always loved you."

His brindled brows moved upward. "Keeping your enemies closer?"

"We're standing at arm's length, Gaius."

He smiled. "You and your Attack Group have a safe and successful journey, Captain."

They parted. Calli called softly after him, "Gaius."

He turned.

Very softly, "Keep Romulus much, much closer."

Calli walked away from Gaius, and suddenly there was Numa Pompeii. A mountain in her way, with that all too familiar supercilious smile. "Teacher's pet."

Calli walked past him. Tried to ignore him. There was a lot of Numa to ignore.

"A lay for an A, Callista?"

Stopped her.

She had always done well in Gaius' classes.

She turned round.

Numa's presence daunted. An adamantly sexual power. The way Numa looked through her. Difficult to maintain a Naval officer's dignity under that penetrating, demeaning gaze.

Numa smiled at her. "There's a reason that saying doesn't rhyme in Latin, American girl."

Calli stalked up to Numa. Gave her nose a kittenish

wrinkle right in his face. "Numa? I'd have gone down on Gaius Americanus for an F."

As Fort Eisenhower Control gave *Merrimack* an exit route to depart, an urgent res signal came in from Fortress Aeyrie.

Farragut muttered, "Romulus had better not be insisting I surrender Augustus."

Not.

Farragut took the call, clicked off. His eyes rolled toward the putative heavens. "Oh, for Jesus."

"Sir?" Gypsy inquired.

Farragut groaned, "Romulus really did send her."

"Who?" said Gypsy.

Colonel Steele reared back, appalled, disbelieving. "The *beard?*"

Farragut nodded. Motioned. Not happy. "TR, go get her."

19

HER NAME WAS AMADEA. No surname. Just Amadea.

She was a mercenary, sent by Romulus to assist the Attack Group in getting to Constantine.

She was one hundred years old. She had known Constantine before his supposed death.

Amadea used to be a professional quarry in the Most Dangerous Game—a typically Roman sublegal pastime for extremely wealthy and ruthless Romans, the idea lifted directly from Richard Connell's short story, "The Most Dangerous Game." The hunters hunted human beings for sport.

Quarry in the game were ranked by the number of games they survived against hunters of a certain skill level. Quarry were never armed. "White tiger" was the rank of an unarmed quarry who had killed or taken the surrender of an armed expert hunter. Technically, the quarry was not supposed to kill the hunter, but sometimes they got angry.

Constantine had enjoyed the game. Was an expert.

Amadea had forced Constantine's surrender. Had pressed his own gun to his forehead.

She was a white tiger.

She boarded *Merrimack* under a Marine watch the whole way.

"What was *that?*" Cain Salvador cried after Amadea was escorted off the dock.

"White tiger," said Ranza Espinoza.

"I mean on her *chin*!"

"That would be a beard," said Ranza.

"Looks cute on her," said Carly, fingers tracing her own chin, speculative.

"No, it don't!" Dak cried.

"The fashion started in Rome," said Ranza.

"They can just keep it!" said Dak.

"It's really an Egyptian fashion," said Darb. "A female pharaoh would strap on a beard so she would be taken seriously."

"If she wants to be taken seriously, then why'd she make herself so darn cute?" said Cain. "I mean, except for that—that thing."

"She's messing with you," said Kerry Blue, giving Cain a push with her whole body. "It's workin', ain't it?"

Physically Amadea had a superficial resemblance to Maryann about her. Farragut's late wife Maryann. Petite. Sunshine blonde. Had what they called an American smile—teeth all perfectly shaped and in perfect alignment and too white. Cute little figure. Young. Maryann would be forever young.

But substantially, this creature was not Maryann at all. Hard, jaded, knowing, old. Refurbished to springy youth. And there was that belligerent beard—blonde, neat, smaller than a shot glass, but about the same shape. A dare, the beard. May as well have glued a penis on her chin.

"Captain Farragut."

Amadea's rejuvenators had not taken enough of the slack out of aging vocal cords. The voice was thin, with a harsh edge. "We got off to a bad start." She thrust out a confident hand.

Farragut, very unFarragutly, kept his fists on his hips. "Ma'am, I don't carry mercs on *Merrimack*, but since Caesar sent you, as a courtesy to Caesar, you'll be traveling with us on board one of Caesar's ships. General Pompeii has agreed to take you aboard *Gladiator*. You will not get in the way of military operations."

Amadea gave a perky nod, with a smile. "Caesar sent me because I know Constantine. I can be useful."

"I don't doubt you knew Constantine sixty years ago. Your information is a little stale. And why should Constantine remember or care about you?"

"I'm the one that got away. Big egos remember that sort of thing. I'm also probably the only person who knew Constantine was still alive. I have known for the last sixty years. But—" with a lifting of wheat-blonde eyebrows, "no one listens to me." And switching her gaze past Farragut to Augustus, she said, "*You* knew, I bet. I look forward to hearing what you make of what I have to tell you, Augustus."

"Look elsewhere," said Farragut. "If you have useful information, add it to the database. Augustus will find it. Talking isn't a real efficient way to get data into a patterner, and I won't have you wasting his time."

"Funny. 'Rude' is not a word I've ever heard spoken in connection with John Farragut."

"Neither is 'mercenary,' " said Farragut, and to the Marines, "Get her off my deck."

Merrimack's crew wanted Augustus off-loaded as well. Rumor had gone round that Augustus was a Heraclid. Augustus had obviously had his mind altered, and he had no old personal memories.

Heraclids were the modern bogeymen. But they were real. They looked like anyone else, and dwelled among normal men. You never knew who they were. The whole idea was that you would never know.

Stories went round and round of Heraclids breaking memory and becoming violent again, but those stories were all modern myth. There had never been a real case of a Heraclid remembering who he was, or attacking anyone after he'd had his brain altered.

Farragut had no patience with rumor. Went straight to the suspect. He could always trust Augustus to speak an ugly truth. In fact, Augustus enjoyed ugly truths. Farragut asked him right on the command deck: "Augustus, are you a Heraclid?"

"I am not," said Augustus, and that should have been that. But Augustus, having been given an opening, could not leave it at that. "You do, however, have a Heraclid on board."

Techs stiffened round the command platform, flinched at their crowded stations. The Marine guards at the door exchanged glances. Gypsy turned round to stare.

Farragut looked as if a round had gone off in his face.

"Thanks a heap, Augustus." If the rumors weren't flying before, they were swarming now. Upsetting people was what Augustus did second best.

"You asked," said Augustus.

"I did. I deserved that." Farragut easily owned up to his up screws.

"Who is the Heraclid?" Colonel Steele demanded, but Farragut raised his palm to cut off any answer Augustus might give. "That information is confidential. It does not *ever* need to be known."

"Sir?" the com tech ventured. "May I say something?"

They were all thinking it. Farragut let young Mister Hicks say it. "Let's have it."

"If we have a baby-killing madman on board, is it fair for us not to know who it is?"

Farragut had the answer ready for all of them: "The Heraclids were all cured. No Heraclid has ever reverted. Our Heraclid doesn't even know who he is, and that's the point. They've been given new lives and I'm fixin' to let ours keep his."

Caught Marcander Vincent exchanging a *like hell* glance with the scanner tech.

Farragut ordered Mister Vincent directly, "You will forget about it. I will brig anyone caught trying to dig up the identity of any supposed Heraclid on my ship. Acknowledge."

A chorus of ayes.

Steele said quietly, for only Farragut, "I think I should know, sir."

"And I don't," Farragut answered back.

"Aye, sir."

The Heraclidae were survivors of a LEN colonial disaster, twenty years ago now. A brain malady in the planet's first settlement had caused the adult men to kill the women and children.

"I was seven years old when that came over the news," Mr. Hicks commented aside to the cryptotech. "I was *sure* my stepmom was a Heraclid."

Qord Johnson shook his head. "Heraclidism only happened to men."

"Yeah, well I was seven and you never met my stepmom."

The best physicians of all the nations of Earth could do nothing for the violent survivors, other than sedate them and prevent them from killing themselves in remorse.

The Roman Empire was leagues ahead of any Earth nation in the area of brain research, because, unlike any nation of Earth, Rome *would* experiment.

Rome volunteered its medical resources to try to help the Heraclids.

And succeeded. They cured the disease, and altered the memories of the guilt-stricken men. Gave them new identities, with bland histories. The Heraclids kept no memory of ever being a colonist, of ever being married, of ever having children. The LEN allowed the cured Heraclids to be inserted into the populations of various member countries, where they had led quiet, unremarkable lives for the past twenty years. No Heraclid had ever relapsed into violence, or sought psychiatric help for hideous phantom memories.

The project was witness protection taken one step further—protecting the witness from himself.

"No Roman mole has even turned out to be a Heraclid," said Farragut. "Hard as it is to believe, it looks like the creation of the Heraclidae was a genuine humanitarian operation on the part of Rome." And because it was so hard to believe, he asked Augustus, "Was it? Purely humanitarian?"

"Mostly," said Augustus. "Not entirely. You know our

researchers seize any chance to experiment on the human brain. In this case, success just happened to benefit everyone."

"It's benefiting the baby-killer," Steele said.

Farragut announced that Commander Dent had the deck, and he withdrew, taking Augustus and Steele with him, leaving the crew to debate whether they would rather remember committing an atrocity or have their brains turned into vanilla.

Marcander Vincent was first. "All respect to the commodore," he did not sound necessarily respectful, "but I don't want anyone who's had his head carved open by a Roman brain butcher serving on this ship. And that sure includes the cyborg. Don't know why we can't just ship 'im over to *Gladiator* with the white tiger."

Chief Medical Officer Mo Shah, lifted large brown eyes at the commodore's entrance in the company of Lieutenant Colonel Steele and the Roman patterner Augustus.

A warm man, but not excitable, not enormously expressive. Mohsen Shah was a Riverite. Measured, patient. Enduring.

Riverism was a philosophy. A religion without dogma. Riverites were seekers of understanding.

Where many religions claimed to have the word of God from prophets—and many of their followers wondered why God never talked directly to them—Riverites held that God did speak directly, to everyone. God's word was the stars, the rain, color and sound, the half-life of elements, the arrow of time. Creation was the firsthand testament of the Creator.

Understanding it was the quest.

The River was a symbol of life. At any point in the river, the water passes through, but the river remains. Motion without end, but not cyclical.

Life flows.

"Mo. Do you know if we have a Heraclid on board?"

Mo Shah took the commodore's question like a rock in the stream. He flowed around it: "Why are you asking, sir?"

"I just want to know if you know if there is a Heraclid aboard the *Mack*."

"I am knowing, yes."

"Do you know his identity?"

"I am knowing," said Mo placidly. "I am not telling without cause."

"Exactly what I wanted to hear, Mo," said Farragut.

And turned toward Augustus and Steele, stern. "This matter is on a need-to-know basis. Mo needs to know. I don't need to know. And TR, you don't need to know. Augustus, it's a crying shame that you know, but I order you not to tell anyone. The witch hunt stops *now*."

Augustus lifted his eyes to the overhead, smiling, as if he had just taken a hit in some kind of game.

Steele stood as rigidly as a man could stand at ease, his jaw locked. His breathing was loud through his flaring nostrils.

Augustus looked down at Steele, smiled. "You are going to be fun."

Augustus' voice exuded the kind of sexual innuendo that makes a man's skin crawl and makes him want nothing touching him, not his clothes, not the air, just get everything off, away, right now. Steele could not stand to be in the same airspace as this creature. Said to Farragut, "Permission to withdraw."

"Go."

The hatch no sooner shut behind Steele when Farragut ordered Augustus, "Leave Colonel Steele alone."

Augustus glared like the cat from whom you've taken a baby rabbit it had just begun to bat around.

"You get out of here, too." Farragut nodded Augustus away.

Alone in the lab with Mo, Farragut sat heavily. "Hell."

Mo brought him a drink. Water. From Mo Shah, it was always water.

"How was it coming to be known that a Heraclid is serving on board *Merrimack*?" Mo asked.

"I stepped in a cow pie Augustus left out for me. The whole thing was just a stupid rumor before I opened my mouth. But a lot of smart people believed it. Mo, why did they think Augustus was a Heraclid? He doesn't even fit the profile."

"He is fitting a misunderstanding of the profile," Mo suggested. "Augustus is having no memories. Heraclids are having false memories. Unless one is being versed in the case of the Heraclidae, then one could easily be confusing a lack of memory with a substitution of memories."

In Heraclids the catastrophic memories had been canceled out with neural white noise. Dreamboxes then gave them dull histories. Altered brain chemistry lowered their aggression and ambition, so none of the Heraclids would become a celebrity or politician or sports hero, which might put him in a position to have his past dredged up by the mass media and falsehoods discovered in it.

"Augustus is having no memories?" Farragut questioned. Heard himself. Shook his head. "I mean, Augustus doesn't have any memories?"

"I asked him where he went to school," said Mo. "He said he was not remembering. Now how, I was asking myself, can one be forgetting school? He is having all the end effects of early learning—speech, socialization (such as it is being)—but the events that created his neural structures, those are being missing from memory. It is as if he has only been existing for less than ten years."

"I'm told he's a sadist."

"He is being so," Mo averred, his face solemn.

One corner of Farragut's mouth pulled up into an ironic smile. "When I heard that, I pictured whips and leather. But that's not it, is it?"

Mo shook his head in agreement. Touched his own temple. "*This* is being his target."

The mind was Augustus' playground. He poked around for suspicions, hypocrisies, something he could stab a psychic knife in and turn slowly.

"Admiral Klein," Farragut murmured.

Augustus had found something to say to Admiral

Klein to make it worth Klein's entire career just to connect his fist with Augustus' smug face.

Fighting with your coworkers would get you sacked from just about any employment you could get in the U.S.A. outside your family business. Admiral Klein was Navy. More discipline was expected. He was not allowed to hit a surrendered allied officer under truce.

Augustus had found just the right nonactionable words, and Admiral Klein tossed his own career into the atomizer.

Admiral Klein had probably been fun.

Mo said, encouraging, "I am being fairly certain there is being nothing that anyone could be saying to be making John Farragut be hauling off and hitting him."

Farragut, after he figured out what Mo said, nodded. "I like to think so."

Not that Farragut didn't love a fight. Gunfight, space battle, sword fight, fistfight. He loved it. But it took more than bad words to get him there. Call his mother a whore, and that's just you blowing wind out your face. Didn't change his mother, and just proved you were a drup. No action required. Farragut was not a puppet. No one could pull his strings and make his arms swing.

"But he is playing mind games," Mo warned. "And Augustus is having a highly organized mind. Be watching your ass, Commodore."

The Attack Group was scarcely underway toward the frontier when *Merrimack* received a communication from Amadea on board *Gladiator*. The hail went first through the com tech, then Gypsy Dent, who passed it to the commodore only reluctantly. "I don't know what the beard is saying, sir, but it sounds like something you should know about."

"Farragut!" Barked his own name into the com. Did not turn on the vid. Did not want to look at Amadea's perky bearded face.

"Just wanted to make sure you picked up the tachyon clicker, Captain Farragut," said the mercenary. She sounded a hundred years old. "Have you?"

"I don't even know what one is."

"It's a faster-than-light communication form used by patterners. You need a tachyon receiver to pick it up. Patterners have them implanted. I carry one. Your friend is communicating covertly with another patterner out here."

My friend. Covertly. "So what is he saying?"

"I don't know," said Amadea. "It's all clicks. It's a patterner code. I don't think it can be broken. I know the patterners have been told by Rome not to communicate that way, but just try to stop them."

"Send me what you have," said Farragut.

He was being played and knew it. Yet it would be militarily irresponsible to ignore such a warning from any source.

Found Augustus in his quarters. There were no sleep racks on board *Merrimack* long enough to accommodate the Roman, so the quartermaster had stowed Augustus in torpedo rack room number six with the spare torpedoes.

Farragut had never seen a rack room decorated before. Augustus had moved many of his belongings in. The deck was carpeted, the overhead draped with a Roman canopy. One torpedo rack had been converted into a sleep pod with richly textured bedding. Augustus, who slept half the day, reclined atop all the cushions. Did not rise at the commodore's entrance.

A reproduction Winged Victory like the original one in the Louvre spread her white marble wings over the spare torpedoes. A graceful female figure. "Interesting choice for you," Farragut commented.

"She speaks to me," said Augustus.

More interesting, given that she was missing her head.

Farragut became aware that he was gripping the recording capsule in his fist as if he could crush it. Asked Augustus, "Did you know we passed through a tachyon clicker?"

"Yes," said Augustus, one hand loosely screening one closed eye, two fingers resting on his brow, two on his Roman nose.

"Were you going to report it?"

"No."

"Why not?"

"It's irrelevant."

"Irrelevant to what?"

"Anything."

"You're communicating with someone beyond this ship."

"No."

"You didn't send a signal to someone?"

"No."

Like talking to a two-year-old. With twenty younger siblings, John Farragut had talked to a lot of two-year-olds. "Did you pick up this signal?"

"May have."

"Yes or no."

Augustus finally deigned to open his eyes. Flicked in the direction of Farragut's fist. "I don't know exactly what you have there, so I don't know if I picked that one up."

"Did you pick up a tachyon clicker message within the last day?"

"We passed through one."

"So I hear. Was the message meant for you?"

"I don't know."

"Are you going to continue making me excavate for answers?"

"Ask better questions."

Farragut gazed up at the headless Winged Victory.

One Admiral Klein. Two Admiral Klein. Three Admiral Klein . . . Ten Admiral Klein.

Held the message capsule lengthwise between thumb and middle finger. "Do you know who sent this message?"

And instead of the answer of a two-year-old, he got complete information, thoroughly compressed, Augustus-style: "He's dead. You killed him."

Took Farragut by surprise. He was some moments in assembling the bits and pieces of information contained in those few words. The sender was dead. So the message could not be current. The message must have been sent some time ago at a great distance from here. The sender had to be a patterner.

I killed him.

Augustus had known the sender, and had obliquely given Farragut his name.

The name flew out of Farragut's mouth, "Septimus."

Rome's patterners seemed to be numbered rather than named. The earliest one, created decades ago, had been called Primus—the First—followed by a patterner called Secundus—the Second. Both of those patterners had died before John Farragut was even born. Following them had also been a Tertius, and presumably a Quadrus, Quintus, and Sextus, because John Farragut had done battle with the patterner Septimus just over a year ago.

The patterner Septimus died in a rundown with *Merrimack*—but not before Septimus had shot a pea hole through *Merrimack* stem to stern, distortion field and all, with a shot that singed the hair on top of Farragut's head.

The days-long chase left Septimus comatose, with a brain hemorrhage. Like an overloaded engine burned out. Farragut remembered the dried-out eyes. The smell.

Here, now, was a tachyon clicker from Septimus just arriving from whatever part of space it had been sent sometime while Septimus still lived.

An old signal, from one patterner to another, that Merrimack happened to pass through. Irrelevant as an old letter. Maybe private. Maybe painful. From someone like Augustus.

A message from a dead patterner. Killed by John Farragut.

"There, but for the grace of God, it could have been you?" Farragut asked.

"No. It could not," said Augustus, sitting up. "*I* would have had you."

PART THREE

Heart of Darkness

20

CRICKETS, KEPT IN TINY cages on the command platform, started to chirp, much faster than any temperature would ever warrant. The ship's status lights turned yellow, with a laconic report from the lab: "We have Hive sign."

Tight beams from all ships of the Attack Group confirmed Hive sign. Farragut turned to Marcander Vincent at the tactical station, "Something you want to tell me, Mister Vincent?"

"Target located, Commodore. Thirty by twenty by one hundred seventy. Vector indicates it hasn't noticed us. And it's not a sphere, sir."

Gorgons in space always traveled in frozen spheres. Marcander Vincent was defending his failure to sight them.

"It's kind of a wad," Marcander Vincent added.

The gorgons had apparently scattered to attack a ship, had been outrun, and were now re-forming into a sphere.

"They don't see us."

"Let's poke 'em," said Farragut. "Signals, give me a res ping."

Merrimack emitted a single resonant pulse on a random harmonic.

The gorgon bunch continued to crawl over each other, but the whole wad, as Tactical called it, veered.

Marcander Vincent reported, "Target has changed vector. Target is now on intercept course with *Merrimack*. Intercept in one hundred twenty seconds."

"Commander Dent, get us on an evasion course—away from Fort Ike. Relay course to the Attack Group. Maintain current distance of separation from the gorgons. Do not engage."

While Gypsy issued orders, Farragut got on the intracom to the lab. "Gentlemen, you may start your experiment."

The Sargasson—Steve Wayne—could now turn his singular sensitivity on the insects in the lab, in an attempt to detect what it was about insects that allowed them to detect a Hive presence.

But after a scant few moments, the lab hailed the command deck. The voice was Patrick Hamilton's. "Commodore Farragut, could you—?" Stopped, started over, "Sir, we have a problem. Can you come down here?"

Farragut exited the command deck, took the ladder down like a firefighter's pole.

First thing he saw upon bursting into the lab was that the xenos had removed the Sargasson from his thousand-gallon tank. Or so it appeared. Farragut had become accustomed to walking in here and seeing the alien's long, long leaves undulating with the water's motion. Blue, green, red, fantastical colors.

The big tank appeared empty. Then he saw it. Had seen it when he first came in but hadn't recognized it. A brown shriveled mass clotted at the bottom corner of the tank, behind a rock, like dead algae. A speaker, mounted outboard the tank to transmit the Sargasson's translated signals, issued a moan.

Farragut nodded at the speaker. "Is that the Sargasson?"

The worried xenos nodded.

"What's he saying? Can you translate that?"

"That *is* the translation," said Patrick Hamilton, the ship's xenolinguist.

Doctor Patrick Hamilton was Lieutenant Commander Glenn Hamilton's husband. A slender, aesthetic man. Handsome in an artistic fashion. Civilian through and through.

Eyed the commodore warily. Knew the reason that the crew called his Glenn "Mrs. Hamilton" was not because she was Patrick's wife. They called the commodore "Admiral Nelson" in the same breath.

Farragut put his hand to the tank where the ash brown Sargasson cringed. "Is he ill?"

"Not exactly," said Patrick Hamilton. "That is the picture of mindless terror."

Farragut stared at Dr. Hamilton, grasping for a direction. Said, "*Talk* to it!"

"How do you give a pep talk to *mulch*?" Patrick cried.

"Oh, for—can he hear us?"

The xenos gave Farragut a microphone. Farragut clicked the mike on. "Steve?" He clicked off. "I feel like an idiot." Clicked on. "Steve. Don't be afraid. We're two hundred klicks from the gorgons, and we're not fixin' to let them any closer. Just relax, collect yourself."

The plant wilted further. Moaned.

"Saddle up, Mister Wayne! You're making a wreck of yourself here. This is fear itself. The gorgons are way the hell out there. Would it help if we increased our distance?"

Gibbering issued from the speaker.

"Give him some time," Patrick Hamilton suggested.

"No," Farragut slapped the microphone into Patrick's hand. "He looks like hash. There'll be plenty of time and plenty of other gorgons where we're headed." And he signaled the command platform, "Mr. Dent, organize parting shots at the gorgon mass from all ships, then get the fleet out of here."

Merrimack, Gladiator, Rio Grande, Wolfhound, Sunlit Meadows, Windward Isles, and *Horatius* moved through the frontier of defended space. The last outpost of civilization—an automated chain relay station—was here. The Attack Group could send courier missiles to this station. The repeater would relay their messages on from here via resonance. The station could also accept res messages from Earth or Palatine, and send them after the Attack Group via courier missile.

The Attack Group passed the *Monitor* at the edge of nowhere. Exchanged signals and received their last transmission by resonance, the *Monitor*'s "God speed."

"And now we go silent. Mr. Dent, take us dark."

The ships' proud running lights blinked out. The Stars and Stripes came inboard to the sound of Taps. Portholes were masked over with one-way light screens.

Already dark and alone in the vastness of space, the big ships became small. The void, the hugeness pressed inward.

There is no mild space, no rough, no warm. It is all the same. Absolute. Ruthless. It does not rage. It does not becalm. It forgives not.

A ship was a world unto itself. Your light, your air, your pressure, your up, your down, all contained within the ship's bulks, in the middle of literal nothingness. The enormity beyond the metal edges of the world lay completely beyond the grasp of the earthbound. The fragility hits in the middle of the dark watch, and makes a man wake up shaking. And John Farragut becomes your mother, your father, your Earth, your shield, the holder of your light, your water, your breath. The mind turns cultish, removed from what you know, the edge of your world close enough to touch.

Actually touch it, and it is cold.

Easy to deify the one who holds all the power and all the answers.

Out of the blue—or out of the black, as things came here—Augustus told Farragut, "You are an inadequate god."

Farragut glanced behind him in the corridor for some other inadequate god. He was alone with Augustus.

Farragut had come up to the top deck of the *Merrimack*'s fuselage, to stand underneath the outer hull, listening to the clunking over his head. The Marines were out there, hull walking.

Farragut absorbed Augustus' words. Decided he really had heard correctly. Nodded. "Yeah. Damn good thing there's a greater power working out here. And I am for sure not talking about the Hive."

"Have you not heard?" said Augustus. "The Hive is the Rapture. Might this not be the hand of God?"

"Is somebody actually saying that? No. This is not God's will."

"How do you know?"

"By using the brains God gave me! —Oh, now that don't sound right." As an ill-sounding rasp/buzz sounded from the distortion field and something heavy thumped the hull and something else scraped, skittered, bounced.

The Marines were out there practicing with a new weapon, called a scythe by those who could pronounce the word, a grim reaper by everyone else. It was a blade mounted on a long pole, designed for slicing off gorgons' mouths the moment they insinuated through the ship's distortion field. Developed directly following Flight Sergeant Kerry Blue's escapade on Thaleia wherein she buried herself alive with a gorgon in her Swift's distortion field and carved off all its mouths.

The space between *Merrimack*'s hull and distortion field was much wider than in Kerry's Swift. It was awkward going out there, the gravity iffy, the atmosphere minimal, so the Marines were all in suits, the only light from their headlamps.

"Anyway," said Farragut, eyes up as if he could watch his Marines through the solid hull. "This can't be the Rapture, most of the people that got rapt so far have been godless Romans."

He was not taking this seriously.

A man with that much power must lose perspective. And how did a man ever gain that much power without having power lust?

Came a teeth-curling metal on metal sound, and a scream. *Merrimack* was notorious for her training injuries.

"And God Bless America, that for sure doesn't sound

right." Farragut was in motion, calling for a medic and charging for the nearest air lock to bring the wounded man in.

The man defied the pattern.

There was a great deal of ship-visiting during the journey to Sagittarius Zero. Early on, Farragut announced his intention to visit first *Gladiator* then *Horatius* in the company of Augustus and Colonel Steele and Captain McDaniels from the *Rio Grande*. Numa countered with an invitation to a formal dinner on board Numa Pompeii's ship.

Gladiator's dining chamber was a grander space than the commodore's Mess on *Merrimack*.

Farragut had been here before. This time he was eating.

And it was Roman style this time, on couches. Eating while reclining was supposed to be better for the digestion. Most Americans found it tough on the elbows and easier to slop their wine. At least the wine did not land in the lap.

Herius Asinius was quiet as a cat. He wore a gray tunic, trimmed in scarlet, but then Herius was a tough enough looking hombre to get away with wearing a dress. The tunic was sleeveless, showing off the SPQR brand on his muscular arm.

Colonel Steele had difficulty breaking bread with the murderer of Reggie, Tad, and Enzo. He would not even look at Herius Asinius. And he was not at all comfortable on the couch. Certain that he looked stupid. At least he'd been allowed Navy blue. Steele had always considered dress whites and food a deadly combination.

Dallas McDaniels, in dress whites, had the couch posture down cold. Looked like he might have been resting by the campfire out on the trail. Should have brought his harmonica.

Augustus coiled easy as a snake on his couch. Maybe because he was currently serving on board a U.S. ship, but he wore trousers instead of a tunic. He was all in black with three blood-red studs. Flavian colors.

Dallas leaned over to Farragut, said for only Farragut to hear, "So, John, old son, what do you think I'd look like with a toe ring?" Nodded ahead.

At Numa Pompeii, arrayed in Roman tunic, toga, oak-leaf crown, and thick bronze bracelets on either thick wrist. He was barefoot but for the toe ring.

"You'd look right purty," Farragut told Dallas. And aloud, to Numa, "Nice crown, Numa. Did Caesar's testament get unsealed before we went silent or something? Should we be expecting an announcement this evening?"

Numa smiled, shook his crowned head. "It doesn't matter whose name is in that testament. The Senate has the last word."

Farragut translated: "Your name's not in there, is it?"

"Not a chance. Magnus and I never saw eye to eye."

"You're a Senator. Who are you voting for?"

"The best man."

"You're voting for yourself."

"Absolutely."

The meat was spiced beyond recognition. So was the wine. "What do I have here?" Farragut asked.

Numa motioned with the pointy end of his spoon, which he had just used to dislodge a snail from its shell. "That is squab. And that there is the dormouse."

Numa Pompeii, Herius Asinius, and Augustus were eating their slugs, pigeon, and rodent, so Farragut followed suit. And Steele followed Farragut.

The honeyed figs were too sweet but not bad. What Farragut really wanted after all that was some black coffee. Got it. Unfortunately, it was also heavily spiced. Cinnamon this time. He pushed his coffee aside. Brought up the reason for his visit.

"The League ships came out here naked," said Farragut. "They're engineers with swords. Just won't keep body and soul together when the gorgons get through their skinny little distortion fields. I'm fixin' to move some real soldiers onto their boats."

"I hope you are not looking to me, Commodore," said Numa. *Gladiator* was an enormous ship with many decks to defend. Numa said he could spare none of her crew or legionaries to defend another vessel.

"In that case, I'm volunteering two cohorts of Heri's Dracs from the *Horatius*," said Farragut. "Herius?"

Herius Asinius carefully measured his words before speaking. "Are your Marines not capable?"

"There are just more of y'all," said Farragut simply.

"My Marines are capable," TR Steele declared. And to Farragut, "We don't need them, sir."

"But do the South Africans and the Malaysians need to know New Jersey quite that well?" said Augustus. Augustus had apparently heard lively stories of a Jersey-born Marine named Kerry Blue.

Became clear that he'd struck farther below the belt than he'd even intended when Colonel Steele turned a deep shade of murderous crimson.

Numa Pompeii did not know anything about New Jersey, but recognized a barb when it flew from couch to couch even if he did not understand a bit of it. "Commodore Farragut, I am happy to see that our patterner is showing you every respect he has ever shown me."

Farragut nodded, grinning into the table. "Numa, if you're happy, I'm happy."

"Eat shit," said Numa.

"Die," said Farragut.

Numa and Farragut reached across the space between couches to touch wine goblets.

Numa said, "Did you know, *Commodore*, that this Attack Group was my idea? Your Joint Chiefs co-opted it and put me under your command."

"Numa, if you weren't reporting to me, then you'd be reporting to Dallas McDaniels or Calli Carmel."

"I would *not* be reporting to Callista," Numa vowed. "As to chain of command, it would be more efficient and appropriate if *Legion Draconis* reported to you through me. You should be asking me about what cohorts to move aboard the LEN ships."

"Not in this man's Attack Group, Numa. I'm not haggling over command structure."

He did not sound provoked, but his tone invited no argument.

Romans regarded themselves as the natural masters of the universe. Always had. Never stopped. Though their tactics changed to stealth when force was not a viable option.

The Roman Empire never fell. In its supposed fall, Romans achieved a death grip on disciplines of power and influence, and embedded their language into them—law, science, medicine, religion.

Unable to withstand the spread of Christianity, Rome infiltrated its power structure. Imposed the Latin language on the Church—the only Church at the time. Kept their hold on the Catholic Church until the late twentieth century, with the end of the Latin Mass.

Appropriate dinner conversation in a place that had a vomitorium was wide open. The Romans talked freely of religion and politics, so it was open season on both as far as Dallas McDaniels was concerned.

"If I remember, Roman priests didn't marry under Roman rule," Dallas said. "What the hell was that about?"

"Control," said Numa. "What else? The Christian prophet Paul said, 'It is good for a man not to touch woman.' A peculiar idea, but politically useful. Rome made that law for men in power. So power would pass by merit, not by blood. Romans chose the heirs of their secrets carefully and not necessarily by blood kinship."

Dallas said, "It's not a nation, it's a conspiracy!"

"You would think so. Adoption was always common in Rome. We were open to forming attachments with the like-minded, rather than simply the same genes."

"Most of us find family ties pretty strong," said Farragut. "Like 'em or not."

"It's a natural inclination, for certain," said Numa. "But Rome is more evolved than that. The impulse remains to preserve others like yourself. But like yourself *how?* Physically like yourself? What exactly of yourself most needs preserving? Plato argued that pregnancy of the soul is superior to pregnancy of the body."

"Now here I thought that was an argument for homosexuality," said Farragut.

"That is the flat-minded interpretation. Pregnancy of the soul is a passionate need to pass on the essence of oneself, what is important. To a degree what you value might find safe harbor in like genetics. But if the fruit of your loins is a doorknob, do you vest what you treasure into *that*? Or into a like soul who will protect what you pass down, whether that soul dwells in a female or male house or a white, brown, black, or yellow house? That is how Rome survived. Rome is more a melting pot than the U.S. has ever been. The U.S. remains more mosaic than actual meltdown. Rome is just as varicolored as the U.S. but not multicultural. Absolutely not multicultural. The important thing, what survived the Long Silence, is Rome itself. The American highest state of being is the individual. We are Roma Eterna and we have more right than you to say *e pluribus unum*."

"Yeah, like to get that off our currency," Dallas drawled. "Aren't you the same boys who brought us the Inquisition?"

"As a matter of fact, we are," said Numa. "For the record however, the Inquisitors tortured and killed seven hundred people, not thirty thousand. The story has been embellished, as if seven hundred were not gory enough. And the targets of the Inquisition were not the openly declared Jews and Moslems. Rome, same as the U.S., reserves the right to seek out and kill moles in its midst—do we not, Commodore Farragut? The Inquisition was a security measure. Those who professed to be Roman and were secretly something else, those we killed."

"The iron maiden wasn't overkill?" said Dallas.

"The iron maiden was not ours. Someone added that to the story to make it more juicy. For those who like that sort of thing."

Dallas leaned over so he could see the patterner. "That wouldn't be *you*, Augustus?"

"Meat screaming," Augustus said dismissively, bored.

"Okay, the Catholic Church gave Rome the shove,"

said Dallas. "Wasn't your God to begin with. So Rome is back to borrowing other peoples' gods."

"We have to borrow them," Augustus said. "No god ever bothered to approach us directly. Everyone seems to see God except us. Anyone here see a pattern in that?"

"Yes, it means you're going to hell," said Steele.

"There is no going, Colonel," said Augustus. "It's already fact."

Back on *Merrimack,* Steele wanted get away from Augustus best speed, but Augustus wouldn't stay out of his footsteps. Steele finally spun on him, "What do you want!"

"I am sensing animosity," said Augustus, disingenuous. "Was it something I said?"

The murderous color returned to Steele's face. There was no mistake.

Steele could muster nothing more clever than, "Drop dead."

"As attractive as that suggestion is, I have orders to the contrary. I also have orders not to torment you. So now you may report my violation of orders to your commodore."

Steele smoldered. "I can fend for myself."

Augustus stepped away, smiling. "You will wish you had accepted the protection."

Kerry Blue in sick bay. Uncomfortable. The bruising and tearing were two days old.

Mo Shah repaired her, frowning. "Kerry, who did this to you?"

"You never ask me that, Mo," she said, perplexed, then, "Oh!" She curled half up on the examination table. "Did he give me VD? I'll kill him!"

"No, there is being no disease," said Dr. Shah. "Kerry, was this voluntary?"

"Hell, yeah. You thought—? Oh. No." She laughed. "Wasn't like that. He was just a little rough. And a lot big."

Mo Shah remained stern. "I do not want to be seeing this again. You may get dressed."

"Oh, trust me. It won't happen again. It was kind of an experiment."

Mo Shah's usually serene brow kept a fretful pinch in it. "Next time this is happening, I will be needing a name and I will be filing charges."

"Really?" Kerry was amazed. "What charge?"

"Destruction of government property."

Kerry fell back on the table, laughing to tears.

"I am being serious."

Kerry had been charged with destruction of government property once before—for getting a sunburn. So this should not have surprised her, but it did. She wiped away tears, thought she was done, but burst into a fresh gale. Managed to squeak out: *"Uncle Sam owns that, too?"*

The story of what Uncle Sam owned spread through the ship in a hydrogen flash. A laughing hydrogen flash.

Red haze and homicidal wrath. Stalking up the corridor. Sick. The bottom had fallen out of his world.

Someone had been screwed, and it wasn't really Kerry Blue.

Helpless fury, hollow anguish that could only be allayed by blood.

A bulk, a sky-blue uniform blocked the way.

"Game of squash, TR?"

Steele could scarcely focus on the commodore. Scarcely talk. Mumbled, "No, thank you, sir." Made to pass.

"It's an order, actually," said Farragut, moving again into his path.

Steele met his eyes, stunned. The eyes looked straight through him.

An angry Farragut was a quiet Farragut. Said nothing more.

Steele replied, the only thing he could say that would

not land him back on Earth without his scrambled eggs, "Aye, sir."

Withdrew into battle stillness. To be in the moment and nothing beyond it. Stay in that cold clarity where nothing exists beyond the range of your own senses.

On the squash court some of it stole back into the disciplined emptiness. He smashed the little green ball about the court as if slashing gorgons. Rammed shots without aim, with such force they had to reach the front wall at some time amid all the mad ricochets. Broke one racquet.

Cracked his head against the wall returning a shot. Touched his head. Looked at his fingers. Blood.

Suspected Farragut might have let him win, though Farragut never let anyone over the age of twelve win anything.

Steele left the court, soaked to his eyelashes, a towel round his neck. Apologized to the commodore for his disrespect in the corridor. Didn't feel any better, but the battle—it hadn't been a game—brought him back to himself.

You are a soldier. You are not the most important thing out here.

Heart, pride, everything was still smeared on the deck by a clueless girl and a soulless monster.

You have your duty.

He had been so quick to fly into action, he hadn't stopped long enough to think that Kerry Blue did not need avenging. Hurting Kerry Blue had never been the objective. Kerry Blue was laughing about it.

Steele was the only one wounded here.

Patterners never miss.

"You could provoke a stone."

"A stone, but not John Farragut."

"Oh, I'm plenty smoked," Farragut moved from the hatchway into Augustus' torpedo rack room. "You disregarded a direct order."

"The Marine refused the protection."

"Colonel Steele cannot countermand any order of mine. You will desist."

"I did nothing to Steele. Anyway, I'm done now."

"You bet you are. You will confine your shots to me."

"I tried. I didn't get any farther with Mrs. Hamilton than you did."

Blue eyes blinked wide.

Hamster. Augustus had gone after his adored Glenn Hamilton.

Farragut blinked again in shock.

And suddenly he was laughing.

"That is not the reaction I was looking for," Augustus admitted.

Still laughing, Farragut turned back to the hatch. Said, "Jesus would've slapped you."

"You are better than your God?"

Farragut shook his head, leaving. "Jesus wasn't Navy."

21

FOR THE SHEER ENORMITY of space, there should have been no difficulty finding a clear path to Sagittarius Zero.

Were a ship to shut down its sensors and fly a straight random vector through the thick of the Milky Way, its chance of colliding with a single star would be remote. The space between stars was vast.

"Hive sign," the lab reported up to the command deck. "We have Hive sign."

"How?" Marcander Vincent beat on his tactical console.

"Evade," Gyspy Dent ordered. "Mister Vincent, who is moving in?"

Marcander Vincent looked at his monitors. "All of them in a ten light-year radius. Nearest sphere is still four light-years galactic north."

Mister Hicks relayed reports from the other ships in the Attack Group. They had Hive sign. "Not sure which ship in the Attack Group caught their attention first, but we have it."

"Someone must have resonated."

Commodore Farragut bounded onto the command deck. Passed the basketball he'd forgotten to let go of to a Marine guard at the hatch. "Where are we?"

"Hive spheres are converging," said Marcander Vincent. "They're making a box."

"Find us a path out of it," said Farragut. And signaled the lab, "Get our Sargasson on the telltales. I want this harmonic identified before we lose this Hive sign."

The Attack Group moved together on an evasion course.

A clatter sounded against *Merrimack*'s distortion field. The ship had plowed through a field of space debris.

A burble disturbed the artificial grav. Bigger than normal.

The ship's distortion field, while protecting the ship and its contents from catastrophic effects of inertia at FTL, still allowed through hints of what was happening outside.

Everyone felt it. A sensation of drag. As if *Merrimack* were running into a head wind, or more as if *Merrimack* were an airplane dropping landing gear in atmosphere. And there was a sound like wind.

Something had attached itself to the distortion field.

"What did we pick up?" Gypsy demanded.

Marcander Vincent hesitated in disbelief. "Gorgons."

Not a sphere. Not a wad. Long strings of the monsters were spread wide, like Herius Asinius' parachuting gorgons at Thaleia.

An individual gorgon was only a meter in diameter. Too small to activate a prox alarm.

Alarms sounded. Lights flashed red.

Gypsy spoke into the loud com: "Prepare to repel boarders!"

Rio Grande jetted hydrogen fire at *Merrimack*.

Gladiator reported boarders, *Horatius* assisting.

Wolfhound tended the smaller *Windward Isles* and *Sunlit Meadows*.

Someone on the com was sounding Mayday.

Farragut looked to the com tech. "Who is that and how is their Day any Mayer than ours?"

"It's the Meadow Muffins," said Mr. Hicks. The League of Earth Nations' ships.

The Mayday went abruptly silent. The LEN ships' coms were out.

"I guess their day *is* Mayer than ours."

Marines clad in atmospheric suits poured out *Merrimack*'s top air lock and fanned out atop the hull. They stood atop the ship, wielding long-poled scythes, dragged the blades against the adamant distortion wall. Sliced off gorgons' heads as they emerged inside the field. Cursed the gore that dripped down on them. Blinked against the lights, weird and confusing—chemical glow from their own headlamps, the bounce back from the distortion field, and the bizarre yellow-white hydrogen blaze from *Rio* striking the other side of the distortion field.

Became very, very dark when the hydrogen fire stopped.

Patrick Hamilton in the lab took the hail from the command deck: "Our Sargasson, Cowboy Wayne, has another chance to be a hero," said Farragut. "What's he make of the telltales?"

The Sargasson guttered in the tank, clutching its rock. Patrick responded: "I think he's speaking Swedish."

Gorgons clotted thicker and thicker on the ship's distortion field. The com failed. Then the lights.

The atmosphere changed. Ears popped. A wind moaned through the corridors.

"Hull breach."

The air inside the ship rushed out to fill the space between the hull and the distortion field. Command dispatched a runner topside to advise the Marines of the breach. But they would already know, having felt the wind, the change in air pressure.

Colonel Steele dispatched two squads of Marines armed with swords to where the gorgons were coming up through the underside of the starboard wing. The monsters had chewed through the air locks and were coming up a flight elevator shaft from the underwing flight deck.

Augustus joined the charge from behind. A Marine turned to see who was behind him. Suddenly not sure which side the monster was on.

The black eyes were not quite there. Not hollow. A wide focus. A terrifying, inhuman expression on the patterner's face. A heavy hand cannon wired into his forearm.

Marines never fired projectile weapons inboard other than a splinter gun, a weapon with which you could change your mind. For the tight quarters and thin bulks, you could never afford to miss, or to shoot through your target.

Augustus opened fire.

Marines swore and hit the deck.

The cannon raked down gorgons, row on row, its projectiles exploding within its targets, and continuing no farther. The shots came close to Marines' ears, shoulders, but did not touch. And the Marines swore at him, even as the gorgons that had been right in front of them dissolved.

Augustus moved to the front, preternaturally swift, and the Marines made way for him, and fell in behind.

Colonel Steele glanced aside at the killing machine now in the fore with him, just as Augustus fired up. Didn't even seem to look. Just turned the cannon up. Fired. And a gorgon splatted down from the overhead.

The masses of gorgons that poured up from the flight elevator were trying to outflank the Marines by climbing up the bulks and skittering along the hangar deck's very high overhead. Augustus picked them off, as Steele and his Marines hacked down the gorgons on the deck.

The cannon fire stopped as abruptly as it had started.

"Colonel Steele!"

Steele fell behind the front line, looked toward the voice.

Found a Marine, several Marines, staring at Augustus who had turned around to face them.

Augustus. Not moving. A vacancy in the black eyes. The hand cannon pointed at the Marines.

It wasn't Augustus anymore. It was a gorgon on two legs with a deadly accurate hand cannon pointed at Steele's Marines. The Marines were hesitating. The man had just a second ago been their comrade-in-arms.

Steele was in motion. Up from behind, he lunged at Augustus, and slashed, a huge stroke, spinning himself off-balance and onto the deck grates.

Two fat, severed cables flopped loose from Augustus' neck.

Augustus' posture slipped. His face changed. Confusion and pain. Awareness.

Seeing someone home, the Marines standing at cannon point lowered their ready swords, and dashed around Augustus to get at the gorgons.

Augustus reached down, pulled Steele to his feet with less effort than lifting a toddler. He unplugged his cannon from his forearm, shrugged out of the straps. Let the cannon drop to the deck. "What else we got?"

Steele gave him his sword. "Do you know how—"

Augustus gave the blade an instantly expert pass, said, "Apparently, I do."

He reached behind his neck, unplugged the severed stalks of cable hanging from base of his skull. He shook the cut ends at Steele. "You *could* have just yanked them out of their sockets."

"I was trying to cut off your damned head!" Steele snarled. Meant it.

"Short again," said Augustus and moved back to the front to hack down gorgons.

Alpha Team patrolled the lower decks, searching for other flanking breaches. Okay, it was necessary duty, but it felt cowardly.

A barking from somewhere deep in the lower sail turned to wild growling and snarling. Ranza Espinoza jerked her head toward the ladder. "Blue, check the mutt."

The sail was one hundred fifty feet down, a narrow shark fin, narrowing all the way down fore and aft, and no wider than six feet wide port to starboard, filled with equipment, most of which was not functioning right now.

Kerry found the miniature shepherd halfway down. Farragut's favorite dog. Snarling and snapping, its hackles raised. Raised hers, too.

The space between the hull and the distortion field was much, much narrower around the ship's upper and lower sails than around the ship's fuselage. No Marines were outside this part of the hull, shaving off gorgon mouths as they insinuated through the distortion field.

The idea was that once the gorgons insinuated through the distortion field, they would not just start gnawing on the nearest section of hull. They would take the path of least resistance to the food—meaning that they would skitter up the hull to the topside where the Marines were waiting for them with scythes and hydrogen torches, where the orientation of gravity favored the defenders.

Kerry shone her chemical light on the bundles of cables and hoses and conduit that ran up and down the sail. The light caught the severed end of a loose hose sticking through the hull. "Holy Mother—"

Hoses don't have teeth.

Started into her wrist com, "We've got a—" The com was out. Kerry faced up and yelled, *"We got a hull breach down here!"*

Steele felt something—maybe that was his soul—drop right out of him.

Post Kerry Blue inside the ship in reserve, and she gets the flanking attack. There was no protecting the woman.

You just can't keep them safe. Commodore Farragut had left his young wife safe on Earth, and she killed herself. You could not win. This kind of thing should just not be allowed to happen.

It was an eternity—probably less than an hour—before Steele could get down into the lower sail where Alpha Team held several breaches, cutting off anything that stuck itself through the hull.

Their voices carried up.

Carly Delgado: "Why is it so hot? How can it be hot? We're in outer space. Open a window."

Cole Darby: "The system is uffed."

Kerry Blue: "What happened to redundance? What happened to redundance? Where is the fox-trotting backup system?"

Darb: "This is the backup system."

Ranza Espinoza: "Colonel on deck."

Steele said, "What do you need down here?"

"Boosters," said Ranza.

Steele had brought them. Intradermal drugs to keep the fighters going. He produced a fistful of them from his pockets.

Glanced over Alphas. They looked good. Shiny. Dragging a little. No serious wounds. "What else?"

Met Kerry Blue's eyes. "If someone could throw some water bottles down here, that would be good," said Kerry. "And something for the dog."

Bloody drool dripped from the dog's mouth. Its muzzle burned from caustic gorgon ooze.

"You'll have it," said Steele. Retreated up the ladder, feeling suddenly stronger, as if he'd taken one of the boosters.

Patrick Hamilton, PhD, was no kind of soldier. He was a xenolinguist. Did not mind playing water boy to Marines and amateur vet to a ship's dog during a gorgon siege. His petite wife, whom they called the Hamster, was a more formidable swordsman than was Doctor Patrick Hamilton.

He'd got that lot in the lower sail taken care of, and returned to his lab. Found the hatch open.

A dog, a Doberman, nearly knocked him over charging out. The bitch plowed into Patrick's legs, then galloped up the corridor, dragging a long gray rag in its mouth.

Took a moment for Patrick Hamilton to realize what he'd just seen. That was not a long gray rag. That was the Sargasson, Steve Wayne. Yelled, "Inga! Bad dog—!"

Spun round at the crashing and thrashing within the lab. Saw the jagged hole torn in the overhead. Water on the deck. The thousand-gallon tank overturned. Gorgons snapping at flying insects loosed from their containers.

Patrick yanked the hatch shut and took off running up the corridor after the dog and the Sargasson.

"We have a second swarm."

"How can you tell one swarm from another?" said Farragut, turning.

Augustus was there, his scalp raked open, a hunk of bone missing from over his right eye, drying blood smeared on his face. "There are soldiers in the galley."

Soldiers. Also called can openers. The second, deadlier form of the Hive. Soldiers were tougher than gorgons, with harder bodies, and giant pincers instead of masses of tentacles.

Farragut shouted for backup and followed Augustus to the galley at a run.

The metal hull overhead the galley angled up, grotesquely curled, peeled back, the shimmer of the distortion field visible through the enormous breach. Pincered aliens jumped down to the deck. A knot of Marines and Chef Zack, blocked from the hatch and backed into a corner, defended a position behind a metal food prep bar with a protective overhang, which kept the soldiers that jumped from the overhead from landing on them.

Chef Zack was there, shoulder to shoulder with the Marines, wild-eyed, grisly, hacking off pincers with his butcher knife.

With all the hand-to-tentacle gore they had witnessed, there were still some blades and some people just more chilling than others. There was Chef Zack, his face spattered with gore, wielding his butcher's knife, howling, nightmarish and barbarous.

Farragut and a team of navvies opened up with hydrogen torches, jetting streams of fire at the overhead to stop any more monsters from dropping in, and trying to burn a path from the hatch to the trapped Marines.

Augustus advanced, plowed into the thick of the soldiers, slashing with two swords, like a walking daisy-cutter. Hacked off a pincer that was tearing his thigh open. The bleeding stopped instantly from the horrendous wound. He continued slashing, limping now, some of the thigh muscles disconnected. He dragged his torn limb, advanced like a zombie, pincers flying off either side. An inhuman monster you want on your side.

He got through the aliens to the Marines and leaped over the metal bar into their refuge with them. Took Chef Zack's knife from him, threw it down. Yelled, "Incoming!" Leaped up onto the bar like a gorgon and bodily threw Chef Zack over the aliens, between the hydrogen jets, and over the navvies' heads.

Zack hit the deck clumsily. Probably broke something, but Zack got to his feet and ran out of the galley even as Augustus was hurling another man up and over. And another.

Augustus paused in his airlift to slice pincers off the nearest aliens snapping at the bar, until there was a layer of maimed aliens in the way of the intact soldiers. He seized up another Marine, stripped his sword from him, and under protest set him flying.

The next Marine Augustus heaved forward but did not let go. The Marine bit his tongue, swore the air purple. As in the space between the bar and Farragut's men, a dozen aliens leaped up to catch a flying man that did not come their way.

"Heads up!" Augustus roared.

As flaming monsters spilled from the overhead, falling into the places Farragut's men just sprinted back from.

No sooner had the aliens dropped, when Augustus hurled two more Marines across the wider space to safety. Heard a bone snap on that landing.

The air roiled now with black caustic smoke. Difficult to breathe. Difficult to see.

When there was no one left behind the bar but Augustus, he stalked back through the jam of soldiers, splitting them open with two swords. The navvies keeping hydrogen jets flaming on either side of him to keep him from being crushed.

A pincer grazed his scalp. Another raked the skin and muscle off his left-side ribs. The bleeding was brief.

When he joined up with the navvies, they executed a controlled retreat from the smoking galley, lobbed fragmentation grenades inside, and sealed the hatch.

In the corridor, the Marines and navvies stared at Augustus, part in awe, part fascination at the open bloody meat and the bared bones and cables.

Farragut eyed the Roman head to sliced-off toe. Said, "If you have anything left in you, I need you."

"I am yours to command."

Farragut told his navvies, "Send Kit Kittering and the Og to the command deck, and somebody find an atmospheric suit big enough for this guy." This guy being Augustus. "Augustus, with me."

"Commodore on deck," Glenn Hamilton announced.

Gypsy's eyes widened briefly at Augustus. Reported to Farragut in the calm, grave voice of someone stating their imminent death, "We have lost navigation."

Chief Engineer Kit Kittering reported quickly to the command platform. A boyish young woman, square shouldered as a toy soldier with short, blunt-cut, dark hair, large doll eyes, and a foul mouth. She glanced at Augustus. Stared in shock. Said, "You look dead." And, at toy soldier attention to Farragut, "Yes, sir!"

"Here's what we're fixin' to do," said Farragut, making eye contact with Gypsy, Hamster, Kit, and Augustus. "We load the irresistible harmonic into a res chamber and equip it with a chemical fuse to turn it on after it has left this ship. Once we start that fuse, we can't miss any step in this plan or we are gorgon chow.

"We dislodge the safe from my quarters and load it on board a skiff. The skiff gets hand-cranked out to the port wing flight deck and prepped for launch. We nock the gyro so the skiff will fly in a circle. A big circle.

"The res chamber with the delay fuse goes into the safe inside the skiff.

"We take down the distortion field over the flight deck and launch the skiff as fast as it will go. The fuse burns down and the skiff starts resonating the irresistible harmonic. We take *Merrimack*'s distortion field down to minimal to let all the gorgons bale out and go chase the skiff.

"We'll have until they catch up with the skiff, insinuate through its distortion field, eat through the hull, and eat through the safe, and eat the resonator to get out of here."

Kit said, "A Star Sparrow is much faster than a skiff."

"Too fast," said Farragut and Augustus at once.

And Farragut by himself, "If the gorgons don't have a chance of catching it, they won't chase. Same reason I want the circle. I want *this* here bunch of gorgons on board *my* boat to respond to that harmonic. Not the gorgons ten light-years away.

"Mister Dent, find Colonel Steele. Have him get all our hull walkers inboard and either tethered down or locked behind an air lock away from any hull breaches.

"I also need some Marines to keep the gorgons off Kit's crew while they get the skiff loaded and onto the flight deck. Augustus, coordinate with Kit on the fuse."

Kit asked, a tremor in her voice, "How do we launch the skiff? Is this a suicide mission, sir?"

"I've got that part," said Augustus.

"You're not committing suicide, Augustus."

"Don't need to. I'll rig a fused launch for the skiff."

Farragut looked to all of them again. His eyes had that bright blue gleam that made you think you were going to live. "Get everything in the right sequence at the right time. All this has to be happening right now. Og! Turn around."

As Chief Ogden Bannerman appeared in the hatchway.

"Get me some big guys and some equipment to move my safe."

Farragut moved the contents of his safe into Gypsy's safe. An act of optimism. That there would still be things to be kept secret twenty minutes from now.

Og's erks unbolted the commodore's safe from the deck. Without lifts, it was difficult to move. Gypsy ran to the command deck to lessen the ship's gravity to make the transport of the safe from the commodore's quarters out to the port hangar deck easier. Surprised that the ship still had gravity.

Marines coming in through the air locks were redeployed to keep the path from the commodore's quarters to the port hangar deck clear of gorgons.

Kit Kittering brought a resonator to the hangar deck where Augustus prepared a skiff to autostart and to fly on a lame duck course. Kit kept staring at him, pieces of him that ought to be inboard hanging out but not bleeding. Naked tendons moved in the back of his hand.

Without looking, Augustus said, "Am I interesting, Mister Kittering?"

"Hell, yeah."

She readied the irresistible harmonic. Checked it four or five times. Had Augustus check it again.

He would not activate the fuse until the last. Kit already had an irrational dread that the resonator would start itself. And she an engineer.

Gypsy arranged a human com chain to relay shouted messages from the command deck to the hangar deck.

Marines in atmospheric suits brought suits for Farragut and the big walking corpse, along with tethers, scythes, and flamethrowers.

A report came shouted down from the command deck: soldiers had chewed their way out of the galley and were spreading through the ship.

Erks pushed the skiff into the flight elevator, sealed the hangarside of the air lock behind it. Augustus, Farragut, and a squad of Marines were sealed in with it, flamethrowers at the ready as they opened the flight deck side of the air lock. The erks manually cranked the skiff up the elevator to the flight deck.

Gorgons were sparse on the flight deck, not much up here to eat.

But up above, the distortion field was clotted with gorgon upon gorgon, slowly insinuating in. The Marines took scythes to the emerging mouths. Other Marines pushed the skiff into a launch slot, clamped its gear down.

Farragut observed the gorgon layer overhead. Could be tonnage up there.

Augustus followed his gaze.

"The moment we retract the distortion field for launch, all those gorgons up there will come *down*," said Farragut. Looked at the little skiff underneath the imminent avalanche.

"Need to get rid of the *down*," said Augustus.

"I need to get the order to Gypsy to kill the gravity before the distortion field goes."

Marines, Farragut, and Kit positioned themselves on the lift, ready for retreat.

Augustus set the fuse on the resonator, closed the safe. Set the skiff to autolaunch. Jumped down to the flight deck on his one working leg, shut the skiff's hatch. Ran/hobbled to the lift. "Thirty. Twenty-nine."

Farragut banged out the signal for the erks down below to crank the elevator back down fast. Marines pulled the topside hatch shut over them as the commodore's team came down.

Farragut ordered through the shouted relays: "Kill the ship's gravity! Now!"

Knew it was done before the acknowledgment came back. Farragut's feet left the deck.

"Retract port flight deck distortion field."

Acknowledgment came back through the relay.

Augustus continued the launch countdown: "Nine. Eight.

"Release deck clamps."

"Releasing—" the erk started. Interrupted himself, "They're stuck! Negative clamp release!"

Farragut started forward to climb up and force the clamps open.

Augustus pulled him back with the words: "Five. Four. I suggest everyone evacuate the hangar deck. Now."

Sudden awareness in all of them of the danger. A

spaceship was about to take off from the overhead to which it was clamped.

All personnel dashed out the big doors that divided the ramp tunnel from the hangar deck. They hooked their tether ends into the deck grates.

Ignition was thunderous against the overhead. The flight deck groaned.

Suddenly part of the hangar deck overhead ripped up and off. Farragut glimpsed open space as the wind started.

The skiff—and deck plates and the deck clamps— shot away.

Farragut's tether went taut. Knocked the air out of him. The outbound wind howled.

Threw him against someone else. Maybe Kit.

The outrush of atmosphere sucked the big hangar deck doors shut with a boom.

Farragut did not drop back to the deck with the doors' shutting. There was still no gravity. But he was no longer twisting and whipping round on the end of his tether in the hurricane wind.

Heard a crash.

Asked, floating. "What is that?"

"The skiff hit us!"

"Where is it now?"

"It is not on course," was all Augustus could say for sure.

"What if it's snagged on us?" said Kit, entangled in Farragut's tether.

Augustus answered, "Then we are irresistible in five. Four. Three. We have fuse burn. And resonance—*now*."

All eyes turned in the direction that up used to be.

22

I**T WAS INSTANTANEOUS.**
Gorgons and soldiers lifted away from *Merrimack*'s distortion field. And kept going.

Lights came on. The coms returned to life.

The first order over the com was Farragut calling the command deck: "Commander Dent, restore gravity on a ten count."

Gypsy acknowledged: "Gravity restore initiated."

Crew, Marines, and loose objects returned gradually to the deck. The ten count gave personnel time to find their feet before the weight set in. Made for a better return to the deck than Augustus' evacuation of the galley.

Farragut ran up to the command deck. Announced over the loud com: "All hands. All hands. Secure personnel from any hull breach. Report immediately if unable to comply. We are dropping the distortion field. *Prepare to expel boarders.*"

And he nodded to Gypsy to make it happen.

"In ten, nine, eight—"

The countdown halted for someone to chase a dog. Resumed.

"Seven, six—"

Halted again for Marines engaged in combat with soldiers. Waited for their retreat behind an air lock.

The count resumed.

On zero, *Merrimack* dropped all but the ship's forward asteroid shield.

Any aliens still insinuating through the ship's distortion field were suddenly released into the vacuum. And immediately hied away. Any alien sucked out a hull breach made no attempt to hold on.

Once free, they all pursued the irresistible harmonic.

"Restore distortion field."

"Restoring field, aye." Then: "Field in place."

"Mister Dent, get us out of here."

Merrimack blazed out of the area, wary now of large fields of small objects.

Marcander Vincent was immediately bucked down from his position at tactical. The kid from the Hamster shift took over the tactical station.

The space battleship executed a wild goose path while the crew and Marines rooted out and killed the remaining gorgons and soldiers on board.

So long as a single gorgon was alive on *Merrimack*, the entire Hive knew where the ship was. Let it see *Merrimack* going in a false direction.

The whole ship knew when the last gorgon died. The telltales stopped chirping and fluttering. And Kerry Blue's euphoric screech filled the ship corridors, because it was her sword stroke that made the telltales go quiet.

Then it was time to search for the wounded and put names to the dead.

The moment that all crew and company were accounted for, Farragut felt all the energy leave him, sudden as a telltale collapsing to rest.

The adrenaline buzz gave way to dead tiredness.

Hamster had taken a booster and told the commodore and the XO that she was good to take the next watch. She dismissed her commanding officers from the command deck.

Farragut made sure Augustus made it to the ship's hospital, then dragged himself to his quarters.

Brain gone muzzy. Not even sure what he was squinting at.

Spoke to no one there: "Why is there a long gray rag in my shower?"

Once upon a time, World War II fighters would get into a melee and suddenly find themselves surrounded by nothing but wide blue sky. The enemy, their comrades would be abruptly nowhere in sight.

Out here, you very quickly became surrounded by absolute nothing.

Merrimack had lost the Attack Group.

Had procedures in place for just such an eventuality. Proceeded to the rendezvous coordinates coded for this leg of the trip.

And found *Rio* already there, scorched but intact.

Dallas McDaniels' voice came over the tight beam: "John, old son! Thought we lost you."

Wolfhound and the LEN ships arrived soon after. Calli came over to *Merrimack* on a skiff. "I don't know what happened. I thought we were dead, and suddenly all the gorgons—" She opened her hands like a magician showing nothing there. "Vanished. Did you do that?"

Calli could not say that the LEN had been disappointing. She hadn't expected much from them to begin with. The LEN had never faced a tentacle before. "But I didn't expect them to be boat anchors!"

"How about the Dracs?" Farragut had stationed two cohorts of Dracs on board the LEN ships.

"What you'd expect from Roman legionaries. The Dracs are the only reason I still have the boat anchors with me."

Gladiator and *Horatius* were not accounted for.

Merrimack, Rio Grande, Wolfhound, Sunlit Meadows, and *Windward Isles* settled in to wait for the Romans.

Circling the rendezvous coordinates in the waiting, the commodore conferred with his senior officers. "How did the gorgons find us?"

"Someone resonated," said Gypsy. "That's the only way."

One of Dallas McDaniels' eyebrows went up, the

other went down, and he looked at Gypsy sideways in complete disbelief. *"Who?"*

There was no way to tell for sure. Resonance only existed in the instant. Once the sender stopped sending, the resonance ceased to exist. Resonance left no trail.

Steele said, "None of the watches on *Merrimack* saw anything suspicious around any res chamber."

Captain Carmel and Captain McDaniels reported the same.

"Then if no one confesses, we won't know," said Farragut.

"Had to be someone stone stupid," said Dallas McDaniels. "How can anyone in this man's Navy be that dumb."

Farragut shook his head. "I'd be willing to offer amnesty to anyone who confessed—because I'd really like to know if it was stupidity instead of sabotage—but if someone other than y'all asked to see me in confidence, that would be a dead giveaway to all these folks in my Attack Group who want this stupid man-jack or jane dead, so I'm not expecting anyone to come forward."

"It had to be someone with a death wish," Colonel Steele said. "Do we know anyone like that?"

Mo Shah patched up Augustus as best he could. The Roman's wounds were ghastly. Whole muscles had been stripped away, his cables laid bare, some of them severed.

"Is that not hurting?" Mo Shah asked.

"I am not caring," said Augustus.

The medical officer filled in the deep wounds with temporary gel. New tissue needed to be cultivated. And Mo Shah needed Augustus' assistance making the repairs. Had drugs and nanites brought up from Augustus' quarters in torpedo rack room six.

Mo Shah scowled and became more and more troubled as he set up the tissue cloning tanks. Finally asked, "Colonel Augustus, what is being your mother's name?"

Augustus reclined, coolly serene, pink gel quivering

in his hideous wounds. Gouged-out pieces of bone from his left eyebrow and left cheek along a wound that just missed his eye gave him a wicked gaze. "Mary Shelley."

"Father's name?"

"Victor Frankenstein."

"I have been thinking so," said Dr. Shah, not overly surprised. Reassured, more the case, that he had not been mistaken somewhere.

Farragut found Jose Maria in sick bay, playing a Spanish guitar at Augustus' cotside.

Saw that Augustus' cables had been repaired. The flesh was coming along more slowly.

The Sargasson had been moved out of the commodore's shower and into a tank in sick bay. Mo Shah was pretty good with houseplants. A touch of green had returned to Steve Wayne's gray fronds. Still the Sargasson did not look well.

There was a junior medic tending Augustus.

"Where's Mo?" Farragut asked.

"I got the short straw, sir," said the medic.

Augustus said, "The MO was being contemplative of being stabbing me."

"Augustus, how in the hell can you torque off a Riverite?"

Augustus did not answer the question. Or maybe he did. He said, "Ever think that maybe you killed Maryann?"

Jose Maria missed a chord.

Farragut said, "I know I did. I live with it. Hurts. I knew I wouldn't be there for her. Never should have married her."

As if Augustus had pointed a gun at him and Farragut took the gun and emptied all the chambers into himself. Left Augustus with an empty gun.

Augustus looked perplexed and weirdly without anything to say.

Farragut pulled up a seat. "Now. Did you learn anything when you were taken over by the Hive overmind?"

Augustus shook his head, scratched at his new scalp. "There is no mind. There is some awareness of Self. Self as in a kind of Us but without plurality. The Hive does not regard itself as many. There is no sense of individual self. What the Hive does—it's a program. But there is no 'die' command."

"Damn. Then how do they die?"

"They don't die when some overmind says die. When local conditions add up to a state that will no longer support an individual expending the energy to sustain itself, it ceases to be. And because the individual doesn't see itself as an individual, it gets suckered into disintegrating."

"Did you identify the Hive harmonic?"

Augustus gave a wry, nasty smile. Pink gel dripped from his cheek. "What is the frequency of your brain waves?"

Farragut shook his head. "I'm not a patterner."

"Neither was I at the time. I was part of It. It never occurred to me to identify and remember the harmonic. It was I. I was it."

"I don't know what kind of augmentation you've got going on there in your skull, but is there any chance of getting the harmonic off your own equipment?"

"Way ahead of you. Tried that. Resonance leaves no footprints."

Jose Maria paused over his guitar. "Is it true, as it seems to be, that the Hive can locate the origin and reception point of a resonant pulse?"

"Yes. It does. I could sense all of them. All of Us. All of me." He rephrased several times, none of the expressions quite fitting. "And let me tell you, it's a vast universe out there."

"How widespread were You?"

"I am reasonably certain the Hive is extragalactic."

Farragut gave a low whistle.

"Is there any chance that the signals we're picking up from Constantine's planet aren't real? Maybe there is no life on Planet Zero, and all this is really a Hive lure, drawing us into a trap?"

Augustus and Jose Maria both shook their heads.

"I mean, think about it. The Hive could be mimicking signals of human life to draw us in."

The heads kept shaking.

"Why not? Even a fish can learn what a lure is."

Jose Maria tried to explain. "If I understand the beast, as Augustus has described it, the Hive cannot conceive of a separate mind—or shall I say the Hive program cannot process a logic set separate from its own. The if/then decisions of the Hive are the only ones possible. A trap requires empathy. The Hive has no empathy. The elseness is the sticking point."

Augustus rephrased, speaking as the Hive, "If I know it, everyone knows it, because I am everything."

"Well, gentlemen, that all flew straight over me," said Farragut.

"The Hive cannot put out bait or set traps," said Jose Maria. "The Hive has no imagination. It can scarcely be said to think. So it cannot imagine that we are even thinking beings, much less imagine what we think. It assumes— without even going through the act of assuming—it just *knows* that we must know everything it does."

Augustus cut to the conclusion. "The signs of life on Planet Zero are not a trap. At least not a trap set by the Hive. The Hive does not lure. The Hive goes and gets what it wants. The Hive will never surprise you on purpose."

Jose Maria added, "I doubt the signs of life from Planet Zero are a trap set by Constantine either. Constantine's choice of lairs has more the appearance of a fortress than a trap. Everything around it screams at us to stay away. Exactly as it did on Thaleia."

"It screams at *me* to just send a planet killer in there and have done with the bastard. But since Constantine seems to be living there without getting eaten, we need him alive. Because what Constantine knows, *only* he knows."

"About your Roman, Commodore Farragut."

"Which Roman, Mo? I've got two whole Roman warships MIA."

"*Your* Roman."

That had to be Augustus.

Augustus was John Farragut's Roman because no one else could stand him. Except for Jose Maria de Cordillera and Jose Maria was a civilian, and therefore did not count.

Not sure what Augustus had done to piss in Mo Shah's river, but Farragut sensed personal animosity as Mo reported his findings to Commodore Farragut, Commander Dent, and the civilian microbiologist Jose Maria de Cordillera.

"Augustus is having two sets of DNA."

"Is he a chimera?" Gypsy asked.

"No, he is not being so."

Farragut turned aside to Gypsy, "What's a chimera?"

"A fused twin."

Farragut felt his chin back up. "That *happens?*"

"The chimera usually doesn't even know," said Gypsy. "Until the children she knows damn well came out of her own body don't match her DNA. The children are often barren."

Gypsy did not sound happy, and she did not sound disinterested. A frown on those bold features looked forbidding.

Farragut stayed on course. Asked Mo, "Augustus isn't one of those chimeras?"

"The body Augustus inhabits is being twenty-five years old."

"Hardest twenty-five years I ever saw," said Farragut.

"Accelerated aging can be happening when a clone is being made from adult cells."

"Like Dolly the sheep," Jose Maria said.

Mo nodded. "Dolly, the world's first cloned mammal, became old before her time."

"So Augustus is a twenty-five-year-old clone?" said Farragut.

"Augustus is not being entirely twenty-five and not entirely a clone. He is having original parts—the brain in particular is being predominantly original. The age of the brain is being uncertain. But the brain is having the original pituitary gland, which is causing the accelerated aging in the body. The body is being an altered clone. It is having different genes activated than in the original man. Some genes have been altered, some have been engineered. This body is being much taller than the original, and this body is being strung with cables. It is crawling with nanites, the function of which is seeming to be the maintenance of the augmentations and the prevention of the body from rejecting them.

"The augmentations are causing considerable pain to the clone body. The implanted brain is being painfully aware of this.

"The assembled unit of clone body and original brain, this man we are knowing and loving as Augustus is being approximately eight years old."

"Eight?" said Farragut with a start. "Augustus is eight? Why did the engineers let the body age? Cloning has come a long way since Dolly the sheep."

Jose Maria suggested, "Maybe his makers wanted a more sedate variant of the original."

Farragut remembered Augustus saying once: *Young men die easily in packs.*

The hormonal storm of a young man was probably not a good quality to have in a patterner.

This operative had not been designed for reckless heroics. A forty- or fifty-year-old disposition was what the creators probably wanted. Not what they got, but may have been what they wanted.

"So where is the twenty-five-year-old brain that came with Ausgustus' body? And why not keep them together?"

"I am not knowing," said Mo.

Jose Maria did. Spoke in sudden insight: "Because the brain was the desired part. Or I should say the mind. A mind cannot be cloned. The vessel—the brain—defines its contents. The experiences of a person, his life, builds his brain and forms the mind. The original brain had the logical inclination and the analytical synapses already formed. The clone body is merely a vehicle manufactured to house that brain. Trauma damages the development of a brain. The clone body developed with embedded cables and painful alterations. The clone brain, scarred by its experiences, was probably not what the engineers were looking for in a patterner."

"Well, somewhere there's a body without a brain and a brain without a body. So what did the Roman Frankensteins do with them? Did they unite the two spare parts?"

"That is a fairly ghastly concept," Jose Maria agreed.

"It's a crime against humanity," said Gypsy.

"Augustus is not the criminal," said Farragut. "He is the crime."

"Are we sure?" said Gypsy.

The grim scenario of brain transplants had been around since before the technology was ever available—body transplants really. The fear had always been that a wealthy egomaniac wanting eternal youth would cultivate a young body, remove the brain that grew with it, and have his own brain moved into the new home.

Any benefit according to that scenario was obviated here in that Augustus did not remember his former self. Augustus knew he had a past life. He had mentioned it once. Farragut hadn't known at the time that Augustus was being literal. But Augustus' memories did not go back more than eight years—which was why the crew had supposed him a Heraclid.

"Why would anyone want that done if he couldn't remember who he was?"

"Maybe the rich bunghole who thought he was buying a powerful new body didn't get what he bargained for," Gypsy suggested.

A voice from behind answered: "That's the thing with coming to life; no one gets to bargain."

Augustus had risen from his cot and come to the MO's office. He stood in the entrance, dripping pink gel and looking very like Frankenstein's monster.

Farragut was the only one who did not give a guilty flinch to be caught talking about Augustus behind his back. Said, "The volunteer rate for becoming a patterner has got to be real, real low."

"No one volunteers to become a patterner," Augustus said.

"I can believe that," Farragut said. "No one—no one in their right mind—would volunteer to have his brain separated from his body."

"Did you commit a crime?" Gypsy asked.

Augustus gave her a withering glare. "I was Caesar's right hand."

"I take that as a no," said Farragut.

"No one would sink that kind of investment into augmenting a criminal mind," said Augustus.

That put to rest any idea at all that Augustus had ever, in any incarnation, been a Heraclid.

"Did you play piano when you were three?" Jose Maria asked.

Farragut and Gypsy darted odd glances at Jose Maria, not sure where that question had come from.

Augustus said, "I was never three."

Jose Maria countered, "Your brain was."

"That person no doubt played piano at an early age," Augustus said.

It had been known for centuries that learning to play the piano when one was three years old greatly improved one's problem solving ability. Roman households may not have a chicken in every pot, but there was a piano in every nursery. It was considered a basic right.

Mo Shah said, "We have been knowing for a long time that Rome is performing prohibited experiments on human beings, but brain transplanting is being far beyond the pale."

"It is only ever done to create patterners," said Augustus. "Opportunities are few and the success rate is very small. Had it failed, I never would have known."

"What happened to the brain that grew up inside the body you're using? The clone whose body you snatched," said Gypsy. "*That* brain had a thought or two."

"I have no first- or secondhand information on the disposition of the clone brain," said Augustus. "But I know the same as you know. They chucked it."

"Maybe they put it in your old body," said Farragut.

"You just won't let anything go, will you, John Farragut?"

"While there's hope," Farragut agreed.

"While there's life," Augustus translated. To John Farragut the words were nearly synonymous. "Then give it up, because that is not what they did. If the 'old body' had been salvageable, then that man would have lived. What you are refusing to grasp here is that the primary prerequisite for becoming a patterner is the quality of being dead."

23

"**I**'**M TOLD HIS NAME** was Cyprian Flavius Cassius," said Augustus without emotion. "He was twenty-three when he died."

"Why do you call yourself *he* and not *I*?" said Farragut.

"I don't remember ever being such a person," said Augustus. "I am quite literally a new incarnation. I am not he."

"You are remembering nothing?" Dr. Mo Shah asked.

Augustus seemed to search his memory. Said at last, "I'm pretty sure I got laid a lot."

"Do you remember anything *in between* being Flavius Cassius and Augustus?" Jose Maria asked, and took a step back, as if afraid to hear the answer.

Augustus gave no indication of remembered horrors. Perhaps a little boredom. "Not really."

"I would think you would be in an utter panic!" said Gypsy Dent. "It's—good lord!—it's *unspeakable*."

"You'll have to 'speak' more than that, Commander Dent. I don't know what you're talking about. What panic am I supposed to be in?"

"You were—*disembodied!*"

Augustus considered panic. Apparently, it had never occurred to him.

"Panic how? As you pointed out—I had no body. I

couldn't even tell you what sort of container my brain was housed in. Without senses, without mouth to go dry and prickle and sour, without stomach to flutter and wrench, without palms to slick and heart to race, tear ducts to burn— What do you *feel*? Emotion is a biochemical reaction. Without the physical expression of fear to feed back into the brain, where does emotion go? How does one panic without the outward symptoms? Besides which, I think my creators must have suppressed my consciousness. I may as well have been in a womb."

"And nothing came through from your subconscious?" asked Jose Maria.

"Nothing specific. I had no time sense, I know that. Music. I think there was music. Some stimulus that evoked an awareness of music in my occipital lobe, because I certainly had no ears. It was a long dream remembered dimly if at all. And I woke up knowing things this other person, this Cyprian Flavius Cassius, could never have known. I suppose I learned things in my—what to call it?—sleep? Gestation? But I don't remember acquiring the knowledge. I simply *have* it. What the creators did, how they did it, is not information I will ever be given access to."

"You were Cyprian Flavius Cassius," said Farragut. "Now with a clone body and reengineered brain you're Augustus. They gave you only one name this time. Like a slave."

"I am not a slave," said Augustus.

"You are programmed to absolute service to the Empire," said Jose Maria. "How is that not slavery?"

"Who gives a rip! I just came in here to get pain medication," said Augustus. He crossed Mo's office, leaving a trail of pink slime behind him, and took from Mo Shah's supply cabinet what he came for. "I was created. And not by God. Who owns this life if not the Empire?"

Gladiator and *Horatius* showed up at the rendezvous coordinates twenty-three Earth hours later, not badly damaged, or else already repaired. The Roman ships had in tow the boxcars filled with explosives. Minus one.

Numa had some words about *Merrimack*'s navigation skills and their ensnarement by gorgons. Farragut asked in return if *Gladiator* was volunteering to take point.

The white tiger Amadea claimed one hundred twenty gorgon kills in the battle on board *Gladiator*.

Kerry Blue couldn't believe it when she heard it.

"She's *counting?*"

Kerry Blue. Posted under the ship again. Not even sure what she'd done this time, but her timing couldn't be worse.

It was after the services for the dead, and the Group was closing in on Sagittarius Zero. The ship was pretty well patched up, and the erks got the hangar decks put back together. Very important, because the hangar decks were where the Marines played basketball. Kerry could hear the basketball up there, thudding. Feet stampeding back and forth. Everybody bellowing.

Kerry's Alpha Team, eliminated way back in the first rounds, would be cheering for Delta against Echo.

Playing the championship game now had been Farragut's idea. After Tad from Delta and Enzo from Echo were killed on leave, the championship match just kind of went away. Farragut proposed that the championship game go on in their memory, with Farragut and Steele filling in for Tad and Enzo.

Thought it would be good for morale, and it sure sounded like it was working.

There was a big party happening up there that everybody—everybody not on duty—was at. Crew gave up their sleep cycles to be there, stomping and hollering in the hangar deck.

And Kerry was down here. She didn't know why. Just knew she wasn't up there.

She didn't get released until the game was over—huge roaring finish and all—and company and crew were going back to where they should have been, laughing and talking about the game.

Not that Kerry Blue didn't like to see her team happy, but their hilarity in the forecastle just smushed her face into the fact that she'd missed the game of the century.

Her mates could scarcely tell her about it because they kept breaking down into incoherent cackles.

Steele. Steele had done something funny. And Steele was never ever funny.

Steele's side—Echo Team—lost the game. Steele had to drink a beerful of Rafe's shoe.

"A what?" said Kerry.

"A shoe full of Rafe's beer."

"Rafe's shoe, filled with beer."

"Beer. From a shoe. Rafe's shoe. They filled it with beer, and Colonel Steele had to drink it."

"Rafe has the biggest feet on the *Mack*," said Kerry.

She pretty well detonated her team with that one.

"WE KNOW!" they all shouted back at her, and next thing she knew they're on the deck howling and laughing themselves to gasps all over again.

And that wasn't the end of it. Darb recovered first, continued the story, "Well, the Old Man chugs down the shoe, and his face is *red*. I mean he's *red*. He slams down the shoe and demands another. Okay, you had to be there, or I'm not telling it right."

"No, no, it sounds really really funny," said Kerry. "I wish I'd been there."

"Well, why weren't you?" said Cain, wiping his eyes.

" 'Cause I got posted under the ship, where else would I be!" Kerry snapped.

Dak explained it to Cain, "What it is, is Colonel Steele hates Kerry Blue. Everybody knows that."

Darb said, in an altogether different voice, "Yeah. Really really hates her."

The change in emphasis the way Darb said it turned a switch in Kerry's head. "Oh, God."

Darb saw her lights go on. "You just now finally noticing that, Blue?"

Kerry met Cole Darby's eyes, rather terrified. Said more faintly still, "Yeah."

The happy baboon, Dak Shepard, blithe and utterly oblivious snorted, "Hell, you gots to be all kinds of real stupid not to know Colonel Steele hates Kerry Blue!"

Kerry sat, numb, "All kinds of real stupid."

Darb patted her shoulder. "Good morning, Sleeping Beauty."

Kerry dropped her head all the way between her knees.

The colonel. He's the damn colonel.

"Oh, *crap.*"

A knock on his hatch. Couldn't really call it a knock. More of a tap. Better not be one of his Marines. It was really a girl sort of knock.

Steele belched. Grimaced.

Nothing like shoe-flavored beer.

"Come in."

And there she was. Kerry Blue.

If she had been at that game, he would have fallen over his own feet. Would have bollixed all his shots. He was supposed to be playing for Enzo. He had done right by Enzo. The game had come down to the last second.

Now he had to face Kerry Blue.

"Sir, I don't want to be posted under the ship anymore."

Steele reacted slowly, smoldering. A disturbed dragon. "Are you questioning my orders, Marine?"

"Yes, sir."

Like being shot. No. He'd been shot. This was worse. Worse than his worst fears. He would rather be shot again.

This must be what it was like to swallow poison. Naked. In front of everybody.

Like talking to a firing squad, he said, "Do you want a transfer?"

"No, sir. You know I don't."

His arms crossed themselves. It was a defensive posture. He could not uncross them now. That would look weak, indecisive. He needed all the barriers he had. Tasted a bitter, stinging sourness in his mouth. Told her, brusque, "Instructions on how to file a charge are in the manual. Look it up."

"Oh, come *on*. I'm not doing that."

Felt the color coming and going from his face like a beacon. No mistake now. They really were talking about what he was afraid they were talking about.

She knew.

She knew, *but she didn't hate him.*

Scarlet, pale, scarlet.

His thoughts whited out. The closest to real panic he had ever come in his entire life. He retreated behind his rank, "Dismissed."

Kerry Blue looked around her as if she'd missed something. He had not answered her question/demand. "But—"

"Get out."

There might have been a little foot stamp there. And don't she dare do cute girl things, or he would lose all control, dignity, all—whatever he had to lose, he would lose it.

Kerry turned to the hatch. Yanked it open to show how angry she was. She looked back, "I don't want to go anywhere." She stomped out, yanked the hatch closed behind her, trying to make it slam.

The hatch reopened in a moment. Just a crack. Only the voice came in. "I don't want you going anywhere either."

The hatch closed again.

Heat blazed, fell away cold. Blazed.

How does it feel to want, Blue?

Jose Maria de Cordillera came to Commodore Farragut's quarters with Augustus during the middle watch. Apologized for disturbing him. "Something odd," said Jose Maria. "If you please, young Commodore. The behavior is odd."

Augustus agreed; there was odd behavior out there worth observing.

Farragut found his command deck crowded with xenos, observing the oddity on the monitor screens, muttering to each other, or muttering notes into recorders.

Showing in several views on the various screens, two Hive swarms moved in very close proximity to each other, with some overlap between the two, the soldier swarm leading, the gorgons following. Neither of the swarms were formed into a sphere. Each was an amorphous mass.

It looked as if the soldiers were eating the gorgons.

Neither swarm appeared to be taking notice of the Attack Group.

Jose Maria advised the commodore, "These images are two years old. We are not seeing this in real time because we are keeping our distance and this is a passive scan."

The gorgons each swelled obscenely, and, slowly, pushed out a bluish-white gelatinous extrusion that curled back on itself until, when the extrusion was all out, it formed the shape of a pretzel.

The gorgon itself was left shriveled down to an empty sack with dead stalks of tentacles hanging on.

The gelatinous extruded loops coalesced into solid larval blobs. The white bodies developed short stubby leggish appendages, with a single large sucker orifice ringed and ringed with little teeth. The oriface clamped onto the empty gorgon sack that had produced it, and sucked it in, tentacles and all. The stubby teeth were visible through their translucent bodies, chewing.

This was the genesis of horror beyond horror.

"Gluies."

A hail came over the tight beam, "John, old son. You awake?"

Farragut took the com. "No, compadre. I'm having a nightmare. Are you *seeing* this?"

The gluies then turned on the soldiers, which had been eating them while they were in their gorgon form. The roles were reversed now. The gluies attached their orifices to the soldiers' hard bodies and sucked the soldiers' insides out.

Dallas' voice sounded on the com again: "And if that don't scare your balls inboard, you just aren't paying attention."

Farragut turned to Jose Maria. "Does this upset your theory of the Hive being a single coherent entity?"

"It is upsetting on a number of levels," said Jose Maria. The gluies chewed the empty shells of the soldiers.

Farragut shook his head. Did not understand what he was seeing. "Gluies are *babies?*"

Augustus said, "It might be easy to assume gluies are larvae because they are white and repulsive and pushed out of a gorgon's ass. But they destroy the gorgons and feed on the soldiers."

Jose Maria added to that, "So between the gorgons and the soldiers, we have a net population loss, which does not qualify as reproduction."

Farragut tried again, "So gluies are parasites laid inside a gorgon host. Something that feeds on the Hive? Now there's a switch."

"Drawing from any Earthly reference is certainly tenuous and probably dangerous," Jose Maria warned.

Augustus, speaking like a machine, said, "More data is required."

"Gluies have been observed feeding in concert with both gorgons and soldiers, so I cannot abandon the assumption that gluies are Hive," said Jose Maria. "And there is nothing to eat in this area of space and much of the Hive. Even the human body will digest itself in starvation."

Gluies were the worst, the most feared form of the Hive. The doomsday version.

"We have few hard facts on gluies," said Jose Maria.

"We have one," said Augustus. A very hard fact, very hard to take. "No ship has ever survived contact with gluies."

The yellow sun of the Sagittarius Zero system grew

visibly brighter and larger than anything else in the star field. Attack Group One had arrived.

The star system was choked with asteroids, which were assumed to be gorgon spheres.

"Why are they here?" Gypsy stared at all the images, baffled. "Shouldn't they be moving toward food?"

The Attack Group had stepped down from FTL, and approached the Planet Zero from orbital north, coming in perpendicular to the system's orbital plane.

The xenos had expected that the gorgon presence would be thinner up here than in the orbital plane, but this was not so. Gorgons haloed Planet Zero like globular clusters around a galactic hub.

Farragut asked Augustus to plug in to the ship's navigation system and guide the pilot in around the masses of aliens.

The Attack Group had penetrated twenty astronomical units into the Sagittarius Zero system when Augustus bolted straight up, yanked his cables from their connections at the base of his skull and said: "They know we're here."

Crickets chirped.

"Hive sign," Gypsy Dent reported.

Farragut got on the tight beam to his group: "Go FTL. Exit star system. Use rendezvous coordinates nine. Execute *now*."

A sound like wet snow on a window.

Farragut looked up. "Now what is *that?*"

He turned to Tactical, but Tactical had gone dumb.

His XO stared as if into headlights. "Um."

Gypsy Dent never ummed.

"Gluies, sir," Gyspy said.

As the lights went out.

24

"**F**IRE ALL JETS. FIRE."

"Firing, aye."

Hydrogen-fueled fire blazed from *Merrimack*'s ports.

"Commander Dent, get another decoy craft organized to resonate the irresistible harmonic and lure the Hive away from the ship."

"Aye, sir."

Crew hastily prepped a new decoy craft as *Merrimack* spewed fire. Fired until the gluies shrouded the ship so thickly that the fire blew back in the barrels and the jets shut down.

The gluies would be oozing through the distortion field next.

"Deploy hull walkers."

Marines clothed in atmo suits and armed with scythes and flamethrowers poured out the topside air locks to take up positions on the hull.

The atmo suits, a glaring international orange, set them apart from the sickly bluish-white aliens that seeped through the distortion field.

The hull walkers had no luck with the scythes. The blades, sharp and smooth as they were, stuck in the gluies' gelatinous bodies. Even when the Yurg managed to slice off a piece of intruding gluie with a swift mighty stroke, the white lump fell to the hull and did not die. It lay there, waiting to be stepped in, corroding the hull.

The Marines fired up their handheld flamethrowers. Carried their fuel in two separate backpacks, one solid hydrogen, another for an oxidizer to make the hydrogen burn.

Gluies did not ignite. They melted, and not quickly. Gave off a lot of smoke. And they kept moving even after you burned a third of their body away. Melt off their feet, and they just kept moving in slow slug fashion.

"Burn off their mouths," Ranza ordered her team. "Try that."

Kerry Blue could not stand to look at those nubbly little teeth. Filled every gaping mouth she saw with fire.

The atmosphere was thin out here between hull and distortion field. Even so, it quickly filled with smoke, roiling thick.

Gluies plopped down from the distortion field to the hull. The hull became coated in gluish white. Left a Marine nowhere to stand. They disintegrated your atmo suit, burned your ankles, let the smoke inside your suit to sting your eyes. You had to clamp your teeth on your rebreather and remember to inhale only through your mouth and out your nose because gluies smelled like death.

When your suit was compromised, you had no choice but to burn out a path to the nearest air lock.

A wind across the hull signaled the first hull breach. The ship's atmosphere exhaled into the space between the distortion field and the hull.

Colonel Steele ordered the rest of his Marines to retreat inside the ship.

Lobbed a grenade out behind him. Paused in the air lock, waiting for the blast. Reopened the hatch to check for effect.

Gluies, peppered with frags, continued to advance.

Steele sealed the hatch.

The ship filling with smoke. The air scrubbers had ceased operating.

Farragut ordered all hands to atmospheric suits.

The order was relayed through the ship by shouts.

A runner came to the command deck to report that the decoy—the wild goose they called it—was partially prepped but that Augustus would not fuse it.

The runner turned, feeling the brush of someone behind him. Gave an involuntary yelp.

Augustus, in chemical light, looked monstrous. The new skin and bone made a slash of lightness across his haggard face behind the face shield of his atmospheric suit.

"What's holding up the fuse, Augustus?" Farragut asked.

"Your wild goose will never leave the flight deck. The moment you open the distortion field for launch, that boat will plow into a solid pack of gluies and stick there and resonate the irresistible harmonic right here."

"Even if I kill the gravity?"

"Won't make a bit of difference. The pressure on the distortion field is immense. The gluies are pushing in. The gluies will fill up any open space instantly, with or without gravity."

"Can something else get through the gluies? Torpedo? Star Sparrow?"

"No."

Farragut accepted the answer. If there were a decoy that could get through gluies, some other ship would have tried this before. And lived.

"Anyone see a way out of this?"

"Go to your God like a soldier," said Augustus.

"I'm not fixin' to roll to my rifle."

The odds of survival weren't long. They were nonexistent.

No ship ever survived gluies.

Augustus waited for some stupid sunshine from Farragut, some there's-always-a-first-time sort of happy dung.

But what Farragut said was, "If this be our Corindahlor, then let's do it right."

And he was giving orders: "Take the fire suppression

system down in the sails and the wings and in the compartments abutting the hull. Any blaze high enough to kill a gluie will activate the fire suppressors, and I won't have *Mack* fighting for the other side.

"Close all hatches to ship's interior fuselage."

Closing the interior hatches in effect created a second hull within the hull.

"Another place to retreat?" Augustus asked as the shouted orders echoed through the corridors.

"No, it's a place for the xenos to figure out how to combat gluies. Tell the Sargasson we need to know what harmonic our insects are listening to, and we need it right now."

A runner delivered the message to the lab, where insects were wildly singing and caroming off the sides of their canisters. The Sargasson wallowed in its tank.

The xenos had been trying scans on the insects, painstakingly charting their physical changes down to the molecular level. But the gluie encasement had shut their equipment down. Without their computers, the xenos wallowed like the Sargasson in the dark, listening to gluies drip down from the distortion field and slap onto the hull.

"Commodore."

Farragut looked to where Gypsy was standing by the clearport on the command deck. A white gelatinous mass pressed against the port, like the underside of a slug.

Farragut addressed his deck crew, "Okay, shut down the command deck. Lock it up, gentlemen." Nothing was functioning anyway: tactical, com, fire control, targeting, nav were all down.

The crew secured their stations and took up H packs and flamethrowers to join a battle at a hull breach.

Farragut's hand grasped the shoulder of a shaky young specialist. Advised, "If you're fixin' to heave, you better do it before we get out there, son."

The specialist tore off his helmet and lunged for a waste port.

Wiped his mouth, replaced his helmet.

"You good?" Farragut asked.

Nodded. "I'm good, sir." Exited the command deck with the others. Gypsy secured the hatch after them.

Farragut led them up to the top deck where gorgons were penetrating the hull.

Some navvies had slapped together sets of mechanical bellows and were pumping them into the vent to clear the interior smoke out to the space between the hull and the distortion field. That sort of worked for a while, but the vents were now clogged with gluies.

"I got this one," said Cain Salvador. Reached up, stuck the nozzle of his flamethrower in the vent.

The blowback of flame sent Cain jumping back into Colonel Steele.

Farther up and down the corridor gluies oozed through the overhead, dropped to the deck. The chemical lamps were going out, or else they were covered by gluies. The Marines of Team Alpha had only the light of their own headlamps.

The light caught on an interior hatch. All eyes followed the light. Considered retreat.

Kerry Blue said, "I ain't dyin' in the dark. I'm gonna go burn shit."

Steele motioned the team to the left and right.

The Bull Mastiffs gave a woof and advanced to face the white death.

On the top deck, Augustus seized the back of Farragut's helmet, swiveled it to force him to look at the passive sensor on his atmo suit. The patch was vivid orange, creeping toward red.

Farragut roared: "Cease fire! Cease fire! Somebody's H pack is leaking! Atmo is almost four percent hydrogen. *Clear the deck!*"

He shepherded his crew down the hatches.

Let the patterner throw the leaking H pack up the hatch with a flash grenade. The hatch slammed shut before the fireball cannoned across the deck.

* * *

The defenders huddled under the hatches, listening for the blaze to die.

It died quickly. Farragut put his hand to the ladder to go back up.

"This way," said Augustus.

"I'm not ready to pull back this far."

"This is the quickest route to the port wing."

Farragut was about to ask why he wanted to get to the port wing. Then he became aware of a Morse clanging. He hadn't picked up on the pattern before through all the other din.

Heard it now. "What's it saying?"

"Engine Five's containment field is fluctuating."

Engine Five was affixed under the ship's port wing, inboard of the underwing flight deck.

"Mister Kittering is attempting to isolate the engine."

"Can we eject anything into this crush?"

"No. She won't be able to eject it. Best she can do is get the engine's containment field on the other side of the ship's distortion field before containment collapses."

The most stable functions on board a spaceship were its distortion fields and its engine containment fields. An engine containment field was just another distortion field with a magnetic component to keep the matter and antimatter separate from each other. The magnetic field in Engine Five had become unstable.

Farragut set out at a run through the dark interior of his ship. Knew the shortest route to anywhere.

"The Hive hasn't gone after an engine in a long time," he said, running.

The Hive learns. And the Hive had learned that breaching an engine's containment field destroys the swarm. Or, perhaps equally important to the Hive, breaching an engine destroys the food the swarm wanted to eat.

But these were gluies. The kamikazes of the Hive.

Farragut and Augustus came out of the ship's interior at the portside ramp tunnel. The wide space radiated heat. There must have been a hydrogen flash here, too. Melted globs of gluies without feet or mouths clung to the deck grates. But there were no human skeletons. Company and crew had managed to get clear before the flash. Underneath the deck grates, water sloshed.

Already, another rank of gluies oozed down from the hull onto the flight deck.

Farragut ran to the sound of the Morse clanging.

It came from inside the air lock to Engine Five's compartment.

The inner hatch was ajar. Farragut gave it a tug.

The signalman inside the air lock fell out of it, dropped his spanner. He had been messing up his signals now anyway. His hands shook. His lips were ashen blue. He stood up. "Commodore."

Chief Engineer Kit Kittering stayed inside the lock, swearing.

"Talk to me in English, Kit."

"They—they've—" Kit's hands moved jerkily.

Augustus said, "That hatch will not shut."

Kit huffed. "I can't get this hatch to shut to seal off the engine!" She came out of the lock, gave the hatch a push.

The hatch bounced back open at her.

The hinges and their pins showed heavy corrosion and warping. Gluies had been here.

Augustus seized the hatch, pulled up. The warped pieces groaned. Bent back toward neutral position.

Cracked.

Broken pieces fell through the deck grates.

Kit walked through the hatchway into the air lock. "So we're ground zero for the matter/antimatter annihilation." She leaned against the hatch to the engine compartment and curled up to die.

Augustus said, "This is probably preferable to getting eaten or burned alive."

Farragut turned and faced the advancing mass of gluies.

Kept his eyes open.

*   *   *

And saw gluies retreat like a foaming ocean wave from a beach.

The white mass pulled away, back to the breach by which the horde had entered the wing.

He could see through the jagged breach to the distortion field. Watched the mountainous crush of gluies lift away like a shroud from the distortion field and move away into space.

The gluies that were still inside the ship, bottled against the distortion field, tried to insinuate their way out.

The containment field around Engine Five stabilized.

The ship's lights went on.

The air systems breathed to life, sucked away the smoke and miasma of burned gluie from the compartments and corridors.

Disassociated globs of gluie remaining on the deck, without mouth or feet, dissolved through the deck grates.

Farragut called into the air lock. "Get out of there, Kit. I have things for you to do."

The gluie at Kerry Blue's toes melted. The one at her heels turned and slithered up the bulk and out the breach the way it came.

A touch at her waist made her jump. Then she saw it was Colonel Steele's hand. She slumped a little, laughing. Leaned against him. "Oh, my God."

Heard someone, somewhere, yelling: "Someone else is resonating the irresistible harmonic! *Someone got a decoy out!*"

"Bet it was *Gladiator*," said Carly.

"Bet it was *Rio*." Dak.

"Give me odds and I'll take the Meadow Muffins," said Darb.

All through the ship gluies pulled back, tried to get out. Crew dove out of their way and opened hatches for them.

Farragut's voice sounded on the loud com: "All

hands, all hands, get yourself tethered down or into the interior of the ship behind an air lock. I'm fixin' to take down the distortion field to let this trash out."

He had returned to his command deck to find it intact. Without the crew inside it, the gluies had not deemed it worth the effort to breach. The specialists were returning to their stations.

"All decks, report. Are we clear to purge gluies?"

Waited for the decks to lock down, hook down, report in.

"Distortion field down in ten, nine, eight—"

Tactical was organizing the sensor signals into images that made sense to the human eye.

"Seven, six, five—"

The systems monitors read normal for all six engines.

"Four, three, two, one—"

The distortion field blinked out. The gluies trapped within it flew away as if propelled.

The air moaned through the hull breaches.

"Restore distortion field."

"Restoring field, aye."

The wind ceased to moan.

Hive sign had not stopped on board the ship.

Gypsy got on the loud com, "All hands. We have a clinger. Find it. Kill it."

The tactical screens presented images of gluies pouncing on a decoy vessel that was moving away from *Merrimack*.

"I hope to Jesus that's a decoy," said Farragut in a sudden horrid thought. Realized he didn't know what was under that mountain of death. All the Hive swarms within the Sagittarius Zero star system moved toward it. Gorgons, soldiers, gluies. Billions of Hive mouths.

"Where is my Group?"

And over the tight beam: "Farragut to Group. Call in."

Wolfhound called in. Mostly intact. They'd had gorgons.

Gladiator called in from the fifth planet. Reported

heavy damage. They had taken on gorgons. Scraped some of them off in the dirt.

Horatius called in. Intact. Gorgons. *Horatius* had spent another boxcar of explosives.

Rio Grande called in. Chewed all to hell. Can openers. Fifty-five deaths that they knew of so far.

Windward Isles The XO called in. Captain Fred was having her arm reattached and did anyone have any type AB negative blood. The gorgons ate theirs.

Sunlit Meadows called in. Hull damage. One death.

"How'd we rate gluie treatment?" Tactical muttered to navigation.

The Group converged on *Merrimack*'s position.

Rio looked a horror. The hull chewed with enormous gaping rents. You could see people inside on the decks.

But most horrifying to the Group was learning that *Merrimack* had gluies.

"Wouldn't have survived it without the interference," said Farragut. "Which one of y'all got the wild goose out?"

No one answered.

Tactical sounded off: "Commodore, bogeys. We have bogeys. A lot of them. Spaceships. Not ours. No IFF."

"The devil comes to collect his due," said Augustus.

They were small vessels, probably drones from their size. Their design elements were clearly human. Clearly PanGalactic.

On the Group's com a mechanical voice sounded. Familiar. Distorted. But Farragut had heard the voice before. It addressed Commodore Farragut by name. "You shall not resonate. You shall follow your escort. You shall not scan the limpets. Touching the limpets in any way whatsoever will destroy them, and my lord's protection will cease."

Specialists at their stations mouthed silently to each other, *"My lord?"*

"Farragut to Group. Follow *Merrimack*."

And *Merrimack* followed its drone escort on a course toward the fourth planet. The techs looked for the limpets they were not supposed to scan. Found them. Small objects hooked to the distortion field. They had to be resonating the Hive harmonic.

"We need us one of those."

"As soon as we figure out how to scan it without losing *his lordship*'s protection."

Merrimack's fabrication plant was already powered up and at work constructing patches for the hull and the decks. The ship was down to three flight decks, the fourth eaten away. And it looked like *Rio* was going to need a lot of help.

Telltales kept flying through the ship, chittering and crawling. The ants would not go to earth. The Zakan moths fluttered. *Merrimack* received reports—the situation was the same on the other ships. Hive sign without Hive on board.

Jose Maria postulated, "Perhaps there are no Hive elements on board. Perhaps the protection of the limpets causes the panic."

"That's real probable, Jose Maria, but I want this ship searched millimeter by millimeter."

Gypsy acknowledged that.

Farragut said, "I'm going down decks to light a fire under those xenos. Augustus, you're thinking real loud. Come with me."

En route to the xeno lab, Augustus said, "We passed through another tachyon clicker on approach to the solar system."

Farragut frowned. Tachyon clicker. That was a covert message between patterners.

"Your white tiger didn't tell you?" said Augustus.

"She's not my white tiger," said Farragut. "And no, she didn't. Is this another signal from Septimus?"

"No. This signal originates from the fourth planet of this system. The clicks have the signature code of Secundus."

Secundus. The second patterner ever created.

Secundus had been the patterner Caesar Daisius sent to Thaleia to rein in Constantine sixty-one years ago. Secundus was believed killed in the same blast that killed Constantine.

Apparently, that belief was mistaken if Secundus was out here in the Deep, sending tachyon clickers from Constantine's world.

"Secundus joined the other side," Farragut concluded.

"He did. Not by his own will. This clicker is a repeating warning. A recording transmitted over and over on automatic. It's directional—streaming toward Palatine. It warns any other patterner not to tap into any of Constantine's systems. Secundus says he was infected by a Trojan Horse program which caused him to serve Constantine. He states it in a way that could get around his programming."

"Are you sure this message is genuine? It would be jolly convenient for Constantine if my patterner is afraid to access Constantine's data."

"Crossed my mind. This is real."

"Does this mean we have an ally on Planet Zero?"

"Secundus is dead. Only the warning survives."

Farragut turned in the corridor to face him. "You sure this time? Did Secundus' last message say 'I'm dead?'"

"Patterners have limited life spans. Secundus died a long time ago. And no, we don't come back for a third time. The second time is final."

Farragut remembered Septimus. That patterner's second death had been brain death.

"How limited a life span? When does your warranty expire?"

"Last year," said Augustus.

The fourth planet of the Sagittarius Zero system appeared on the ships' monitors. White clouds scattered over oceans of blue. The land masses showed part barren brown, part green with vegetation.

In addition to the glut of PanGalactic sentinels circling the planet, there was a spaceship in orbit.

Roman.

Farragut was about to hail *Gladiator* to ask Numa Pompeii if he could identify the ship.

Then saw that he did not need to ask a Roman. Jose Maria had turned white, rigid. Stared in unmistakable recognition. Nostrils flared. A quiver started under his chin. His dark eyes held a coal fire burn.

"Jose Maria?"

Jose Maria's voice came out a vibrating rasp: "That is *Sulla*."

25

THE UNKNOWN MACHINE voice on the com addressed Farragut again. This time with a vid to go with it. The image of a man, cabled like a patterner, his expression vacant, gray eyes dull. His voice was flat, mechanical, but still familiar. He invited the ships which were able to land to do so in the protected zone. He invited all ships' personnel to the surface. Said that his lord Constantine would grant Commodore Farragut an audience.

Commander Gypsy Dent saw recognition all around her on the command deck. She had never met the man, but she had seen his picture once. "Is that Sebastian Gray?"

The late Sebastian Gray had been XO of the *Merrimack* in between the service of Calli Carmel and Gypsy Dent.

Farragut answered, his mouth dry, "Looks like."

The patterner who looked and sounded like Sebastian Gray said, "You have seen the power of my lord's invention."

Farragut muted the audio and clicked off the vid. "He's saying Constantine invented the Hive." He looked to Augustus for comment.

"Bullshit," said Augustus.

"I appreciate a concise report. Jose Maria?"

Jose Maria, looking fragile, said, "I concur with Augustus."

Farragut clicked audio and visual back on. "What does your lord want?"

"My lord needs nothing from you. My lord invites you to land your ships and be restored. You have a patterner on board. I would like to interface with him."

Farragut muted the com again, shut off the vid in surprise. Looked to Augustus.

"Of course he would," said Augustus.

"How does he know you're here?"

"Does he?" said Augustus.

Farragut clicked the link back on, spoke, noncommittally, "I have a patterner?"

"His name is Augustus," said Sebastian Gray.

Constantine had more intelligence of the Attack Group than the Group had of him. Farragut did not want to say anything else. "Mister Gray, thank your lord for us. Farragut out." Clicked off. "Damn."

Augustus said, "Right neighborly for a man who claims to have created the Hive; displaced gorgons to Thaleia; and cabled up a patterner. I take it Sebastian Gray *does* meet the primary prerequisite for becoming a patterner?"

"Yeah," said Farragut. Sebastian Gray was dead. "Jose Maria, are you all right?"

Jose Maria was breathing into his hands. Shook his head, no.

Gypsy said, "You're not going down are you, sir?"

"At some point I'll have to. Someone who has his secretary refer to him as my lord will only talk to the top guy. And that's why we're here. I could use you, Augustus."

"So could Constantine. He wants me. He needs a patterner."

"He has one. Are you sure that wasn't Bast instead of Secundus warning you on the tachyon clicker?"

"The clicker has Secundus' signature pattern. That kluged together Sebastian Gray thing is nothing. Constantine just trotted that out because he doesn't want to look like he needs a patterner."

Jose Maria said, "If Constantine has done that to

your man, young Commodore, what has he done to the people on *Sulla*?"

Augustus answered that one. "Don't worry, *Don* Cordillera. And I mean this benignly, your wife is dead. He wants me. His patterner Secundus is dead. Constantine needs another patterner. I won't be taken. I would be more secure on my own vessel. Permission to launch Striker."

Steele reinterpreted Augustus' request, "Commodore, he's going down to the planet to join *his lord*."

Farragut spoke to his patterner, "Augustus, go."

In a short time, the little red-and-black Striker launched.

And immediately moved toward the planet.

Steele did not speak. Grinding teeth, muscles bulging at his jaw, his glower all shouted silently *I told you so*.

"There he goes," said Gypsy. "Never would have guessed Augustus to be a traitor to the Empire."

Tactical reported, "Sir! The Striker isn't moving under its own power. It's being dragged. That's a hook."

Farragut moved to the tactical station to see the read-outs. "Here's the distortion hook. Here's the Striker's output. The Striker's force is working in the opposite direction. Augustus is trying to get away. Constantine is dragging him toward the planet."

Steele blurted, "Why doesn't the Roman cyborg shoot his way free!"

Tactical said, "Why don't *we* shoot him free?"

"We can't afford to shoot," said Farragut. "We could hit Constantine. Or piss him off enough to feed us back to the Hive."

The Striker continued slowly toward the atmosphere. The readings from its engines' output indicated the engines were red lined.

Farragut sent: "Augustus, stand by to shut down engines. We're going to hook you."

It was a command you could only give to a patterner. The engine shutdown needed to be precise. A millisecond too soon, Constantine would reel the Striker to the ground. Too late and the Striker's maxed engines would be bottled, their energy turned inward, and Augustus boiled away.

"Standing by," Augustus answered, laconic.

"Hook him!"

"Deploy hook, aye."

Merrimack threw out an energy field—like a fist closing round Constantine's energy fist closed around the Striker—as Augustus cut engines.

Much slower now, the Striker still moved toward the atmosphere.

"We did tug-of-war with a black hole," Tactical cried against his readouts. "How can we be losing against this guy?"

Someone murmured, "This guy controls everything."

"I don't ever want to hear that," said Farragut.

Gypsy said, "Constantine has the better grip. He has a seamless hold on the Striker. Our distortion hook has a gap in it where it fits around Constantine's hook."

"Then let's close our grip," said John Farragut. "Extend our hook down to the planet to enclose his hook's generator. We'll pull the whole installation right out of the ground."

Smiles broke out on the command deck at the scale of the operation. The smiles faded as it became clear that Commodore Farragut wasn't the only one thinking huge.

Tactical reported reluctantly, "Commodore. Constantine's distortion hook is anchored halfway to the planet's core. If we tug, we'll just move the planet."

Farragut had not expected to be outflanked. And hadn't expected that Augustus wouldn't come up with a better idea.

Augustus' voice sounded on the com: "You must know I have a mandate to self-destruct before allowing myself to fall into enemy hands."

A new voice sounded on the com. John Farragut had never heard it before but could guess immediately who was speaking. "Augustus, I am not your enemy."

Augustus' voice went on: "Self-destruct sequence loaded. Engaged. Ten. Nine."

Farragut shouted, "Augustus, I override your mandate!"

"Six. Five."

The voice of Constantine cajoled, "Give me a moment to reason with—" at the same time that Farragut shouted, "Augustus, abort self-destruct!"

"Three. Two. Hail Caesar."

Farragut looked to Gypsy who instantly ordered, "Drop hook!"

Constantine did not drop his hook. The blaze of bottled fire traveled down the hook to the ground installation that erupted in the shock wave from the Striker exploding within its distortion field.

When the second hook vanished, the glowing debris expanded in a glittering sphere before going completely black.

Farragut stared at the darkening screen from within a numb shield of disbelief. The mind threw up a wall against it. Wasn't real.

Watched in a strange detachment. It was all just something viewed on a screen.

"Tactical," Farragut said. "Current status of the Hive."

"Unchanged, sir."

Farragut hoped Constantine wanted something more from the Attack Group than Augustus.

"Elaborately staged," Constantine's voice came over the com, humor in it. "I suppose the patterner set that one up."

Farragut had only thought he was numb. Sudden fury poured out before he even knew he had it. "You bastard son of a bitch, you killed my officer!"

Constantine's reply sounded less certain. "I had no intention of harming you. If you were listening to his transmissions, then you know that man killed himself. Please note that it was you who acted with hostility, even after I saved you from my legions."

Farragut shouted, "You shipjacked my Striker!"

"Do not shout at me. Do you know who you are talking to?"

"I'm taking a guess here that I'm talking at Constantine Siculus."

"This is my world. You came to me. Land your ships. I will repair them all. My automatons will fabricate anything you want."

"Land where?" Farragut demanded, curt.

Gypsy had words bulging out her eyes, but she would not cross the commodore on his command deck.

"Anywhere in the green zones. Follow my signal to my palace. Bring *Don* Cordillera."

Farragut clicked off. "Now how in blazes does he know about Jose Maria?"

Gypsy said, "Sir, we *aren't* putting down?"

"We are no safer in orbit than on the ground. In fact, the closer to Constantine's palace, the safer. Take him up on his invitation to park some heavy artillery in his backyard. Send *Wolfhound* and *Horatius* down. TR, take the Wing down in their Swifts. The Battery goes down with *Wolfhound*. Set up a field camp. Cozy it right up next to the source of Constantine's transmission. I don't have to tell you this is hostile territory. Secure the perimeter, get a dome up, secure the ground. Accept *nothing* from Constantine. No gifts, no food, no technical assistance. Take *nothing* inside the perimeter. Herius Asinius will report to Colonel Steele on the ground."

He paused to ask Gypsy, "Do we have jammers on?"

"Yes, sir."

Jammers prevented displacement into the ship.

"Does Constantine?"

In a moment, Gypsy answered, "Yes, sir. He does."

Nothing would be displacing either way.

"Don't drop jammers for anything.

Well staged.

Farragut could not believe how angry that remark made him. And the assumption was true, actually. That fiasco had been staged, but not by John Farragut.

Augustus should have been able to get out of that tug-of-war. Should have known how never to get in it.

How many times had Augustus expressed the willingness to die? Even under orders not to commit suicide, he had found a way to get the job done anyway. An honorable excuse. He had to self-destruct so as not to fall into enemy hands.

Damn him.

Farragut felt weirdly directionless. Lost. With Augustus you always knew where you stood. When you lost your up, your down, your horizon, Augustus was there to slam you to the deck and show you *down*.

An indispensable thorn in his side, painful for its absence.

And Jose Maria, his moral compass, had been taken out, too. The sight of *Sulla* had knocked Jose Maria's world sideways.

Farragut found himself at Augustus' torpedo rack room six. Looked for him here. Something of him. Augustus had not taken his things back to his Striker. As if he had meant to come back here. The carpets were still down, the Roman canopy still up. The tapestries hung from the torpedoes. A cushion, fitted into one torpedo rack, made his bed. The headless Winged Victory marble still loomed over the torpedoes.

Augustus was really gone.

Ad patres.

Farragut did not understand. It was pointless. Unnecessary.

Augustus could have predicted that would happen. That Constantine would hook his Striker. Had he manipulated Farragut and Constantine into sending him into a situation in which he could get himself killed?

Surrounded by Hive, living at the mercy of the enemy, Farragut could not hold a service for Augustus right now, which was just as well because Farragut was the only man in the Group who could stand him, and he was so mad at Augustus he would just tell him to go to hell.

When he came out of the rack room, Gypsy was there in the corridor. She saw his face. "You *can't* be crying for him."

"You're right, Gypsy. You're right. So I don't know

what this is." He roughly dried his face with his palm heels. "I am just so almighty *pissed*, GOD BLESS AMERICA!" He shouted back through the hatchway into the rack room.

"Find anything in there, sir?" Gypsy peered through the hatch.

"I wasn't really looking. I was blessing him from here to Gehenna. I have been played. I trusted him."

"That may not have been real smart, sir," Gypsy said gently.

"He was always honest with me. I *thought*. How can you mistrust someone who calls you an idiot to your face? I am so angry with him for not being what I thought he was."

Gyspy listened, lending a sad, calm strength. "What was that, sir."

"Defender of Rome. I thought I could count on him to be that."

Farragut's anger was always fleeting. This anger lodged in his heart and stayed. He turned around and went back into Augustus' compartment. He had more things to call him.

26

A WEEK HAD PASSED since Attack Group One arrived at Sagittarius Zero. The Group ships had assumed a wider orbit around the fourth planet than the ghost ship *Sulla*.

Sulla sent no signals other than its running lights. Jose Maria de Cordillera watched the ship drift underneath *Merrimack* every time around.

Rio still looked hellish. The erks were using *Windward Isles* and *Sunlit Meadows* as platforms to effect repairs on it.

PanGalactic ships moved in to offer assistance. Were told to move away.

The Marines and Dracs had established a field camp on the ground.

Time was coming for Commodore Farragut to face the god of Sagittarius Zero.

First, Farragut took a skiff from *Merrimack* to *Gladiator*.

A giant scarab cricket swooped down on his head as he disembarked on *Gladiator*'s dock. Farragut ducked. "Ho! Numa! Call off your bug!"

Numa Pompeii apologized with a deep chuckle. "We still have a Hive presence, but we can't find it. We're starting to think Constantine's limpets are provoking our crickets."

"Yeah, that's our thought, too," said Farragut, brushing his hair back into place with his hand.

There was a Roman shuttle in the dock. Herius Asinius had come up from the field base to listen in on what the merc had to say about Constantine Siculus.

Amadea had changed her appearance. Still had the beard. A very fine gold chain threaded through it now to make it gleam. Her eyes were now as gold as her hair.

The voice was an old woman's.

"Constantine craves respect and recognition of the powerful," Amadea told the commanders. "If he doesn't get it, he tends to kill them."

She paused, because Farragut and Numa were talking behind their hands.

"Is that what became of Caesar Magnus?" Farragut whispered to Numa Pompeii. "Magnus failed to respect or recognize Constantine?"

Numa shook his head, muttered back, "Magnus never knew Constantine. Caesar Daisius put the hit on Constantine."

Amadea continued, "He thinks he's a great hunter. He isn't. Don't bother lying to him. He'll think you're lying, no matter what you tell him. He cheats at everything. He's not a good chess player. He needs to clear off most of the board before he moves in for checkmate."

"So he's bad with too many variables," Numa said.

"How does he play baseball?" said Farragut.

"He doesn't."

"Football?" said Herius Asinius.

"No. Neither kind. He considers them thuggish."

Thuggish. From a mass murderer who hunts human beings for fun.

"How did you get him to surrender to you in the game?" said Herius Asinius.

"Gun barrel pressed between the eyes," said Amadea. "That usually does it."

Merc talk. Farragut hated it.

"What does he want?" said Farragut. "We know he wanted Augustus. Now that Augustus is dead, why are we still alive?"

"He will want all the technological developments of

the last sixty years. And he is thinking that Augustus' death was a show. Was it a show?"

Farragut stared back at her, said harshly, "What is wrong with you?"

Amadea continued, "He may want your ships."

"For what? An invasion?"

"He sees himself as Caesar. All he's missing is the empire. I think Thaleia was meant to get a last minute rescue like we got here. You weren't supposed to win at Thaleia. I think Thaleia was meant to see the Second Coming of Constantine."

Farragut and Numa looked at each other. Farragut lifted his eyebrows. Numa gave a facial shrug.

"I think it was a bad idea to put troops on the ground. Constantine will try to buy your men. And he *will* buy them."

"My men are not for sale," said Farragut. "And Rome has its pride." He exchanged glances with Herius Asinius.

"You have no idea what Constantine can offer," said the white tiger.

"We know you're for sure for sale. That's why you're not going down. How does Constantine know my name? How did he know I had a patterner? How does he know Jose Maria de Cordillera is with us?"

"Moles," said Amadea. "You have them. Romans always use them. Constantine is Roman."

"Are you one?"

"I am Roman."

"Are you a mole?"

"I am working for Caesar Romulus. Put a lie detector on me. Are you going down to meet with Constantine?"

"In time."

"I'm coming with you."

Farragut did not bother to tell her again that she was not setting foot on the planet. As he joined the skiff to return to *Merrimack*, he told Numa Pompeii, "Take the tiger up on that lie detector. Find out who she's really working for."

Caught the edge of a brooding scowl from Herius Asinius, who offered no comment. Herius shared little with anyone except his cousin.

Farragut's demand had made Herius Asinius remember a furtive girl with ash brown hair and matching ash brown eyes—no beard—who clutched a landing disk to her chest back on Thaleia.

Jose Maria de Cordillera did not respond to the tapping at the hatch to his compartment.

The hatch opened.

Jose Maria was kneeling, his back to the hatch, his feet crossed beneath him, backs of his hands resting on his thighs, thumb and middle finger touching. He held his back straight, shoulders wide. His long black hair was held back in its silver clasp. He presented an artistic Zen figure. Still. But there was a terrible tension in the stillness.

"I'm sorry to interrupt your meditation," said John Farragut in the hatch.

The silver clasp moved side to side, no. "There is no interruption. Nothing to apologize for." Jose Maria rose to his feet in a fluid motion. Faced Farragut with red-rimmed eyes. "This man is evil."

"We knew that."

"It is a fraud. I recognize it as such. That ship cannot be *Sulla*. So why do I react with anger when an evil, deceitful man tries to deceive me?"

"I'm just fixin' to take the bastard out as soon as we get his secret."

"Amen."

"Of course that plan is complicated by the possibility that Constantine has the same plan for us."

Jose Maria's voice trembled, "How dare he use the *Sulla?*"

Farragut signaled the command deck. "Get a hold of Sebastian Gray. See if his Supreme Self will grant me that audience now."

*   *   *

Under Constantine's sun, insects flapped and chirped in crazed chaos. Friendly resonance was not friendly. The Hive was here. And while the bugs were a big pain in the face, they were helpful reminders that territory just didn't get any more hostile than this.

Wolfhound and *Horatius* had set down a scant one klick from Constantine's palace. There was a low hill between the camp and the palace, so you couldn't see it. Still, Constantine was real close. Behind the camp, another half klick in the opposite direction from the palace, stretched an open sea.

No one challenged Colonel Steele's choice of sites, so the Marines and the Dracs constructed their field camp here, threw up their energy dome, and placed the big guns, ready to fire in any direction.

The line in between the U.S. side of camp and the Roman side of camp was even hotter than the force field perimeter that divided all of them from Constantine's world.

Inside the Roman half of the camp, the Legion carrier had detached and put down four boxcars in a square, forming a makeshift legionary fortress. It blocked the view from the U.S. side.

Outside the perimeter, even closer than the palace, just across the river from the Roman side of camp, PanGalactic automatons were building, busy as ants and as fast. They threw up structure after structure. Marines paused between watches to see what was going up now.

The automatons were building just about everything except guns and defenses. There was already an amusement park. Several bars for different tastes. A pool room. An elaborate swimming pool with swim up bar. A whorehouse. A stable with pretty horses and a riding trail. A golf course. A casino. And several pedestrian boulevards lined with buildings that looked like shops.

A shuttle had come down from *Merrimack*. Brought Farragut and the beautiful Jose Maria de Cordillera. They had gone outside the perimeter. Steele was really torqued that Farragut would not take a Marine guard with him.

Kerry Blue heard Farragut tell Steele before he left, "Constantine already has us captive. I go unarmed. He'll either take it as sign of trust or a sign of my recognition of his superiority. And, TR, I want you to remind everyone: no one kills Constantine."

Kerry was outside the perimeter with Cole Darby, setting up listening devices meant to pick up sounds and filter out everything but the voices. Problem was nobody out here was talking. A lot of smiling people over there across the river in their fantasy town and not one of them chattering, which was okay because what the Marines really wanted to pick up was Constantine in the palace.

But Constantine and his patterner Sebastian Gray weren't talking either.

And just what was Constantine supposed to say? "As you know, Sebastian, the resonant code I use to control the gorgons is doo dah day." Yeah, that would be great if he said that.

Kerry struggled with the spindly array, snarling.

A robot approached. Kerry and Darb drew weapons. The automaton recognized the gesture, the weapons. Halted. A human voice came out of the machine: "May I assist?"

"No. Move it out, bolt-hole."

The robot apparently understood slang. Inclined its body in a mechanical bow and glided away.

Darb and Kerry got the array set up. "They can try this thing out on Commodore Farragut and *Don Cordillera*. You just know Farragut's gonna be talking."

Batting insects away from their faces, Kerry Blue and Cole Darby requested reentry through the perimeter.

Entry required two checks of identity. One by a human guard, and a confirmation by a handheld identification device. Kerry got a green from the handheld, but the Yurg challenged her:

"How do I know that's really you, Blue?"

Kerry, hot, uncomfortable, impatient, snapped open

her jumpsuit, pulled down the top, and tied the sleeves around her waist. She shook down her sweaty hair on her bare shoulders. Glared at Yurg from under sweaty brows.

"Uh, yeah, those look like Blue." Yurg let her in.

But he barred Darb.

Cole Darby shrugged out of his jumpsuit, tied the sleeves around his waist. Did not have the same effect.

"Pleased to say that doesn't help me, my man."

The Yurg did a full scan on Cole Darby before letting him inside the perimeter.

Kerry dragged her sweaty arms back into her sticky sleeves, looked over at the Roman camp. The Dracs had a soccer field staked out and were kicking a ball around.

A voice carried across the camp from the other direction: "Blue! You brought that uffing weed down here!"

Kerry snapped up her jumpsuit, and trotted over quick time to see what she'd done this time.

Found TR Steele, fists on his flanks, his glare fixed on something on the ground. Kerry followed the blue dagger gaze down to a clump of green leaves.

Froggy toes and big eyes peeked out from under the foliage.

A lizard plant.

Kerry owned a lizard plant. Native of the planet Arra in the Myriad.

"That's not mine," said Kerry. She crouched down with her arms outstretched. "C'mere, boogs."

The lizard plant did not reach for her, cooing. This one turned leafy tail and ran for the nearest tree. As there were no trees, it scampered up Colonel Steele and took refuge atop his buzz cut head, one webby foot just above one glaring ice blue eye.

"Looks good on you, sir," said Kerry, standing back up. She grinned at him. Saw through his snarl now. Tried not to laugh at him, but he looked really sweet. She suggested brightly, "I could bring my lizard plant down from the *Mack*. Yours and mine could get together for some wild weed lovin'."

Steele turned utterly scarlet. Bellowed, "*They will not!*"

The lizard plant snugged down on Steele's head.

Kerry nodded up. "Where'd you get him, sir?"

Commodore John Farragut and Jose Maria de Cordillera walked to the palace slowly, observing the land. The ground was a different color on the hillock than in the camp, yellower here. The trees on the rise were Earth trees, willow, cypress, tamarisk, sumac, the weeds goldenrod and thistle.

Then the flora changed again as they neared the palace. Iron-red earth, with spongy blue, green, and yellow bushes that looked like coral formations.

The palace was like no other building in the world, though there were few enough buildings on the entire planet. Most of those were factories.

The palace was unique. Nothing PanGalactic about it, with its soaring marble pillars, high clerestories, wide graceful stone steps curving up the rise. It was tall, but not so grandiose as something Roman.

Farragut and Jose Maria mounted the wide, wide steps. Guards in Roman regalia did not challenge them.

Open graceful arches led from a wide terrace into a great hall.

Farragut dropped to one knee, hand to the jewel-encrusted floor.

"Are you well, young Commodore?"

Farragut was speechless. Ran his palm over the mosaic of gemstones—precious emerald, ruby, and sapphire, semiprecious opal, zircon, lapis, tourmaline, garnet, topaz—the whole jewel box, all lined in lead.

Without rising, Farragut abruptly turned his eyes up. And there it was, the mural on the ceiling, white gaps in the picture where earthquakes had taken out pieces. The marble columns showed cracks.

And the floor. The floor. Farragut got to his feet, looked for it. Found it.

A U.S. landing disk embedded in the gemstone floor.

He met Jose Maria's concerned gaze, astonished.

Grand interior doors groaned in parting, robes rustled, whispering against the gemstones. A leonine figure swept in, crowned in a golden laurel wreath. He stood before the throne, arrayed in gold and red, and looking half his 120 years. Constantine Siculus, grand as Caesar.

Announced in booming voice, "Commodore Farragut. *Welcome to Arra*."

Farragut brushed the dust from his hand. He had not recognized the palace from the outside. He had only ever been inside.

In the star cluster known as the Myriad, Farragut had displaced landing disks down to the Archon Donner's throne room. One errant landing disk had come in too low, displaced itself into the floor. And there it was.

At the time that *Merrimack* departed Arra, a radiation storm was approaching and a LEN evacuation of the planet was underway.

Here Constantine claimed to have moved the whole planet Arra almost a thousand light-years across the galaxy, and set it in orbit around a new sun with a survivable rotation deep in Hive space.

Constantine seated himself on Donner's throne. His lion's mane of hair and beard were coppery gold and Zeusly. His forearms were encased in truly gaudy golden gauntlets decorated with gemstones and colored lights. Behind his crowned head rose Donner's monumental black plaque engraved with alien script.

Sebastian Gray entered quietly, cabled, plugged in and vacant-eyed as a patterner. He took up a post at Constantine's flank, exactly as Farragut had seen Augustus stand by Caesar Magnus.

Constantine took pleasure in Farragut's amazement. Terribly casually he said, "You know Sebastian Gray."

"I did," said Farragut. And to Gray, "I got that keettrig out of the attic for your widow."

Gray gave no reaction.

"It is difficult to talk to a patterner when they are connected. But you know that. Is your patterner truly dead?"

Farragut's eyes flared, burned; mouth pulled into a

wolfish set of teeth, jaw tight, breath deep and furious. Fought down an eruption of words.

Constantine *caused* Augustus' death. What kind of idiot question was that: *Is your patterner truly dead?*

Constantine pushed on, "But where is the Triumphalis?" Farragut heard irony in it. Sensed rivalry.

General Numa Pompeii was a Triumphalis, crowned, robed, and imperial. Constantine was not except by his own decree.

"Upstairs," said Farragut.

"Your *Rio Grande* wants repair, and I have constructed a cradle for *Merrimack*. Bring your ships down."

Farragut shook his head. "Mighty neighborly, but my birds are better off flying."

"Do not resonate," Constantine warned. "And do not try to analyze the limpets."

Constantine's eyes were now on Jose Maria de Cordillera. Waiting for a question.

Constantine had left *Sulla* in orbit to be seen. And he knew who Jose Maria was. A learned man. A Nobel Laureate. Widower of a passenger on board the long-missing *Sulla*.

Everyone knew that *Sulla* was the first victim of the Hive, though *Sulla* had never been found. Till now.

Jose Maria refused to play this game. Stayed silent, dignified, contained.

Farragut asked, "Constantine, what do you want?"

"I want nothing. I do anything. I move worlds to suit my purpose. Where was the might of Rome when Telecore was dying?"

Got a flinch out of Jose Maria with that one. His wife had helped terraform Telecore.

"*I* am the might of Rome," said Constantine. "I conquer death. Is that not what gods do?"

Farragut felt the muscles of his face move into a peculiar set. He inhaled, did not speak. Thought loudly: *Are you mad?*

Constantine answered the stare, "I have seen that look before."

"Bet you have," said Farragut.

* * *

The camp's energy screen opened to receive Farragut and Jose Maria back inside.

"I don't ever want that opened without verification," said Farragut, walking in.

The Yurg started after him, uncertain, "Uh, sir? Is this a test?"

Farragut stopped. "What do you think?"

"Can I scan you, sir?"

"You had better, son."

Scanned and verified, Commodore Farragut met up with his Marine CO, Colonel Steele, who had a plant on his head.

"That's an interesting look for you, TR."

Webbed feet held on to the gunsights fixed on either side of Steele's eyes.

"It's not Flight Sergeant Blue's, sir," said Steele. "It lives here."

"Significance?" Jose Maria asked Farragut, his voice unnaturally soft.

"That lizard's an Arran life-form," Farragut explained. "The Archon Donner had a shelf full of them in his palace."

"Convergent evolution?" Jose Maria speculated.

"It's not a verge," said Flight Sergeant Kerry Blue. "That's the real thing. I have one just like it."

Steele pried the plant off his head. "You don't seem surprised, Commodore."

"Already had that shock, TR."

Steele looked troubled, daunted. Asked, "Is this Arra?"

Farragut shook his head. "I don't know. We're a long way from the Myriad."

Moving worlds. That was a big one to swallow.

"Air pressure's wrong. Show me around the camp."

Steele and Farragut started out along a pond, which was wholly contained within the perimeter. Jose Maria, isolated within himself, walked a few steps behind. Remote, distressed, he took only half notice of their alien surroundings.

In the pond a train of baby fluff balls, gold and brown and cute as ducklings, paddled with tiny webbed feet after a grotesque adult. The Marines called the adults skaterays, or mudskates, or bubblebacks, or wartrays, or flying uglies. The adults were shaped like a skate or a ray, but warty and toad-skinned, blotched a gray-brown sort of green, with tufts of warthoggish hair bristling from their warts. And the warts *pulsed*. Fully grown, they were a yard long with broad wings and a lizard tail. The tiny baby feet must be temporary.

The trees around the pond were breathing. Stout, rubbery growths—also warty—but prune textured. The warts opened to inhale. The tree exhaled out a central stack in its very wide trunk. The branches, gnarled as an ancient oak's, spread wide, with black-green rags for leaves.

Farragut, Jose Maria, and Steele walked along the perimeter. Farragut asked about the detection arrays. There was nothing to report from those.

Farragut entered a text message into his com and showed it to Steele.

Be careful what you say outside of the ships. Constantine is listening to us, too.

"Yes, sir," said Steele. Then, "What's he like?"

Farragut changed the text. Showed Steele:

Barking mad.

They walked on. Came to a trench. Farragut looked across it to the Roman side of the camp. Looked around him for someone playing a joke, but no one was laughing.

"What," Farragut began, not even sure what to say, "is *this*?"

Herius Asinius answered from across the trench. "It's a trench, Commodore. Traditional in a Roman encampment."

"Not down the middle of *your own camp*."

He glowered at Steele for explanation.

"This is new, sir," said Steele. Then, "I should have known about this."

The trench ran the entire width of the camp, dividing the U.S. from the Roman side.

Farragut said, very, very softly, "Fill it in."

And stood at the edge of the trench, and waited.

This was not Have-this-filled-in-by-sundown. Or Fill-it-in-when-it-fits-your-schedule. This was the commodore is waiting for the damned thing to disappear right now.

Equipment appeared. Men and machinery could not have moved faster had they been under gluie attack and making this trench as if it had never existed was the only thing that could save them.

Farragut walked across level ground to the Roman side.

He paused at the far end to observe the new town across the river. A Roman passed him field glasses for a better look.

"Is that a baseball diamond?" said Farragut.

"Yes, *Domni*," said the Roman. "New today."

It even had lights for a night game. "That's really low," said Farragut. Turned around to finish his walkabout.

He had come full circle with Jose Maria and Steele. They were back to the pond with the breathing trees.

In the water, a mud-colored adult skateray chased a fluffy baby with murderous intent, flapping and hissing. The fluff ball keened piteously and paddled frantically with tiny feet in a tight, tight circle, too tight for the adult to turn and line up a bite. A clutch of other babies milled together nearby, cheeping.

A sudden sploosh made the officers look.

Kerry Blue at the water's edge. She had thrown a rock.

Steele thundered, "Blue! What are you doing!"

"It's an orphan! It just wants a mama!" Then "Sorry, sir. Tryin' to help, sir."

Jose Maria noted the scene. The players. An adult with its own brood. An orphan child trying to join the family.

Jose Maria explained to Kerry, "An orphan is competition for that creature's own young. This one has lost its mother. This is survival of the strongest. It is natural selection."

Farragut, also watching the little drama, declared, "*I* am natural. No less than the trees and the stars, I have a right to be here. And *I* select the fuzzy thing. Flight Sergeant Blue, go rescue your . . . thing."

John Farragut despised a bully.

Kerry Blue splashed into the pond. The water came up to her waist. She scooped the keening orphan into her hands, kneed the brute adult in the chin, and trudged ashore. The adult hissed, incensed, flapping its flaps against the water.

Kerry climbed out of the water with a bright smile that left Steele dizzy. Kerry Blue, her clothes clinging to her body, face beaming, hands cuddling something helpless. Steele turned to stone.

Kerry gushed, laughing. "Thank you, sir."

"My pleasure, Flight Sergeant," said Farragut. Because she had charmed a smile out of Jose Maria.

Jose Maria had not said a word about *Sulla*. Had not asked Constantine about survivors. He knew he was being baited. Filled him with a storm of grief and outrage.

A young woman's tender heart under that Marine uniform made him smile.

He warned Kerry gently, "You realize that will grow up into *that*."

He pointed at another adult, this one in full view on the land, humping across the short scrub grass, its flapping body undulating up and down. At the pond bank it launched itself into the air, glided low over the water and landed in a breathing tree, there to drape itself over a low branch to hang like Dak's socks over the water.

"Don't care," said Kerry. She named the baby Barnacle Bob.

"He's not coming with us," Steele commanded, scowling his worst who-let-girls-into-the-Fleet-Marine scowl.

And could not believe he called the thing *he*. The woman made him crazy.

"Aye, sir," said Kerry. "*Don* Cordillera, what do these eat?"

Jose Maria nodded at the other babies in the pond. "Well, the algae look appetizing."

Kerry skimmed a heaping handful of pond scum off the water, and set the green mess with Barnacle Bob in the shelter of some woody reeds.

On his way back to the shuttle with the commodore, Jose Maria glanced toward something beyond the camp perimeter. His glance held, became a stare.

His smile faded. He became very still, except for his chest, which rose and fell with deep, wounded breaths.

No one dared approach him, except Farragut who would approach a snarling musinot if it were one he cared for. Jose Maria cut off anything Farragut might say. "Do *not*."

Farragut followed Jose Maria's hard stare.

To a woman, approaching the camp with a light, dancer's step, her flowing trousers fluttering about her legs like scarves. She was perhaps fifty or sixty years old, naturally aged, her brown skin softly lined over elegant facial bones. Her long, long black hair was threaded with gray. She held one artistic hand over her heavy silver necklace to keep it from bouncing on her chest. A large blue diamond sparkled on the ring finger of her left hand.

A Marine asked Jose Maria, "Will you be going back out, sir?"

All the Marines sir'd Jose Maria, even though he was a civilian.

Jose Maria shook his head, mute. No, he was not going out.

The woman came right up to the energy field, searched past the sentries who refused her entry. She leaned to see around them, caught sight of Jose Maria, and she tilted her head with a gentle smile.

Jose Maria stopped breathing. May as well have turned to stone.

A sentry strode in from the perimeter to Jose Maria. "The lady is asking for you, sir. What should I tell her?"

Jose Maria stared back at the young man blankly.

Then made a motion like a shrug. "Shoot it," he said, and walked back to the shuttle.

The shuttle returned to *Merrimack* in thickest silence. Upon arrival, Jose Maria went straight to his quarters without a word.

Gypsy Dent met the commodore at the dock. Informed him quietly, "We have a possible situation, sir. Signals picked up a tight beam from *Gladiator* to the planet surface—*not* directed to the field base."

"To where, then?"

"To the palace. Was that to you, sir?"

Farragut shook his head. "I didn't get a hail from *Gladiator*. When was this?"

Gypsy glanced at her chron. "Twenty minutes ago."

"No. We were back in camp by then." He signaled the command deck. "Hamster. Get Numa on the com for me. Ask him what he's doing."

He was on his way to the command deck, when the ship's alarms went off. He was running anyway. Charged onto the command deck, Gypsy on his heels. "What are y'all doing to my boat?"

"We've been pinged," said Lieutenant Glenn Hamilton. "Res pulse. The gorgons have noticed."

She already had the ship moving out of orbit.

"What idiot—?"

"Caesar Romulus, sir," Glenn answered.

"Oh, for Jesus."

"I wasn't able to contact General Pompeii, Commodore," said Glenn.

"To hell with Numa. Hail *Rio*."

In a moment the com tech said, "I have Captain McDaniels on the tight beam."

Farragut took up the com: "Dallas, we have a problem."

27

FARRAGUT PASSED THE FLAG to *Rio Grande* and told Captain McDaniels to find out who Numa was talking to on the surface. Turned to his res tech: "Give me Romulus."

Romulus was on the resonator demanding a status report. "Numa Pompeii has already informed me that the Attack Group has made contact with Constantine Siculus, *and* that you managed to lose the patterncr Augustus. I expect to hear updates from *you*, Commodore Farragut."

Farragut told Romulus, "I sent my report to the Joint Chiefs on the repeater. You'll have it in a couple weeks. I don't have anything to add to what General Pompeii told you except that it is a military *imperative* that no one resonate on any of our harmonics. Farragut out." He jammed the link off with a "Lord Almighty!"

Said to the res tech: "Disable this thing."

Wondered how in hell Romulus got word of all that so quickly. It could only be that Numa Pompeii had his own repeater—a lot closer than the Group's repeater back on the frontier. Numa's repeater would have to be disposable, because it would be aswarm with gorgons right now, just like *Merrimack*.

To Gypsy he requested, "What are we looking at?"

"Gorgons converging from all directions. Apparently, any other res pulse trumps the protective one.

That's why Constantine told us not to resonate. And those limpets we weren't supposed to touch? Those disintegrated the instant Romulus pinged us. And we are running out of directions to jink, sir."

Farragut nodded. "Take us toward the sun."

The listening station outside the Marine/Drac camp picked up a conversation. From the direction of the palace, very rough, garbled, but the techs on board *Wolfhound* were able to clean it up enough to get the words.

There were two speakers.

One: So you are here after all. Are you here to serve me or to serve me to my enemies?

Two: Before I cross that Rubicon, you must make me a promise.

One: What am I to promise you?

Two: The pretender Romulus' head. Detached from the rest of Romulus.

One: You needn't have insisted. I already intend to do that when I am Caesar.

Two: If he lives, I am destroyed. There's not a corner in the Empire I could go. Your word. Give me your word as Caesar.

One: You have it.

Two: Then you have me.

And that ended the voices. The first speaker was undoubtedly Constantine, but who was the other?

Steele tried to raise Farragut on his wrist com, but got nothing. Stalked on board the groundbase ship *Wolfhound.* Told the XO, "I need to get a message to *Merrimack.*"

Was told: "*Merrimack* has left orbit. We just heard from Captain McDaniels—*Merrimack* has gorgons."

Steele kept a measured calm exiting *Wolfhound.* Found Flight Leader Ranza Espinoza monitoring the perimeter. Demanded, "Who is outside the bead?"

"From our side, only Captain Carmel. From the Roman side, I don't know. I'll need to ask the Dracs."

* * *

Acting Commodore Dallas McDaniels hailed *Gladiator*. Requested to speak with General Numa Pompeii.

Gladiator's frosty XO answered instead. "The Triumphalis is not available."

"Get him," said Dallas.

"He is not here," the XO said.

"Not here as in not *where*? If he's not on the command deck, then get him there."

"The Triumphalis is not on board *Gladiator*."

"Where is he?"

"The Triumphalis did not see fit to file an away plan with this officer."

Dallas McDaniels signaled down to *Wolfhound* and *Horatius*, asking if Numa Pompeii were with them. Numa Pompeii was not to be found on either the U.S. or the Roman side. He also learned that Captain Carmel was somewhere outside the bead. At that, Dallas ordered all the ground troops under lockdown.

"I want every man-jack and jane confined within the perimeter until the return of the *Merrimack*. Acknowledge."

"Aye, sir."

Steele marched toward the Roman side of the camp. Sensed someone behind him, and whirled. Almost drew on her.

"Jesus, Marine!"

It was Kerry Blue.

"Mack *left*? Without *us*? How can they do that, sir? They can't do that!"

"They have gorgons," Steele growled at her.

"We have to go with them! Those navvies can't hack their way out of a swarm of butterflies! They don't have more than two sword arms in the whole crew."

"What do you want to do, Marine? Commandeer *Wolfhound* without Captain Carmel, take off, and go rescue *Merrimack*?"

"Yes!" Kerry cried.

One of the things that drew him to this woman—she said what he felt and could not say.

He motioned her to about-face. "Get back to your post, Marine."

On the Roman side, Steele discovered the perimeter not locked down.

"Why not?" Steele roared at Herius Asinius.

"I have men still outside the perimeter," Herius answered, gazing outward, not at his commanding officer, hands clasped behind his back.

"Doing what?"

"Recon," said Herius Asinius, his expression sullen, smoky. Muscles stood out in high definition under his bronze skin. Romans bred their men that way. This one was built like a stallion.

"Recon," said Steele in high disbelief. "I thought Romans did everything by remote."

"Our remote equipment is PanGalactic make," Herius Asinius said silkily. "It makes sense to use Pan-Galactic products against their inventor—*if* your brain is made of pig iron."

Steele did not credit for a moment that the missing Romans were surveilling anything. They were playing with the toys or dealing with the enemy. He challenged, "Then what have they found out?"

"They have not come back yet," Herius Asinius explained, almost sweetly.

"Bring them in immediately."

Steele waited for Herius Asinius to comply.

Herius moved with surly slowness. Spoke into his com. In Latin. Could have been reciting *Mary Had a Little Lamb* for all Steele knew.

Dark sultry eyes watched Steele watching him. A defiant gleam in the eyes. The Roman knew Steele couldn't understand him. Probably did start reciting *Mary Had a Little Lamb*.

"Report to me."

"I am told I do," said Herius. "Report to you."

"Is General Pompeii with your men?"

The question made Herius blink. "Not to my knowledge, no."

"Is he in your camp?"

"No," said Herius. And the blink made Steele believe him.

"Where is he?"

Herius Asinius said, "The Triumphalis is wherever he has decided to be."

Calli Carmel had heard a thunderclap under a blue sky. She knew the sound of displacement. She also knew that Constantine had jammers in place, so whoever was displacing was doing so at the pleasure of Constantine.

Calli had immediately informed her XO she was leaving the perimeter.

She left from the Roman side, ran over the new bridge across the river into the new town that had mushroomed up over the last several days.

She prowled the construction sites in the direction from which she had heard the thunder, between the brothel and the beer garden, the pool and the bowling alley. There were many people in the streets, silent people, smiling at her.

She glimpsed a figure different from the rest. Big. Moving with a distinctive commanding stride.

Calli sprinted closer. Hid behind a wall, peered around it.

There was Numa Pompeii, walking with a purpose, straight through the town and out the other side to wild fields of alien grass and black rocks.

She tailed him at a distance. Debated catching up with him, but she wanted to see where he was going first.

Waited while he hiked over a hill.

When he was out of sight, she dashed across the open space up to the summit. Fell down flat in the weeds to spy and to encrypt a text message into her com to her XO.

From here she could see a small PanGalactic transport in the middle of a field. Sebastian Gray peered from the open hatch, and beckoned Numa Pompeii to hurry.

Numa strode at his own pace. Swaggered up the ramp.

Calli sprinted. She ran full out across the scrub weed, and jumped through the transport's hatch as it began to close.

"Whew," she said blithely, guiding her long hair out of her face. She sat in an empty seat. "Where are we going?"

Sebastian Gray, in the pilot's seat, swiveled round. "You will leave your com behind, or I will report myself abducted. If I am caught aiding the enemy, I will be dismantled."

Calli hesitated. She could not be tracked without her com.

In her indecision, Numa seized her wrist, stripped her com off, and pitched it out of the transport. Then put it to Calli: "Coming or staying?" Poised to pitch her out, too.

Calli said, "I'm with you."

Numa double-tapped the back of Sebastian's seat. "Let's go."

The hatch closed.

"John was right not to trust you," Calli said as the engine started up.

"Your commodore trusts me."

"He didn't let you go with him to interview Constantine. In fact, do you have orders?"

"Commodore Farragut did not limit my initiative."

"You don't have orders," Calli translated. She leaned forward to address the pilot, "Sebastian."

The pilot did not respond to the name.

"*Are* you Sebastian?"

"I am told I was," said the pilot, eyes ahead, the small craft moving low to the ground, almost brushing the tops of the weeds.

"Do you remember me?"

"I know who you are, Captain Carmel."

"Where are we going?"

Sebastian did not answer.

Numa answered for him, "To the main resonator, to get the Hive's harmonic."

"Why doesn't *Sebastian* just *tell* us the harmonic?" said Calli.

"You don't know much about patterners, do you?"

Numa Pompeii had been the man who gave Augustus to Farragut.

"I've heard bad things about Augustus," Calli confessed the sum of her knowledge.

"Certain inhibitions are hard coded into a patterner. The man may *want* to help us, but coding prohibits an outright breach of orders. I must ask him for something Constantine hasn't thought to forbid him from doing. Sebastian can't *tell* us the harmonic. But he can show us."

The transport skimmed across a wide desolate region, across the river, and out of the safe zone.

Calli moaned. "This is bullskat." She leaned forward, elbows on her knees. Her head hung forward so the tip of her long ponytail curled on the tops of her boots. "I should brig myself for this."

Merrimack circled the sun on one of the Trojan points of the innermost planet.

Gorgons and soldiers could only approach in spheres. A Hive sphere's nominal distortion field protected its members from the sun's irradiation. The sphere's members could not separate out without burning away.

This close to the sun even the spheres had to rotate to maintain a tolerable inner temperature.

Merrimack's Navy gunners took target practice at them. The gorgon sphere's normal defensive tactic of breaking up before incoming beams was self-destruction here. The navvies played games with them.

The ship was as happy as the goat on the roof. It just could not ever leave the roof.

The xenos had started breeding the miniature cows.

Commodore Farragut seized a moment to confront his civilian adviser in his quarters.

Jose Maria de Cordillera had filled his living compartment with a holoimage of wide, wide sunlit fields. He stood, leaning pensively against a partition, but the partition was eclipsed by the holoimage, so that Jose Maria appeared to be leaning on sunlit air when Farragut let himself in.

Uncharacteristically, Jose Maria did not turn to acknowledge the commodore's entrance. So Farragut got right to the point: "Why did you tell my Marine to shoot your wife back there on the planet?"

Jose Maria straightened from his lean, turned. He looked calmer now, sober. The smoldering fury had burned down to sad ash. "Did you notice her ring?"

"The boulder?" said Farragut. A large blue rock of some fourteen karats had glittered on the woman's left hand. "Couldn't miss it."

Jose Maria reached into his breast pocket, withdrew a ring. The stone was a big pear-shaped blue diamond surrounded with little round white diamonds that made it ignite blue fire in the light. "Mercedes left the boulder home. This is the Blue Empress."

He handed the ring to Farragut. The stone dazzled blue before blue eyes, a natural diamond, one of the named stones from Earth itself.

Doctor Mercedes de Cordillera would not have taken such a ring with her to a secret Roman terraforming project in the Deep End. Jose Maria de Cordillera kept his wife's ring over his heart.

"The silver necklace you saw is still in her jewelry box on Terra Rica. Those dress clothes are in the back of her closet. She took khakis and denim and hiking boots and lab shoes with her on her voyage."

Farragut shook his head, suggested, "Constantine could have replicated her favorite things after he rescued *Sulla*."

"Those clothes are not her favorites. And that smile—"

Jose Maria broke off a moment, the anger welling again. He took a breath. "That was her awards ceremony smile. Mercedes did much philanthropic work. She was often invited to recognition dinners, and she could not bear them. She practiced a gracious smile so she would not look too strained accepting awards she did not want. I told her she looked like a plastic Virgin Mary. But people love the Virgin, and the practiced smile recorded well. That was the smile she used in public when she accepted awards.

"That was the smile that *woman* gave me. That was not my smile."

He put out his palm, and Farragut replaced the diamond ring in it.

The palm closed into a fist over Jose Maria's heart.

"That was not my Mercedes."

Commodore Farragut did not attempt to communicate with his Group, for fear of compromising their safety. He could see them on his monitors—see them as they were eight minutes ago.

"Commodore, the Hive has a new trick," said Tactical, and reported a gorgon sphere hiding in the shadow of the innermost planet. Pushing out glue.

"Fry 'em," Farragut ordered.

Merrimack sent a nuclear warhead into the mass of them. The gluies died in one sun's light or the other.

Navvies barked like Bull Mastiffs.

Xenos noted the precise distance from the sun where a disassociated gorgon could rotate itself to maintain a survivable temperature and where turning just made it into a rotisserie, and *Merrimack* parked herself in orbit there.

The ship's insects calmed.

The crew relaxed.

The stay in the sun gave time to continue repairs, to hold a service for mates lost to the gluies, and to figure out how to get back to Planet Zero, which Farragut refused to call Arra.

Farragut received a request from Jose Maria over the com. "Will the young Commodore join me in torpedo rack room six?"

Farragut told him yes. Announced to the command deck, "Mr. Dent has the com and the watch."

He slid down the ladders, barreled through the corridors. Crew moved out of his way. They were accustomed to the commodore in motion, so his speed did not alarm them.

Farragut hoped that Jose Maria had found something useful among Augustus' things.

As he neared the torpedo rack room that had served as Augustus' quarters, he slowed almost to a stop. Strains of a Spanish guitar sounded from inside the hatch. But Jose Maria was waiting outside in the passageway for Farragut. So who was playing the guitar?

A recording, of course, Farragut realized. Impossible hopes did leap.

Still, *Don* Cordillera had the look of a diabolical cat. "Jose Maria?"

"After you, young Commodore." Jose Maria motioned toward the hatch.

The music stopped as Farragut opened the hatch.

Augustus barely had time to say, "Don't touch me," when he was wearing John Farragut.

"Augustus, I never thought I'd be happy to see you!" Thumped him on the back.

"Get off me."

A man who had no use for affection, Augustus did not appreciate the too-enthusiastic welcome back from the dead, like the zealous greeting of a big dog. At least no licking was involved.

"Ha!" Farragut seized his shoulders, pulled back to beam at him, gave him another bear squeeze and whomp on the back before letting go. Stood back marveling with the brightest of Farragut smiles. "How in the hell?"

"Constantine is not the first or last person to arrange his own death," Augustus said.

"You could have told me!"

"I needed you to sell the truth of it. You're a very bad liar."

"I'll work on that. I mourned you, you bastard!"

"And did an outstanding job."

Now that Farragut thought of it, an annoying number of people, upon learning of Augustus' death, had asked: *Are you sure he's dead?*

"Who *does* know?" Farragut asked.

"You and the *don*. You are the only people I trust other than the flattop, and he is too stupid to be useful. *Don* Cordillera is useful because he is smarter than Constantine. You, because you are unpredictable."

"Your voice came from the Striker. It wasn't a remote relay. We checked."

"As did Constantine, I have no doubt. My voice was a recording. I programmed several messages to be triggered by different situations or prompts. I miss my Striker, but it was necessary for it to be destroyed to convince Constantine of my death."

"Where have you *been?*"

"Here." Augustus motioned to the racks of torpedoes behind the Roman tapestries. "Hugging torpedoes."

"Do you know what's been going on? Constantine has managed to load our bases."

"No," said Augustus. "He hasn't."

Not sure of the basis of that flat "No," but Farragut liked the authoritative sound of it.

"Constantine is not as all mighty as he appears," said Augustus. "He's a puff adder."

"How much is puff and how much is real adder?"

"Equal parts venom and vapor. Constantine is a user, not a creator.

"His planet is not Arra. There is only one transplanted trench of Arra down there, and that is the parcel that included the Archon's palace.

"That ship in orbit is not *Sulla*. It's a reproduction shell. The power output is all wrong and it's not even constructed of the same material as *Sulla*.

"There are no *Sulla* survivors here—"

"Mercedes—" Jose Maria blurted.

"Is not here," said Augustus. "You knew that."

"I did." Jose Maria nodded, placed his hand over his heart. Closed his eyes as if praying. "I do. I thought I had let her go." He opened his eyes, resolute. "She is gone."

"There is more agriculture and animal husbandry on board *Merrimack* than there is on the whole of Constantine's planet. The people in his town are not people.

I'm pretty sure that Constantine is the only human being alive in his realm."

"What about Sebastian Gray?" said Farragut.

"That thing?" said Augustus. "That is not Sebastian Gray. That is not a patterner. I don't think that thing is even alive."

28

SEBASTIAN GRAY PILOTED the skimmer over rocky fields of scrub grass that gave way to barren hardpan, then up and over a lush jungle.

At last he brought the skimmer straight down through the jungle trees to land in a tight clearing.

There was a building tucked in the trees. Calli did not see it until the craft was on the ground. A low concrete structure hidden from the air by the jungle canopy.

The skimmer's hatch opened. Moist air rolled in, warm.

Numa unstrapped from his seat and swaggered down the ramp. Jungle calls sounded in the sweet dense air.

His voice carried back into the open hatch of the transport: "Callista, are you waiting to see if I get eaten?"

Calli called out, "I'm waiting for Sebastian to get out before I leave this boat."

Numa's footsteps crunched closer. "What's he doing?"

"Sitting in the pilot's seat," Calli called out. "This is a trap, you idiot."

"Of course it's a trap, you silly American cowgirl. This could be the last foolish thing you ever do."

Numa marched up the ramp, unstrapped the patterner from the pilot's seat, and hauled him bodily down the ramp.

Roman leaders took wild risks. It was expected.

Not the sort of thing someone with Calli's brass was supposed to be doing.

Calli finally climbed out. "I'm not the one who got out of the transport and left the pilot in it."

She followed Numa Pompeii, who kept his hand closed firmly on Sebastian's elbow.

They had not gone more than ten steps toward the hidden building when the skimmer lifted off the ground, ramp still hanging off its side, hatch still open. It ascended above the treetops, and flew away, stranding the three of them in the jungle.

Sebastian gazed straight ahead while Calli and Numa watched the transport go.

"Constantine is big on dead man switches," Calli commented.

All PanGalactic products had bomb dates, fail safes, and dead man switches, rigged so that, in the absence of a controller, something happened.

"Constantine is big on dead men," said Numa.

And the jungle began to shiver, snap, and shred. A tree fell. Winged animals rose screeching above the noise of thrashing foliage, savagely consumed.

"The gorgons will eat the evidence," said Numa. "Constantine will make up any story he wants about our disappearance."

Calli pointed at Gray, "But what about him? How does Constantine's patterner get out of this?"

"Apparently, he is expendable."

"Let's spend him," said Calli.

Numa drew his side arm, shot Gray in the head and the chest.

Gray's eyes, already glazed, did not blink. He didn't die so much as he ceased to function, folded into a cumbersome pile on the ground.

Calli started under the trees toward the shelter of the building.

Numa seized her arm, yanked her back hard. "We are meant to go there." He let go of Calli, tossed Gray over his shoulder like a duffel bag, and broke into a run in the direction back toward the barren zone.

The sound was enormous, everywhere. The jungle become voracious, devouring itself. Animals squealed.

A million thoughts whirled within a single moment of decision. Calli could dash into the shelter or follow Numa.

Sebastian Gray had brought them to the building.

Calli plunged into the jungle after Numa.

She quickly ran into advancing gorgons. They were coming from everywhere. Seemed to be closing in a ring toward the building.

She spied Numa, up ahead, throwing Sebastian's carcass at a mass of gorgons in his way.

The gorgons trampled over Sebastian, showing no interest whatsoever in the carcass. They kept coming at Numa, who dodged wide, big as a defensive back, agile as a punt returner.

Calli saw that once Numa got past the advancing gorgons, the gorgons did not turn around to chase. They kept coming toward the building. Toward her.

"Don't turn back!" Numa shouted from somewhere up ahead in the underbrush.

Calli threaded a path between trees, skirting around gorgons where she could, cutting off their mouths with her knife when she couldn't.

It became clear that Numa was on the right course. Just get around the gorgons, and they lost interest. Meet them head on; they try to eat you.

Calli slashed off giant fronds from the trees, pushed them into the many mouths that reached at her, as she leaped, shoved, crashed through the wide waves that she could not sneak around.

Sunlight gleamed ahead through the thinning jungle.

Scratched, bleeding, breathless, Calli broke into bright sunlight.

Wide-open, featureless hardpan stretched away to the horizon, with nowhere to hide. The thrashing and screaming was all behind her in the murky jungle. A small moving dot ahead, wavering in desert heat, was Numa Pompeii.

Calli ran flat out and kept running.

Calli caught up with Numa in the night. The winds were dead calm, the sky clear. Moonshadows edged heavy Numa Pompeii's heavy footprints into clarity.

She came upon him where he rested, miles from the gorgon-choked jungle they had escaped.

She dropped to sit by him. Lungs burned. Throat stung. "I would have headed into that death trap building."

"Is that a thank you, Callista?"

"No. You knew that Sebastian Gray's offer to bring you out here was a Trojan Horse." And she yelled at him, "*Why are we out here!*"

"The thing with Trojan Horses is to be ready to beat the hell out of whatever comes out of the Horse."

"What would be the point of luring you out here?"

"To kill me, of course."

"Constantine? He can kill all of us at any time."

"Just me. Without alienating my men. Constantine wants followers, not rival leaders. Constantine means to be Caesar. And he knows that will only happen over my dead body." He squinted at her in the moonlight. "Callista, what have you got there?"

Calli had brought with her, miles into the hardpan, a very large pulpy green leaf.

"It's my frond," she said, and lay down for a few minutes with the big leaf over her like a blanket.

The sun was rising. Numa stood up.

Calli pointed ahead, "That way?"

"That way is the palace and field camp. But that way," Numa pointed off to the left, "is the shortest route to the river. How thirsty are you?"

"River," Calli pointed her frond left.

Numa nodded. "River."

They set out toward the river, the rhino and the gazelle, Calli carrying her frond over her head like a parasol.

* * *

Eight bells sounded on *Merrimack's* third day in the sun. Navvies had slept soundly without expecting an alarm.

Farragut considered sending a resonant message to the JC. But that might upset a balance. He sent a courier missile instead, wondering if it would make it out of the star system, then turned to his patterner.

"Augustus, can you calculate how many gorgons I can pack onto *Mack*'s shell without losing the helm?"

Kerry at the pond's edge, listened to the trees wheeze, and watched adolescent wartrays pumping up their warts.

"Which one is yours?" Carly asked, joining her at the bank.

"I can't tell."

"What kind of mother are you?"

Kerry lifted her shoulders, let them drop with a sigh. "They grow up so fast."

Darb came up alongside Kerry. Watched the wart creatures. "How long can we live like this?"

Kerry shaded her eyes at the sun, as if she could really see *Merrimack*.

Captain Carmel was MIA. Carmel's XO had heard nothing since Carmel left the perimeter. The Dracs had found her com out in a field on the other side of the new town.

The Dracs also reported that all those black rock formations out there in the scrub grass were piles of dormant gorgons and can openers.

Tandem shouts sounded through the camp:

"Incoming!"

And *"Hold your fire. Do not fire!"*

A fireball in the sky, roaring down, flaming pieces of it flying off, till the fireball became a flaming spearhead.

"That's *Merrimack*!"

Gorgons in burning shreds peeled off the fiery shape. *Merrimack* in a blaze thundered over Constantine's palace, shook the ground, and cracked pieces of the mural off the throne room ceiling.

Got Constantine's attention.

Farragut hailed Constantine, "Could use some assistance here, sir."

Constantine's voice rumbled and quaked: "How *dare* you!"

"I'm just tryin' to get these burrs off my hide. Why'd you let them come after me?"

"You betrayed me!"

"How did I do that, sir?"

"You resonated! You were told not to, and you defied me!"

"No, sir. And no, sir. I did not. Caesar Romulus resonated *me*. Gorgons home in on a receiver same as they home on a sender. Caesar didn't get the order not to resonate and he doesn't much obey me either."

"Caesar? Caesar! Go aloft and see what I can do that your *Caesar* cannot!" Constantine declared.

Merrimack ascended out of the atmosphere. Before the gorgons could close back in on her, limpets attached themselves to the ship's distortion field, and the Hive lost interest again. The ship's protection had been reinstated.

"Well played, sir," said Gypsy when the com was off.

Farragut made a motion of casting out a fishing line and reeling it in. "Not my favorite sport."

And it nearly strangled him to signal Constantine, "Thank you, sir." Shut the com off. Leaned over the arm of his chair and spat on the deck.

"Must you, sir?"

"Ass kissing," said Farragut. "Leaves a taste."

"Commodore" McDaniel hailed *Merrimack*. "Where you been, old son?"

"Hell, Dallas. Just went for a walkabout. Anything happen while we were gone?"

A hesitation. "Red Rover."

"Come on over, compadre."

Dallas took a skiff over to *Merrimack*. Boarded gingerly, expecting the deck to come up and hit him.

Dallas McDaniels brought a recording. Taken from the Marines' listening array on the planet. "I didn't want this out there for anyone to pick up."

One: So you are here after all. Are you here to serve me or to serve me to my enemies?

Two: Before I cross that Rubicon, you must make me a promise.

One: What am I to promise you?

Two: The pretender Romulus' head. Detached from the rest of Romulus.

One: You needn't have insisted. I already intend to do that when I am Caesar.

Two: If he lives, I am destroyed. There's not a corner in the Empire I could go. Your word. Give me your word as Caesar.

One: You have it.

Two: Then you have me.

Farragut started with the obvious question, "Who was outside the perimeter when this recording was taken?"

"Captain Carmel."

"Oh, Cal." Farragut put a hand to his face like a cage.

Gypsy bridled. "Sir, you *don't* suspect—"

"No, I do not," Farragut groaned. "She has a talent—no, it's a gift. Cal has a *gift* for getting herself into compromising positions."

"She does that, sir," Gypsy agreed.

"How long has she been missing?"

"Three days."

"Not good."

Had they not been told: Constantine clears off most of the board before he moves in for checkmate.

Farragut trusted Cal could get herself out of whatever she had got herself into this time. Though historically, that had not always been the case.

"Numa Pompeii is also missing," said Dallas.

"What of the recording?" Gypsy said. "Where's the merc?"

"Amadea is not on the planet," said Farragut.

"Neither, supposedly, is Numa Pompeii. Maybe that's Numa talking?"

Farragut nodded at the recording. "Honestly, I don't think that's anyone. I think Constantine wants us to suspect our own. He wouldn't let us pick up anything he didn't want us to hear." He withdrew the recording bubble from the player, gave it back to Dallas.

"The idea of the Attack Group was so we could support each other. It's not serving this scenario. In this situation it just gives Constantine more hostages. Just as soon as the gorgons and the can openers settle back down and clump back together into their spheres, Dallas, I want you to take *Rio* and the LEN ships and take a walk. Get out of this star system.

"I'm going downstairs to give Constantine something else to look at. Commander Dent, announce me to the Self."

Farragut arrived in camp by shuttle. He summoned TR Steele inside. Told him not to be alarmed if *Wolfhound* or *Horatius* noticed *Rio Grande, Windward Isles,* and *Sunlit Meadows* missing from orbit. "Don't announce it. Just keep it quiet."

Then he left camp, alone, from the Roman side, over the bridge and into the town, through all the forbidden fruits Constantine laid out before his men.

The Marines objected loudly after he was underway. The commodore needed a guard, they said.

Steele barked all of them to attention. "*You want something to do!*" he roared at them.

They didn't. Expected a drill now. They had been drilling evacuation ever since *Horatius* and *Wolfhound* set down.

Instead, Steele picked up a soccer ball and started toward the Roman side of camp. "Fall in!"

The Marines followed the colonel over to the Roman side. Herius Asinius came out to meet the approaching front. His Dracs fell in behind him.

Steele threw the ball, hard, at Herius Asinius, who caught it.

"Put up or shut up," said Steele. "Lupes versus dogs."

Herius Asinius spun the ball on his fingertip. "You are on, Colonel Steele."

Constantine made Commodore Farragut pace a smooth spot into his gemstone floor, waiting. When at last Constantine deigned to appear, he said, "You have come to thank me for sparing your ship yet again." He had arrayed himself in a toga of gold cloth over a tunic of brilliant red this time, but wore the same atrocious golden gauntlets encrusted with gemstones and blinking lights. The wreath on his head was golden oak.

"I have come to demand you stop trying to seduce my men," said Farragut. "I want that amusement park removed from my camp."

"You are accusing me of seduction? If you cannot control your men, that indicates a want of leadership, does it not?"

"I am controlling them," Farragut fired back. "Remove the toys."

"This is my world," said Constantine. "Not yours. You came here. I did not summon you."

"You displaced gorgons to Thaleia!"

"Also my world," said Constantine.

And with a sudden suspicion, Farragut threw out a guess, "And to Telecore!" Telecore, the Deep End planet secretly terraformed by Rome and devoured by the Hive.

"Also my world," said Constantine.

Farragut could not interpret the answer. Had Constantine really sent the gorgons to Telecore? Puff? Or adder. "Telecore wasn't yours."

"It was in my territory. You exist in my domain with my permission. With me, you are safe. Without me—"

Constantine's head jerked back, a red spot suddenly there in the middle of his forehead.

Constantine blinked. Touched the red. Not blood and not from a hole.

Paintball.

Constantine's gaze locked beyond Farragut. He rose from his throne, volcanic. "*Amadea!*"

A second crack appeared in Constantine's almighty calm. This one a roaring fissure. To the automatons in the chamber, he thundered, "Get her!"

The automatons moved with inhuman speed, but by the time Farragut turned, the tiger had vanished.

Constantine growled at Farragut, "You will hand over the white tiger."

"It's not my world," said Farragut. "And she's not my tiger. She belongs to Caesar."

Caesar, and not meaning Constantine.

Farragut turned and strode out, braced for a shot in the back, but he made it outside to the light.

He jogged down the wide steps from the terrace.

Did not want to return to the camp too quickly. He took the route through town.

The automaton guards were darting about like Keystone Kops. The white tiger had got away. But that was what she was good at.

In his brooding walk through the town, he became aware that he had picked up a shadow.

He halted suddenly. Spoke without looking round, "I hate to say this to a merc, but: good job, gal."

He swore he could hear a smile.

Not sure who threw the first punch—because it was probably really a kick. This *was* soccer, after all. And it was probably Kerry Blue. At Kerry's size, down, dirty, and first was the only way to survive.

It was supposed to be a soccer game, Marines versus Dracs, but when the shouting started, well, Kerry Blue don't shout at big guys. Took one down curled round his family jewels. And now it was an almighty brawl.

The game was gonna be no decision, but the U.S. of A. was gonna win the fight. Do you Romans understand *semper fi*?

Silence descended in a wave. Shouts and thudding fists damped down till there was only one voice shouting.

The Voice of God.

Oh, hell, Commodore Farragut had returned from Constantine's palace. He was back in camp calling down holy Jesus

Marines and Dracs scrabbled up from the dirt. You never saw a bunch of U.S. Marines and Roman legionaries try to look so small.

Farragut prowled the settling dust. Lightning bolts flashing from his blue eyes.

"WHAT IS THIS?"

"Soccer game, sir," someone said. Had to be an American, because the Romans called it football.

Everyone stood at rigid attention. Stomachs drawn way in—expecting to be gutted. Eyes a thousand yards away. Don't make eye contact or you'll burn to a cinder.

The Archangel Farragut stalked the forest of them. Closed on the COs—Colonel Steele and the legate Herius Asinius—neither of whom had dirty knees or bloody knuckles.

"I take responsibility, sir," Steele began. Got cut off.

"No, you won't, Colonel Steele. Shut up."

Never heard the commodore call Steele anything but TR. He was mad as hell.

And then, glory hallelujah, the wrath of God fell on the Roman, Herius Asinius.

Raked him up and down and reamed him through the middle, screaming. Struck Herius Asinius dumb. "I should have expected this, Hairy Ass Asinine-us!"

Kerry Blue gasped so hard she thought she'd inhaled her teeth.

Farragut suddenly stopped in mid-roar. His gaze caught on Constantine's spy monitors outside the perimeter.

Farragut drew his side arm, stalked outside the bead, and blasted the monitors more times than were needed to make sure they were dead, dead, dead.

As soon as he'd gone outside the perimeter, Marines had jumped to make sure he could pass back in. In he came, holstering his side arm, thank God, but still roaring at the legate, this time for allowing Constantine to set up monitors outside the camp.

"With respect," Herius had reached his limit. "Perimeter security is U.S. reponsibil—"

Farragut had lifted a forefinger. Stopped Herius' voice in mid-word as if there were lasers jetting from that finger.

Farragut's eyes shifted, seemed to become aware of all the stupefied Marines and legionaries.

He rasped to Herius Asinius, "Come with me." He stalked to his shuttle, the Roman legate following stiffly. The shuttle hatch banged shut like the door to the woodshed.

Colonel Steele commanded everyone back to duty.

The crowds broke up in muted obedience. Resentment emanating from the Romans, worse than in wartime.

29

THE RIVER FLOWED wide, lazy, and clear, showing the color of its rock bed. Calli knelt at the bank to drink. Reared back on her heels. "Fish!"

"You intend to catch one?" said Numa, snide.

"They mean the Hive isn't here! We must be inside the protected zone." She took off her boots and her jumpsuit. Numa blatantly stared at her.

She knotted her jumpsuit and inflated it into makeshift water wings. She waded out to deep water, floated with the current.

The river ran right between Constantine's new town and the camp. The current would carry her there.

In moments, Numa bobbed up beside her, like an elephant seal. Floated on his back, head first. Stayed near Calli so he would not need to look where he was going.

A distance down the river, a cloud of insects blew into them. Numa submerged. When he came up for air, he shouted at Calli, "What the hell are you doing?"

Calli was grabbing at the air, catching insects, popping them into her mouth. She answered with her mouth full, "Eating!"

Numa regarded her like an odd lab experiment. "Do you even know what those are?"

"They're seventeen-year locusts."

"Are you sure?"

"My funeral, right?" She gave him a smile with a bug wing stuck between her teeth.

She was sure. John Farragut had once regaled her with several locust recipes from back home in Kentucky. Any of those now sounded better than live bugs, but Calli carried very little in the way of a fat reserve. She was shivering most of it away in the river. And when she stopped shivering, she would know she had hypothermia. "I don't know where my next meal is coming from."

"I'll skip this one, thank you."

"Not like you couldn't afford to miss a meal or twelve."

Then, after awhile, Numa said, "Damned noisy, your lunch."

"Locusts are always like that. Even without the Hive around."

All insects perceived Hive proximity. Most of a locust's abdomen was a drum, with the drumhead just behind the base of the wings. The internal structures of the males vibrated the drum to make the distinctive noise.

"Why would Constantine bring locusts to his world?" Numa growled.

"Accident," said Calli between bugs, as if it were obvious.

"Twice?" said Numa, pulling a powerful sidestroke.

Calli stopped bug-catching to stare at him.

Numa said, "Herius Asinius told me there were locusts on Thaleia."

Calli frowned. "I heard the same thing from the Marines."

Why would Constantine make the same mistake twice? Unless he wanted locusts here.

Come evening, Herius Asinius left the perimeter without notifying anyone or asking anyone's permission, soccer ball under his arm. He crossed the bridge over the river, strode into the forbidden town to the forbidden soccer stadium and turned on the lights.

Kicked the hell out of the soccer ball.

After a time, a hologram flickered onto a team bench.

Constantine might have chosen to look realistic, but he chose to appear like a glowing apparition, with a nimbus around his shining form. The voice sounded like it was coming from the apparition: "He had no right."

Herius Asinius snorted. Said in a surly tone, "You saw that?" Gave the ball a hard boot. Farragut had humiliated him in front of everyone. Apparently not just his own camp.

"This is my world. I see everything. I can help you."

Herius glowered at the apparition from under wilted dark locks, his face shining with sweat. "Go plant those lips on someone else's butt." He jogged away to collect his ball and kick it downfield.

The voice followed him, a disembodied spirit. "I don't understand why yours are still attached to that swaggering Yank."

Herius picked up the ball, stalked back to the bench. "I only take orders because—" He didn't really have an end to that sentence. He put the ball through the hologram.

"You don't need to put on a show for the U.S. spy arrays," the hologram spoke. "They cannot detect us here."

Herius shouted at the image. "I know what you're trying to do. You are so obvious! So get this clear: I am not a traitor."

"And Commodore Farragut is not Caesar."

Herius went silent. Stood like a nervous stallion, nostrils flaring. Lips twitched. Had he been a stallion, his ears would be intently forward.

"He is not even Roman," said the image of Constantine.

Herius mumbled something unintelligible, shut his mouth again.

"Would you like to deliver *Merrimack* intact to Rome? Haul it under racked spears to Palatine?"

An inadvertent sound like a moan of hunger escaped Herius. He said nothing. His gaze stayed fastened on the image of Constantine—looking at him from the corners of his eyes, as if he wanted to rip himself away, but he was stuck.

"You came out here to save Rome from the Hive. If you can do that without helping your conquerors, well. You needn't answer me now. Think on it."

Constantine blurred to a glow that brightened, too bright to look at. Rose like a star into the darkening sky.

Steele sent a shuttle up from the surface in the middle of the camp night. He signaled *Merrimack*. Told Hamster to wake up Commodore Farragut and have him personally meet the shuttle. "Tell Commodore Farragut these are authentic."

Farragut woke up like a struck match. Got to the dock before the shuttle arrived.

The hatch opened to Captain Calli Carmel and General Numa Pompeii, wet, but no longer dripping. They had left puddles under the grates on the shuttle deck. The skin of their hands was puckered, as if someone had scrubbed a deck with them. Calli shivered, her lips blue; Numa was sunburned to blisters.

The perimeter guards who had tested them as authentic accompanied them from the shuttle.

Farragut said, "Where's the cat that dragged y'all in?" He quickly got his jacket off and settled it round Calli.

"We're dead, sir."

"Looks like," said Farragut. Got on the com and summoned Doctor Mo Shah to the dock.

Calli held the warmth of the jacket round her. "I'm keeping this this time."

Numa's eyes shifted from Farragut to Farragut's jacket and back. "Marking your territory, Commodore?"

"There are worse ways," said Farragut.

Calli's brows flew up. She didn't add a word to that exchange.

"Where have y'all been?"

Calli answered, teeth chattering audibly, "Numa

thought the best way to find the nature of a trap was to step in it."

"And you, Cal?"

"Oh, me? I'm an idiot."

There was an *um-hm*, from Numa.

"Didn't say you weren't," said Calli. "That was not Sebastian Gray. Not even a piece of him. There was not an edible part of his body. Sebastian lured Numa out. I wanted to see who Numa was meeting. And I got caught in the same snare."

"We did not get caught. We are here. Reporting back to the commodore," Numa told her, then told Farragut, "We're dead. I thought it might be helpful to let Constantine go on thinking so."

"Popular tactic these days," said Farragut. "And not that I don't admire independent action and initiative, but cutting our people off from their leadership in the face of an intimidating power just ain't the course of action I would ever approve."

"Calculated risk," said Numa.

"Error in judgment," said Calli.

"Cal, your pocket is whirring."

"Oh." Calli fished in her pocket. Brought out locusts. "I—we—were thinking these might have helped Constantine get the Hive harmonic. He brought them to Thaleia by accident. Then he brought them here. They have a drum behind their heads. Maybe it could be acting as a res chamber."

Farragut nodded to a guard to collect Calli's bugs from her shaking hands. "Take those to the xenos. See what they can detect. Have Augustus look at the data."

Numa's head turned whiplash quick.

Augustus was alive.

Farragut ordered Calli and Numa, "Get cleaned up, patched up, ready for action. We are about to get hairy."

His com sounded an emergency buzz. "But not this soon," he said, concerned, and took the hail. "Talk to me."

Gypsy on the command deck advised, "I have Captain McDaniels for you. Patching through."

Farragut felt a thickness in his throat. *Rio Grande* was supposed to escape. Something had gone wrong. Farragut yelled into the com, "Dallas! You still here?"

"Not for long, old son. We got through the thick of it, passed the last planet, thought we were clear, and got mugged. We've got gluies."

Farragut's throat closed up.

"Power's gonna quit any second. John, old son, look in on Joleen and my boys if you get the time."

"That's a promise, compadre."

"And Meadow Mouse and Sunny Thing won't leave us, so you might better look in on Captain Fred's and Ram's folks too."

All three of them. They were the ones who were meant to get away.

Tried to maintain a strong voice, "I sure will."

"*Vaya con Dios,* pardner."

"See you on the other side."

Didn't know if Dallas heard him. An empty quiet answered back.

PART FOUR

The Corindahlor Bridge

30

WHEN AT LAST CONSTANTINE deigned to respond to the hail, Farragut demanded: *"Help them!"*

The pause that followed was long. Very long.

The answer was spoken slowly, "Commodore Farragut. What exactly would you have me do?" Almost sounded as if he didn't know what Farragut was talking about. But of course he did.

Urgently, frustration bleeding, not too proud to beg, Farragut said, *"Rio Grande, Sunlit Meadows,* and *Windward Isles*! Give them their protection back!"

The following pause was even longer. Finally: "Just what did they think they were about?"

Farragut's eyes crushed shut. *Rio* had gluies, for the love of God. "I'll order them to come back. Just put the protection back on."

"Why?"

Why? What could he say to this monster? "Please."

The god liked pleading from the powerful.

But Constantine answered, "No. I *choose* not to. You must realize I do not brook defiance. Your ships got what you asked for. You cannot change your mind now."

The link severed.

In the silence, Farragut imagined he could hear the gluies chewing on *Rio*'s hull. The screams of the dying.

*   *   *

Kerry Blue on sentry duty. Walked the bead on the U.S. side of the camp with Cain Salvador under the noon sun.

They had been told to stay alert, as if trouble were on the horizon, but no one would give any clue of what exactly they were supposed to be watching for.

The systems monitor called in a perimeter breach, Three hundred yards to the east along the bead. That was Roman country.

"Don't Rome got its own sentries?" said Blue to Cain. She returned systems' call: "Inbound or outbound?"

"Unknown."

"Great."

Cain had his field lenses on. "I got him. Outbound. We got ourselves a Roman walker."

"Yeah, I feel like a walk," said Kerry, starting out after the figure.

"Don't get close, Blue. Do not engage."

"I know. I know. I just want to see if that's who it looks like. And where the hell he thinks he's going."

"Blue!"

"What!"

"Last time anyone saw Captain Carmel, she was following a Roman to see where he was going."

"Yes, Mom."

She gave the walker a wide lead. He never looked around or back. Apparently didn't give a squid's butt who might be watching him. Kerry had a hard time believing this sortie could be authorized.

Constantine's town grew larger and spread closer to the camp every hour. Looked even bigger from inside it. Looked like places you saw in travelogues. It was hard not to gawk, but Kerry kept her attention on the Roman—who wasn't really that hard on the eyes—strong shoulders and a hard sculpted ass that was poetry in motion.

The forest of buildings ended abruptly. Kerry stopped right there. The back side of Constantine's palace was just across another bridge back across the river. It led off to the tree-lined approach to the back steps of Constantine's palace.

The Roman started up the palace steps. Kerry saw the SPQR brand on his arm flash in the sunlight.

Kerry withdrew into shadow. "Alpha Three. This is Alpha Six."

Cain's voice returned: "What'd you get, Blue?"

"I am looking at Hairy Ass Asininus walking up the steps to Constantine's palace."

"Get back here, Kerry!"

"On my way."

She turned around, back through the city. Thought for a moment she had taken a wrong turn because nothing looked familiar.

Looked up at a building, taller than most of the others.

A figure stood outside, on the balcony, gazing in the direction Kerry thought the camp lay.

She knew him.

Had known him well. Tried to call his name, but her voice failed her.

Cowboy.

Android guards flanking the approach to the palace let Herius Asinius pass. He was not terribly surprised to find Constantine on the terrace. Expecting him.

The tunic was saffron yellow. The toga brilliant red. The crown was gilt laurel. The overwrought gauntlets were blinking.

"Ave," said Herius Asinius.

"What do your masters think of this visit?" Constantine greeted him, also in Latin.

"I don't care what the Americans think."

"I knew you would come."

"Don't think you know me," said Herius, sullen.

"I do know you."

From the direction of the camp, sirens wound up, blared.

Herius spun round in a defensive crouch.

Constantine looked in the direction of the sound. "What is the alarm for?"

"That means the camp is under attack," said Herius, on edge. "Are you attacking my men?"

"Not I," said Constantine. Puzzled, curious, but not concerned. "Perhaps your crazed American commodore has launched an attack on your Legion."

"The sirens are American," said Herius dryly.

The com on Herius Asinius' hand was blinking a silent demand for attention. He ignored it.

Constantine's eyes flickered toward the blinks. Ordered Herius, suspicious, "Answer that."

Herius lifted his hand. Snarled into the com, *"What?"*

"Domni! Where are you! We have been ordered aloft. We have gorgons inside the perimeter!"

Herius Asinius turned on Constantine with a look of betrayal. "Why?"

"There are no gorgons in your camp," said Constantine, condescending.

A roaring of engines sounded from the direction of the camp. Clouds of rising dust billowed over the hillock that blocked the view.

Constantine snapped to Herius, "I don't care what the American is doing. Order your ship and your men to stay."

"Not if you're attacking them!" Herius cried, starting down the steps.

"You shall stop!"

Herius froze.

Impatient, annoyed, Constantine said, "Come with me."

Automatons had moved to block the base of the stairs.

Herius turned on the steps, glaring up, fear, anger in his dark eyes.

"Come, come, come," Constantine beckoned him up, with the attitude that all this pother was trivial and Herius was upset over nothing.

Contantine mounted a narrower set of white stairs up to the roof of the palace, from where they would be able to see the camp. As he climbed, Constantine activated his own com and demanded to speak to Commodore Farragut.

A terse answer sounded from his com: "Farragut."

Constantine said, "Remember what happened to your other three ships that tried to run."

"*Wolfhound* and *Horatius* were *not* trying to run! They were sitting where you invited them! And you set your gorgons loose on them anyway! Why wouldn't they run now!"

Constantine opened his mouth to object. Shut off the com. His authority slipped. He seemed confused.

From the direction of the U.S./Roman camp, a Roman legionary came running, sprinted through the automatons, and up the palace steps to the terrace. He wore a German-made displacement collar and carried a second one along with a landing disk.

He hastily searched about the terrace. Glanced up. Spied Herius Asinius and Constantine on the steps to the roof. And ran up, taking the narrow steps by twos and threes.

"*Domni!* We need to go. I brought these in case the gorgons cut off the way back." He presented the second collar and the landing disk to Herius Asinius.

Herius took the collar from the messenger. Put it on. Then reached to the runner's neck and took the other collar, too.

The runner blanched. "But that one is for m—" Stopped himself. Hand to his neck. Looked like a naked slave thrown to the lions.

"Get out of here," said Herius.

The man flew down the steps.

Herius offered the second collar to Constantine. "If you want."

Constantine declined. "Those will not work here." He continued up the steps to the roof.

"If you will not drop the jammers to let me out, then I would rather displace into oblivion than be eaten by gorgons."

"The gorgons are contained," Constantine snapped peevishly.

Constantine reached the rooftop. Turned toward the encampment.

The serenity fell off his face.

Herius Asinius arrived at the top. Followed Constantine's stare.

The U.S./Roman camp was overrun with gorgons.

Kerry Blue heard the sirens. Took the call on her com. It was Cain: "Kerry! Haul your pretty ass back here! We have gorgons!"

"I'm coming! I'm coming!"

Then she shouted up to the balcony. "Cowboy!"

Cowboy abruptly withdrew from the balcony without answering.

Kerry ran inside the building to meet him at the bottom of the stairs—only to catch sight of him—wayward prick that he had always been—bailing out a back window.

"Cowboy, you ass! We have to scramble! The gorgons are loose. You don't want to stay here!"

Alive. Cowboy was alive. Just like Sebastian Gray and *Sulla*.

But what had Constantine done to Cowboy that Cowboy didn't know her?

Cowboy, that lying, cheating married bastard had probably laid every woman survivor of *Sulla*. Didn't matter right now. Marines don't leave their own behind. Kerry ran out the back door. "Cowboy!"

Other people in the street were acting weirdly normal. Oblivious to the sirens, or to Kerry Blue shouting and chasing Cowboy.

Kerry heard the *Wolfhound* and *Horatius* power up. They had been practicing evac since they first set down. They could all be gone in four minutes.

"Frag it to hell, Cowboy, we're dusting off!"

Cowboy went into the casino.

"Oh, for—!" Kerry stumbled over her own words. Tempted to just leave the bastard here. Then thought: Had Constantine made Cowboy immune to gorgons? If that was true, then she really had to get him back to *Merrimack*. Kerry ran into the casino.

The doorman, who seemed deaf to the sirens, asked her if she felt lucky.

And for all the lights and bells and merry little machine tunes in the key of G, no one seemed to be talking to each other in the casino, though they were drinking a lot and winning a lot.

She picked out Cowboy from among the gamblers. Saw him slipping through a door.

Kerry heaved out a growling snarl. The man wasn't worth it. Had never been worth it.

She charged through the door. Expected to see him with a *linda* back here. But Cowboy was alone in a back room.

"Cowboy, you dick! Do you have the gorgon harmonic?"

He looked at her strangely. The face was Cowboy's. The way the face moved was not.

"You are not Colonel Steele."

Two dozen smart retorts came to mind before reality set in. Kerry Blue felt cold. "And you're not—"

Oh, Kerry Blue, don't ever tell the android imposter you have smoked his cover. Never been accused of being a brain, but this was a depth of dumb she did not know was in her.

She started to back away slowly.

Cowboy's face did not change expression. Quicker than a gorgon, he had her side arm in his hand, aimed at her. Pulled the trigger.

No one had programmed him to know that U.S. weapons were coded to their bearers. The side arm did not fire for him.

Kerry spun for the door, felt herself wrenched short, her left hand caught in a crushing grip. She heard/felt the snap. That was her com crushing under the android thumb. Her sweaty palm slipped from Cowboy's grip, and Kerry Blue was out the door. Slammed it and dashed through the casino.

She yelled into her com, but got no reply.

Burst out to the street at a dead run. The doorman told her better luck next time.

Heard the Cowboy thing coming after her. Faster than human.

Kerry Blue ran for her life, hard as she had ever run. Even knowing that no human could ever outrun a well built android.

"Do not do this," Herius Asinius pleaded. "Make your monsters stop."

Constantine did not seem to hear him. Drifted to the railing, jerkily, in a disbelieving kind of stagger. Staring at the gorgons invading the camp. His lips parted in amazement, denial.

Tentacles snapped. Black bodies rolled, spidered in their blundering, ravenous advance.

Gorgons within the safe zone.

"You must have resonated," Constantine accused. "I told you not to resonate."

"Then it had to be the Americans," said Herius. "Not us!"

The Roman ship *Horatius* lifted from the ground.

Constantine pulled back his broad sleeve, glanced fretfully at the lights on his jeweled gauntlet, then back at the gorgons, entirely at a loss.

Herius gestured with the runner's displacement collar. "If you can't stop them, can you drop the signal jammers? I can have us displaced to my ship."

Constantine shook his head, eyes fixed on the gorgons.

Gorgons tumbled into the pond inside the U.S. camp. Mouthed tentacles snapped at the wartrays and ravaged the breathing trees.

A slow acidic smile spread across Constantine's lips. His shoulders moved with a couple of spasms of suppressed laughter. A malevolent knowing.

Herius Asinius did not know what exactly it was that Constantine saw, but he knew what the smile meant.

Constantine had recognized the gorgons as programmed fakes. And Herius Asinius could forget about living out this day.

Herius made a quick grab for Constantine's gauntlet, got hold of it, and gave a mighty yank.

The gauntlet pulled loose from Constantine's forearm.

As it came free, the glowing lights went instantly dark.

Constantine breathed deep with wrath, spoke with measured, feline patience, "Herius Asinius, do you know what a dead man switch is?"

Constantine was big on dead man switches.

And there was an instant change in the ambient sounds. The sound of a million mouths rose from all around. Birds took to the air, screaming. The forests moved. Black rock formations in the fields uncurled and sprouted legs.

"This is what a real perimeter failure sounds like," said Constantine Siculus.

Like crashing blades of a gargantuan harvester.

"And soon you will see what real gorgons do."

Kerry Blue ran. Air raked her throat. Pulse thundered in her ears. Eyes stung, watered. Footsteps thudded right behind her.

She tripped. Went sailing forward. Grit gouged her palm heels. First chest, then knees hit the ground.

She writhed over onto her back, with her legs cocked. Kerry Blue was going to go out kicking.

31

KERRY BLUE BLINKED grit and tears from her eyes. No Cowboy loomed over her to kick. She scrambled to her feet. Tried to stop bleating. Turned a three sixty.

The people in the town had all stopped moving. The street was creepy and still.

There was Cowboy, back a few steps, stopped and fallen over like a plastic doll.

Anyone who was not a real human being had stopped. And that was everyone but Kerry Blue.

She laughed a little. Cursed a little.

Tried to brush the grit out of her bleeding palms.

Noises beyond the town were horribly familiar. Sounded like Thaleia used to sound. Like gorgons. Lots of gorgons, eating.

Wolfhound rose above the rooftops into the sky off to her left.

Then a squadron of Swifts shot into the air.

Then another squadron.

"No!" *Oh, no. Oh, God.*

Kerry ran in the direction of the launching spaceships.

Ran to where the damned river and a damned sheer terrace on the other side of the damned river blocked her damned way.

She had to backtrack to get to the bridge.

Another squadron of Swifts streaked overhead.

Kerry Blue screamed.

Told herself Colonel Steele would have left a Swift for her. Alpha Six would be waiting for her where she landed it.

She zigzagged through the town's labyrinthine streets, growing more and more frantic.

Glimpsed it between buildings—the bridge.

She charged across the river.

Ran to the empty camp, over wide patches of flattened grass where the big ships used to sit. She couldn't see for the breathing trees, but she knew there must be a Swift waiting for her on the far side of the pond.

She ran harder, while a mass of gorgons closed in on the pond from the fields behind the abandoned camp.

On the palace rooftop, Constantine put out a demanding palm to Herius Asinius for his gauntlet. "Now give it back."

"You mean without it, you will die?" said Herius Asinius. The gauntlet was Constantine's control panel. The controls were inoperative at the moment, but Herius Asinius knew what he had.

"No. *You* will die. Give it back." The palm waited.

Herius backed several paces away from Constantine on the flat white rooftop.

Constantine snapped his fingers at his guards, enormously annoyed. "Retrieve the gauntlet."

Dead man switches did not apply to Constantine's bodyguard. The guards responded with the empty precision of androids.

Before the androids could get up the steps, Herius clamped one of the displacement collars on the gauntlet and sent it.

The gauntlet/control panel vanished. A thunderclap of air closed on the instant vacuum in its wake.

With only one displacement signal and Constantine's jammers still active, the gauntlet's scattered pieces would arrive irretrievably nowhere.

Herius Asinius said, "Hail, Caesar."

Constantine's breathing heaved up to a roar. "You *idiot!*"

The android guards had halted, finding their orders now impossible to execute.

Constantine ordered, "Get that man!"

Herius tried to run. The androids caught him immediately. Herius was a brawny man, but the machines were heavy and implacable.

"Kill him," Constantine ordered. Then, immediately, "No! *Don't* kill him!"

The androids paused over the conflicting orders. The latest took precedence. The androids kept their grip on Herius, hard.

"Hold him here," said Constantine, gathering up his billowing red robes. "Hold him here until he is eaten!" And to Herius Asinius and anyone monitoring him he pronounced: *"Sic semper malefidelibus!"*

Merrimack's com tech received a hail from Herius Asinius on the surface. Farragut jumped on the com: "Heri! Talk to me, son."

Herius spoke fast. "Constantine smoked us. I'm dead in another hundred ticks. Constantine's control panel was in his left gauntlet. I had to destroy it. But he must have another control center. If you can track him to wherever he is going right now, that should show you the location of his backup controls. Here they come."

Gorgons. He meant gorgons.

Farragut lifted his face, met Gypsy's gaze. "Get a loc on the source of this transmission and *hook him*. Track Constantine."

Targeting worked for a fix on Herius Asinius' com transmission. Gorgons, real ones, had eaten past the fake gorgons and were closing on Herius' position on the palace rooftop.

"Targeting, talk to me."

Targeting was sweating. "Commodore, I think I'm running into Constantine's jammers. His jammers are still operational. I can't get an accurate solution on Herius Asinius."

"Get a messy one. I don't care if you take the whole palace, just get a hook on him!"

The hook was an extension of the ship's force field. It would encase Herius in the ship's defenses.

"Aye, sir," said Targeting. "Ready hook."

"Deploy hook."

"Hook away." Then. "No good. Negative hook. Negative hook."

The hook bounced off a ceiling field which Constantine maintained over the palace.

"God bless America! Fire on the gorgons approaching the palace!"

"Acquire gorgons," Gypsy ordered Targeting.

"Not happening, sir."

Farragut ordered: "Take your best guess and fire."

"Firing, aye."

Beams rained down on the palace grounds. Deflected uselessly off of Constantine's overhead defenses.

Gorgons, well below Constantine's skyward shields, had reached the palace steps.

Herius Asinius' voice came again over the com: "Thank you for that. Get Constantine. It has been an honor, sir."

Farragut kept the com open. Listened to his screams at the end, because he could not leave him to die alone. When nothing sounded over the com but crunching, he turned the com off, his face wet.

He inhaled an angry sniff. "Do we have a loc on that royal bastard?"

"I have a visual." Tactical threw the image of Constantine onto the main screen. The command staff saw Constantine walking—strolling—across his compound. Gorgons moved toward him, but Constantine's mouth moved, speaking orders to his android attendants, and instantly the gorgons lost interest in Constantine, to swarm instead on the inedible androids with a special fury.

Numa Pompeii had come to *Merrimack*'s command deck. Watched the screens. "Apologies, Commodore Farragut, we have seen this behavior before."

"We have," said Farragut. "We sure have."

The androids were resonating the irresistible harmonic. Had to be.

On the monitors, Constantine strolled, fearless. Pointing to his attendants, who sacrificed themselves to the Hive, suicidally resonating.

Numa said, "Augustus discovered that resonating the complement of a harmonic cancels out both harmonics."

"We found that out the hard way," said Farragut.

Rome had used that information against the U.S.

Farragut said, "Commander Dent, let's share that discovery with Constantine."

"Calculate complement to the irresistible harmonic," Gypsy ordered.

The res tech and the cryptotech started calculations.

"Complement calculated and loaded," the res tech reported.

Farragut looked to Numa. "Is this going to work?"

"If Constantine *is* using what we call the irresistible harmonic, it will work."

"Send it."

Gypsy ordered, "Resonate complement."

"Resonating, aye." Then, "No good. Negative signal."

"It didn't work?"

"I didn't send," said the tech. "I don't have a green."

Tactical spoke up, "It worked. Look."

The gorgons down on the palace grounds lost interest in Constantine's androids as quickly as they had gained it. They turned round to pursue the moving lifeform on the walkway.

Constantine glanced aside. Glanced twice. Broke from his haughty stride and ran, chased by demons.

Bitter laughter rippled across the command deck.

Constantine scrabbled and ducked into a concrete bunker.

"Okay, there's his hideout. Constantine's backup controls will be down there."

Gorgons clotted *Merrimack*'s distortion field. Navigation lined up a dive into the atmosphere to burn them off before the ship could lose her helm.

The res tech reported brightly from his station, "Commodore, I know why I didn't get a green light."

"So do I. A harmonic and its complement cancel each other out. When you resonated the complement, neither existed."

The tech deflated. "I wanted to show off, Commodore."

"Sorry, son."

Wolfhound was rising from the atmosphere. Gorgons swarmed on *Wolfhound* as soon as she was spaceborne.

Horatius was still in the atmosphere.

As *Merrimack* porpoised out of the atmosphere, Gypsy ordered the pilot to steady the ship's course to receive the Swifts returning from the planet. It meant collecting gorgons again, but there was no other way. The Swifts could not survive out there on their own.

Navigation tried to calculate a run to the sun. The escape route was closing. A wall of gorgons eclipsed the sun. He tried to figure if the ship could get up enough inertia to carry her through the gorgon wall to the safety of the sun's blaze. *Mack* could accelerate to FTL. So could Hive spheres. And the gorgons had mass on their side. He looked at flanking maneuvers. And the data kept changing. He would not have solid numbers until all the Swifts were back. While gorgons continued to mass between *Merrimack* and the sun.

Gypsy called to the flight decks, "Did we get all Swifts inboard?"

"We are light one," said Colonel Steele.

"We're light *two*," said Chief Ogden Bannerman.

Kerry Blue raced against an oily black-brown wave of gorgons marching in from the field behind the camp. She had to get to her Swift first. Knew her Swift had to be there. Colonel Steele would not strand her.

If Colonel Steele knew she was alive.

Kerry's com was fuzzed. She couldn't tell Steele she was still alive.

If Steele thought she was dead, he could leave her.

The sunlight dimmed, though there wasn't a cloud in the sky.

She made it to the pond. Saw tentacles on the far bank. This was going to be close. She ran along the bank. Heard a roar from above.

A Swift entering atmo. "Here! Here!" Kerry jumped up and down waving her arms. "Colonel, I'm here!"

The Swift passed low, right overhead and sped onward.

"No! No! I'm here! Oh, no! Oh, skagit!"

Stepped wrong on the wet embankment. Foot slid, leg buckled. She fell sideways. Water surrounded her up to her shoulders.

Gorgons spilled over the banks.

Kerry splashed, scrambled for footing in the slimy mud. Tore at the reeds to climb out.

Suddenly her face, her whole head, was enveloped in slimy wetness. She couldn't see. Couldn't breathe. Her foot skidded again. Knee dropped in the mud. She fell into the woody reeds. A whip-hard gorgon tentacle hit her back. Knew she was dead.

Merrimack dove once more into the atmosphere.

As the shroud of gorgons burned off in the friction, the ship's sensors returned to life—just in time to detect Constantine's bunker opening, and a small ship launching out of it.

The little craft hit escape velocity and shot past *Merrimack*.

Too late to get off a shot, *Merrimack* signaled any ship in the Attack Group: "Fire on unidentified craft! Get him!"

Horatius failed to get a lock. Fired anyway. *Horatius'* shots went wide and wild.

Wolfhound was dark, and did not even receive the order.

Gladiator, clotted with gorgons, could not fire solid ordnance. Could only get out beam shots, and beam shots were useless shooting from behind a fleeing enemy.

You had to catch an FTL craft coming. Once he was past you, a ship that small was almost as fast as a Star Sparrow.

As *Merrimack* climbed out of atmosphere, Farragut ordered, "Get a Star Sparrow out there!"

"Launching Star Sparrow, aye."

But Constantine was ready for that. One shot from a beam cannon out the stern of Constantine's escape craft detonated the Star Sparrow well short of its target.

Tactical watched Constantine getting away. The small PanGalactic racing craft showed on the screens. Tactical reported solemnly, "Target will reach the edge of the solar system in one minute."

Watched it go in a grim vigil, as navigation reran his numbers, because his first calc said *Merrimack* could not reach the sun.

"Constantine is passing the ninth planet. Will clear in fifteen, fourteen—"

The escape craft exploded in a double blast—one on its bow, the other from its engine losing shielding.

Tactical stood right up at his station and crowed, "It's *Rio* and the Meadow Muffins!"

32

THE IMAGE OF *RIO* Grande resolved onto the monitors, riddled with holes, but carrying no gluies, limping between *Sunlit Meadows* and *Windward Isles*.

Dallas McDaniels' voice came over the com. "John, old son, why didn't you kill *all* these buggers while you were at it?"

"*Dallas!* Glory be, Dallas, I thought you had gluies!"

"We did. They melted all to piss. Now here I thought you did something to rescue us."

"It was nothing I did."

"Do not be so sure, young Commodore," said Jose Maria, who normally said nothing on the command deck.

Farragut turned, surprised.

Jose Maria continued, "Remember, *Merrimack* blanked out a harmonic a few minutes ago."

"Oh, my God," someone said. Could have been anyone. Hope leaped across the command deck—

Only to be quickly damped down by a sound they all knew, of gorgons snagging the force field again, clustering impossibly thick.

"Dallas, bag your ass to the sun if you can. Don't come anywhere near us. We are caged here. Circle wide and get yourself in a close orbit to the sun. Then try to shoot a way clear for us from the sun side. Gypsy, take us on another dive into atmo. Jose Maria, keep talking."

"Two events occurred a short time ago. *Merrimack* canceled out the irresistible harmonic, and the gluies on *Rio Grande* died. Did those two events coincide?"

Farragut called into the com, "Dallas, do you have a chron mark on exactly when your gluies quit living?"

"Sure do. Sending."

Merrimack received the chron reading at the moment of the gluies' death. Farragut ordered the res tech: "Match time against the time we resonated."

"It's a match, sir."

"A perfect coincidence," said Jose Maria. "But not a coincidence, I think. Cause and effect is strongly indicated."

Farragut was not following. "What does this mean? Gluies aren't Hive?"

Gypsy said, "Gluies must be Hive. We saw gluies come out of gorgons."

"Two," said Jose Maria. "There are two Hives. There *were* two Hives."

"*Rio Grande* ran into a rival gang?"

"I believe so. And I believe the Hive produces gluies to kill rival Hive soldiers. I have heard gluies called antibodies. That may not be a bad analogy. The Hive uses gluies to attack foreign bodies within its space. And that is why the irresistible harmonic was irresistible."

Farragut said, "One Hive's resonance is another Hive's 'Die monster die.' "

"Yes, young Commodore. I believe that is the case."

"The irresistible harmonic pissed the holy hell out the first Hive, because it was the signal of the second Hive!"

Jose Maria nodded. "And when you blanked out the irresistible harmonic, the second Hive died."

"Then, God Almighty, we need the harmonic of *this* Hive!"

"How do we get that?" Gypsy asked soberly. "We killed Constantine and blew up his escape ship."

*   *   *

Kerry Blue groped at her face, blinded and suffocating, and trampled by what felt like stampeding sticks. Her fingers found the edges of her shroud. She peeled the wet film off her mouth and nose. Inhaled a cry. Pulled the slithery shroud out of her eyes.

Opened her eyes to a gorgon tentacle. Right in front of her. It moved away. Stepped on her foot. Tentacles walked over her.

Another set of tentacles stepped on her back. She felt each mouth jab and lift away, then saw the whole monster stump up the mud embankment.

Gorgons marched over her, around her, till the shoal of them were all passed. Left her sitting in the reeds, drawing quavering breaths.

As if they could not see her. Or did not care.

The wartray, Barnacle Bob, grown very large, stuck to Kerry Blue, draped over her head and shoulders, his warts pulsing.

More gorgons moved by the pond, ignoring the wartrays, ignoring the reeds, the algae, the breathing trees.

Imported Earth trees were going down as if in a hyperactive sawmill—willows, tamarisks. Gorgons buzzed through the thistles and the goldenrod but left the alien bluish purple stalks and red-orange fronds.

Kerry huddled in the pond with the native life.

She lifted her com. Tried it again, shaking near to convulsions, her body in mutiny. Her voice was not coming out very well. "*Merrimack. Merrimack. Merrimack.* This is Alpha Six. I—I think I got something."

Merrimack did not respond. Kerry saw now that the Cowboy thing had crushed her com.

Kerry Blue got up unsteadily, teetered on her feet. She caught two more of the wartrays. They hissed at her. She balled them up in their own flaps and tucked them under either arm like a pair of footballs, and she tiptoed, cringing, through herds of gorgons. She held her breath, tried not to whimper when she really just wanted to scream her head off. Knew, just knew, that any moment the gorgons would realize she was not one of them.

Or they could decide to take a bite out of her anyway. She had seen gorgons in a feeding frenzy get careless with their mouths.

Revulsion got the better of her, and she had to pause and throw up. Spat.

Had to dart away from that spot, because another gorgon thought she'd found something to eat and wanted it.

She crept to where her Swift, Alpha Six, sat, right where she left it. Knew it would be there.

The gorgons had already pulled the canopy back and fished out the emergency rations and one pair of leather gloves. Everything else looked intact.

Kerry stuffed the two unwilling wartrays into the cockpit, then scrambled in herself. She caught the wartrays as they tried to escape, stuffed them back down, and pulled the canopy forward.

She tried the Swift's com. "*Merrimack. Merrimack. Merrimack.* This is Alpha Six. I think I have something."

The signal went, but no response came back.

They left!

She sat in the cockpit, quaking. Gorgons stalking by. The two wartrays trapped with her, hissed, warts pulsing fit to burst. Barnicle Bob throbbed on her head.

"*Merrimack. Merrimack. Merrimack.* This is Alpha Six."

It was getting steamy in here.

She started her Swift's engine. Did not know where she thought she could go.

Merrimack's com tech reported, startled, "Sir. I have Alpha Six."

Steele's expression, to anyone looking at him at that moment, was a bald confession. He moved to the com, shouted into it, "Alpha Six, what is your situation!"

Farragut muted the com to tell Steele quietly, "I'm sorry, TR. That cannot possibly be your Marine. It has to be one of Constantine's fabrications, like Sebastian Gray."

Farragut clicked the com back on and said warily, "Alpha Six, how are you still alive?"

"Captain! I mean Commodore! Sir! Bob landed on my head. The gorgons don't eat wartrays! Or some of the trees and some of the swamp reeds!"

Farragut muted the com again. "Who the hell is *Bob?*"

Jose Maria supplied, "Barnacle Bob. The little creature Kerry Blue rescued, by your leave. Apparently, it has grown up to be Androcles' lion."

"This can't be real," said Farragut, though the incoherent voice sure sounded true Blue. Into the com, not certain quite what to ask, Farragut said, "Flight Sergeant, you have 'Bob' there with you?"

"No, *no*. I made him shoo on home. I didn't want the xenos poking at him. But I have two other ones. They're mean, but they seem to be keeping the gorgons away."

Farragut confessed to Steele. "That is, without any doubt, Kerry Blue."

Jose Maria nodded. "And what this implies makes sense."

"It *does?*"

"Life emerges to survive conditions present. With the Hive here, life would emerge with natural defenses against the Hive. The natives are resonating—on the Hive harmonic."

Something else made sense. How Constantine had recognized the fake gorgons as fake. The fake gorgons had attacked native life in the pond *which Constantine knew were immune*.

"Alpha Six, you are clear to dock, portside flight deck." And to the flight deck crew, "Get Alpha Six aboard quick and get my ship moving again. I don't think two little wartrays are going to keep the gorgons off the whole space battleship." To the lab: "Get the Sargasson functional. We need him *now*. Have him do whatever it is Sargassons do to detect what harmonic the wartrays are resonating."

The battle had changed. Before now the xenos had only insects to work with, which could detect Hive resonance. Now they had creatures that truly appeared to be *sending* Hive resonance.

"Augustus, report to the lab."

Alpha Six arrived without gorgons. But *Merrimack* picked up a blanket of gorgons on her force field while allowing Alpha Six to dock.

Colonel Steele was waiting on the dock. He jumped up on the icy Swift, slid the canopy back.

Saw Kerry Blue's brown hair, wet and stuck close to her head, looking like a chick just out of the egg.

"Watch it, sir," said Kerry, handing up wartrays. "These guys are really mad."

Steele handed the wartrays down to xenos, who were also waiting on the dock in dancing impatience. They accepted their hissing charges and ran to the lab.

TR Steele reached down into the cockpit, hauled Kerry up by her armpits. Set her on her feet before him atop the Swift.

She trembled, her heart beating fast between his big hands. She bewildered him with her scared kind of courage. Her maddeningly soft feminine cheek leaned close to his chest. Good thing she stank like hell or he would have kissed her right there.

Her bleeding palms touched him as if making sure he was real. She was smiling and crying.

Steele handed a very unsteady and smelly Kerry Blue down to big Dak Shepard, who said up to Steele, "She's gooey."

"Bob peed down my neck," said Kerry.

Steele snarled.

Two xenos charged into the lab like a pair of running backs with their wartrays. "Where is Steve Wayne!"

"Who?" said the Marine guard.

"The Sargasson!"

"John Wayne's brother!"

One xeno rapped on the Sargasson's tank. "Come on, Mr. Wayne, time to ride! Wake up!"

Doctor Patrick Hamilton hurried in protectively. "Don't—" He put his hands to the tank to keep it from sloshing. He searched the bottom for the unhappy alien. "Steve? *Steve?*"

A lot of short black hairs, like a hundred eyelashes, floated inside the tank. A great deal of water lay splashed outside the tank, standing in puddles on an adjacent worktop and on the deck.

The wetness trailed to where one of the ship's dogs, Inga, the Doberman, lay curled in the corner of the lab compartment, chewing on an old sock.

The xenos became suddenly aware it was not an old sock.

Patrick Hamilton stared at the bulks, which were spattered with tiny droplets as from the shaking of a wet dog. His hands vibrated, open and useless. He mumbled, "I'll shoot her. I'll shoot her."

Farragut hailed the lab demanding status.

"We're dead," said Patrick Hamilton. He habitually left off the "sir" when addressing Farragut.

"Explain that."

"Steve Wayne has been murdered."

"Put Augustus on the com."

"Augustus is not here."

"Didn't he report to the lab?"

"No."

Chief Ogden Bannerman was on the com now, "Commodore, Augustus is not on board *Merrimack*."

"How is that possible?"

"There is a Swift out without leave. Alpha Two."

"Alpha Two didn't come back?"

"Alpha Two came back. I ticked that crate in myself. And Alpha Two's pilot, Flight Sergeant Dak Shepard, is on board. Some time between the return of the Swifts and our last descent into atmo—when all *loyal* hands was manning our swords—Alpha Two disappeared from its slot without leave."

"You can't just exit space dock while all ship systems are down and we are on manual!"

"Well, sir, *you* can't, and *I* can't, but somewhere in

the same time period, that half-human piece of Roman spytech stopped registering inside our force field. He is *not* hiding in the torpedo racks."

Farragut sent over the loud com: "Augustus, report to the command deck."

Received no acknowledgment.

"Augustus went to rejoin his master," said Colonel Steele, who had returned to the command deck. "I just hope Augustus was with Constantine when *Rio* blew his escape ship to hell."

33

THIS, *THIS* IS HOW Jehovah felt during the Deluge. Damn them. Damn them all.

Constantine paced his bunker, waiting for all of them to die.

He had watched the plot of his decoy escape ship blink out from his monitor. Somehow the traitors had managed to destroy the decoy. Disturbing. That should not have happened. His decoy should have got away.

Connecting ordnance to a vessel traveling FTL should have been beyond their technology. He needed to get that technology.

He would be able to glean it from their ships' dead carcasses once the traitors were all eaten.

Mean little rodents. All of them. How difficult was it for them to recognize a superior power? His dominance was self-evident. And apparently too much for their little rodent brains to conceive.

He got up to check his resonator. Made dead certain that all the limpets outside his sanctuary had self-destructed. He would not have his protection used by those parasites any longer.

He would need to play this differently next time. Deal with rodents as rodents. The mistake had been offering friendship. Next time he would cut off the heads of the commanders first and in front of everyone, then proceed from there.

He passed from one chamber into another. The lights, which should have automatically illuminated, didn't.

In the dark, something flew into his open mouth, lodged in his throat.

He gagged, instantly afraid. Could not help but swallow. The object felt round and rubbery going down.

He blinked in the dark. Someone was here.

Dread gave way to elation.

Augustus.

Constantine laughed out loud. "You weren't in your ship either! Great minds think alike." He touched his own throat. Still felt the impact of the ball. "What was this?"

"Goodwill insurance," said Augustus. "That could have been a bullet. But it wasn't."

"I'm glad it wasn't a bullet," said Constantine. Swallowed uncomfortably. The bruised sensation was still there. "What was it?"

"You don't know if it's anything at all," said Augustus. "But you can't afford to kill me until it finds its way to the head. It's not a popper, so don't try to cough it up. It expands. It will choke you coming back the way it came in. The other way is merely unpleasant. If you live to see it."

Constantine smiled past the death threat. Chided him, "Augustus, harming you is the last thing I wanted. I need you. I am your best friend. With you, I can rule Rome as it should be ruled."

Augustus had few expressions other than disdain. "What do you know of Caesar Magnus' assassination." It was a demand, not a question.

"*You* weren't behind that?" said Constantine, a little surprised.

Augustus gave no reaction except to repeat, "What do you know?"

Constantine hesitated, irritated, reluctant to confess. But it was not worth spending a lie. "Nothing at all. I'd have got Magnus sooner or later, but this? This was just bad timing. Killing him now opened the door for that weasel Romulus instead of *me*. It just adds a complication. I will prevail." Then thought to add Augustus. "*We* will prevail."

"So you are not guilty but not innocent," said Augustus.

Constantine did not really understand the question. Thought he was all done with that Magnus thing. "How is that?"

"You wanted Magnus dead," said Augustus.

Constantine laughed. Bellowed, "Who didn't!"

"Who didn't," Augustus echoed softly. "That information would have been vital for you to have before you started talking."

Augustus moved toward the bunker's second exit.

"What do you want!" Constantine cried. "With me, you can have *anything*! Name it!"

Augustus answered, "Justice."

"You'll have it!"

"I know."

Clawing, breaking, scritching, and shattering sounded behind Constantine, and suddenly he knew he had swallowed a resonator.

Any harmonic would do.

Augustus passed through the second exit.

Constantine cried after him. "Have it your way! I'll do anything!"

"Really?" said Augustus. Shut and bolted the door. "Die horribly."

34

THE HIVE HAD MOVED like a mud slide into the space around Planet Zero. All calculations indicated that gorgons could and would catch *Merrimack* if she tried to return to the sun. Most tricks only worked once against the Hive.

Farragut could not be sure if the other ships of the Attack Group were still alive. He could only make sporadic contact when another ship entered the atmosphere at the same time as *Mack* to shed its latest gorgon coat.

The gorgons had already learned to bail from a ship's distortion field when the ship began its dive. Finding a clear spot to come back up was getting harder and harder. Like an arctic sea icing over. There were not many breathing holes left. The masses of aliens clustered round the tenuous outer layers of atmosphere, thick as pond scum, so ships collected another coating of them the moment they returned to space.

"Figure about a seven-thousand-klick radius for the planet, including atmosphere. Gives a surface area of six-hundred-sixteen-billion meters squared. That's sixteen hundred sixteen billion gorgons to cover the whole sky."

"Darb?" Carly Delgado squinted at him, gorgon gore stinging her eyes under her face shield, her sword and her hair dripping. "Nobody needed to know that."

*　　*　　*

Gorgons clotted the distortion field again. The lights failed again. The command deck operated under the lurid chemical glow of the emergency lights.

A white light flashed on and off, falling on the faces of the command deck crew. Most of the faces were very young. So intent on seeing anything at all by any light that at first no one noticed the light itself. One of those things you see but forget to question, because everything else is abnormal.

Became aware of it. It was white and it kept going on and off. And it was coming from *outside*.

A tech squinted at the clearport, it finally occurring to him to wonder how there could be a light in outer space flashing through a solid coat of gorgons. He turned round at his station to stare at Commodore Farragut who noticed it, too, said: "Is that *Morse?*" Gestured at the air. The light. On and off.

The com tech and the cryptotech started counting the blinks. Dit Dit Dah Dit.

Gypsy Dent moved to the clearport, tried to see past the light to the source behind it. Reported, "There is a Striker out there, sir."

"Augustus?" Farragut started forward. But Augustus' Striker had been destroyed.

"It's a Striker," Gypsy repeated. "It's blue and white." Augustus' Striker had been red and black. "It's touching our distortion field." She turned to meet the commodore's gaze. "There are no gorgons on him."

"He has the Hive harmonic."

The command deck stirred.

Calli Carmel was on the command deck now, in borrowed clothes. Farragut asked her instead of Numa Pompeii, "Calli, what *gens* is blue and white?"

"Sempronius," said Calli. "The patterner Secundus was a Sempronius. Secundus is dead."

Numa Pompeii, haunting the command deck like a beached whale, said in heavy irony, "So is Augustus."

"That could be Constantine in Secundus' Striker, for all we know," said Colonel Steele. "Or one of Constantine's androids."

Farragut asked, of the flashing dits and dahs. "Is anyone getting this?"

"Yes, sir," said Qord Johnson, the cryptotech. "It's Morse. Telling us to enable our res chamber and giving us a harmonic to resonate."

Farragut turned to Gypsy. "Make it happen."

Gypsy Dent immediately ordered the res tech to enable the ship's res chamber.

"Enabling res chamber, aye."

"Commodore Farragut, may I speak?"

"General Pompeii?"

"I don't know who that is out there. We can see he *has* the protective harmonic. *Doesn't mean that is what he is giving to you.*"

"Res chamber enabled."

"Load the Striker's harmonic."

"Loading harmonic, aye."

"Sir!" Colonel Steele was unable to restrain himself. "Let's have it, TR."

"This Roman knows who is out there." Steele would not call Numa Pompeii by name or rank. "He *knows* we're being fed something deadly. He just never intended to be on board *Merrimack* when it happened."

Farragut looked to Numa for reaction. General Pompeii assumed the posture of a serene and lofty mountain. He would not die sniveling. He would not live sniveling. Said, "I cannot tell you what the person in that ship is thinking. The command is yours, Commodore Farragut."

"The thing in that ship is Augustus," said Steele. "He's going to deliver *Merrimack* to his Caesar."

"It is Augustus," said Farragut, certain.

Gypsy noted softly, "Augustus wants you dead, sir."

"Not arguing. But not this way."

"Harmonic loaded."

Calli spoke to Farragut, "We're back at the Myriad."

There had been a moment in the Myriad when *Merrimack* was at the mercy of Augustus' Striker. Augustus could have taken the battleship out right then. Instead he let *Merrimack* escape.

There was a sin that needed atoning.

"You won't get away with this twice, John."

"Resonate harmonic," Farragut ordered.

"Resonating, aye."

Eternity passed in the red emergency lights, the white Morse flashing. Shouts of the crew, battling gorgons, carried up to the command deck.

"It's a garbage harmonic," Tactical concluded.

Just as the lights went on in the command deck and the gorgons peeled off the distortion field around the command deck.

The monsters moved aft, joining the attack on the sail and wings.

Someone realized aloud, with a nervous laugh, "It's a big ship."

"She's a big ship," said Farragut. "Pull the res chambers from all the Swifts, all the launches, everything we have aboard, and disperse them through my big ship with the new harmonic. Make it fast."

The ship's intracom was not working. Steele quit the command deck at a bellowing charge, calling for techs and Marines.

Farragut shielded one side of his face from the incessant flashing from the clearport. "Get Augustus on the com. Make him stop blinking."

"Receiving a signal from the Striker," said the com tech as the Morse stopped.

"Let's have it," said Farragut, gesturing to his own com.

Augustus' voice requested permission to dock his Striker in the cargo deck.

"Permission granted." And to Gypsy, "Let him in as soon as we have power on the cargo deck."

"Aye, sir."

Numa Pompeii spoke. "Commodore. We need to get this harmonic to the other ships. Mine, in particular."

Calli gave a sign like an auction bid that said: Mine first.

The res tech asked, "If *Wolfhound* and *Gladiator* and

Horatius didn't make it to the sun, then their coms are down right now. How do we get the harmonic to them?"

"We don't," said Farragut.

Numa looked like he'd been shot. The rest of the command crew gave small flinches, sounds and stares of shock.

No one voiced protest, but the stares waited for explanation.

"Mr. Johnson. Calculate the complement to Hive harmonic. Load and resonate."

Shock gave way to murderous enthusiasm. Even some cackles.

Farragut was going to kill the enemy all at once.

"Point of consideration," said the crypto, even as he obeyed, calculating the complement. "We don't have to kill the Hive. We can just stop them and learn how they do what they do."

"I don't want the Hive stopped. I want it dead."

Qord Johnson verified his calculations. Glanced over at the Roman general. There was to be no privacy here, so he just said it to the commodore: "If we're successful here, the secret of how the Hive determines the location of the source of a res pulse dies with the Hive. Does Augustus have that? If he does, when the hot war breaks out, the Romans will have it." Qord looked at Numa "And we won't. Complement calculated. Ready to load."

"Load complement," Farragut ordered.

"Loading resonant complement, aye."

Jose Maria moved in very close to murmur to the commodore. "This is genocide."

"I can live with that."

"As can I," said Jose Maria, stepping back. Reminding him was all.

"I will sleep very well tonight. My only nightmare is right now if this *doesn't* work."

"How could it *not work*?" said Numa.

"The Hive learns. They saw us kill the other Hive with the complement of its resonant harmonic. Is this group ready and waiting for this? When we resonate;

they could all switch to channel B. Then we have nothing at all."

"Complement loaded."

An awful silence stretched an eternal second.

"That scenario cannot happen," said Jose Maria. "The Hive is not aware that the Hive harmonic is a secret. It cannot conceive of a secret."

Did not sound convincing.

"Any message, sir?" the res tech asked.

"A ping worked for the gluies. Just a ping."

"Standing by to resonate complement."

"Execute."

"Resonating. Aye."

And waited.

Nothing happened.

"Do we have green?"

"Negative, Commodore," said the res tech. "Resending. Green. I have a green light now. Harmonic sending. We canceled out *something*."

But nothing had changed on the monitors.

The sensors were all clear and functioning. Showed images from space. Gorgons still entombed the *Horatius*. Pretty sure that was *Horatius*. It was a ball of gorgons clotted on something the size of *Horatius*, but it could be *Wolfhound*. The huge ball would be *Gladiator*.

Shouts from the inner decks had changed to outbursts of disgust.

There were still the billions of gorgons in space. Tentacled monsters in chaotic motion.

But there was something different in the motion. Not obvious at first. Gorgons moving in space, but the tentacles were not whipping. The tentacles were breaking off from the bodies. Opening mouths kept opening, breaking off the ends of the tentacles and fanning into tenuous rings of debris.

The gorgons, all of them, had instantly frozen in the perfect cold of space. The inertia of their last motions kept their thrashing limbs moving in many directions at once. They were now dreamily shattering.

The haze of gorgons at the edge of the atmosphere

slowly fell, igniting. Would become six hundred billion meteors.

The com burst to life.

"*Merrimack. Merrimack. Merrimack.* This is *Rio Grande.* John, old son, did you do this?"

"Any ship. Any ship. This is *Wolfhound.* Our outboard gorgons have stopped coming in. Inside, we have a mess. Inboard gorgons melted. Request the location of Captain Carmel."

"*Gladiator* has dead gorgons on board. Request the location of the Triumphalis Numa Pompeii."

Calli got on her hand com, answered her XO.

Numa on his hand com, signaled *Gladiator* that he was on board *Merrimack.*

Marcus Asinius was not requesting the location of his commanding officer. He knew.

"*Merrimack* to *Horatius,* are y'all still with us?"

"We live," said Marcus. Grief suppressed, suffused, in the hollow voice.

"All ships, this is *Merrimack.* Get rid of your gorgon jackets. You look bad. Then annihilate the gorgons round the planet before they hit atmosphere. They'll destroy the climate with all those burning corpses."

He clicked off. Regarded the rest of the images from outside. All the frozen spaceborne corpses. "I don't like seeing them out there." Ordered Steele: "Break 'em up."

Steele gave the order: "Wing. Battery. Secure space junk."

Yelling, crowing, laughter crackled over the com from the Swifts and the gun bays, as explosions lit up all the monitors in a barbaric frenzy.

Gypsy Dent murmured to Farragut, "Isn't that a little . . . unseemly?"

"No, it's not," said Farragut, moving toward the hatch. "I'm fixin' to man me a gun and see if I can still hit a target."

Gypsy gave a wry moue, then said, "When you get back, sir, can I have a go?"

*   *   *

Farragut clambered up the ladder to the ship's gun blisters, eager as Christmas morning. Ran down the corridor. Skidded to a halt.

Augustus stood in his way, in the middle of the corridor, still and expressionless as a sphinx.

Farragut's smile was jubilant. He talked too fast to finish a sentence, "Augustus! You were— I can't even— You did it! God bless America! Come with me. Tell me how you did it. I'm fixin' to take target practice on frozen gorgons. Come on if you want a shot."

Augustus did not move from Farragut's path. With surreal slowness he drew his side arm. Lifted its muzzle toward Farragut.

Farragut asked, uncertain, "Is that a yes?"

Augustus' voice was flat as his expression. "I have a commission to kill you."

"No," said Farragut.

Heard the shot.

Felt the heat singe against his ear.

Heard a body slump and drop to the deck behind him.

Farragut turned round.

The white tiger Amadea lay dead on the deck, gold eyes open and staring, a burn hole in her forehead.

She had moved so quietly, Farragut had not heard her come up behind him. She gripped a gun in her dead hand.

Augustus spoke, "She offered me half."

Farragut cried, bewildered, "Half of what? Who put a hit on me?"

"In order: half of nothing, and probably no one."

"Do you want to explain that?"

"No."

"Do anyway."

Augustus stalked back to the body, kicked the weapon out of the corpse hand. "I don't think you were the end target. Your death was incidental."

"Not to *me*."

"You were a means to an end. I believe our mercenary set me up to kill you in order to give her an excuse to kill me without facing prosecution." And with false innocence: "Who could want me dead?"

"A lot of people, Augustus. But there's only one who demanded that Amadea be attached to my Attack Group."

Romulus wanted Augustus dead. Romulus sent the white tiger with the Attack Group. Amadea would not have collected payment for Augustus' death unless she did the killing. And Augustus said, "She was even happier than you were to see me alive."

"How did she get on my ship?"

"Did you search every craft *Merrimack* took aboard during the planetary evacuation?"

He hadn't. Of course he hadn't.

"You need to tell me how you got the Hive harmonic."

"From Constantine."

That jolted Farragut. "Constantine is still *alive?*"

"No. I'm ninety-nine percent sure, not. Request permission to go to the surface to look for his teeth."

Didn't even ask what Constantine's teeth would be doing on the surface. "I'm coming with you." Farragut started back down the corridor, talking into his com. Called for a shuttle and called for security to collect Amadea's body.

Farragut then looked up at Augustus with a huge shaky smile, about to speak. Augustus cut him off. "You know I took an oath to goddam Caesar. Do *not* thank me."

35

CONSTANTINE'S RES CHAMBER was still resonating the Hive harmonic when Augustus returned with Commodore Farragut to the bunker to look for Constantine's teeth.

Farragut turned the resonator off.

Contantine's teeth lay scattered, mostly on top of the res chamber. Constantine had been hugging it, trying to be one with the source of the friendly harmonic. But the resonator that Augustus had forced inside him was sending another harmonic. Any other harmonic trumped the friendly harmonic.

Constantine's polymer shoe soles were here, with some torn polymer clothing. Bloodstains darkened the concrete floor.

The small resonator he had swallowed was still here, on the floor, without its spongy covering. Still resonating in a wide pool of melted gorgon residue.

Augustus crushed it under heel. *"Sic semper malefidelibus."*

"Ever thus to the faithless," Farragut said.

He climbed out of the bunker and up to the palace roof to find Herius Asinius' teeth.

Merrimack's technicians were copying Constantine's database onto an independent device, where it could not corrupt any of *Merrimack*'s own data. Numa Pompeii's people were doing the same.

Victory was perilous. Now that the threat which united the U.S. and Rome was dead, no one was quite sure where anyone stood.

Debate had begun over who owned the world and the factories on it. Rome, the U.S., and the LEN each planted a flag in the soil and made their declarations.

"It won't be long before we stick our gluies on each other," said Farragut. "But I don't want it to be here."

Intelligence officers from several ships, picking over Constantine's database, discovered that the attempt by *Rio Grande* and the LEN ships to leave the Sagittarius Zero system without Constantine's notice had actually succeeded.

Constantine had *not* known that the three ships were gone until Farragut begged him to restore the protective harmonic to save them from the attacking gluies.

Constantine's refusal to help had not been his own choice. Constantine could not restore the protective harmonic to *Rio* and the LEN ships because he had never removed it.

Rio's limpets never stopped resonating Constantine's harmonic. Upon leaving the solar system, *Rio* and the LEN ran into the rival Hive. The harmonic that was friendly on Constantine's world made the rival Hive want the three ships dead.

Constantine had not been above painting events out of his control to look like the result of his own conscious will.

So, too, he had claimed responsibility for the Hive's destruction of the planet Telecore. His database spoke otherwise. Constantine had not even known of the existence of Telecore until Rome surrendered to the United States and the catastrophic events at Telecore became public knowledge.

The puff adder had been puffing.

Displacement equipment was found in Constantine's bunker. PanGalactic of course. And there were records of messages from Amadea to Constantine, going back decades.

"Amadea was working for Constantine," the Naval intelligence officer reported. "She planted the landing disks on Thaleia."

Farragut put that one to Augustus. "I thought you said Amadea was working for Romulus."

"She was," said Augustus. "On and off. She worked for whoever was on top at the moment. And always for Amadea."

Amadea had been Constantine's source of information from Near Space. She had sent him the story of the disappearance of *Sulla*, and a picture of it, from which he manufactured a replica. There was also a recording in the database of Doctor Mercedes de Cordillera, taken before her fateful journey on board *Sulla*, receiving an award for advancements in medicinal botany. Her flowing trousers fluttered as she climbed the steps to the podium. The Blue Empress glittered on the hand that accepted the plaque. Doctor Cordillera smiled beatifically for the recorders.

When Attack Group One mustered at Fort Theodore Roosevelt for an unspecified destination deep in the Deep End, Amadea knew exactly where they were going.

Because Romulus wanted Augustus dead, it was easy for Amadea to get Romulus to attach her to the Attack Group. From there, she could either take credit for delivering Augustus to Constantine, or she could kill Augustus for Romulus, depending on how events turned.

Hers was the voice on the garbled surveillance recording insisting that Constantine kill Romulus. She could not afford to have both of them alive in the end to compare notes and find that she had been playing them both.

Amadea had sent Constantine public records of personnel in the Attack Group—John Farragut, Jose Maria de Cordillera, Numa Pompeii, along with obituaries of personnel killed on *Merrimack* during battles with the Hive. Commander Sebastian Gray was one. Flight

Sergeant Cowboy Carver was another. Cowboy had been a colorful, popular man. For some reason, Constantine thought that would have made Cowboy special to the commander of the Marines on board *Merrimack*.

"Cowboy wasn't even killed by the Hive. He got himself blown up," said Farragut. "Rank that scheme down there with my fake gorgons taking a bite out of a wartray."

"And your lame tirade at Herius Asinius at the soccer brawl?" Augustus suggested.

"Lame?" Farragut pulled back. "My tirade *worked*. Constantine believed it. And you said I wasn't a good liar."

"You're not. You're wretched. That charade only worked because you were dealing with an opponent who did not—would not—know you. John Farragut never castigates his men in public, and he never messes up a name. Hairy Ass Asinine-us? That was way under the bottom. You were strident and nervous, two states in which I have never seen you. Luckily, you were putting on a show for a blind man. But I will admit the brawl looked real."

"That *was* real. I gave TR orders to pick a fight with the Dracs, and I wanted a full scale melee by the time I got back from Constantine."

"Insults don't normally break a Roman's discipline," said Augustus.

"TR challenged Herius' men to a soccer game. The fight broke out by itself."

Augustus muttered in self-irony, something that sounded like: *too stupid to be useful.*

"*Heri believed me*. Heri didn't know my lame tirade was a sham until I took him into my shuttle away from Constantine's surveillance equipment and told him what I was about. Heri did what he had to do. Even after everything went to hell." Farragut became solemn, lips pressed together hard. Said, "We call that uncommon valor where I come from."

Commodore Farragut sent his report to the Joint Chiefs by res pulse, proposing that the Attack Group continue on to Telecore, the first human outpost destroyed by the Hive, to make certain the Hive threat had been neutralized.

General Numa Pompeii requested to separate from the Attack Group. "I should like to be back in Near Space for the Senate vote on the new Caesar."

John Farragut's blue eyes went completely blank for a moment. Information was not getting where it needed to go. Or had this disconnect been intentional? Farragut said, hesitant, "Numa, you'll need a time machine for that one."

The Triumphalis seemed to grow larger in affront.

The Roman Senate had held the vote without him. Numa had been in contact with Rome. He, the Senator, the great Triumphalis Numa Pompeii, and no one had thought to tell him.

More likely his contacts had been told not to tell him.

Numa sounded betrayed. "Romulus was not to unseal his father's testament until after our victory." He darted an accusatory look at Augustus.

Augustus said flatly, "You told Romulus I'm dead. No one is sending *me* messages. I know less than you."

Numa, in umbrage, said, "Apparently there was some sudden need for haste. And apparently there was a quorum. And apparently there was a clear majority. And *I* need to ask an *American*: who am I to hail as Caesar now?"

"Same guy as before," said Farragut. "Romulus."

Numa looked disgusted.

It was Augustus who stood straight up and vibrated like a spear just stabbed into the deck.

From that, Numa's expression turned to mixed surprise, suspicion, and realization.

Numa and Augustus weren't talking—not in front of an American—but Farragut could connect some of these dots.

Romulus had not waited for a victory against the Hive to unseal his father's testament.

Romulus had waited until he knew Augustus was dead and not a moment longer.

Augustus had sealed Magnus' testament. Augustus knew what was in it.

And Farragut had a fair idea that the document Augustus sealed probably wasn't the document Romulus presented to the Senate before the vote.

Farragut looked from Numa to Augustus, their silence saying all that needed saying. "Glory be, y'all have got yourselves an Almighty coup."

Celebrations broke out all across the human-settled portion of the galaxy upon news of the destruction of the Hive.

Romulus planned an enormous festival for his coronation. On that subject, Numa and Augustus remained as secretive as only Romans could be.

And on Planet Zero, the Dracs and Marines were finally allowed to play with all the toys.

Roman legionaries were using the soccer field. U.S Marines used the football field and the baseball diamond. They had to be day games. The lights weren't working. Constantine's dead man switches had shut off most of the power. Most of the automatons had ceased functioning, and Constantine's personal guards were unresponsive.

Insectoids were quiet for the first time in forever.

On the last day on Planet Zero, Farragut held a feast in the open air.

The ships in orbit ran on skeleton crews with guards. Everyone else was down at the party. And everyone was allotted time downstairs at one time or another.

Merrimack's Chef Zack entered into competition with *Rio*'s Mama Beau and *Wolfhound*'s Minister of Foodage for the favor of the celebrants. And all hands partied like they had just saved the universe.

You could hear Numa Pompeii holding court at his end of the party. His booming voice carried the length of the clearing. The Americans couldn't understand what he was saying because he was speaking in Latin, but all the Roman men around him roared with laughter.

Calli Carmel stopped by Numa's table. "I brought you dessert." She left a locust on his plate.

Inga the Doberman had been stripped of her rank and her dog tags, and drummed out of the Navy. Jose Maria de Cordillera, down on the planet, walked his new pet dog.

Dak Shepard was reunited with his Swift, Alpha Two, which Augustus had parked near Constantine's bunker.

"Hey, who ate all my pretzels?"

Cole Darby told Kerry Blue, "Good thing Bob thought you were his mama."

Cain and Dak looked at each other, suppressing snickers.

"Uh," Cain said. "Bob didn't think Kerry was his ma."

Kerry curled her lip. "Well, why do you think he saved my life, bozon?"

"Uh," said Dak. "Your hair was really slimy when you came back, Kerry."

"Bob peed down my neck."

"Kerry, the xenos say that wasn't pee."

"Oh. Oh. *Oh*. Aw, no. Eeyeew!" Kerry got up, brushed herself off as if she had ants, and stalked away.

The demoted tactical specialist Marcander Vincent approached Commodore Farragut, requesting a transfer.

"You got a reprimand and a demotion, Mister Vincent. You deserved it. Transferring to another ship won't help anything."

"That's not it, sir. You're allowing a Heraclid to serve on your ship, fine." His eyes flickered to Augustus with suspicion and hatred. "Let me serve elsewhere. I just can't serve on board with a baby killer."

"Denied. Learn to live with it. Unless you are giving me your resignation."

Marcander Vincent looked shocked sick. Had not expected that at all.

"But I wish you wouldn't," Farragut went on. "I need you where you are, Marcander."

"Yes, sir. Thank you, sir."

Marcander withdrew, rattled.

Augustus wore a crocodilian smile. "You asked Mo Shah."

Farragut shook his head. "Didn't have to."

An unremarkable man, Marcander Vincent was older than Farragut and advancing nowhere. "He can't outrun this one. If I transfer him, he'll find out wherever he goes, there will be a Heraclid on board. I won't let that happen. And *you* aren't going to tell him."

"Me?" Augustus wore innocence like a cobra in a tutu.

"You're a sadistic bastard, Augustus."

Augustus nodded; this was so.

Kerry wandered away from the party. She had brought her pet lizard plant down to the planet to visit its own kind, and now wasn't sure where it had gone off to. She walked along the river, through a thin forest of native trees, where couples were trysting.

Came to where the river fed into open water, and she walked along the sea strand, the yellow sun glancing with diamond brilliance off the wide-open blue.

Something odd moved ahead. Closer, it resolved into a mast rocking side to side.

Kerry came to a sailing boat tied to a dock.

Had to be one of the toys Constantine had built to tempt the Marines and the Dracs.

Kerry walked out to the end of the dock. In her Marine boots she gingerly stepped from the dock, over the gunwale to a polished wood deck. Sounds rose from below. She called down tentatively, "Ahoy?"

Up the steps from the cabin rose a buzz cut white-blond head. Arctic blue eyes lifted. Steele's big hand motioned. "Take in that line."

Kerry looked where Steele gestured. The rope was probably "that line." She unwound it from its brass cleat on the dock, and pulled it on board.

Steele used a deck hook to push off from the dock. The sloop drifted out.

Kerry helped Steele haul up the white sail. It filled, billowed. The deck canted. Kerry kept her footing easily. She'd had much worse from the *Mack*.

The wind carried them out to the deep water.

Kerry Blue didn't know a boom from a broomstick, but it was clear that Steele had done this before. He handled the craft with masterful ease. Kerry felt as if she had stepped out of her own life into someone else's.

They sailed over shining water under an alien sky.

Kerry mostly watched Steele move. Nothing prettier than a man who knew what he was doing.

He was wearing shorts so she could see the muscles in his hard legs flex, the blond hairs gleam in the sunshine.

She felt an expectancy. Waiting for something to happen. Afraid to breathe on the moment.

Steele had secured a couple of beers from the party. He brought the bottles up from the cooler in the cabin, gave one to Kerry, and they sat on the deck watching the sun paint the sky as it sank toward the water.

Kerry asked, "How do you know how to do all this?"

Steele did not look at her. His eyes fixed into a squint at some faraway point on the horizon. "Some rich man got a tax write-off on his little yacht if he took underprivileged kids out of the Midwest—who would never *ever* have a need to know any of this—took them out to the Atlantic and taught them how to sail." He sounded angry.

"Sounds like fun," Kerry said.

"I *loved* it. I didn't know whether to thank him or hit him. So what was the point of it all if I would never ever get to touch another yacht in my life?"

"Guess you better thank him," said Kerry.

Blond brows lifted like a shrug. "I decked him. Waiting for the shuttle to pick us up and take us back to Oklahoma. Laid him right out."

Kerry laughed, leaned her cheek against his hard, hard upper arm.

Steele stood up. Turned the sloop around toward land.

The sky turned deep velvet. There ought to have been stars, but there were probably too many dead gorgons out there for that. One of the moons rose bright and swollen on the horizon. Solid ground felt odd underfoot after being on the water. Kerry walked back upriver with Steele toward the camp, where the party was still in full rev.

Passing through the trees, Kerry saw moving shadows and heard giggles in the dark. Made her wistful. Steele was not pausing here. And she'd thought maybe he might.

They approached the lights and noise. Kerry got in front of him and stopped short, faced him, palm to his chest. "I had the best time."

Steele grunted.

Kerry searched his face. "Do I have a great big wart on my forehead, 'cause you're not looking me in the eyes."

"Big wart," said Steele. "You need to get that looked at."

"Colonel—"

A rustling in the underbrush made him look.

A cluster of green leaves scampered out of the dark, scrambled up the tree that was TR Steele, and perched atop his head.

Steele gruffly pulled the lizard plant off him, set it down snarling with a bullying bluster, but he didn't crease a single leaf.

"I'm taking the next watch topside," said Steele and left Kerry there.

Kerry took a step after him, started to call.

Another rustling of leaves and patter of quick feet neared. Kerry's lizard plant galloping toward her, joyous to see her.

Kerry crouched down with open arms.

Her lizard plant jumped on Steele's lizard plant and the two twined into a single leaf ball, tails entwined, trilling.

Kerry stood back up, hands on hips. "Oh, now that's just not *fair*."

In the morning, *Merrimack, Rio Grande, Wolfhound, Gladiator* and *Horatius* left Sagittarius Zero in the custody of the two LEN police ships.

Farragut had embraced Ram Singh in parting, gave him a kiss on both cheeks. Kissed Captain Fred on the mouth. Fredrika bid all of them, "Don't shoot each other on the way home."

THE ATTACK GROUP was underway to the dead world Telecore. A tense journey. A lot of things not being said.

In a briefing room on board *Merrimack*, Farragut watched the stand of the Roman Tenth at Corindahlor.

The bridge spanned two miles across the Corindahlor Channel, a choke point between land masses. U.S. forces held either side and hemmed in the Tenth Cohort of the Praetorian Guard on the bridge. The Guard could have withdrawn, lowered their dome, and displaced out. They did not have to die. But they would not go. Kept launching ordnance at the surrounding enemy.

One of the three centuries of the famous 300 was Flavian. You could spot them by their black-and-red colors.

Unfortunately for the victors, who made this recording, the record showed the Romans at their most tenacious, their most valiant. The damned thing was a more stirring piece of propaganda than the Romans themselves could ever have staged.

In the end, the U.S. won the bridge but lost the planet.

Came to the famous scene. The U.S. troops had penetrated the dome. Facing certain death now, the defenders refused to surrender.

A young Flavian stud, very like Cowboy—even had

his shirt open like Cowboy in the icy air—leaped onto the bridge railing with a savage smile, fired his weapon, roaring at the oncoming troops.

His field armor flickered out.

And he laughed. Fighting to the death. Ferociously alive.

Projectiles tore into his chest and he fell over the rail into darkness. Below would be the icy water of the Corindahlor Channel.

"There ought to be a legal limit on the number of times anyone can play back that damn thing."

Farragut turned to Augustus. "You really can't tolerate national heroes, can you?" Nobody ever disparaged the Roman Tenth.

And then suddenly the dawning. Obvious now that he saw it. How could he not have seen it. "You were there."

"*I* was not."

Farragut asked the computer if there was a Cyprian Flavius Cassius in this record. The recording backed up to the cowboy making his stand on the rail, laughing. Froze on his image.

Farragut looked from him to Augustus. The only man alive with a right to scorn these men.

No wonder he was so angry. The others were in Elysium. He was here, serving the enemy.

Cyprian Flavius Cassius on the bridge, eternally young, laughing at death.

"Why didn't you keep your name?"

"It is not my name. I know of this the same way you do—from seeing that recording."

"You don't remember this? It's not possible. How can they erase a memory that vivid? Neurons in the brain talk to each other."

"It is not I. I was not there," Augustus said, dispassionate, detached. Dead inside. Nothing left of the life that was.

Telecore still had its atmosphere. There was still nitrogen fixed in the soil. The radiation from the neutron hose had long since decayed. There was free water. The planet could be terraformed again.

The Marines set down a field base. Checked the former settlement sites for residual Hive presence. There were no buildings. The Romans had destroyed everything that the Hive did not.

The Dracs pulled the dead man switches from some PanGalactic builder equipment and set it to constructing a stone mausoleum on Telecore, undisputed Roman ground, for their legate Herius Asinius.

It was a handsome building, built like a temple, of local limestone and marble, big but not overweening.

There was nothing left of the Legion commander but his teeth. His men put them in a small urn of pure gold. The purity made the urn soft, but it would hold its luster for the best part of eternity.

Dracs in full regalia carried the urn on a bier to the mausoleum under the scarlet-and-gray legion standard and the silver eagle. They laid the urn in a vault under the floor.

John Farragut made his formal public apology to Herius Asinius at his funeral in front of God and everyone.

He placed a grass crown and a bottle of bourbon over Herius' resting place.

"You don't have authority to bestow a crown," said Augustus. "A crown is a Roman award. It doesn't mean anything coming from you."

"It means I think he should have it. And I am more legitimate than your Caesar."

"Thomas Ryder."

Thomas Ryder Steele glared at Kerry Blue as she joined him behind the windbreak he was setting up.

Without trees or grass to slow them, the winds of Telecore swept dirt and sand into the field camp with an unrelenting clatter.

Thomas Ryder Steele seldom heard his own name. "How in the hell'd you find that out?"

"Augustus told me."

The thought of Kerry Blue with Augustus turned like a bullet lodged under a bone a long time ago and forgotten. Something he lived with until it moved.

His emotions must have read on his face because Kerry said, "Augustus never really wanted me. That was really a cheap shot at you, wasn't it?"

She knew. She knew he could be got at through Kerry Blue. Cornered, his voice dropped. "It wasn't cheap. That *cost*."

She had never seen a look like those cold-hot blue eyes. Stopped the breath in her throat.

She had hurt him.

"You're still mad at me for that, aren't you?" She felt the dizzying abyss here between them.

He shook his head. Wanted Augustus dead again, yes. But Kerry didn't love Augustus, so to hell with all that. He croaked, "No."

"But you *are* mad at me."

Blond brows lowered, eyes narrowed, mouth turned down, chin pushed forward. Steele nodded. Had no intention of ever saying it, but it was coming out of his mouth, "Cowboy! You almost got yourself killed *chasing fucking Cowboy!*"

Kerry flinched, startled. Then smiled. Her shoulders shook.

"*Don't* laugh at me."

She did laugh. Not a mocking laugh. A nervous giddy laugh. "We're having a lovers' quarrel!"

"No. That would mean we—" Couldn't finish that sentence. "That you—" Definitely couldn't finish that one either.

"I do," said Kerry. One of them had to jump first into the abyss; guessed it was gonna be Kerry. "I love you. I've always adored you. You're so far above me I never ever thought we would ever ever even have this conversation."

Steele fought like a drowning man. "This conversation is not happening."

Her voice quavered with fear. "Yes, it is." She felt cold. Cold like alone in a space suit in deep space with no ship in sight. He was hanging her out here alone. Her voice shook. "Yes, it is happening, Thomas Ryder. Yes, it is. Don't do this to me again."

"I am your commanding officer. I have a duty not to abuse my rank."

"I ain't being abused."

"You don't get it."

"Got that right, sir."

He drew himself up before her, forbidding, commanding. Duty was his life. "There is a line I can't cross."

"You were pushed," said Kerry. She jumped. Her arms were round his broad shoulders, her mouth on his, one leg round his waist. If not for their clothes, she presented point-blank.

The line dissolved. Rational thought AWOL.

Steele caught her to him. Shoved his tongue into her mouth. Wasn't romantic. Wasn't art. It was naked need, raw passion breaking. His hands were in her hair, on her ass, pressing her to him. Trying to feel every part of her at once. Felt her arms holding tight, heard the passion in her breath, caught the gleam of tears at the corners of her almost-shut eyes.

A frantic insect whine with a patter of wings made Kerry convulse, jerk free. Shut Steele down cold.

Kerry swayed. Laughed weakly. "Sorry." The reaction was reflex now.

Zakan moths.

"No," said Steele glancing around, alert, guarded, grim.

The Zakan moths in the canister at Steele's belt were fluttering madly, keening.

"The Hive's all dead." Kerry traced a finger down his arm, wanting to get back to where they'd been.

Steele shook his head, his big hand warm and firm on her waist. He began slowly, "Marine—"

The ground around them pocked, moved. Crumbling dirt gave way to living holes, ringed with teeth.

A tentacle lashed free into the air.

"Run!" Steele pushed Kerry toward camp as he roared into his wrist com: *Hive sign! Hive!*

* * *

Merrimack signaled Planet Zero, ordered Ram and Fredrika to get their people spaceborne. *Yesterday!*

Fred and Ram reported back from a safe orbit that Hive elements were emerging from the ground of Planet Zero.

Merrimack also sent the alarm to Thaleia, which so far showed no Hive sign. But the alerts threw the entire area of Near Space into panic. No one knew where the Hive would erupt next.

"Are these galactic seventeen-year locusts?" said Farragut.

Jose Maria de Cordillera answered, "I do not believe this could be a cycle. It may be that when the parent Hive goes silent, that silence provides the trigger for the rise of the next Hive. Why would something so vast, so ravenous, need to reproduce unless it were dead?"

Marines during dust off shot at the gorgons and observed that the gorgons did not dodge. This was a brand-new Hive—born yesterday. They didn't know a damn thing. There was no jamming of weapons. No avoiding shots. Neither former Hive harmonic meant anything to these.

But insects knew what they were.

There was nothing to eat down there on Telecore. The new Hive hadn't figured out how to fly yet to chase the resonance in the sky, but you saw tentacles straining upward in the direction of ships in orbit.

The impulse was to take another neutron hose to the planet and scour them off. But that would not kill the entire Hive, and Farragut did not want to teach the new monsters anything before he turned all their lights out.

"And we thought genocide was going to be easy."

On the screen in the briefing room was the image of Herius Asinius' mausoleum.

Farragut was standing before the screen, brooding, his arms crossed, when Augustus entered the compartment.

Farragut did not move his gaze from the lonely image. "They ate the crown and drank his bourbon."

"He doesn't know," said Augustus.

"*I* do. We will take this world back. For good."

"It's Roman ground."

"Don't care. It's human ground. They can't have it."

Augustus regarded him strangely. "How did you know to come here?"

"I didn't," said Farragut.

Augustus disagreed. "There are patterns you see that I don't." He paused. "I hit the water backward."

Farragut got lost on that turn. And abruptly caught up to where Augustus had gone.

The Corindahlor Bridge.

Stopped the air in Farragut's lungs. He did not even dare move.

What had happened to Cyprian Flavius Cassius after he went over the side of the bridge was not in the recording.

"I remember getting water in my ears."

Farragut turned slowly to face him.

"You know that last stretch of your ear canal when the water threads up to your eardrum? It's only this far." He pinched the distance between his fingernails. "Felt like a bloody yard. I remember that."

"What happens to you now, Augustus?" said Farragut. "When the Attack Group disbands. I really don't want to send you back. Romulus charged you with the murder of Caesar."

"I did not murder Caesar," said Augustus. "But I am going to."

"Augustus, did I ever apologize to you for all that crap I called you in the torpedo room when I thought you self-destructed?"

Augustus shook his head, not important. "Commodore Farragut."

Farragut could not remember Augustus ever addressing him as that. "Augustus?"

Tried to read the gaunt face, the lined brow. As imperially proud, remote, and bitter as on Thaleia. Head high, the dark eyes looking down on him.

Augustus spoke as from a great hollow.

"You have the respect of the dead."

Now in Hardcover from DAW Books

The Fourth Exciting Novel of
The Tour of the Merrimack:

STRENGTH AND HONOR

R.M. MELUCH

Read on for a sneak preview.

★ 1 ★

LIEUTENANT GLENN (HAMSTER)
Hamilton was Officer of the Watch when the
Emergency Action Message came in.

She passed the EAM to the cryptotech for confirmation, and immediately paged John Farragut on his personal com. "Captain's presence requested on the command deck."

Captain Farragut's voice came back, "What's this about?"

An instant's blank panic showed on Hamster's face. The captain was often in Roman company. Hamster could not afford to explain. She answered quickly, "Gypsy's hair." And immediately clicked off.

She stood over the com, feeling the eyes of the command deck upon her. With her eyes set dead ahead, she spoke to anyone in range of her quiet voice, "If what I just said gets back to Commander Dent, every man jack and jane on this deck will walk the plank." And she took the com back up, "Commander Dent, your presence is requested on the command deck."

The lieutenant had not requested speed from either the captain or the exec. She did not want to sound alarmed.

And the captain was going to arrive like a missile anyway.

John Farragut blew through the hatch to the command deck like a gust of fair wind, wearing the sky blue uniform of ship's captain.

One of the Marine guards at the hatch announced, "Captain on deck."

Farragut's presence announced itself. He was a big

man, fair-haired, blue-eyed, an irresistible force. Energy radiated from him. Nearly forty years old now, he kept the bright enthusiasm of a boy.

Captain John Farragut had lately been Commodore Farragut, but that had been a field promotion and temporary. His Attack Group One had disbanded after fulfilling its purpose. The two League of Earth Nations ships of the group had stayed behind at Planet Zero. The U.S. ships, *Rio Grande* and *Wolfhound*, were headed back to Fort Eisenhower. And the two Roman ships, *Gladiator* and *Horatius,* that had been under Farragut's command separated out on orders from Caesar Romulus.

The space battleship *Merrimack* remained alone in very deep space, in orbit around the dead world Telecore.

Telecore had begun life as a Roman colony. Before anyone had ever heard of the Hive, the Romans built a secret outpost on the planet to outflank American expansion in the Sagittarian arm of the galaxy.

Telecore had ended life consumed by the Hive. The Hive was a great soulless evil that existed only to eat. What the Romans planted on Telecore, the Hive came to reap.

The Romans were gone. The Hive was still there.

Captain Farragut liked to know his enemy. He had been in *Merrimack*'s lab with the xenoscientists, observing how newly emerged gorgons behaved, when he received Hamster's summons.

Farragut spoke before anyone could tell him, "The balloon went up?"

Specialists at their close-packed stations on the command deck traded looks. Somehow, from what Hamster said, John Farragut had figured out that the United States was at war.

"Looks like it, sir." Lieutenant Glenn Hamilton nodded toward the forward communications shack, where the cryptotech had cloistered himself with the EAM. "Waiting on confirmation."

Commander Egypt "Gypsy" Dent entered the deck.

She had left her ferocious hair in her cabin. Her head was smooth. Her brown eyes were narrowed into a squint, half-asleep. Strong-boned, tall and frowning, Gypsy scanned the monitors for some sign of the emergency that had roused her here. Hamster advised her softly, "It's war, sir."

The eyes opened at once. Gypsy was awake now.

"Who declared?" said Farragut. "I'm fixin' to be almighty unhappy if it was us."

He could not believe the Joint Chiefs would strand him out here in the deepest end of the Deep End, sitting on the biggest warship in the U.S. Naval Fleet, while the U.S. declared war without so much as a stand-by-for-heavy-rolls to warn him.

But Hamster answered, "*They* did, sir."

They. Rome.

The Imperial Government of Rome establishes the following facts:

Although Rome on her part has strictly adhered to the rules of international law in her relations with the United States during every period of the recent Emergency in the common defense against the Hive, the Government of the United States has used the Emergency to abridge the right of Rome to its own government, and continues to usurp the lawful authority of Rome over her own armed forces under pretext of a common defense against a threat that has been diminished to inconsequence in order to perpetuate oppression and to enforce a treaty coerced under most extreme circumstances. The United States violates Roman borders at will, and denies Rome the autonomy and security to which every nation is entitled, in actions consistent with an organized crime racket rather than a civilized nation.

Pledges extracted upon threat of being fed to monsters cannot be bound by law.

The Government of the United States has thereby virtually created a state of war.

The Imperial Government of Rome, consequently,

discontinues diplomatic relations with the United States of America and declares that Rome considers herself as being in a state of war with the United States of America.

VIII.xiii.MMCDXLVI

CAESAR ROMULUS.

"And you are all rotten people and don't deserve to live no more," Tactical added in a low mutter into his console.

"Thank you, Mister Vincent," said Farragut, a warning in his voice. Loose comments were what got Marcander Vincent bucked down to the Hamster Watch in the first place.

Farragut asked Lieutenant Hamilton, "Where do we stand?"

"We have the text of the President's request to Congress to declare back at 'em," said Hamster, and fed the text to his station.

To the Congress of the United States:

On the morning of August 13, the Imperial Government of Palatine, pursuing its course of galactic conquest, declared war against the United States.

The long known and the long expected has thus taken place. The forces endeavoring to enslave the entire galaxy now are moving into free space.

Delay invites greater danger. Rapid and united effort by all free peoples who are determined to remain free will insure a victory of the forces of justice and of righteousness over the forces of inhumanity and of totalitarianism.

I, therefore, request the Congress to recognize a state of war between the United States and the Imperial Government of Palatine.

MARISA JANE JOHNSON.

"Congressional recognition is 'imminent,'" Hamster added.

Farragut looked to the com tech, "Nothing from

Congress yet?"

"Not yet, sir."

"'kay." Farragut drew alongside Commander Dent, his hand between her shoulder blades. He spoke low, "If approval comes in before I get back, keep it quiet. There's something I have to do first."

"Understood, sir." Their heads were close together. Gypsy's brown eyes flicked, her focus shifting across his face, assessing.

There was a time, during the last hostilities, when Farragut had standing orders: Should *Merrimack* ever fall into enemy hands, Captain Farragut must kill his cryptotech. During that time, *Merrimack* had in fact been captured by Romans. Yet the cryptotech, Qord Johnson, was still alive to this day and authenticating the EAM in *Merrimack*'s communication shack right now.

Someone *else* had orders regarding the cryptotech in case of capture now.

You never could trust John Farragut to kill his own people.

Farragut still had his orders regarding the Roman patterner, whom *Merrimack* carried on board.

In case of war, the captain's first task—to be carried out immediately and without question—was to take Augustus down. The Roman patterner was the single biggest threat to U.S. security. Farragut's order was clear. Neutralize the threat. Do not try to capture Augustus or to salvage information from him. As Admiral Mishindi said, "Just drop him."

Qord Johnson emerged from the communications shack. He looked to the captain, the XO. "Sir. Sir." He passed the EAM to Farragut. "Emergency Action Message confirmed. Rome declared War. President Johnson presented her declaration to Congress."

Then it was real. War.

Gypsy studied the captain's eyes. She asked quietly, "Do you want me to do it, sir?"

Farragut shook his head. "If Augustus hears anyone but me coming to visit him, he'll know something's up."

That was true. Normally the crew and Marines on board *Merrimack* went out of their way to avoid crossing Augustus' path.

Most men on board would *like* to have these orders.

Captain Farragut could not ever delegate something like this. The day he delegated because he could not carry out an order for himself was the day he delegated command of his ship.

He motioned to one of the Marines who flanked the hatch. "Do you have a single stage piece on you?"

The sergeant fished a small backup weapon from his boot pocket. Surrendered it, grip first.

Farragut checked the load. Head busters. Low velocity projectiles, only meant to pierce a human body, not tear through and through. The point detonated only upon abrupt contact with human DNA.

The sergeant reminded Farragut uneasily, "That piece is coded to me, sir." He felt stupid saying that to the captain. Would feel stupider if he hung the captain out there pulling the trigger of a gun that wouldn't fire for him.

Weapons on board a space battleship were coded to their proper users. A weapon would not fire for anyone other than its coded owner.

But everyone on board *Merrimack*, company and crew alike, belonged to Captain John Farragut.

Farragut assured the Marine benevolently, "Son, there's nothing on this boat I can't shoot."

Even so, he depressed the trigger halfway. A green light confirmed recognition. He let up the trigger, clicked the safety off, cocked the piece, and slipped it into his jacket pocket like a street thug.

"Do you want a Marine guard?" his XO asked.

Farragut shook his head, no. "Gypsy, he can hear a gnat spit."

"He'll hear *you*," said Gypsy.

"Good bet," Farragut agreed. "He'll hear me coming. But that's okay. He likes to pretend I don't exist."

Augustus never stood up when the captain entered

his compartment. Most times Augustus did not even bother to look at him at all.

"I'll be right back."

Farragut moved out fast. He did not try to soften his footsteps. He needed to sound normal.

This task had to be done. He saw the wisdom and necessity of it. And he knew how to kill—and not just at a distance. Farragut had beheaded the Roman Captain Sejanus on the command deck of his own ship with a sword. He knew how to do this.

This was just another Roman.

The most abrasive, off-pissing, caustic, sadistic son of a Roman bitch he had ever known.

The most loyal. With a courage beyond question.

He was having a son of a hard time with this one.

Farragut would get only one shot, if that. He would not be able to say anything. No regrets. No good-bye. He could not even look him in the eyes. Augustus could read Farragut's eyes. And Augustus was extremely fast.

No one outdraws a patterner.

Just shoot him. A shot in the back if Augustus' back presented first.

A prickle like fear stung his mouth. He tried to blank out his thoughts. Stop thinking and just move.

Sounds of his ship around him were all normal. Booted footsteps on eight decks. Voices through thin partitions—fewer voices at this hour of the mid watch. The steady low hum of six mammoth engines. The sharp thunk of rubber balls in the squash court. Air rushing in the vents. Water moving through conduits. Hiss of hydraulics. Clicking of a dog that needed its nails cut.

His ship was an industrial beauty. Spare. Utilitarian. Thin partitions were only in place to keep things from passing compartment to compartment. Any equipment that might be tucked within walls on a passenger ship— conduits, pipes, struts—was all on view here. There were no ceilings, only the undersides of the decks above along with more of the ship's inner workings clustered up there in the overhead. You could see what this ship was made of. Except for things dangerous, secret, private, or requiring heavy containment, *Merrimack* was right there for you to see.

Farragut slid down the ladder to the corridor that accessed the torpedo rack room. At six foot eight in height, Augustus was difficult to billet. A torpedo rack was the only place he could fit horizontally.

Farragut made a conscious effort not to slow his stride. He wondered if Augustus could read deadly intent in a man's footsteps.

He hoped Augustus would not look when the hatch opened. He couldn't remember a time when Augustus ever did look. Augustus' pattern of disdain for Farragut's authority would serve now.

The patterner slept most of the day and all the mid watch. There was a good chance Farragut would catch him sleeping. He was probably going to murder Augustus in his rack.

Farragut kept his right hand in his pocket, gripping the sidearm.

Don't even show the piece, he decided. Just point and shoot through his pocket. The interior space beyond the hatch was tight. The instant that hatch opened, Farragut would be very close to his target. Point-blank, in fact.

His throat tightened up as he neared the hatch. He fought off the personal reaction. *To hell with it.*

Big breath. Hold it.

His left arm was supposed to be reaching to pull the hatch open, but he suddenly could not move it.

He hadn't heard a thing.

Two invincible, cable-reinforced arms had locked around him from behind, pinning his left arm across his chest, his right arm locked against his side. A large hand closed over Farragut's right hand, the one gripping the sidearm inside his pocket.

Squeezed.

The weapon discharged.

The bullet lodged in Farragut's deck boot. The head did not detonate.

The shot itself had made barely a pop. No one was going to come running to investigate.

The rough cheek pressing hard against Farragut's temple pushed his head to an unnatural turn, forced his chin into his own shoulder, immobile.

Augustus' breath puffed against his ear in a whispered growl. "I have the same orders."

RM Meluch

The Tour of the Merrimack

"An action-packed space opera. For readers who like romps through outer space, lots of battles with gooey horrific insects, and character sexplotation, *The Myriad* delivers..."　　　*—SciFi.com*

"Like *The Myriad*, this one is grand space opera. You will enjoy it."　　　*—Analog*

"This is grand old-fashioned space opera, so toss your disbelief out the nearest airlock and dive in."
　　　　　　　　—Publishers Weekly (Starred Review)

THE MYRIAD　　　　　0-7564-0320-1
WOLF STAR　　　　　0-7564-0383-6
THE SAGITTARIUS COMMAND
　　　　　　　978-0-7564-0490-1
and now in hardcover:
STRENGTH AND HONOR
　　　978-0-7564-0527-4

To Order Call: 1-800-788-6262
www.dawbooks.com

CJ Cherryh
The Foreigner Novels

"Serious space opera at its very best by one of the leading SF writers in the field today." —*Publishers Weekly*

FOREIGNER	0-88677-637-6
INVADER	0-88677-687-2
INHERITOR	0-88677-728-3
PRECURSOR	0-88677-910-3
DEFENDER	0-7564-0020-1
EXPLORER	0-7564-0165-8
DESTROYER	0-7564-0333-2
PRETENDER	0-7564-0408-6
DELIVERER	0-7564-0414-7

"Her world building, aliens, and suspense rank among the strongest in the whole SF field. May those strengths be sustained indefinitely, or at least until the end of Foreigner." —*Booklist*

To Order Call: 1-800-788-6262

www.dawbooks.com

CJ Cherryh

Complete Classic Novels in Omnibus Editions

THE DREAMING TREE
The Dreamstone and *The Tree of Swords and Jewels*
0-88677-782-8

THE FADED SUN TRILOGY
Kesrith, *Shon'jir*, and *Kutath*.   0-88677-836-0

THE MORGAINE SAGA
Gate of Ivrel, *Well of Shiuan*, and *Fires of Azeroth*.
0-88677-877-8

THE CHANUR SAGA
The Pride of Chanur, *Chanur's Venture* and
The Kif Strike Back.   0-88677-930-8

ALTERNATE REALITIES
Port Eterntiy, *Voyager in Night*, and *Wave Without a Shore*
0-88677-946-4

AT THE EDGE OF SPACE
Brothers of Earth and *Hunter of Worlds*.   0-7564-0160-7

THE DEEP BEYOND
Serpent's Reach and *Cuckoo's Egg*.   0-7564-0311-1

ALLIANCE SPACE
Merchanter's Luck and *40,000 in Gehenna*   0-7564-0494-9

To Order Call: 1-800-788-6262
www.dawbooks.com

DAW 9

Tanya Huff

The Confederation Novels

"As a heroine, Kerr shines. She is cut from the same mold
as Ellen Ripley of the *Aliens* films. Like her heroine,
Huff delivers the goods." —*SF Weekly*

A CONFEDERATION OF VALOR
Omnibus Edition
(Valor's Choice, The Better Part of Valor)
978-0-7564-0399-7

THE HEART OF VALOR
978-0-7564-0481-9

and now in hardcover:
VALOR'S TRIAL
978-0-7564-0479-6

To Order Call: 1-800-788-6262
www.dawbooks.com

DAW 73